Praise for *New York Times* bestselling author Jillian Hart

"Jillian Hart's compassionate story will most certainly please readers."
—*RT Book Reviews* on *Everyday Blessings*

"It's a pleasure to read this achingly tender story."
—*RT Book Reviews* on *Her Wedding Wish*

"A heartwarming story with likable characters."
—*RT Book Reviews* on *His Country Girl*

"Jillian Hart conveys heart-tugging emotional struggles."
—*RT Book Reviews* on *Sweet Blessings*

Praise for Catherine Palmer

"Palmer adds spice and unpredictability to this love story, making it fresh and wonderful."
—*RT Book Reviews* on *The Maverick's Bride*

"Heartwarming… Palmer knows how to write about a sensitive subject with wisdom and kindness."
—*RT Book Reviews* on *Thread of Deceit*

"Rich in historical details only Catherine Palmer can convey."
—*RT Book Reviews* on *The Briton*

New York Times Bestselling Author

Jillian Hart
and
Catherine Palmer

Homespun Bride
&
The Briton

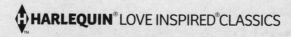

H HARLEQUIN® LOVE INSPIRED® CLASSICS
™

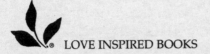

LOVE INSPIRED BOOKS

Recycling programs for this product may not exist in your area.

ISBN-13: 978-1-335-89584-4

Homespun Bride & The Briton

Copyright © 2018 by Harlequin Books S.A.

The publisher acknowledges the copyright holders of the individual works as follows:

Homespun Bride
Copyright © 2008 by Jill Strickler

The Briton
Copyright © 2008 by Catherine Palmer

CONTENTS

New York Times bestselling author **Jillian Hart** grew up on her family's homestead, where she helped raise cattle, rode horses and scribbled stories in her spare time. After earning her English degree from Whitman College, she worked in travel and advertising before selling her first novel. When Jillian isn't working on her next story, she can be found puttering in her rose garden, curled up with a good book or spending quiet evenings at home with her family.

Books by Jillian Hart

Love Inspired

The McKaslin Clan series

Precious Blessings
Every Kind of Heaven
Everyday Blessings
A McKaslin Homecoming
Her Wedding Wish
Her Perfect Man
A Soldier for Keeps
Blind-Date Bride
Montana Homecoming
Montana Cowboy
Montana Dreams

Visit the Author Profile page at Harlequin.com.

HOMESPUN BRIDE

Jillian Hart

The Lord is my shepherd; I shall not want.
—*Psalms* 23:1

Chapter One

Montana Territory, 1883

The tiny railroad town of Angel Falls was a symphony of noise. Because she was blind, Noelle Kramer had gotten the knack of separating one sound from another. There was the chink of horseshoes on the hard-packed snow and ice as teamsters and riders hurried on their way. The merry bell in the church steeple clanged a melody, marking the late-afternoon hour. The businesslike clip-clip of ladies' shoes on the swept-clean boardwalk was like a metronome tapping the meter. The low-throated rumble of the train, two blocks over, added a steady bass percussion as it idled on steel tracks.

It all painted a picture, of sorts, but there was so much missing. She could not see the colorful window displays of the shops. Were they bright with spring colors yet? While she could not know this, not without asking her dear aunt, who was busy fussing with their horse's tether rope, she tried to picture what she could. She hadn't been blind so long that she couldn't remember the look of things. She only had to pull it up in her mind, the main street with its cheerful window displays, awnings and continuous boardwalks.

What she couldn't picture was her friend Lanna, from their school days, who'd been in the dress shop when she and her aunt had stopped to pick up a new hat. Lanna had been bursting with happiness. The brightest notes of joy rang in her voice as she'd been fitted for her wedding dress.

Noelle closed her eyes against the pain; she closed her thoughts and her heart, too. She'd never asked what had become of the wedding gown she'd had made. The one she'd never had a chance to pick up for her wedding day.

She rubbed the fourth finger of her left hand, so bare beneath the thick woolen glove. She understood why Shelton had changed his mind. What surprised her was that her heart wasn't broken; she'd not been deeply in love with him but she'd hoped for happiness anyway.

No, what had devastated her had been his words. *You're damaged goods, now.* Her blindness was the reason she would never have a hope of marrying. Of being a wife and a mother. Her affliction was a burden to others. She, alone, could not tend fires and watch after servants or see to the dozens of details in the running of a household and caring for small children.

Still, she had a lot to be thankful for.

"Now, you settle down like a good horse." Aunt Henrietta's no-nonsense scolding easily drowned out the street noise. Even her gait was a sensible brisk stride and her petticoats rustled as she climbed into the sleigh.

"Is he giving you more trouble?" Noelle asked, trying to hide her worry.

"He won't if he knows what's good for him." Henrietta settled her heavy hoops and plentiful skirts around her on the seat. "I gave him a talking-to he won't soon forget. He's a Worthington now, and he has a standard of conduct to uphold. I won't be seen around town wrestling a horse for control like some common teamster."

Noelle bit her lip trying to hide the smile for she knew her aunt was dreadfully serious. To Henrietta, appearances and reputation were everything. "I'm sure he'll be fine. He's probably just not used to all the noise in town."

"I don't care what he's used to!" Henrietta huffed. The seat groaned beneath her weight as she leaned forward, perhaps in search of the lap blanket. "Where has that gone to? Wait, here it is. Cover up, dear. There's a dangerous cold to the air. Mark my words, we'll see a blizzard before we reach home, if we make it there in time."

Noelle bit her lip again. She was endlessly amused by Henrietta's drama. A blizzard? Surely that was a dire assessment of the situation. She held up her gloved hand but couldn't hear any telltale *tap, tap* against the leather. "I smell snow in the wind. It is falling yet? I can't tell."

"Nothing yet, although I can hardly hear you. I shall never get used to that newfangled contraption."

"Which newfangled contraption is bothering you now?"

"Why, the train, of course." Henrietta took delight in her complaints, for her voice was smiling as she gathered the thick leather reins with a rustle. "I can tell by the look on your face that once again my disapproval of modern progress amuses you."

"I wonder why the Northern Pacific Railroad didn't ask you before they laid track through our valley."

"That is exactly my complaint with them." Henrietta

gave the reins a slap and the gelding leaped forward, jerking them to a rough, swift start. "There, now. That's more like it. I don't put up with a horse's nonsense."

Or any nonsense, Noelle knew, which was why she hadn't asked about Lanna's dress when they'd left the shop. Why she tucked away her sadness. Henrietta didn't have a mind to tolerate sadness. She always said that God knew best and that was that.

No doubt that was true. Sometimes it was simply difficult to understand.

The wind changed, bringing with it the fresh wintry scent of snowflakes. Noelle could feel them, as light as a Brahms lullaby, and she lifted her face to the brush of their crisp iciness against her skin.

Henrietta snapped the reins briskly, intent on directing their horse. "Do you smell that?"

"Yes, isn't the snow wonderful?"

"Goodness, not that, dear. It's the train. At least you're spared the ugly view of the trailing coal smoke that hovers over the town like a black, poisonous, endless snake. What are we expected to do? Expire from the discharge?"

"I doubt the men in charge of the rail company are concerned by the smoke cloud."

"Well, they can afford not to be! They are not here to breathe it in! And why do we need such progress? Gone are the days when a person labored to get to their destination. I walked beside my parents' wagon halfway to Missouri, and it put the starch in my bonnet. It's what's wrong with young people nowadays. Life is too easy for them."

The train whistle blasted, drowning out her words. And there was another more frightening sound—the high-noted terror in a horse's neigh. Noelle cringed, panic licking at her. Years ago, their mare had made that terrified, almost-human scream when a rattlesnake had startled her and she'd run with the family buggy over the edge of the road. On that day, Noelle had lost her mother, her father and her sight.

Surely, that sound wasn't coming from their horse? She glanced around the street, as if she could see; it was habit, nothing more. She gripped the edge of the sleigh tight in reflex and in memory, but there was no time to open her heart in prayer. The sleigh jerked forward. Wind whizzed in her ears and snow slapped against her face. The sleigh's runners hit grooves in the compact snow at a rapid-fire pace, bouncing her on the seat.

"Good heavens!" Henrietta sounded deeply put out. "Calm down, you ill-behaved brute—"

The train whistle blew a second time. The sleigh jerked to a sudden stop. Noelle slid forward on the seat and something hard struck her chin. Pain exploded through her jaw, as she realized she'd hit the dashboard. Was that high, shrill bugling neigh coming from their horse? Sure enough, she could feel his huge body block the wind as he reared up. For one breathless moment, she feared he might fall on them. Henrietta's terrified gasp confirmed her suspicions.

"Quick!" She found her aunt's arm and gave her a nudge. "Out of the sleigh. Hurry! Before—"

Too late. The whistle blew, the sleigh lurched and the horse came down running. The train's loud chugging and clamoring only seemed to drive the gelding to run faster, right down the middle of Main. Shouted exclamations and the sudden rush of other horses and vehicles to get out of the way overrode all other sounds.

The sleigh swayed from side to side in a sickening way. They were going too fast for the vehicle. She braced her feet and held on tight. Fear tasted coppery and bitter on her tongue. The past rose up in a colorful image in her mind's eye. Her mother's cry as the buggy broke apart. The horrible falling at great speed. The sudden blinding pain—

No. Not again. Lord, stop this from happening. Please. Panic beat crazily against her ribs. Fear felt thick on her tongue. It was too late to jump from the sleigh, and she wouldn't abandon Henrietta. She tried to make her mind clear enough to form another prayer but only one thought came. *Help us.*

Somewhere, over the sound of Henrietta's continued demands for the horse to stop and stop now, a man shouted out, "Runaway horse! Grab him!"

Maybe someone *could* stop them. Hope lifted through her panic, and Noelle clung to it. *Please, Lord, send someone to help us.*

There was no answer as the sleigh began to buck harder and rock from side to side. Had they left the road? Soft snow sprayed against her face. She held on to the edge of the seat with all her might, but her stomach gripped from the sleigh's violent rocking motion. Foliage crumpled and crunched beneath the runners.

Had they gone off the road? Fear shot through her heart. They were going too fast, they were going to overturn and the sleigh was going to break apart. Henrietta must have realized this, too, because she began sobbing. That only drove the horse to run faster. Noelle squeezed her eyes shut. A sob broke through her, and the seat bucked beneath her. They would be hurt—or worse—and she could not stop it from happening.

The Lord hadn't answered her prayer last time, either, and look at what she'd lost. Her heart squeezed with pain. She could not lose so much again, and yet she had no choice. The sleigh rose sharply upward, and tipped violently to the right, slamming her hard against the dashboard again. She felt no physical pain, only an emotional one. It was too late for answered prayers now.

Then, through the rush of her pulse in her ears, she heard something else. Something new. The drum of hoofbeats.

"Whoa, there, big fella." A man's voice, a deep vibrant baritone rumbled like winter thunder from the sky, overpowering every other sound until there was only silence. Only him. "Calm down. You're all right, buddy."

The sleigh's bumping slowed. Noelle hung on to the dashboard, drawn to the sound of the man's confident and powerful voice coming as if from the sky.

Am I dreaming this? Noelle had to wonder. None of this felt real. The sleigh tipped dangerously and listed to a stop. The dizzying sense of movement stopped.

There was only the blast of the winded gelding's ragged breaths and that soothing baritone. She could hardly believe that they were safe.

Safe. Because of him.

She heard the creak of his saddle as he dismounted. The sensations of Henrietta clutching her, the wind's low-noted howl like a lonely wolf's cry and the chill that set in all faded into the background. She was riveted to his voice; there was something about his voice, but as he spoke low to keep the horse calm over the clatter of the harnessing she couldn't place what it was. Maybe he was tethering the horse.

Relief flooded her. The remnants of fear jarred

through her, making her blood thick and her pulse loud in her ears. She turned toward the faint squeaking sound his boots made on the snow. His gait was even and confident; not too fast, and long-legged. Already her mind was trying to paint a picture of him.

"Are you two ladies all right?" The man's baritone boomed.

It wasn't a cold tone, Noelle heard, but warmth in that voice, character and heart. And something more, indefinable like a memory just out of reach.

"F-fine. Considering what c-could have happened." Was that really her speaking? She probably sounded so breathless and shaky from the aftereffect of fear, that was all, and not because of the man.

Henrietta still gasped for breath, frozen in place, but still managing to talk. "We're a little worse for the wear, I d-dare say. I hate to think what would have happened if you hadn't intervened, sir. You s-saved us just in time."

"Looks like it," the rider answered easily as if it hadn't been his doing. "What's important now is that you two try to make as little movement as possible. I'm going to get you out one at a time. Don't worry, you'll be safe."

Safe? Noelle gulped. Did that mean they were still in danger? She could tell they were tipped at an odd angle, but her hearing had failed her. Her ears seemed to be ignoring everything, save for the man's voice. It was strange, as was the feeling that she ought to know him, and how could that be? If he wasn't a stranger, then Henrietta would have called him by name.

"D-dear hea-vens!" Her aunt sounded quite strained. "A-are you q-quite sure that we're not about to plunge into the river?"

The river? That took her thoughts off their rescuer. Fear shivered down her spine. Only then did she realize there was another sound above the raging howl of the wind—the rush of the fast-moving river.

How close were they to the edge? She tried to breathe but her lungs felt heavy and the air in them like mud. As her senses settled, she could better hear the hungry rush of the river alarmingly close.

"Let me help you, miss."

His voice seemed to move through her spirit and, confused, she didn't realize that he was taking her hand until suddenly his fingers closed around hers. His touch was strong and as steady as granite. Every fear within her stilled. It seemed impossible to be afraid as his other hand gripped her elbow.

Stunned, she could feel the faint wind shadow as he towered over her. She knew he was tall, wide-shouldered and built like steel. She knew, somehow, without seeing him. It was as if she was familiar with his touch. How could that possibly be?

"Careful, now." His calm baritone boomed. "Step up a little, that's right."

She could feel his strength as he lifted her out of the tipped sleigh. For an instant, she felt weightless as if there was no gravity that could hold her to the ground. As if there were only wind and sky. She breathed in the winter air, the faint scent of soap and leather and wool. Her shoes touched the snow and the impact jarred through her, although he'd set her gently to the ground.

Who was this man? The last time she'd felt like this, suspended between earth and sky, between safety and the unknown was so long ago, she dared not let her mind dig up those buried dreams.

With a whisper of movement he released her. "Stay here while I fetch your mother."

She stood wobbling on her shaky legs, feeling the kick of fear still racing through her veins. Riveted, unable to think of anything else, even her aunt's safety, she listened to the crunch of the snow beneath his boots as he moved again. The wind and snow lashed against her nose and eyes like tears. She tucked the muffler more snuggly around her face, shivering not from fear or cold but from something else.

She heard Henrietta's sob of fear, she heard the jingle of their rescuer's horse's bridle and that low reassuring baritone, although the howling wind stole his words.

Never had she so sorely missed her sight. Every fiber of her being longed to be able to see him. Then she heard the squeak of the sleigh's runner as it moved against the snow and she realized the rush she heard was the swift-running river and roar of the falls—the highest waterfall in all of Montana Territory.

A prayer flew to her lips, but before she could give it voice, she heard the crunch of her aunt's sturdy gait. "Let me take a look at you. I have to see with my own eyes. This is like an awful nightmare." Henrietta grabbed her and turned her around, like a mother hen checking on one of her chicks.

Love for her aunt filled her—she'd learned that love made everyone perfect. What were flaws? They hardly mattered when she could have lost Henrietta as she had her parents. Emotion burned in her throat, emotion she dared not speak of, since Henrietta did not approve of outbursts of any kind.

"I'm fine," she told her aunt to reassure her. "But are you all right?"

"Worse for the ordeal but right enough. I saw you hit the dashboard. Are you bleeding?"

"I'm fine, I told you. It's blizzarding, and—"

"You ladies need to get safely home." He spoke up. "The storm is likely to get worse before it gets better."

"Young man, you saved our lives."

"I was at the right place at the right time is all." He took a step, which made it easier to keep his eye on that high-strung horse. "Are you sure you're both all right? A ride like that could shake anyone up."

"I have nerves of steel." The woman's chin firmed as she tugged at the daughter's scarf, which obscured her nearly completely. "My niece, however, is quite fragile as she's blind."

"Niece?" Not daughter. And blind at that. Wasn't that too bad? Thad thought. Sympathy filled him as he watched the aunt fuss.

"My dear, let me see. I have to make sure you've not broken anything."

"As long as you two ladies are safe enough, I'll just see to the horse then." He stepped back. His mind should be working out how to get that vehicle out of the bushes, but he couldn't concentrate on it.

There was something about the young woman—the niece—something he couldn't put his finger on. He'd hardly glanced at her when he'd hauled her from the family sleigh, but now he took a longer look through the veil of falling snow.

For a moment, her silhouette, the size of her, and the way she moved reminded him of Noelle. How about that; Noelle, his frozen heart reminded him with a painful squeeze, had been his first—and only—love.

It couldn't be her, he reasoned, since she was married

and probably a mother by now. She'd be safe in town, living snug in one of the finest houses in the county instead of riding along the country roads in a storm. Still, curiosity nibbled at him as he plowed through the knee-deep snow. Snow was falling faster now, and yet somehow through the thick downfall his gaze seemed to find her.

She was fragile, a delicate bundle of wool; snow clung to her hood, scarf and cloak like a shroud, making her tough to see. She'd been just a little bit of a thing when he'd lifted her from the sleigh, and his only thought at the time had been to get both women out of danger. Now something chewed at his memory. He couldn't quite figure out what, but he could feel it in his gut.

The woman was talking on as she unwound the niece's veil. "We were tossed about dreadfully. You're likely bruised and broken from root to stem. I've never been so terrified. All I could do was pray over and over and think of you, my dear." Her words warmed with tenderness. "What a greater nightmare for you."

"We're fine. All's well that ends well," the niece insisted.

Although her voice was muffled by the thick snowfall, his step faltered. There *was* something about her voice, something familiar in the gentle resonance of her alto. Now he could see the top part of her face, due to her loosened scarf. Her eyes—they were a startling shade of flawless emerald green.

Whoa, there. He'd seen that perfect shade of green before—and long ago. Recognition speared through his midsection, but he already knew she was his Noelle even before the last layer of the scarf fell away from her face.

His Noelle, just as lovely and dear, was now blind and veiled with snow. His first love. The woman he'd spent years and thousands of miles trying to forget. Hard to believe that there she was suddenly right in front of him. He'd heard about the engagement announcement a few years back, and he'd known in returning to Angel Falls to live that he'd have to run into her eventually.

He just didn't figure it would be so soon and like this.

Seeing her again shouldn't make him feel as if he'd been hit in the chest with a cannonball. The shock was wearing off, he realized, the same as when you received a hard blow. First off, you were too stunned to feel it. Then the pain began to settle in, just a hint, and then to rush in until it was unbearable. Yep, that was the word to describe what was happening inside his rib cage. A pain worse than a broken bone beat through him.

Best get the sleigh righted, the horse hitched back up and the women home. But it was all he could do to turn his back as he took his mustang by the bridle. The palomino pinto gave him a snort and shook his head, sending the snow on his golden mane flying.

Yep, I know how you feel, Sunny, Thad thought. Judging by the look of things, it would be a long time until they had a chance to get in out of the cold.

He'd do best to ignore the women, especially Noelle, and to get to the work needin' to be done. He gave the sleigh a shove, but the vehicle was wedged against the snow-covered brush banking the river. Not that he put a lot of weight on the Lord overmuch these days, but Thad had to admit it was a close call. Almost eerie how he'd caught them just in time. It did seem providential. Had they gone only a few feet more, gravity would have done the trick and pulled the sleigh straight into the frigid, fast waters of Angel River and plummeted them directly over the tallest falls in the territory.

Thad squeezed his eyes shut. He couldn't stand to think of Noelle tossed into that river, fighting the powerful current along with the ice chunks. There would have been no way to have pulled her from the river in time. Had he been a few minutes slower in coming after them or if Sunny hadn't been so swift, there would have been no way to save her. To fate, the Lord or to simple chance, he was grateful.

Some tiny measure of tenderness in his chest, like a fire long banked, sputtered to life. His tenderness for her, still there, after so much time and distance. How about that.

Since the black gelding was a tad calmer now that the sound of the train had faded off into the distance, Thad rehitched him to the sleigh but secured the driving reins to his saddle horn. He used the two horses working together to free the sleigh and get it realigned toward the road.

The older woman looked uncertain about getting back into the vehicle. With the way that black gelding of theirs was twitchy and wild-eyed, he didn't blame her. "Don't worry, ma'am, I'll see you two ladies home."

"Th-that would be very good of you, sir. I'm rather shaken up. I'm of half a mind to walk the entire mile home, except for my dear niece."

Noelle. He wouldn't let his heart react to her. All that mattered was doing right by her—and that was one thing that hadn't changed. He came around to help the aunt into the sleigh and after she was safely seated, turned toward Noelle. Her scarf had slid down to reveal the curve of her face, the slope of her nose and the rosebud smile of her mouth.

What had happened to her? How had she lost her sight? Sadness filled him for her blindness and for what could have been between them, once. He thought about saying something to her, so she would know who he was, but what good would that do? The past was done and over. Only the emptiness of it remained.

"Thank you so much, sir." She turned toward the sound of his step and smiled in his direction. If she, too, wondered who he was, she gave no real hint of it.

He didn't expect her to. Chances were she hardly remembered him, and if she did, she wouldn't think too well of him. She would never know what good wishes he wanted for her as he took her gloved hand. The layers of wool and leather and sheepskin lining between his hand and hers didn't stop that tiny flame of tenderness for her from growing a notch.

He looked into her eyes, into Noelle's eyes, the woman he'd loved truly so long ago, knowing she did not recognize him. Could not see him or sense him, even at heart. She smiled at him as if he were the Good Samaritan she thought he was as he helped her settle onto the seat.

Love was an odd thing, he realized as he backed away. Once, their love had been an emotion felt so strong and pure and true that he would have vowed on his very soul that nothing could tarnish nor diminish their bond. But time had done that simply, easily, and they stood now as strangers.

He reached for Sunny's reins, mounted up and led the way into the worsening storm.

Chapter Two

Huddled against the minus temperatures and lashing snow, Noelle clenched her jaw tight to keep her teeth from chattering.

The whir of the frigid wind and the endless whisper of the torrential snowfall drowned out all sound. It deceived her into imagining they were being pulled along in a void, cut off from the outside world, from everyone and everything, including the stranger who had helped them. She knew he was leading the gelding; Aunt Henrietta had assured her of this fact as soon as they'd set out.

It was only concern, she told herself, because she'd been behind two runaway horses in her lifetime. She did not wish a third trip. Of course she wanted to make sure they arrived safely home and that the stranger would keep his stalwart promise to lead them there.

The stranger. She couldn't seem to rid him from her mind. Her thoughts kept turning over and over the moment she'd first heard his buttery-warm baritone and the strange, vague sense of recognition she'd felt when he'd lifted her from the sleigh.

You know who he reminds you of. She shivered against the cruel cold and swiped the snow from her lashes. No, it couldn't be her old beau. Thad McKaslin was probably in Texas by now, judging by how fast he'd left her years ago. Her heart cracked in small pieces just thinking his name.

No, there was no possibility—none—that *he* was the stranger. Their rescuer was a Good Samaritan and a dependable, mature man, not a boy who only saw to his own concerns.

"Henrietta?" Uncle Robert's bass boomed through the sounds of the storm. "Noelle! Thank God you're here safe. I was just about to ride out looking for you. Didn't you see the blizzard cloud, Henrietta? You are both half frozen."

"Oh, Rob." Henrietta stumbled off the seat with a thud and clatter.

The storm blocked any other sounds, but Noelle knew her aunt had flung herself into her husband's arms. Though stiff with cold, she waited in the sleigh to give them a private moment.

"Do you need help?"

She turned toward the sound of his voice, thinking of all the ways his baritone didn't sound like the Thad she remembered. It was deeper, more mature, made of character and depth of experience. Besides, if it was Thad, he would have said something. See, it *couldn't* be.

"Miss?"

She ignored the knot of foreboding in her stomach and answered him. "I would appreciate the help. Storms with winds like this tend to disorient me. I get a little lost on my own."

"Me, too, but I don't need a storm for that." There was a touch of warmth to those words.

She wondered if he were smiling, and what kind of smile he had. Just for curiosity's sake, of course. She began to shake the snow from the lap blanket.

"Let me get that for you."

He blocked the storm as he towered beside her. She felt the weight of the snow-caked blanket fall away. She breathed in the wintry air, the faint scent of his soap and leather and wool and remembered that boy she'd once loved.

His hand cradled her elbow to help her step out of the sleigh. Cold snow sank to the tops of her ankle-high shoes. For a moment, she felt a strange quiver of familiarity and denial seized her like a fist. Thad McKaslin here, in Angel Falls? Could it be?

She took one step, and he moved to her side to block the worst of the wind and snow. And the way he towered beside her made recognition shiver through her.

I don't want it to be him, she thought, her stomach tightening even more. But just because she didn't want it to be Thad, didn't mean it wasn't. She took another step. "Should I know you?"

"Not really," his comforting baritone rumbled.

"When a man saves a woman's life, well, two women's, she likes to know what name to call her rescuer when she thanks him."

"Maybe some things are better left a mystery." Friendly, that's what his voice was and cozy, the way a fire crackling in the hearth was cozy. "Careful, now. There's a deep drift coming up."

His grip tightened on her and he responded so quickly and gallantly, he must have thought she was truly helpless. It was a common misconception. "Don't worry," she said, easily correcting her balance. "I've gotten used to tottering around. I'm fine."

"The snow drifts high here. Lift your steps a little higher," he said with concern.

Concern she didn't need, not from him. She tried to concentrate on feeling her way over the crest of the snowdrift with the toe of her shoe. Her feet were numb from cold, making it only a little more difficult.

"You do this very well."

She recognized the surprise in his words. "When I lost my sight, I realized I had two options. To see it as a reason to give up or as a reason to go on. Of course, I walk into a few walls and catch my toe on the top of snowdrifts, but I do all right."

"I'll say."

She could feel the flat level of the brick stone walkway that her uncle kept carefully cleared. Snow had accumulated on it, but not more than a few inches, and the walking was easier. She released her rescuer's arm. "Thank you, but I can get in from here."

"No, I should see you to the door."

"You've done enough all ready."

"But you're blind."

"Yes, but I'm not incapable."

"No, I see that." What did he say to that? Thad didn't have the slightest notion. It was breaking his heart in every way. He cleared his throat to ask the question most troubling him. "How long have you been like this?"

"Tripping in the snow? Or blind, do you mean?"

"I'm sorry for your loss of sight." Her smile was still the same, he realized, modest and sweet as the finest sugar, and how it transformed her lovely face the way dawn changed the night sky. But something *had* changed. She no longer held the power to render him a love-struck fool. No, he thought stoically, her smile had no effect on him whatsoever.

"It's been over four years, now."

"Four years?" That surprised him. He'd been gone just about five.

"I hit my head when our buggy rolled and I lost my sight. It wasn't the worst thing I lost. My parents were killed."

"I—I'm sorry to hear that." It surprised him that the venom he'd felt for Noelle's parents vanished. Whatever they had done to him aside, they had loved their daughter dearly. She was their greatest treasure. Hard to blame them for it; harder now that they were gone.

The venom had died but not the bitterness. It was hard to keep it buried where it belonged. "I guess that had to be hard for you."

A single nod, nothing more.

His feelings aside, he knew it had to have been an unbearable loss for her. She had loved her parents deeply, which was one reason why he'd made the decision he did five years ago and why they stood together now as strangers. The only decision he could have made.

Despite her condition, she looked well. Very well. Soft lamplight glowed from the wide windows, gilding her in light. Snow had gathered like tiny pieces of grace on her hood. She looked beautiful, more lovely than ever. Vibrant and womanly in a way he'd never seen her before.

She's happy, he realized with a punch that knocked the air from his lungs and every last speck of regret from his heart. He'd done the right thing in leaving. Her father, rest his soul, had been right.

He didn't like what that decision had done to him, but he'd learned a hard lesson from it. Be wary of the woman you give your heart to.

He took a moment to capture one last look of her, happy and lovely and matured into a sweetheart of a woman. Knowing this only made him feel colder. Glad for her, but cold in the way of the blizzard baring its teeth.

"Won't you come in? You must be half frozen." Concern was there on her face for the stranger she thought he was. "Come in and warm up. We have beef soup and hot tea."

"Can't. My horse is standing in this cold."

"You could put him in our stable."

"No." Would she still ask him in if she knew who he was? What did she think about the man who'd broken his promise to elope with her? Did she even remember him?

Probably not. The bitterness in him won out, but it wasn't *only* bitterness he felt. That old tenderness, a hint of it, remained. No longer a romantic tenderness; that had been surely destroyed, but his feeling of goodwill surprised him once more.

He lifted her free hand, small and disguised by her woolen glove. He knew by memory, still, the shape of her hand from all the times he'd held it in his own. It was with well wishes for her future that he pressed a gentleman's kiss to the back of her hand.

"Now that I've got you and your aunt home safe and sound, I've done my good deed for the day."

"Only one good deed per day?" She withdrew onto the brick walk. "You remind me of an old beau of mine."

"Pardon me, but he couldn't have been the brightest fellow. I can't imagine any man passing you by."

"I must be mistaken, then." She shook her head. Why had she been so sure? But as she swiped the snow out of her eyes, she realized he hadn't answered her question. "How long have you lived in Angel County?"

"I, uh, just moved back to the area. Haven't been here long."

So, it was as she thought. The voice she remembered had been an eighteen-year-old's voice, manly, yes, but still partly boyish, too, not in full maturity. This man's voice was deeper and confident and wholly masculine, but still, it was Thad's.

"Miss, you take care of yourself. No more riding behind runaway horses."

"I think my uncle will see to that."

"Where is your husband? Shouldn't he be the one seeing to your safety?"

"My husband? No. I've never married." Was he moving away? The wind was gathering speed so she couldn't hear him move. "The blizzard is growing worse. You can't go out in that."

"Don't worry your pretty head about me, Noelle."

Noelle. The way his baritone warmed like wild honey around her name made her absolutely certain. "Thad?"

But there was no answer, just the moan of the wind and the hammering of snow falling with a vengeance. It pounded everywhere, on the top of her hood, on the front of her cloak, on the steps at her feet, and the sound deceived her.

Had he already disappeared into the storm? She couldn't tell. She stood alone, battered by howling wind and needle-sharp snow, feeling seventeen again.

Those feelings of love and heartbreak and regret were a lifetime ago. She'd had enough of all three these past years to last her a lifetime. She knew it was foolish of her to wonder about Thad McKaslin now. He had rejected her, too.

She turned on her heels and waded through the snow to the covered porch steps. They were icy, so she took them with care. It was best to keep her mind focused firmly on the blessings in her life. On what was good about this moment and this day. No good came from dwelling on what was past and forever lost.

"Young man, where do you think you are going?" Henrietta demanded from, what sounded, near the bottom of the porch steps. "You'll come back here and warm up with a cup of tea in front of a hot fire."

"I've got stock to see to before the storm gets much worse. Good day, ma'am." Thad's voice came muted by distance and the thick veil of snow.

"Mark my words, you'll freeze to death before you make it to the end of the driveway!" Henrietta humphed when no answer came. "What a disagreeable man. He may have saved us, but God help him. We'll likely as not find him frozen solid on the path to town come morning. Terrible thing," she said, leading the way into the house.

Apparently back to her usual self. Noelle gave thanks for that.

After following her aunt into the warmth of the house, she found herself wondering about Thad. He'd disappeared back into the blizzard, just as he'd come to them.

A narrow escape.

He wasn't bitter, Thad told himself as he nosed Sunny north. No, he was as cold to the past as the wind.

But he was unprepared. Unprepared to have seen her. Unprepared to accept the fact that she'd said the words that kept playing over and over in his mind. I've never married.

Wasn't that why he'd left Angel Falls? To do as her father wanted and get out of her life? So she could marry the right kind of man? Because there was no way an immigrant's son like him could give Noelle the comfort she was used to. There had been many times over the past lonely years that he'd seen the older man's point.

The love he thought they had was a fool's paradise. A dream that had nothing to do with the hard reality of life.

They'd been two kids living on first love and dreams, but the real world ran on hard work and wages. He'd driven cattle from all over the West to the stockyards, from California to Chicago. He'd eaten dust and branded calves and tucked away every spare dollar he could and, except for a few months every winter, he'd lived out of his saddlebags. He'd learned what life was about.

The icy wind gusted hard, pulling him out of his thoughts. He'd gone a fair ways down the driveway. There was nothing around him but the lashing wind and the pummel of the iced snow, which had fallen around him like a veil. He gave thanks for it because he couldn't see anything—especially the house he'd left. Noelle's house. The twilight-dark storm made it easier to forget he'd seen her. To forget everything. Especially those early years away from her and how his heart had bled in misery until one day there'd been no blood left. Until he'd felt drained of substance but finally purged of the dream of her and what could have been.

Sure, there had been times—moments—since then

when he'd thought of her. When he saw a woman's chestnut hair twisted up in that braided fancy knot Noelle liked to wear. Or when he saw an intricate lace curtain hanging in a window, he would recall how she'd liked to sit quietly in the shade on the porch and crochet lace by the hour. Anytime he heard a piece of that fancy piano music she liked to play with the complicated chords and the long-winded compositions, he would remember.

It was the memories that could do him in, that were burrowing like a tick into his chest. He tried to freeze his heart like the winter's frost reaching deep into the ground. Usually that was the best way to handle those haunting thoughts of her and of the past.

He would never have come back to Angel Falls except for his kid brother. The boy didn't know what kind of a sacrifice Thad was making in coming back here and in his decisions to stick around, help the family and start to put down roots for a change.

Roots. He'd been avoiding doing that all this time, aside from the money it took to buy the kind of land he wanted—because settling down would only remind him he wasn't building a life and dreams with her.

Don't think about Noelle. He willed the words deep into his heart. Now, if only he were strong enough to stick by them. Whether she was married or not, their past was dead and gone. He was no longer that foolish boy thinking love was what mattered. He was a man strong enough to resist making a mistake like that— like her—again.

The whiteout-strength winds blasted harder; Sunny shied and veered off the faint path of the road. Not a great sign. Thad pulled his mustang up, so he wouldn't lose his sense of direction. It wouldn't take much for a man to get himself lost in a blizzard like this. He shaded his eyes from the wind-driven downfall to try to get a good look, but he couldn't see a thing. Still, he dismounted, to make sure. Something could be in the road—like another rider driven off track by the storm in need of help.

The curtain of snow shifted on a stronger gust of wind, and something red flashed at the roadside only to disappear again. Keeping hold of Sunny's reins and his sense of direction, Thad knelt to find a lady's hatbox tied up with a fancy red ribbon and, next to it, a small flat ice-covered package.

Must be Noelle's things, he figured, scanning what little he could see for landmarks. This sloping slant of ground was probably at the junction of the main road. The sleigh had made a sharp turn onto the driveway here. Combined with the wind, the goods had probably slid right over the edge of the sleigh.

It looked as though he wasn't completely done with Noelle yet. The small package fit into his saddlebag, but not the bulky hatbox. That he had to hang over his saddle horn by the ribbon.

Just his luck. Now, as he nosed Sunny north into the storm and toward home, there was a reminder of Noelle he could not ignore. The blizzard grew with a ruthless howl, baring its icy teeth. He was cut off from the world. He could see only gray wind, white snow, brutal cold and the cheerful slash of a Christmas-red bow, making it impossible not to think about her. To wonder, but never to wish.

No, not ever again.

Shivering between the cold sheets, Noelle burrowed more deeply into the covers. Her toes found the metal bed warmer heating the foot of her bed. Ah, warmth. Above the background drone of the blizzard, she heard the hiss of the lamp's flame as it wavered, pausing to draw more kerosene up its wick.

On the other side of the bedside table, her cousin's mattress ropes groaned slightly as she shifted, probably to keep the lamplight on her Bible page. "'The Lord does not look at the things man looks at. Man looks at the outward appearance, but the Lord looks at the heart.'"

There was a gentle whisper of the volume closing and the rasp as Matilda slid her Bible onto the edge of the table. "I didn't want to say anything when Mama was around, but did you two almost drown in the river? You know how she exaggerates."

"We didn't fall into the river. The sleigh stopped before that could happen. Fortunately." Noelle knew she would never understand why this runaway horse had been stopped short of disaster, when another one hadn't. Why the stranger had been in the right place at the right time to help them—this time. There was a greater mystery troubling her, though. Their rescuer. She wouldn't stop wondering about that man—against all reason and all wisdom.

"Divine intervention, beyond all doubt." Matilda sounded so sure. "Mama said that man was an angel. She said she wasn't sure how he'd been able to come through the storm like that and to stop that new horse of Papa's just in time. Then he disappeared like he was called up to heaven."

"He took my hand to help me out of the sleigh and, trust me, he was a man and nothing more. He was no angel."

"Then how did he disappear?"

"It was a blizzard. All he had to do was walk three feet and he would be invisible. You know how your mother is."

"Yes, but it's a better story that way." Matilda sighed, a girl of nineteen still dreaming of romance. "Do you think they exist?"

"Angels?"

"No, of course *they* do. I mean, dashing, honorable men who ride to a lady's rescue."

"Only in books, I'm afraid."

"But the stranger, he—"

"No." Noelle cut her cousin off as kindly as she could and pulled her covers up to her chin. "He was probably mounted up and at the edge of town when the gelding broke away. I heard other men shout out to try to stop the horse. He himself said he only did what anyone would do."

"You don't sound grateful."

"Oh, I am. Deeply." She'd done her best to try to keep her calm; as she'd told her aunt, all's well that ends well. But the truth was, about midway through supper the calm had worn off and she'd trembled in delayed fear and shook through most of the evening. Now, she felt worn-out and heartsick.

Why hadn't Thad introduced himself? Why had he used her blindness against her? He knew she couldn't look at his face and recognize him, so he'd chosen to stay safely in the dark. Certainly no hero, not in her book, she thought, knowing that was the broken pieces of her heart talking, apparently still a bit jagged and raw after all this time. He'd been the one to leave her waiting at her window, with no note, no one to break the news to her, nothing.

She squeezed her eyes shut, as if that could stop the hurt from flooding her spirit. It was a long time ago, and it didn't matter now.

Put it out of your mind, she ordered, but her heart didn't seem to be listening. She would never forget the way it had felt to wait through the heat of the September afternoon and into the crisp twilight and refuse to give up on him. Vowing to wait however long it took, that's how much she believed in him. How strong her love. But as the first stars popped out in the ebony sky and the cool night set in, she'd had to accept the truth.

Thaddeus McKaslin, the man she'd loved with her entire soul, had changed his mind. Not the strong stalwart man she'd dreamed him to be, but a coward who couldn't tell the truth. Who couldn't commit. Who'd changed his mind, broken his promise and left town without her.

Why was he back after all this time?

Sharp footsteps knelled in the hallway. "Girls! I know you're in there talking. Lights out! It's past your bedtime."

"Yes, Mama," Matilda answered meekly.

Noelle knew her cousin was rolling her eyes, greatly burdened by her mother's strict role in her life. She herself had been that way once, but it had taken tragedy and maturing into an adult for her to understand the love that had been behind her mother's seemingly controlling behavior. Love, the real kind, was what mattered.

"Good night, girls." Henrietta's steps continued down the hallway to check on her other children.

"Good night, Matilda." Noelle curled onto her side,

listening to the rustle of bedclothes and the squeak of the mattress ropes as her cousin leaned to put out the light.

She tried to let her mind drift, but her thoughts kept going back to Thad. To his questions as he'd walked her to the door. He'd asked about her blindness and her parents and her unmarried state. She added one more silent prayer to the others she'd said, as she did every night before she fell asleep, kneeling beside her bed moments earlier. *Please watch over him, Father. Please see to his happiness.*

If a tear hit the pillow, then she was certain it was not hers. The storm droned and, finally warm enough, Noelle let sleep take her.

Thad put away the last of the dishes and hung the dish towel up to dry. "You all set for the night, Ma? Is there anything else I can do for you?"

"Not one thing. You've been a great help. You've had a long day, too. You go put your feet up and read some of the newspaper with your brother."

His older brother, Aiden, gave him a forbidding look over the top of the local paper.

"I'll go on over to the shanty, then, where my books are. Good night."

"I'll make pancakes tomorrow morning just the way you like them." Ida glowed at the prospect and untied her apron. "Good night, son."

Aiden didn't look up from his reading. "'Night." The clock was striking nine as he closed the back door behind him. He had to fight the blizzard across the yard and through the garden to his dark, frozen shanty. Typical Montana weather, snowing just when you thought there couldn't be any more snow left in the skies.

He found his home dark and empty and cold. As he knelt to stir the banked embers, air fed and sparked the coals. They glowed dull red and bright orange and he carefully added coal until flames were licking higher and bright enough to cast eerie shadows around the tiny simple dwelling.

He left the door open and the draft out, keeping his eye on the fire as he pulled the match tin down from the high corner shelf. Ice shone on the nail heads in the walls and on the wooden surface of the table. The lantern was slick with ice when he went to light it.

This was not the Worthington manor. Then again, he wouldn't want it to be. He hooked his boot beneath the rung of his chair and gave it a tug. Noelle was as unwelcome in his thoughts as the bright red hatbox on his corner shelf.

Just showed that what he'd come to believe in the past five years was true. The good Lord had better things to do than to watch over an average working man like him.

The shanty was warmer, so he closed the stove door and drew his Shakespeare volume down from the bookshelf. While he read of lives and love torn apart for the better part of two hours, Noelle was never far from his thoughts. He knew she never would be again.

When the shelf clock struck ten, he closed the book and got ready for bed. He shivered beneath the covers trying to get warm, and he prayed for her as he did every night. As he had for the past five years.

Chapter Three

"Three whole days trapped in this house by that blizzard." Aunt Henrietta bored through the parlor like a locomotive on a downhill slope. Crystal lamp shades trembled on their bases with a faint clink and clatter. "Three whole days I could have been sewing on Matilda's new dress, and instead I had to spend them in idleness."

"Well, not in complete idleness," Noelle couldn't resist pointing out as she paused in her crocheting to count the stitches with her fingertips. "You spent a lot of time composing letters to the local newspaper and to our territorial lawmakers."

"I hardly expect them to listen to a woman." There was a *thwack, thwack* as Henrietta plumped one of the decorative pillows on her best sofa. "But I will have them know what a danger that contraption is. What newfangled invention will they think up next? I shudder to think of it."

"Well, you should," Noelle said as kindly as she could. "With that dangerous contraption on the loose, do you think we ought to risk another trip to town?"

"It gives me pause." Henrietta moved on to pummel another pillow on Uncle Robert's favorite chair. "I must post these letters of complaint immediately. Noelle, I am sure, poor dear, you are frightened beyond imagining. Perhaps you ought to stay home with Matilda. No sense the two of you endangering your lives. I shall be fine."

Across the hearth from her, Noelle could hear Matilda struggling to hold back a giggle.

"I'll come with you. I'd like the fresh air." Noelle gathered her courage. Driving was a fact of life. She couldn't stay afraid of one thing, because she'd learned the hard way that fear easily became a habit. It had nearly consumed her after she'd first gone blind.

"No, I won't risk it." There was that smile in Henrietta's voice again. "Although my trusty mare is now reshod, so we shall not have to take that wild gelding, there is no telling what peril we could meet with."

"If that's true, then I must come, or I'll sit here worrying over you the entire time you're gone."

"You are a sweetheart." Henrietta blew a loud kiss across the room. "Now then, I've got my reticule. It's a shame about your new winter hat. Perhaps we can find another."

"The one I have is serviceable enough." Noelle carefully anchored her needle in her lacework, so she wouldn't lose any stitches or her place in the pattern, and folded it into the basket beside her chair. The floorboards squeaked beneath her weight as she stood.

"Maybe you'll catch word of the dressmaker's nephew," Matilda whispered, sounding a little breathless and dreamy. Perhaps she wasn't aware that her affections for the handsome teamster weren't well hidden. "Or, maybe you'll happen into the stranger's path again.

If he's new to town—Mama didn't recognize him and you know she makes it her business to know everyone—then perhaps he's looking to settle down. Homestead. Marry. He did rescue *you*."

"He stopped a runaway horse, it was nothing personal. Besides, he's probably already settled down with a wife and kids at home." But Thad married? She couldn't imagine it. She told herself it wasn't bittersweetness that stung her like an angry hornet as she crossed the room. Because she was steeled to the truth in life. It was best to be practical. She almost said so to Matilda but held back the words.

Once, like her cousin, she'd been young and filling her hope chest with embroidered pillow slips and a girl's dreams. Maybe that was a part of the way life went. Maybe she would be a different woman if she'd been able to hold on to some of those dreams, or at least the belief in them. She reached for her cloak on the third peg of the coat tree.

"Goodness! I've never seen such poor manners!" Henrietta burst out and threw open the door so hard, it banged against the stopper. "You! Young man! Where do you think you're going? You get back here and do this properly."

Thad. Noelle knew it was him. Somehow, she knew.

"Uh, I didn't want to disturb, ma'am." His baritone sounded friendly and uncertain and manly all at once. "It's too early to call, but I was on my way to town and didn't want to make a second trip to drop this by."

"Still, you ran off before we could properly thank you the other evening."

"There was a blizzard raging, ma'am. I had livestock

I had to get back to. The storm was growing worse by the second."

He sounded flustered. She really shouldn't take any pleasure in that. If only she could draw up enough bitterness toward him—but now that he was here she realized that she couldn't.

"I'll have to forgive you, young man, seeing as I am standing here alive and well to scold you, because of you." Henrietta's voice smiled again. "Are you coming in?"

"I, uh, was planning to get on with my errands." Noelle could feel his gaze on her like the crisp cold sunshine slanting through the open door. She wanted to say his name, to let him know she had figured out who he was and that he couldn't hide behind her blindness any longer. She also wanted to hide behind it, too. It made no sense, either, but it was how she felt.

Maybe it was easier to let him go back to his life, and let it be as if their paths had never crossed. What good could come of acknowledging him? What good could come from not?

Henrietta persisted. "We are on our way to town, too, but I'm willing to put aside my pressing concerns to thank you properly. You should come in. I'll have the maid serve hot tea and you may meet my oldest daughter."

"Uh, no, thank you, ma'am." Thad scooped up the box and package he'd left on the swept-clean porch. "I found these in the road on my way out the other night."

"Oh, the new fabric. And, Noelle, your hat. How good of you to bring them. And to think we thought we'd lost these forever. It wasn't a tragedy, mind you, but a bother to have to go back to town and risk whatever peril would befall us this time around. Bless you for sparing us that."

"No trouble at all, ma'am." Thad wasn't sure what to make of this woman who stood as straight as a fence post and had the air of an army general, but there was one thing he did recognize. The way she was sizing him up and down as a husband candidate. He could spot a matchmaking mama a mile away. This one was so eager, she was giving off steam.

Or, he thought, maybe that was from his near state of hyperventilation. He was no good at social calls. "I'm more at home in a roundup, ma'am, or riding a trail. I don't get invited into parlors much."

"Then you're not married." She sounded real happy about that.

"No." He reckoned she would be glad to help him remedy that, so he backed up a few steps doing his best to escape while he could. Dragging his gaze from Noelle, who looked even lovelier in the soft lamplight. He didn't want to bring her more pain. Best just to leave. "Well, I've got to be on my way. Nice seein' you again, ma'am."

"Soooo," she dragged the word out thoughtfully. "You're *not married*. We have not been properly introduced. I'm Henrietta Worthington, that is my lovely daughter, Matilda, in the parlor and you already know my niece, Noelle."

"Yes. Good to meet you, miss." Tongue-tied, he tipped his hat, backing away, avoiding looking at Noelle again. The frozen tundra of his heart remained solid. In place. It was probably best if he didn't notice how her apple-green dress brought out the emerald flawlessness of her eyes and emphasized the creamy complexion of her heart-shaped face. Or how the dark hints of red in her chestnut hair gleamed in the firelight from the hearth.

No, it was best not to notice all that. Which was why he'd planned on leaving the goods on the front step and riding away without announcing himself. Too bad it hadn't turned out that way. He didn't know how, but he had to disappear from Noelle's life the way he'd come into it. He hadn't forgotten that he'd been the one to leave her waiting to elope with him.

"Let him go, Aunt." Noelle looked at him with a quiet, confident air as if she saw him perfectly. Her gently chiseled chin hitched up a notch. "I'm sure you have Mr. McKaslin trembling in his boots at the thought of being alone with so many eligible young ladies."

So, he hadn't been as nameless as he'd hoped. She *had* recognized him. Don't let that affect you, man, he told himself, but it was impossible. He'd hoped to spare her this, nothing could come of digging up the past, re-hashing things that could not be fixed. They were both changed people now. Strangers.

Why, then, was the small flame of tenderness in his chest struggling to life again? It was tenderness in a distant sort of way, in a wish-her-well sort of way. It could never be anything more. He wouldn't let it be.

All he had to do was to look around. When he'd been here before, a blizzard's heavy downpour had cut off his view of this grand home, the elaborate spread, the plentiful fields that would yield quality wheat. Such a place could not compete with the claim shanty he lived in now, behind his brother's modest home. Such a place could not compete with the land he planned to buy—when he found the right place that he could afford, that is.

No, there was no storm now to hide the differences between him and Noelle. The differences, which had always separated them, always would.

Henrietta Worthington gasped. "Noelle! Shame on you. You've known who this man is this entire time? Why haven't you said anything? And why don't we know this friend of yours? Come in—"

"He is no friend of mine. Not anymore." She cut off her aunt with her gentle alto, giving no real hint of the emotion beneath.

Anger? Bitterness? Or was it nothing at all? Probably the latter, Thad realized. Lost love first left hurt and anger in its wake, then bitterness, and finally it was forever gone, leaving not so much as ashes to show for it or an empty place for all the space and power it had taken over one's heart.

Proof that love was simply a dream, not real or lasting at all.

"I'd best be going." He gave Noelle one last look. Figured this would be the last time they would come face-to-face. He didn't intend to spend much time on this side of the county. He didn't intend to play with fire; he'd only get burned if he tried. He knew that for certain. All he had to do was gauge it by the narrowing of the aunt's gaze, as if she were taking his true measure.

And Noelle, what would she see in him now if she had her sight? Probably the man who sweet-talked her out of one side of his mouth and lied to her out of the other.

He took a step back, already gone at heart. "Not that it's my business, Mrs. Worthington, but don't go driving that black gelding again. He's no lady's horse. It's not worth your lives if he bolts a second time."

It was Noelle who answered, who'd stepped into the threshold with her wool cloak folded over one arm, staring directly at him. "That sounds as if you care, and how can that be?"

"My caring was never in question." He took another step back and another. "I'll always want the best for you. Take good care of yourself, darlin'."

"I'm not your darling." She tilted her head a bit to listen as he eased down the steps. "Goodbye."

His steady gait was answer enough, ringing against the board steps and then the bricks and the hard-packed snow. She felt the bite of the cold wind and something worse. What could have been. Thad was a lost path that would be forever unknown, thank the Lord. She thought of all the reasons why that was a good thing, but his words haunted her. Was he simply saying the easiest thing, or part of the truth, or was there more truth to tell?

She told herself she wasn't curious. Truly. She didn't want to know the man he'd become. So why did she wait until she heard the creak of a saddle and the faint jangle of a bridle, a horse sidestepping on the icy crust of deep snow before she stepped back into the warmth and closed the door?

"Noelle Elizabeth Kramer!" Henrietta burst out. "Why didn't you tell me you knew that man?"

"I don't. Not any longer. That's simply the truth." Why did she feel emptier as she hung her coat back on the tree? "I knew Thad long ago before, from my school days. As it turned out, I did not know him very well at all."

Henrietta fell uncharacteristically silent, and Noelle wondered if her aunt was compiling a list of questions on the man's character and wealth. Which would be completely expected, but Thad was bound to be a disappointment to her aunt's high standards for an acceptable beau for one of her daughters.

From the corner of the parlor, Matilda gasped. "Do you mean he once courted you?"

"No, there was no courtship." No official one. Why it shamed her now, she couldn't begin to explain. It had all seemed terribly romantic to a sixteen-year-old girl with stars in her eyes and fairy tales in her head, to secretly meet her beloved.

Oh, it had been terribly innocent; Thad had been respectful and a complete gentleman, had never dared to kiss her even after he'd proposed to her. But now, looking back with disillusionment that had forever shattered those fairy tales and dimmed the stars, she could see a different motive. Not a romantic one, but a less than noble one. He'd courted her behind her parents' backs, purposefully fooling them, and for what?

In the end, he'd chosen to run instead of marry. In the end, if there had been any truth to his courtship, then his affection for her had paled next to the strength of his fear. At least, that was the way she'd rationalized it. That's why his words were haunting her. *My caring was never in question.*

Perhaps his caring had been only that. Caring and not the strong, true love she'd felt for him. Either way, it hardly mattered now. She knew his true measure beneath the handsome charm and solid-appearing values. Thad McKaslin was not a man of his word. He was a coward. A man who ran instead of stayed.

"What about his family? Does he own property?" Henrietta persisted. "That's a fine young man. And handsome. Don't you think, Matilda? Noelle, you must tell me what you know about him. Here's your cloak. We're still attending to our errands in town. I'll not be put off my cause, you know."

Noelle fumbled with the garment Henrietta pressed into her hands. Certainly she knew that; why had she re-hung her cloak in the first place? It simply went to show how tangled up her emotions were. A mess of them, threads of old hurt and confusion and the sharp tang of lost love were as hopelessly knotted. "I'm afraid I know very little about Mr. McKaslin. He left town long ago. I never knew what became of him. I never cared to."

After she'd finally accepted that he'd broken his vow to her. That he'd left her waiting for a promise he'd never meant to keep.

"Perhaps he left to make his fortune." There was the rustle of wool as Henrietta slipped into her coat. "Per-haps he has very respectable family back East."

"I'm afraid I don't know." Noelle lost count of her steps and had to reorient herself. Three more steps and she was at the door. The handle felt warm from the ra-diant heat of the fireplace, which was blazing on this frigid, late-winter morning—like her emotional tie to Thad. "But if I were you, I wouldn't depend on Thad McKaslin as a reliable kind of man."

When she stepped outside, the still morning air seemed to wait expectantly, as if some wonderful thing were about to happen. But what? She lived a quiet life teaching piano and crocheting and sewing for her five cousins' hope chests. The days, while happy, were predictable and routine. Why did it feel as if something was about to change?

Simply her wishful thinking, no doubt. Before she'd lost her sight, she had a love for romantic novels. Or, she reasoned, maybe spring really *was* right around the corner. It was, after all, late January. A month and a few weeks more and March would be storming in. It had been her father's favorite time of the year.

Her father. She missed him so strongly, it was like taking an ax to her midsection. She gripped the rail and froze a moment, drawing in the fresh, icy air. He'd been at her side when she finally accepted that Thad had abandoned her. He'd run away from marrying her. After she confessed, her father had comforted her and reassured her as she cried for the pieces of her shattered heart and broken dreams. Only the death of her parents had hurt with that same keen-edged grief.

I miss you, Papa. She felt the lonesomeness for him as solidly as the boards at her feet. Her knees felt weak as she tripped down the steps. Thad had brought all this up. Simply waltzing into her home, pretending he was such a good dependable man. Why the pretense? She already knew the kind of man he was.

An opportunist, her father had said to her, kindly, while she'd sobbed. She remembered how her mother had come into her room with a steaming pot of tea for all of them. She sure ached for her parents' comfort, their company, everything. They had held her up after her innocent illusions had been so thoroughly destroyed.

If they were still alive, they would be the first to reassure her and to send Thaddeus McKaslin back on his way to wherever it was he'd run off to. Good riddance.

But as she reached the brick walk, she heard the low,

deep-throated nicker of a horse's greeting and the chink of steeled shoes shifting in the ice-crusted snow. Was it Thad's horse? Was he still here? And why was she allowing herself to be so upset by him that she hadn't paid enough attention to remember if she'd distinctly heard him riding away or not?

The horse's bridle jingled and she could hear him take a step her way. She held out her hand and the steel-shod hooves padded closer. This time the low nicker was accompanied by the radiant warmth of a horse's big body, and the tickle of whiskers against her fingertips warned her a second before the horse scented her palm and rubbed against her.

Oh, she loved horses. She cherished the warm-silk feel of his muzzle and stroked the animal's nose.

"You are a handsome one," she said, running her fingers over the length of his nose to his forelock. He snorted as if in answer and pressed into her touch. Joy, warm and quiet, flowed through her. "I miss riding the most but you'll just keep that secret, right? My aunt does not approve of women horseback riding, even side-saddle."

The horse seemed likewise offended as he snorted and leaned in, lowering his head to give her better access; at least that's how she chose to think of it. "It's a pleasure to be with a well-behaved horse. That's not usual around here now that my uncle has—"

An angry, buglelike whinny shattered the morning's peace. Noelle spun toward the sound—the stable. That new stallion of Uncle Robert's was so spirited, he was dangerous. "—has decided he's a horseman," she finished.

Please, don't let my uncle get hurt, Lord. She took a

step off the brick walk and stopped, unsure of the uneven drifts of snow that would be no challenge if she could see them. Not that she could help if there was a problem, but she wanted to help. Robert knew next to nothing about horses, although he was certain he knew everything, the poor, dear, misguided man. Perhaps that's where Thad was, giving her uncle a hand and a word of advice. Robert needed it.

The front door slammed shut and Henrietta barreled down the steps with the speed of a tornado. "Where is my horse? Why hasn't Robert brought out Miss Bradshaw?"

"I don't know why your mare is not hitched up yet. It sounds as if he's having problems with the stallion again."

"The stallion? What about my mare? He'd best not even contemplate the possibility of my driving to town behind that—that creature! As if that new gelding hadn't been bad enough of an experience. We shall meet peril for certain. Wait here, dear." Henrietta tromped by on the walk, her shoes striking against the brick and then muffled by the snow.

Noelle imagined her aunt lifting her skirts and wading through the snowdrifts like a Viking conquering the fjords. Since she had to stand alone in the cold, she may as well get better acquainted with Thad's horse. As if the horse agreed, his bridle bit jingled—perhaps he was shaking his head—and then he nosed her hand for more affection.

How could she resist? She savored the little joys of it. The alive feeling of the warm, velvet coat. The rhythmic breathing hot against her hand. The ticklish muzzle whiskers. The heart of the horse as he politely lipped at the pocket of her cloak. She liked him; it was hard not to. Once, in simpler times, she had dreams of horses and living all her life with them—and Thad.

Thad. At least she didn't have to worry about him lingering around, or coming back into her life to stay. His leaving was a certainty. She ran her fingers through the horse's coarse forelock. What was keeping Henrietta's sleigh?

Chapter Four

Seeing her haloed by the frozen mist and chatting with his horse was like being kicked by a bull. He'd been kicked several times, so he knew exactly how it felt. The sight of her knocked the wind from his chest. She looked like his dreams. She looked like his idea of heaven. Always had. Always would.

"So, McKaslin," Robert Worthington said from the finely built stable's main aisle where he fastened the last buckle on a docile mare's harness. "What do you think of my fine purchase in that stall over there?"

Thad looked up and down the aisle; only a few stalls were occupied and one by a white horse showing his teeth. He wasn't sure exactly what to say to compliment the ill-tempered colt. The scent of newly cut wood and fresh shavings at his feet told him this enterprise of Worthington's was brand-new.

Noelle's aunt marched into sight. "Is that fine purchase the reason my sleigh is not ready? Poor Noelle is out there half frozen in this cold. She's fragile, you know that."

"I know, dear. Just had a bit of a problem is all. McKaslin gave me a hand."

"A problem? It looks like a wild bull got loose in this stable—"

Noelle. Thad's attention swung back to her and stayed there. She was petting Sunny. The mustang was no fool. He was nosing her hand affectionately, looking as though he wanted nothing more in the world than to win a smile from her. Poor fella. Thad knew how he felt. He'd once felt the same way.

Seeing her again— Whew. He froze in place. He'd wanted to avoid her this morning so he wouldn't cause her any pain, but now he realized he wasn't as tough as he liked to think.

He could resist making a mistake like her again, but what he couldn't seem to do was to stop the pain. Why, it was impossible to forget how his love for her had once filled his spirit the way a rising sun filled the hollows of a mountain's peak.

Time to leave, man. He nodded in Worthington's direction. "Good luck with that wild boy of yours."

Robert looked up from rechecking the bridle buckles and grinned. "You say that like you think I need good luck."

I think you're gonna need more than that. Thad glanced at the big white stallion, teeth bared and ears plastered flat against his head, and was glad he didn't have to deal with that animal. "I hope you got a good price for him."

"Cost me a pretty penny."

That's what Thad was afraid of. "I meant a low price, sir."

"Well now, he's got excellent confirmation. And his pedigree. Why, it's about as impressive as it can be."

"I'm not about to argue with you, but personally I like a horse who isn't keen on biting me when I get anywhere near him." Thad tipped his hat. "Good day to you, ma'am."

"Uh, well, thank you, young man." With the ferocity of an army general the fine lady squinted her eyes and looked him up and down. "Do you have relatives up north?"

"I believe so. My father's side of the family."

"Very well. It showed a fair amount of character to deliver our lost packages. You went out of your way when you didn't need to."

"I just did what anyone would do." He took a step away before she could invite him back into the parlor for supper or some such nonsense. He didn't figure that she'd want much to do with him if she knew the truth about the way he'd treated Noelle. "Again, good luck, Mr. Worthington. You be careful when you're handling that stallion."

"I intend to." Robert straightened and took the mare by the bit to lead her, but seemed frozen in midstep. He glanced through the wide, open double doors to the picture Noelle made, befriending the gold-and-white mustang. "You wouldn't know a good horseman you could recommend to me, would you? I could use some help around here."

"I, uh—" *Me.* He clamped his mouth shut before the words could escape. He needed a job, but not that bad. Besides, Noelle wouldn't like that idea. And the notion of facing who he was every day—the man she made him remember. The man she saw as a coward. That's what he felt like, even though he knew it wasn't true.

Maybe Noelle's opinion of him meant more than he'd ever thought. He steeled his chest and took a step back, staring hard at the ground, at his scuffed boots, anywhere but where she stood, framed in silver light. "I'll let you know if I hear of anyone."

He left the husband and wife to their chatter, keeping his eyes low, feeling the ache of regret tug at him. There she was. He could sense her somehow like warmth on a spring breeze. What did he do? Walk up to her and make pleasant conversation? He didn't reckon she wanted that. He didn't, either.

The trick was to keep control of that spark of caring in his heart. Keep it small and eventually it would snuff right out. That was his hope anyway.

She must have heard him coming because she turned toward him. There was no smile on her face and she stood in shadow. He'd always remembered Noelle as she'd been when he'd left her—she'd never aged or changed for him in memory, but time changed everyone.

He saw that now. The way hard loss and sorrow had changed the shape of her mouth and eyes, no longer wide with an easy, assumed happiness. Her face was as soft as a rose blossom still, but leaner. Time and maturity had sharpened her high cheekbones. Her emerald-green eyes, still so lovely, did not twinkle and smile at him with good humor, the way they once had. The way they never would again.

She was lovelier than ever, but changed. It was the change now he saw, not the similarities to the young woman he remembered.

"You have a very polite buddy," she said gently, politely. "Unlike my poor uncle's horse."

"Sunny's the best. I'm lucky to have him." He didn't bother to hide the affection he felt. "Pardon me, your uncle seems like a fine man but not that good with horses. I'm worried about that stallion in there."

"As am I. My uncle is inexperienced with horse handling. He's city raised." She turned her attention back to Sunny, who didn't seem to mind more petting a bit. "My aunt is not pleased with this notion of his to quit the bank and realize his dream of raising horses."

"Pleased? Nah. It's worse than that. When I left, she was lighting into him real good." Thad came close to reach for the reins. "Doesn't a family like this have hired stable help?"

"We're between hands right now. Henrietta disapproved of the last one's interest in one of her daughters—my cousins. Two are in town at school, and two more were sent away to finishing school. That's where Angelina will be next year, especially if another stable boy becomes interested in her again."

"Of course. I suppose a family has to be careful of its reputation."

"My aunt seems to think so. Listening to her, it would be impossible to find anyone good enough for her daughters to marry." Noelle kept a careful lid on her heart. Hearing the creak of the saddle and the jingle of the bridle as he obviously gathered the reins so he could mount up, she stepped back so he could leave. Good. She didn't have anything to say to him that hadn't already been said.

He was the one who seemed to be lingering. "Well, now, I'd better get along."

"Yes."

Perhaps she'd answered too quickly. Perhaps that single word had been too sharp. She hadn't meant it to be, but it was too late to change the awkward silence that settled between them like the frigid air. She was sorry about that. "I shouldn't have—"

"No, don't." He stopped her with a hand to her arm. "You have every right to hate me."

She didn't hate him, but she couldn't seem to correct him, either. His touch made a sweet, heartfelt power sweep through her, and it was unsettling. In memory came the summer's heat beating on her sunbonnet, casting a blue shade from the bonnet's brim, the scent of fresh cinnamon rolls and ripening wild grasses, and the pleasantly rough texture of Thad's large hand engulfing hers. Grass crushed beneath her summer shoes as they left their picnic basket and strolled near the river's edge.

The memory of color and shape and sight came, too. She remembered the way Thad's thick, collarlength hair shone blue-black with the sunlight on it. His eyes were the honest blue of the Montana sky before sunset. She could see again the shape of his sun-browned, handsome face, rugged with high slashing cheekbones and a strong blade of a nose. His jaw had been cut square and stubbornly; she supposed it still was.

The horse—Sunny—gave a low nicker of complaint. Thad's hand fell away from her arm, the bridle jingled and Thad spoke. "Looks like your horse and sleigh are ready to go."

The past spiraled away, bringing her solidly into the present with not even the memories of images and color before her eyes.

In darkness, she stood shivering in the cold, listening

to the *clip-clop* of the mare, Miss Bradshaw's gait and the faint hush of the sleigh's runners on the icy crust of snow. Hurt rose up like a cold cutting fog until it was all she could feel.

As if from a great distance she heard her aunt and uncle saying goodbye to Thad, she heard the beat of his steeled horseshoes on the icy ground and felt the tears of the girl she'd used to be, the girl who believed in love and in the goodness of the man who was riding away from her. Even now.

Please let him move on, Lord, she prayed as Henrietta's no-nonsense gait pounded in her direction. *Please take this pain from my heart.*

She didn't want to feel, especially after all this time, the ragged pieces of her spirit broken. She'd waited at the window for Thad watching the moon rise and the stars wheel across the sky. She stood waiting, shivering as the September night turned bitterly cold. Still she'd waited, believing in the goodness of the man she loved—a goodness that didn't, apparently, exist. She'd believed in a love that wasn't true.

Now, five years later, she felt the burn of that old heartache and gulped hard to keep it buried. The pieces of that shattered love still cut like tiny shards of sharp glass.

At least I know he will move on, she thought.

Please, Lord, let that be soon.

Her world was dark and pragmatic. She set her chin, gathered herself and turned toward her aunt's approaching steps. "You have your letter? I wouldn't want you to face such a perilous trip to town and realize you'd left the letter behind."

"Exactly." Henrietta sounded cheerful and it was no

trouble at all to imagine her delighting in the prospect of more drama. There was a rustle and shuffle as she gathered her skirts. "I certainly pray we shall not run into any further trouble. Now that Robert has agreed to take that beast of a runaway to the sale this very day, I am most relieved."

"Yes, but think of whoever buys the gelding," Noelle pointed out, struggling to put a smile on her face, as Robert took her elbow and helped her into the sleigh. "There is more peril awaiting that unsuspecting buyer."

Robert chuckled, warm and deep, a sure sign he was amused. "I will make it clear the gelding has certain training problems, so that we won't have that on our consciences."

"Good." Noelle patted his hand before she let him go. "Thank you for that. I don't want anyone to get hurt the way—" she swallowed hard, forcing the past back where it couldn't hurt her "—we almost did."

"And I'll drive you two lovely ladies to town myself, just to make sure there are no more mishaps."

Henrietta's humph of disapproval was loud enough to disturb the placid Miss Bradshaw. The mare sidestepped in her traces with a quick *clip-clip* on the ice. "Robert, you'll not hitch that beast to this vehicle!"

"Now, my dear, I'll just tie him behind the sleigh. There will be not a single thing to worry about."

"We shall see when we get safely to town. *If* we get safely to town." Henrietta gave the lap blanket a sound snap, shaking it out.

Noelle felt the rasp of the blanket fall across her knees. Whatever her losses and lessons in her life, she was so grateful for her wonderful aunt and uncle. Their love, their acceptance and their funny ways reminded her of her own parents. She hooked her arm through Henrietta's and held on tight.

By noontime, the freezing fog had been blown apart by a cruel north wind bringing with it the look of snow. Thad reckoned the growing storm cloud in the northeast might bring another whiteout. With the responsibilities at the home place partly his now, too, Thad worried about the livestock. He blew out a breath, knuckled his hat back and glanced around the busy town street.

Angel Falls was still a small town by most standards, but it had grown in the time he'd been away. There were more shops, and the look of the street was fancier, as if the whole place, despite the current recession, was managing to thrive. Fancy ribbons brightened up one window, colorful ladies' slippers another, even here at the far end of Second Street, making him feel out of place as he looked for the land office. But he did spot a bookstore. He'd have to go in there another time.

Was he on the right side of the street? He tugged the piece of paper from his trouser pocket and squinted at the address Aiden had scribbled down for him. A woman's gruff voice lifted slightly above the drone of noise on the street. A familiar voice.

"I shall never become accustomed to this weather!" Mrs. Worthington was climbing out of their sleigh a good half-dozen shops up ahead. "You're likely to freeze sitting still in this wind. You must come in, dear."

"I have a difficult time in a crowded place. No, I'd best stay here and try not to freeze in the wind." There was a note of humor to Noelle's voice.

A note that was like an arrow to his heart. Just a hint of humor, but without the brightness and the gentle trill of laughter he remembered so well. They truly were strangers, he reminded himself, surprised how much losing the last little piece of Noelle—the way he'd kept her in memory—hurt. So much for the notion of love. Not only was it ashes, but even long after the ashes had scattered, blown into nothing by the wind, the scar from the burn remained.

Yes. He rubbed at the center of his chest with the heel of his hand. The burn remained.

Mrs. Worthington hadn't see him; her back was to him as she marched along the boardwalk and disappeared into a doorway. He stared at the numbers written on the paper. Sure enough, he'd have to head in Noelle's direction. The last thing he wanted to do was to hurt her more. Chances were he could walk right by her without her knowing, since she could not see him. The boardwalks were fairly busy, and the noise from the street would disguise him well enough.

He headed on in her direction. It was best not to say howdy to her, or the burn on his heart would start hurting fresh. He kept his gaze focused on the icy boardwalk ahead of him and did not look her way, but there she was in his side vision, alone and lovely and sitting in the cold, blind and alone. He had to fight the powerful urge to stop and stay with her, to watch over her until her aunt's return.

She's not your lookout, remember? Not when her father forced him out of town the way he did. Not when her father had threatened his family's land. The trouble was, his heart didn't seem to care about all those sensible arguments. His spark of caring remained. There was a brightness within him that remembered, that would always remember, the schoolgirl who'd laughed so easily, saw wonder and joy everywhere, hummed with every step she took and was full of love and dreams.

Maybe his notion of love being nothing at all was a poor one, when put to the test. Seeing Noelle made his heart cinch up tight. Did she still matter to him?

The embittered part of him wanted to say no. No a thousand times. But as a gust of wind hit him square in the chest, he had to admit the truth.

He'd gone through a lot of misery for her sake. He'd left home, his family and everything he'd ever known. He'd slept on hard ground in freezing weather and in mostly unheated bunkhouses come winter. He'd ridden hard from sunup until sundown in blazing summer heat long day after long day. He'd lived a life he did not like or want because somewhere beyond his unhappiness was her joy, bright and shining and everything she deserved.

Yep, a wise man would just keep on walking and not give her another thought. He forced his boots forward on the icy boardwalk and kept on going.

"Thad?" Her gentle voice said his name the way it always had.

He could tell himself he didn't remember, that she was a stranger to him, that the past was past. It didn't matter so much for deep down in his heart, he would always know her.

She turned toward him as if she saw him. Her sightless eyes looked at him but did not see him. He stopped in the middle of the boardwalk. "How did you know it was me?"

"I'd know your gait anywhere. Do you see my uncle? He's at the horse sale." She sounded hopeful.

She looked that way, too. She might not notice how

easily her emotions played on her lovely face. He might not want to think about how easy it was for him to read her feelings. It always had been for him.

Aching at all the things that had changed between them, he leaned over the hitching post to peer down the alley. Robert Worthington in his fancy tailored suit stood out in the crowd of cowboys and ranchers. "He's right ahead, but he's looking at a half-crazed mare. Doesn't he have any horse know-how at all?"

"My poor uncle means well, but he's city born and bred. He's spent his life reading books on wranglers and cowboys, so he has a lot of fictitious notions in his head." Fondness shaped her soft face. "It's been a life-long dream of his to be a great horse trainer. The poor man has no notion of ranching or real experience handling horses."

"Where does he hail from?"

"St. Louis."

"Your parents came from here," he remembered.

"Yes. When they passed away and I was so injured, Henrietta came straightaway. She took charge of everything until Robert could settle things enough at his work to come help. He took over Papa's interest in the bank, started managing my investments, which I had inherited, and finally sold my family home."

Her family home? It had been a mansion and not a home, but he didn't comment on that. To her, it must have been jammed full of memories. "Was it too painful to live there, afterward?"

"Yes. You *would* know that about me." There was no mistaking the sorrow shadowing her face. "Robert moved his whole family to Montana Territory. He didn't want to take me away from this country where I grew up."

"You had to have been gravely injured."

"Yes, at first, but then I began to recover. God spared me my life, and I am thankful. I have to believe He has some purpose for my life yet."

"I'm sure of that, Noelle." He sounded so sincere, it was impossible not to believe him, impossible not to be touched by that. He shook his head once and cleared his throat. "Well, now, this mare looks much more suitable for a lady's driving horse."

"Yes, that's Miss Bradshaw. She's very sensible."

"So I see." His step drummed closer. "Miss Bradshaw?"

"Henrietta doesn't believe in calling a horse by his or her first name. She prefers a more formal relationship."

"Best not tell her all the nights I slept beside my horse."

"Best not." Noelle couldn't think of more to say; at least more that she wanted to. She wanted to be unaffected, beyond the pain of her schoolgirl's broken heart and above holding on to old anger. She'd healed from his betrayal and moved on, truly. But there, beneath the lid she kept on her heart was something more devastating than anger. She didn't know how to fill the silence between them.

And what a silence it was. Five long years of silence. She didn't know how to break it. She was fairly sure she didn't want to. It wasn't easy holding back the memories of how wrong she'd been about him, about love.

"McKaslin!" Robert's bass boomed cheerfully above the noise and motion on the street. His boots drummed quickly as if he were in grand spirits. "Glad to see you're still here. I was just telling my wife how well you handled that stallion. I've never seen anything like it."

"It was nothing. I've been around horses all my life, is all." A note of humility deepened his baritone.

Noelle knew he was being modest; Thad had a way with horses and an understanding of them she'd always thought was a divine blessing.

Not that it was her business anymore. She carefully drew the lap blanket more tightly around her, leaning to listen. Even when she told herself she shouldn't want to hear. His voice was deeper, manlier and rang with integrity, enticing a long-forgotten part of her to want to believe in him again. But she could not let down the guards on her heart.

"Say, Thad," Robert boomed out jovially, "you're good with horses. You wouldn't happen to be looking for work?"

Noelle's heart forgot to beat. No, her uncle couldn't be about to hire Thad. No, that was simply not possible—

"Rob!" Henrietta scolded above the sudden staccato of her steps. "How can you offer Mr. McKaslin a job? It's as if he isn't successful in his own right."

Noelle could hardly hear anything above the panicked rush in her ears. Surely, Thad would not accept Robert's offer. He had no interest in anything permanent, she was certain.

Thad's friendly chuckle rumbled with amusement. "Pardon me, ma'am, but do I look successful to you? I'm a simple cowboy, nothing more."

Noelle fisted her hands around the hem of the lap blanket. A simple cowboy? He had never been that.

"You can't fool me, son," Robert answered. "You are

a born horseman. I've never seen anyone calm down a horse as fast as you calmed the stallion this morning in my stable. You must make your living training horses." Noelle felt as cold as the rising wind as she waited for Thad's answer, although her heartbeat filled her ears so loudly, she didn't know if she would be able to hear him when he answered. She turned toward where he'd been standing on the boardwalk and wished she wasn't wondering. Wished she didn't want to know the pieces of his life and if he'd found his dream without her.

"No, sir," Thad said at last, his baritone heavy with regret. "I've been making my way as a drover. Riding cattle is hard work but it pays well enough."

"Cattle!" There was no mistaking the excitement in Robert's voice.

Noelle gulped in a bite of air, feeling oddly lost. She wasn't sure if it was worse to know Thad hadn't lived out his dreams than hoping he'd found them without her.

"I imagine that's a hard life, living on the trail," Robert went on to say. "Imagine you've gained a lot of experience."

"Yes, sir. I'm a good all-around man. I know my way around a cattle ranch. I mostly rode cattle. Spent March through October in the saddle on the trail."

She hadn't known she was holding her breath until the air rushed out of her lungs. Riding cattle? Was that what he left her for? To live a cowboy's life wandering from job to job far away from his responsibilities to his family and his promises to her?

Maybe she hadn't forgiven him as much as she'd thought. Shame filled her. There was this hardness in her heart she hadn't realized was there. She shivered beneath the layers of wool and flannel she wore. Determined, she tucked the sheepskin-lined robe covering her lap neatly around her and anchored it so the wind wouldn't creep beneath it. It didn't help. She still felt as cold as a mountain glacier.

Thad's words, calmly spoken, continued to ring in her ear. "Yes, I did like it very much. It's a tough life. Not as romantic as the dime novels make it seem."

"I should think not!" Henrietta humphed as she marched up to the sleigh, her steps quick and confident. "Not at all a preferable livelihood."

Judging by her uncle's chuckle, he was completely amused. "I keep telling my wife that it's the mark of a man how he handles hardship, not what he does for a living."

"Robert! You know that I don't completely disagree with you." By the sound of her voice, half shocked and half smiling, Henrietta was probably shaking her head fondly at her husband.

She could also imagine Thad standing quietly, hands on his hips, in that patient way of his.

"Riding cattle." Robert sounded impressed. "Now, that's excitement. Is it like they say? Singing the cattle to sleep and using your saddle for a pillow?"

"I mostly use my saddlebag, as it's a might softer." Thad's baritone rang with an equal amusement.

That was the sound she recognized—the ring of Thad's easy, warm, good humor. If she'd met him anywhere else, and not in a blizzard with fear thrumming in her ears, she would have recognized him no matter what.

"A saddlebag, eh? That doesn't sound much better. I suppose it's true what they say about the dust in the air and those long hot days."

She waited for Thad's answer, realizing that the lid on her heart was a little ajar. Had Thad found whatever he'd been looking for? Down deep, beyond her disillusion and her hurt, she truly hoped he had.

"Sir, that doesn't begin to capture it. Hundred degrees in the shade, a herd of cattle, say anywhere from a hundred to a thousand kicking up dust, why, it makes a Montana blizzard look like a clear day."

"That does not sound quite as thrilling. I imagine there's a lot of gain to that lifestyle despite its hardships. Sleeping under the stars must be nice."

"It surely does make for a good night's sleep. Nothing like having the heavens and the wonder there for your roof."

Yes, there was the Thad she remembered from long ago. A pang of longing and remorse knelled through her, and she was surprised by the intensity of it. It was a longing for that sweet, innocent time in her life when the world had been so sunny and colorful. When her future was nothing but a long stretch of happy possibilities.

Not anymore. Noelle heard the catch in her throat, like a sob, although it wasn't. She hadn't realized how much she had changed from the girl who knew how to dream, that was all. How much she had lost.

"Goodness, are you all right, dear?" Henrietta dropped onto the sleigh's seat, all motherly concern. "Are you catching a chill? I predicted the wind was too cold for you to sit here and wait for me, and now I fear the worst."

Ashamed, Noelle nodded. What was wrong with her? She did not know, and she had the feeling that if she did, she could not find the right words to describe it.

She cleared the regret from her throat before she could speak. "I'm not too cold. Truly."

She feared Thad had noticed, that he was watching her even now. What did he think about her blindness? Did he pity her? Did he think that she was damaged, less than whole? How could he not? "D-did you post your letter?"

"Certainly I did. Robert, untie Miss Bradshaw for me. I intend to get Noelle out of this bitter wind. In her delicate state, this cold cannot be good for her. If she does not succumb to pneumonia, I shall be amazed!"

Robert's chuckle was loving. "Yes, dear, go on. If you two lovely ladies wish to frequent the dress shop, I'll come by for the horse and sleigh and fetch the girls from the schoolhouse."

"Mind you don't be late! The school bells ring promptly at four o'clock." Henrietta took up the reins with plenty of shuffling. "Good day to you, Mr. McKaslin."

"Good day to you both." Kindness enriched his voice.

She imagined he was tipping his hat's brim once, the way he always used to do. She tried to picture more of him, tried to imagine the young man she'd known, in his prime now. It was hard to do, for he had surely changed as much as she had. Maybe more.

"Goodbye, Noelle."

His words sounded so final. "Goodbye, Thad."

As the cold wind scorched her face, she listened to his boots strike crisp and steady on the boardwalk as he walked away. She could not allow herself to imagine how his wide shoulders would have broadened, how his lean frame would have filled out with muscle and a cowboy's strength. Something cold struck her cheek as she tried not to see—and yet could not help drawing up the image of how he would look seasoned by experience and a rugged, active life.

"It's snowing yet again." Henrietta's voice carved into Noelle's thoughts. "When will winter end? I shall never become accustomed to these Montana storms."

"Yes, sadly we are all likely to be snowed over until Armageddon if this continues." Noelle knew that dire prediction would make her aunt happy, who huffed decidedly, pleased to have such problems to discuss.

Determined to leave Thad McKaslin out of her thoughts, Noelle set her chin and swiped at the cold wetness on her cheek—tears, and not snow after all. "Then your letter shall never reach the territorial governor."

"Exactly my brand of luck. Listen to that! That contraption! How blessed we are to have a sensible mare who will not bolt at the clamor and dank coal smoke." Only then did Noelle hear the clatter of the incoming train and smell its choking coal smoke. She did not notice much else, not the harmony of the traffic noise or the melody of the town's people going about their busy ways. Her heart was too heavy to hear any music. Snow began falling in earnest with sharp, needlelike hits that had no rhythm or song as they fell, driven on a bleak wind.

Chapter Five

As Thad circled a dappled gray mare at the sale—he'd let Robert Worthington talk him into giving his opinion on a few animals he was considering—not even the steadily falling snow could clean away the grit of emotion that clung to him.

This wasn't how he'd reckoned things would be. Seeing Noelle again was going to happen—he knew that when he'd made the decision to come back to Angel Falls. But he figured she'd be a wife and a mother, busy with the fanciful tasks that kept privileged women occupied, like book clubs and church fundraisers and whatnot. What he didn't figure on was having to realize how complete her father's plan had been. Mr. Kramer, rest his soul, must have known that Noelle would never understand or forgive, even with her generous heart. He'd hurt her then, and he was hurting her now. He hated it. He wished—well, he didn't know what he wanted, but he would do anything, or be anything, to keep her from hurting.

Impossible, he realized. His nearness made her sad. It was as plain as day.

"McKaslin, what's your opinion?"

"Wh-what?" He blinked, realizing he must have been staring at the horse's withers for a rather long time. The sights and sounds of the busy horse sale chased away most of his trail of thoughts, but not all of them.

"She's too old but, McKaslin, you seem to like her better than the gelding."

Thad knocked back his hat and the snow accumulating on the brim slid off, giving him time to think of the best way to answer. "You'd do well to go with an older horse. This mare is a little long in the tooth, but she's steady and gentle."

"I suppose I like the brash younger ones. More of a challenge."

Yep, Worthington had even less horse sense than he'd figured on. "Well, sir, you might not want to gamble your womenfolk's well-being like that. This old mare has a lot of good years in her, she'll be suited to pulling a light sleigh or buggy. Besides, look at the kindness you'd be doing. If no one buys her, she might be sent to the stockyards. That is one sad end for a nice horse."

Robert gulped at that. "I hadn't considered that before. I'm glad I asked your opinion. You have sound reasoning and a lot of knowledge. You know I'm looking to hire a good horseman to teach me what I haven't learned in books. If it's stable work you mind, I'll find someone to muck out the stalls—"

"You've got that wrong, Mr. Worthington. I don't mind stable work." Thad shoved his fists into his coat pocket, Noelle filling his thoughts. She was the biggest reason he had to say no, but there were others, too. "Truth is, I've got family trouble to help straighten out and then I've got my own plans."

"I understand." Robert pulled his billfold from his pocket. "I need permanent help, but more than that, I need someone like you. It's hard for a man like me to admit, but this horse business is not like banking."

"No, sir, it's very different. Stacks of money don't kick you in the chest."

"You're right there. I don't want to tell my wife how many times I've come close to getting seriously hurt. Maybe you'd consider working temporary, if that suits you. I'd be grateful for as long as you could stay."

It sounded mighty fine, except for Noelle. Remembering the look on her face whenever he was near cinched it. Nothing could make him hurt her like that. "I see you're considering it." Robert sure looked pleased.

Thad cast his gaze around the sale. Rows and rows of horses standing in a spare lot between a boarding-house and the smithy. Men and boys milled through the aisles, the sounds and colors muffled by the softly falling snow.

He thought of what to say to Robert and then of the land office he had yet to get to. He didn't know if he had a blue moon's chance of finding and affording his own place.

"Then come work for me. You can start right now by helping me figure out a good price for this mare."

"It's sure tempting, but I can't take the offer." There was no other answer he could give. "I wish I could."

"Could I ask what the reason is?"

"It's personal, sir." Out of the corner of his eye he caught sight of his older brother ambling along the boardwalk, probably heading to the land office, where they'd agreed to meet.

Best to hurry this along. He'd spent over an hour with

Worthington, and the man had yet to take his advice. "Robert, buy this mare. I'd offer low first, say twenty, but she's worth more. If you pay seventy-five for her, it's not too much."

"Well, I appreciate that." Robert tipped his hat as Thad did the same.

He left the man bargaining with the horse trader and waded through the fresh snow to the boardwalk. Aiden was leaning over the rail, one eyebrow arched in question.

"I heard that." He didn't blink, and his dark eyes kept careful watch as Thad hit the icy steps.

The ice gave him something to put his mind on instead of Noelle. "What did you hear?"

"Worthington trying to offer you a job." Aiden pivoted and crossed his arms over his chest. "Why would you turn down a good wage? Even if you find land to buy around here—"

"Land that I can afford," Thad pointed out. That was the catch. He'd worked long and hard to put aside every dime he could of his wages, and it didn't add up to nearly what he needed it to be. "I'm not going to work anywhere near Noelle Kramer."

"Ah, so you've seen her. I wondered what would happen when you did."

"You could have told me."

"About her blindness? You could have asked. You left town before because of her." Aiden nodded in the direction of a shop two doors down from the postmaster's. "Are you going to be leaving for the same reasons now?"

"No. I gave you my word I would stay and I will." Thad let his brother fall in step with him. There was a lot he hadn't told his brother five years ago and now. Time to change the track of the conversation. "How's Ma?"

"She's at the mercantile buying fabric to start sewing for Finn." Aiden didn't sound too happy about that.

Thad had learned that Aiden wasn't too happy about anything. "We'll make sure he doesn't let her down this time."

"We'll do our best. I got his train ticket taken care of. He ought to be arriving two weeks from tomorrow." Aiden's wide shoulders sagged a notch.

It was quite a burden. Thad could feel it, too. "I'll do my best, too. We'll get him straightened out."

"It all depends on how the territorial prison has changed him."

Thad didn't know what to say about that. Life had a way of changing a person in the best of circumstances. "I wish I would have come back sooner."

"The wages you sent home made the difference between losing our place and keeping it, so put that worry out of your mind. Between us, we've got enough of them as it is." Aiden checked his watch. "Let's hurry up. I've got to pick up Ma and take her to her church meeting in thirty minutes."

"Hey, I thought you were going to look at property with me."

"I'm not going to leave you to do this on your own, little brother. You need a wiser man's opinion."

"And where would I be gettin' this wise opinion? Surely not from you?"

Aiden smirked—the closest to a smile he ever got. "I've been keeping an eye on the land prices around here. Figured we would take a peek at the sale sometime, too." He gestured toward the sale. "When Finn gets home, he's got to have something to ride. He's not using my horses."

Or Sunny. Thad nodded in agreement.

Aiden cleared his throat as they started walking. "You wouldn't be thinking about beauing that woman again."

"Noelle?" Beauing her? There was an outlandish thought. "No. I learned my lesson and I learned it well."

"Now it's time for me to worry about you, brother. If it's not Miss Kramer, then what else has put that look on your face? There are the Worthington daughters. A few of them are of a marriageable age."

He'd hardly noticed the one in the parlor—then again, he would never notice anyone else when Noelle was in the same room. The pang that ached in his heart was best left unexamined. He spotted the land office. "The real question is, brother, why are you mentioning those daughters? Say, you wouldn't be sweet on one of the Worthington girls, would you?"

"Me?" Aiden spit out the word. "You've been gone a long time, brother, or you'd remember my opinion on most women."

"I remember just fine. But I reckon that you've been alone a long time. That might have changed your opinion some." Thad tried to say the words kindly, knowing his brother hurt for the wife and the newborn son he'd buried. Years hadn't chased the haunted look from Aiden's face. "Even I think about marrying now and again."

"You?" Aiden's jaw dropped in disbelief. "Didn't figure that would be likely."

"Now, I didn't say I was serious about it right this moment, but I've considered marriage from time to time." He stepped to the side to allow two women to pass by on the boardwalk. "The real trouble is finding a *sensible* female."

"Brother, there isn't a one of them on this green earth. God didn't make a woman that way, and if you think otherwise then you are just fooling yourself."

"Spoken like a man destined to live alone for the rest of his life."

"And you aren't?"

"No, not me." Thad blinked against the sudden sharp glare of wintry sun as the road curved northeast. "I'm holding out for the kind of woman a man can count on. Maybe someday I'll find a woman who understands that life is a battle you've got to fight every day."

"Good luck with that one, little brother." Aiden shook his head. "You've been riding the trail too long. You've forgotten what females are like. They're not like us."

"And you've been working in the fields alone too long."

"Then there's no doubt about it, little brother. We are a pair."

That was something he couldn't argue with. He did his best to steel his heart, to let go of what was past and hope that there would be a new start in life awaiting him. The truth was, he could never forget the pain he'd put on Noelle's lovely face. He had to do his best to stay away from her, for both their sakes. Knowing his luck, there wouldn't be land he could afford—at least the kind of land he wanted—and he'd be moving on after things on the home place were better.

The land office was nearly empty, he noticed as he yanked open the door, but the potbellied stove in the center of the room glowed red-hot. Thankful to be out of the bitter cold, Thad shook the snow from his hat and stepped inside.

* * *

"I can't tell you how this cheers me up!" There was no disguising the joy in Uncle Robert's voice from atop the mare he'd just bought for himself at the sale. "I feel alive again, I tell you."

Henrietta tsked as she pulled closed the dressmaker's door. "Robert, of course you are alive. You are driving me to distraction with this nonsense. You are no longer a young man, no matter how many ill-mannered horses you purchase."

Noelle felt a strange chill shiver down her spine, although perhaps it was the turn of the wind. Another storm was on the way, she could smell it brewing in the air. While her aunt and uncle battled good-naturedly, which was not unusual for them, her cousins spilled ahead of her down the steps and into the family sleigh. Their footsteps and chatter, lively and pleasant, counterbalanced the worry she had for her uncle. She wanted to ask Robert to dismount and join them in the sleigh, but it was hard to get a word in edgewise.

"*Two* more horses?" Henrietta sounded stunned. "How many horses will we need to pull our sleigh?"

"Now, Henrietta, you know I'm trying to start my own ranch."

"Yes, but you're a banker," Henrietta pointed out. "This is lunacy, Robert."

"Our Matilda is old enough to drive. The gray mare is for the girls' use."

"What? For us?" The chatter halted and footsteps herded away from the sleigh, Noelle presumed, where the old mare was tied.

"What's her name?" Angelina cried out.

"She's sweet!" fourteen-year-old Minnie cooed.

"She's really ours?" Matilda's hand slipped from hers.

Noelle froze in place on the sidewalk. So, Robert really had taken Thad's advice. That was a relief, but now she felt, well, grateful toward the man. She didn't want to feel the hint of gratitude toward the man. A hard knot coiled up in her stomach, and she wished, how she wished, it would stop. Her normally placid emotions were all snarled up ever since Thad had ridden back into her life.

Without Matilda to guide her, she dared not take a step for fear of falling on a patch of ice. She stood alone, waiting while the family inspected Matilda's new mare. Why was one ear searching the sounds on the street for Thad? Searching for his confident, steady gait, and for the low rumble of his voice?

Longing overtook her. Longing for those sweet, carefree days of her youth, for the dizzy happiness she'd felt when Thad had been beauing her, and for the shining future she'd wanted with him. The shining future she could not have now.

It was all Thad's doing, she realized. Making her remember her lost dreams. Making her look at memories filled with color and love. He made her realize how dark her life and how alone her future. Because of him, she saw her future so clearly—a future she tried not to look at.

"Noelle?" Matilda's touch at her elbow drew her from her thoughts. "Are you all right?"

"Y-yes." It took all her strength of will to bury her feelings. She turned in the direction of her cousin's voice. "No need to worry about me. Do you like your mare?"

"She's a darling. Papa promised he'd teach me to

drive once the weather turns warmer. I'm so excited. I've been waiting to learn to drive for ever so long. Mama still thinks I'm twelve."

"She loves you," Noelle said simply.

"I know. I'm glad I finally get to learn." Matilda sounded as if she was glowing. "Oh, I wonder if I'll be able to drive to Lanna's wedding. Probably. It will be the first wedding of the year!"

"Probably, although learning to drive might also mean that you have to fetch your sisters to and from school now and again."

"True, but I don't mind." Matilda fell silent, and the chatter from the rest of the family remained a background symphony of conversation. "Perhaps there's a good chance I'll run into the dressmaker's nephew while I'm out driving."

"That would hardly be proper," Noelle cautioned, remembering. With all the pieces of her heart, she was remembering her own mistakes. Mistakes she wanted to wipe out of her life like chalk from a blackboard, to rub away every flaw, every wrong choice and every foolish romantic notion. "It's one thing to admire an available man's good qualities—but you don't want to get yourself into trouble, Tilly."

"What trouble could I get into?" Matilda said, all innocence, for she'd been gently raised.

As Noelle had. So innocent, she could not imagine all the consequences of one innocent crush on a nice man. Somehow, Noelle could not separate the feeling that if she'd never fallen in love with Thad, if she'd never strayed from her parents' expectations for her, if she'd never been so headstrong and determined and stubborn, then her parents would still be alive. And she would still have her sight.

Right now, she could be sensibly married to a fine, dependable man, and have several children of her own. More lost dreams that were hard to swallow. Her arms empty, her heart empty, she swallowed hard to keep it from sounding in her voice. "We're commanded to honor our parents, Tilly. You oughtn't to be placing so much importance on something as frail as love. It's like a snowflake in the air, lovely while it's swirling on the wind, but it melts and vanishes into nothing."

"Oh." Matilda sounded stricken. "I didn't mean to disrespect Mama and Papa. I only meant—" She sighed. "I'm not sure what I meant. I just want to be married and happy."

She fell silent. Noelle didn't know what to say. More remorse filled her up. She hadn't meant to hurt her cousin. "I know you do, Tilly. I pray every day that the right man will come calling for you."

"And I appreciate it." There was a smile in Matilda's voice, as if trying to cover her hurt.

"I shouldn't have been so harsh. I didn't mean—" She felt the brush of snow against her cheek, as gentle as grace. This is what came from being anywhere near to Thaddeus James McKaslin. Everything was upside down. Her sensible life, her sensible thoughts. She was choking on the pain and memories she'd buried for good reason.

She squared her shoulders and said as kindly as she could to her cousin. "Am I hearing this right? Uncle Robert *doesn't* want to drive us home?"

"He wants to ride that beautiful new mare of his home. Oh, she is a beauty." Matilda sighed. "Jet-black.

She's so well formed, even I can see it. She's like perfection. Except she keeps trying to bite everyone."

"Is she tame?" Was it a mare Thad had approved of?

"Aside from trying to bite, she *seems* well trained. Come, I'll help you to the sleigh."

The late-afternoon chill seemed to blow right through her layers of warm clothing and penetrate her very bones. "I'm sorry I was so harsh, Tilly."

"No, I appreciate your guidance, Noelle. I just—" Sad. That's how Matilda sounded. "I want to believe there's a real hero meant for me. A great man who will love me for who I am and will never let me down."

"It's a nice dream, Tilly." But it was only a dream. Noelle knew that for a fact, but she held back her words. She didn't know what to say to protect her cousin; and the last thing she wanted to do was to take away her hopes for happiness. "There is a good man out there for you. I'm sure of it."

It was best to accept love for what it was, and marriage, she realized, her aunt and uncle's dissatisfaction with one another adding a sour note as the girls climbed silently into the sleigh.

Thad knocked the snow from his hat brim and felt his hopes fall to the ground, too. The land he was looking at—even buried in snow—was in sorry shape. The fencing—what was left of it—was tumbling over from neglect. The stable was sod. The house nothing more than a tumble-down shanty with no roof. If his guess was right, then where he was standing would be marshland when spring came. Most of the hundred and sixty acres were in a gully, which made him worry about floods from winter snowmelt and spring and autumn rains.

Yep, it was far from ideal property and for an unreasonable price, too.

Aiden ambled over from inspecting the buildings, leading his horse by the reins. "I hope you aren't thinking about laying down good money for this place."

"No. It would be hard to raise a profitable crop here. Livestock can't graze if the pasture's knee-deep in water."

Aiden nodded in acknowledgment, casting his gaze around, frowning severely. "The barn is ready to fall in. This place isn't worth what the bank wants for it." And this was the last property on his very short list.

Thad blew out a lungful of air and stared down at the toes of his scuffed boots. "I want to pay cash. I'm not going into debt for land. Not after what we've been through with the home place."

"Wise decision." Aiden cleared his throat, choosing not to speak of what they had struggled with.

The family mortgage had been the leverage Noelle's father had used to fully convince Thad to leave town without her. His ma was fragile; she had always been. The family had been desperate—Aiden's wife was expecting and sick with the pregnancy, and they needed their home and their land to make a living on. Thad had vowed he'd never let anyone have that kind of hold on him again, especially a banker.

He swallowed hard, glad he'd done the right thing— the only thing he could do. And yet, remembering the pain on Noelle's beautiful face, it had been the wrong thing, too. He'd been caught between a rock and a hard place, and he still was.

"I guess I'll look farther out in the county. Maybe the prices will be better there. Something close enough to ride in and help you with the wheat—and our brother, but far enough away from bad memories." That and the fact that he could see the county road from here, the road the Worthingtons also used to go to and from their spread. A lone horse and rider cantered along the lane.

"Sounds sensible." Aiden mounted up and swung his horse toward the driveway.

Some days reality was a tough thing. Thad gave one last look at the property. His hopes had been higher than he'd thought. He eased his boot into the stirrup and grabbed hold of the saddle horn.

"Would you look at that fool?" Aiden sounded concerned. "He's gonna get himself killed."

Thad slid into the saddle and looked up. Sure enough, it did look as though that horse and rider were in serious disagreement. They'd come to a stop in the road. The black was head down, tail up, bucking like a wild bronco. The man clung to the saddle. There was something familiar about that man. Thad reined Sunny toward the driveway, fighting a bad feeling in his gut. Robert Worthington had a brown wool coat like that, and he was not in control of his horse.

Aiden had already pressed his mount into a fast trot. "That man needs help. Is it—that looks like Mr. Worthington. He's a banker, not a horseman. What's he thinking?"

Thad couldn't answer, as he pressed Sunny into a fast gallop. Could he get there in time to help? The long stretch to the road seemed a hundred miles. Sunny's mane and stinging snow lashed his face as he pushed the mustang faster.

Hold on, Robert. Thad watched the black horse's nose nearly touch the snowy ground as the hind end rocked up high and then higher. Thad was close enough to see Robert scrambling to stay on, but he was slipping. Looked as if he was clinging to that horse with all his might. Chances were that Worthington was going to be unseated. Since he didn't know how to sit a green-broke horse, then he likely didn't know how to take a fall from one, either. Didn't he understand how dangerous that was?

"Faster, Sunny." Thad willed the mustang on, and Sunny went full out, his gallop so fast, they could have been flying.

It was not enough.

With the cold wind in his ears and tearing his eyes, it was hard to tell the exact moment Worthington went flying. But the bad feeling was back in his gut when he saw the man lift off the horse's back end and take a hit from those powerful, carefully aimed rear hooves.

Worthington hit the ground like a rag doll and didn't move. The black, freed from its rider, didn't run, but stayed, stomping and bucking and rearing up to paw the air, dangerously close to the fallen man. Thad winced, hurting for the man, knowing what this could mean. Robert looked unconscious. Maybe worse. Maybe dead.

Please, Lord, not that. A rare prayer filled his heart. Adrenaline chugged through his veins as Sunny's hooves ate up the distance. The instant Sunny hit the main road, he swung out of the saddle, keeping one eye on that black horse. His boots hit the hard-packed snow and he dodged just in time to miss a well-aimed, angry kick to his head.

Thad stood between Robert and the enraged horse and caught the mare by one rein. The instant his fingers tightened on the leather strap, he yanked straight down, pulling the bit with him. The mare fought him with an angry scream, sidestepping and half kicking and baring her teeth, fighting to get in a good bite.

"Whoa there, filly. Whoa, now." Beads of sweat broke out on the back of Thad's neck, strong-arming the powerful horse farther away from Robert. The man was still unconscious. Sunny stood by the fallen man, nosing him gently. Where was Aiden? As the mare fought, trying to knock him off balance, he heard hooves striking nearer.

"I said whoa, girl." The beads of sweat began to roll down his back. His arm muscles burned as if they'd been set on fire. He stood his ground, gritting his teeth, trying to use what leverage he had to force the mare even farther away from Robert.

"Hold on," Aiden called out from behind him.

Not sure how much longer I can do that. Teeth gritted, the mare surged upward into a full rear. His feet left the ground. Pain shot through his arms. *C'mon, Aiden.* He couldn't hold on much longer.

A lasso whizzed through the air and hissed around the mare's neck. The rope yanked tight. Thad's feet hit the ground, and he shortened the rein.

Thank the Lord. Out of the corner of his eye he saw his brother riding close, keeping the rope taut. Free to let go, Thad left the mare to his brother and ran.

Sunny, standing over the unconscious man, gave a snort of alarm. Thad dropped on his knees at Robert's side. His guts clenched. Blood stained Worthington's hair, chest and the snow around him.

Was it too late? Hard to tell. It didn't look as if he was breathing. Thad, dreading the worst, thought of Noelle as he tackled the buttons on the man's thick wool coat. What would she do if she lost her uncle, too? Who would take care of her? Protect her? Look out for her?

Thad tore back the coat, icy fear making his fingers clumsy. Robert's chest was still—too still. And then there was the faintest movement. Shallow. Slow. Unsteady. But it was a breath.

Relief nearly drowned him. Worthington was alive. There was some hope to cling to.

"Robert!" He unwound his scarf. "Mr. Worthington, can you hear me?"

No answer. No movement. Nothing. He was hurt bad, Thad knew it. Sweat broke out on his brow. The icy air made him shiver. The snowflakes landed on his nape as he leaned forward to try to bandage the wound. "I'll go for the doc!" Aiden drew up his horse. Behind him, the temperamental mare, squealing in angry protest, was tethered to a fence post. "Or, is it too late?"

"He's alive. Barely." Thad nodded toward his mustang, who stood patiently waiting at Robert's feet. "Best that you take Sunny. He can run faster than your draft horse."

"I'll be fast." Aiden slid off and gave the old draft horse a fond pat on his neck before he took Sunny by the reins. He mounted up, leaving without another word, for there was no time to waste.

"Robert?" Still no response. Thad shrugged out of his coat, debating what to do. At least those years of experience on the trail would come in handy. Thad figured the cut to Robert's head looked bad enough, but it was the blow to his chest that troubled him. He'd been around enough of this kind of injury to know it was often lethal. His heart could have been damaged.

The wind gusted, blowing colder. It was likely to be

worse before it got better—and not good for Robert. Thad whistled for Clyde.

The big gentle Clydesdale ambled close, his nostrils flaring at the scent of blood, but he wasn't startled. He was a wise horse as he stood and blew out his breath in a whoosh, as if accepting his new burden.

The wind was kicking up, and the snow began to fall like rain. In the haze of the downpour, Thad took a moment to gaze down the road, where the Worthington ranch lay.

Noelle. He hurt for her. He knew that she loved her uncle very much.

Clyde nickered, scenting the wind. Someone was coming. Thad was no longer a religious man so to speak, but that didn't mean he wasn't given over to prayer now and again. He sent one more plea heavenward, *Lord, let that not be his family. Let them not see this.*

A dark horse broke through the veil of snow. There was no mistaking Miss Bradshaw's fine lines and sensible demeanor. He leaped to his feet and grabbed the horse's bridle bit. "Whoa there. Is that you, Mrs. Worthington?"

The snow shrouded her, and her voice was sharp. "Who dares stop us? We have no money, for we spent it all in town. Unhand my horse, you—"

"Thad?" Noelle's gentle voice seemed louder than the storm. She was already moving out from beneath the lap blanket, looking at him as if she clearly saw him. "Something's wrong. What is it?"

"It's Robert." So much for his prayers, Thad thought, steeling himself to face her again. "The horse threw him. He's in the road, and we—"

"Robert?" Mrs. Worthington cried out. "What's happened to my Robert?"

"No, stay where you are, ma'am." He released the bit to stay the woman's arm. "He's injured. I need you to stay collected."

"Injured?" The woman began to hyperventilate, breathing deeply and rapidly.

"Noelle, my brother's riding for the doctor, but we cannot leave him in the road. I was about to put him on the back of this horse, but the sleigh would be best for him."

"Of course." She looked stricken. Instant grief had carved its way around her emerald-green eyes. "Minnie, crowd the lunch pails and books into the backseat. Tilly, come help me. Angelina, see to your mother."

Thad turned on his heel, rushing the few paces back to the fallen man's side. There was so little he could do for Robert, but do it he would. He crouched down beside the fallen man and knocked aside the snow. A fine layer had begun to accumulate on Robert's body as if he were already gone.

Taking gentle care with the injured man, Thad lifted him carefully, determined to get Robert home. With the big man's heavy weight in his arms, he gave one final prayer. *Help him, for his family's sake. Noelle has had enough losses.*

A low note rose in the strengthening wind, and he feared his faith was not strong enough to lift his request to heaven's ear.

"Thad, lay him here." Noelle had deftly collected the lap blankets and had lined the center seat.

As the wife and daughters caught sight of their loved one, battered and bleeding and unconscious, their renewed cries rose up and echoed around him. Thad hardened his heart, fearing a sad outcome, and carefully laid down his burden, holding the man's head in one hand so there would be no further injury.

He was concentrating so hard, he didn't notice Noelle's touch until her hands bumped his. Her fingertips feathered over the blood-soaked makeshift bandage.

"We've got to wrap him up well." Thad spied the last lap blanket lying over the back of the front seat and pulled it onto the unconscious man. "Make sure to keep him as still as you can. I'll be riding right behind the sleigh."

Noelle nodded. Snow clung to her everywhere, gracing her with a pure white luminescence. Her sadness eked into his stone-hard heart and he gruffly moved away, leaving so much—leaving everything—unsaid.

"Getup, Miss Bradshaw." He reached out to give the mare a light pat on the flank and the mare took off, drawing away the sleigh and Noelle.

His Noelle. He could tell himself a thousand times that she was no longer his. That he didn't love her, wouldn't care about her, that the past was done and gone.

The truth was not so simple. The truth left him feeling as hopeless as the bitter winds howling in from the north. He mounted up and pressed Clyde into the teeth of the growing storm.

Chapter Six

Noelle had never felt so useless. While they waited for the doctor to come, the maid and cook hustled back and forth from the bedroom to the kitchen and back again bringing all sorts of necessary items. The best thing she could do was to sit in a chair by her uncle's bedside.

"Robert? Oh, my Robert, please wake up." Henrietta clutched her husband's hand, tears streaming down her face. "You wake up. You hear me? It's the least you can do for not listening to me. If you had, you wouldn't be d-dying."

Lord, please don't let that happen. Noelle swiped at a falling tear. She sat straighter on the ladder-back chair the maid had brought up for her and steepled her hands together.

Please let him be all right.

She could not see to bind his wounds, cook and prepare a poultice or tend to cleaning his abrasions. The most she could do was to keep out of the way of those who could. The only thing she could do with her hands was to pray. As important as that was, it didn't feel like enough.

"If you l-leave me, Rob—" Henrietta choked on a sob "—I shall never forgive you. Mark my words! I will hold it against you for all eternity, that's wh-what I'll d-do."

Her aunt broke down again, all tears and incoherent fear. Noelle unfolded her hands from prayer and rose to find a fresh handkerchief from the top bureau drawer. The eerie, waiting silence of the room and of the house made her padding footsteps seem louder than a herd of horses at feed time.

"Here, Henrietta." She felt her way to the other side of the bed, where her aunt sat sobbing. "What more can I do for you?"

"There's nothing you can do, child. All I want is to see my Robert awake and alive and as good as new. That's what I want." She took the handkerchief and blew her nose with a trumpeting sound. "That man! Why did he go and do that? Mr. McKaslin told him not to buy that mare. Not a lick of sense. He's at *that* age." Knowing her aunt needed to talk, that it would comfort her, Noelle knelt on the wood floor. "What age?"

"Selling the house in town, moving out here to this wilderness is trouble enough. But he quit his job at the bank. Quit. We still have our girls to raise and marry off, every single one of them. This is not the time to begin a horse ranch. Weddings are expensive and we'll have five of them, *and* Lydia's and Meredith's finishing-school costs. Next year Angelina will be attending the academy in Boston, and the year after that Minnie. How will we find good matches for the girls and their lasting happiness if we cannot afford it?"

Noelle found Henrietta's elbow and from there, took her aunt's hand in both of hers. She knew her aunt well enough to know it wasn't the finances she was so distraught over. Henrietta's love was so deep for her husband she could not speak of it.

Noelle wished she knew how to comfort that kind of pain. She felt inadequate as she gave Henrietta's hand a loving squeeze. "One worry at a time. You're not alone, my dear aunt."

"You are a blessing to me." Henrietta sniffled. "What is keeping that doctor? Doesn't he know my Robert needs him? What kind of a physician takes his own sweet time? I should write a letter of complaint." She heard the echo of an approaching step at the far end of the hallway.

"The doctor's riding up now." Cook charged into the bedroom, breathing hard with her exertion. Water sloshed in a basin and she plunked it down on the top of the bureau. "Out of the room, missy. The doc will need room to work."

Yes, she was in the way. Noelle released her aunt's hand and pressed a loving touch to her uncle's forehead. He was such a good man. He had taken her in when she'd had nobody else. He was a good husband and father.

As she slipped from the room the doctor was hurrying up the stairs, perhaps let in by the maid, Sadie, and once again, Noelle was in the way when she wanted so badly to do something to help. She took several paces back and waited in the hallway's cool corner until the medical man strode through the doorway in a great hurry and clatter.

Only then did she make her way downstairs. With a trembling step and a heavy heart, she retreated to her chair in the parlor. The low crying and quiet sniffles told her she wasn't alone in the room. The fire was low,

judging by the dull hum of the flames and the lazy oc-
casional pop, but she could not see to add wood to the
grate.

"Matilda? Would you like me to pray with you?"

Another quiet sniffle. "N-no. I just left Minnie and
Angelina praying in the library. I j-just hurt s-so mu-uch."

"What can I do for you?"

"There's nothing that you can do. Only the d-oc-tor.
And G-god."

"Should I make you some hot tea?"

"That would be l-lovely." Matilda stifled a sob.
"Cook's lemon mint?"

"Of course." Relieved to have something construc-
tive to do, she headed to the kitchen, counting her steps
as she went, ticking off the number of paces from her
chair to the dining room and from the table to the
swinging kitchen door.

Thad. She knew he was there by the change in the
air, by the scent of horse and leather and hay. Against
her will, her heart tugged as if he'd cinched a rope
around it.

Split wood tumbled into the fuel box with a roll and
thunk. She waited, holding herself very still as Thad's
movements seemed loud in the still and empty room.
The fire's voice grew to a crackling roar.

"That'll do." Cook's grudging approval was a rare
sound. "That was mighty Christian of you, Mr. McKaslin."

"Just helping out while I'm here." His baritone
tensed, as if he knew she was in the room. "I guess I'd
best see to the other fires in the house."

His footsteps knelled closer with the unhurried,
strong beat that she knew so well.

She stepped aside, knowing she was in the way

and expected him to walk on by. After all they'd been through, what could there be left to say? She wouldn't trust him, wouldn't allow a friendship, would do nothing but to wish him well. She was certain he felt the same way.

But his gait halted, and she could feel his calming presence towering over her.

"I'm sorry for your uncle," he said gruffly. "I don't suppose there's any word from the doc yet?"

Her eyes watered at the tender caring in his voice—a tender caring she well remembered through all the years and disillusionment. It had been the great gentleness in the powerful man that had once won her heart completely.

If only her heart did not remember that now. She nodded, not trusting her voice, wishing him to go on his way before the burning in her eyes turned to tears.

"I'm no longer much of a praying man, but I've been keeping him in prayer."

"That means a lot." One hot tear rolled down her cheek. "More than you know."

"I care more than you know."

The rough, calloused pad of his thumb brushed featherlight against her cheek to stop her single tear. He'd moved closer, and he leaned in closer still. She could hear the rhythm of his breathing and smell the faint scent of soap on his shirt.

"I know Robert is like a second father to you. I don't want you to lose him, too."

Noelle shook her head, too overcome to speak. She recognized the soft note in Thad's tone, and she knew how his face would look, his eyes caring, his jaw squared, a combination of strength and heart that had always dazzled her.

Another tear rolled down her face, and he caught that one, as well, brushing it away with a kindness that made her ache with all that she had lost. All that had never been.

"Are you going to be all right?" Thad was all the stronger, in her view, for his kindness. "I can sit with you."

"No." How did she tell him the truth? She ought to be crying for her uncle, but the tears were for herself. For him. For the fragments of the past she'd never truly let go. She held on to those bright pieces of joy like a miser did his last pieces of gold. They were slivers of happiness she could not stand to remember. They were bits of sorrow she could not forget.

"N-no." The word scraped against her raw throat. "You go on home. I shall be fine."

"All right, then, but I'm not about to leave. You sure you're okay?"

"S-sure."

"You don't look all right."

Those pieces of sorrow felt brighter, bigger. It was not him she needed.

The door swished open and shut, Thad was gone, and she was achingly alone. She could hear the striking of Cook's shoes on the stairs echoing rapid-fire. Dully, she heard Thad pass through the house before the kitchen door swung shut and cut off the sound of him.

She felt adrift. She longed for the comforting words of her Bible. She ached for the days when she could have run her fingertips along the edges of the fragile, gold-edged pages, treasuring all those wonderful words and passages.

It was no trouble to locate the everyday teapot in its place on one of the many kitchen shelves or the tins of tea. A few quick sniffs helped her to find Tilly's favorite blend.

While she worked, she heard the younger girls clattering down the hall from the library and questioning Cook.

What had the doctor said? She plucked an oven mitt from the top drawer next to the stove and strained to listen.

"The doc has said nothing yet, only that the fall should have killed him. Perhaps there is still hope."

"What if Papa n-never w-wakes up?" Minnie's thin, fragile voice held a note of pure anguish.

Footsteps pounded up the stairs, drowned out by sobs.

"Angelina, Mama said we all had to stay downstairs," Minnie called out. "Angelina, I'm telling on you."

"I don't care." The strike of shoes on the staircase had to be Angelina's, while Minnie cried.

I know exactly how much it hurts to lose a father. Lord, I hope You can spare her, spare them all, that pain. She hurt for them in too many ways to count, this loving family who had taken her in as their own. She had done her best to accept a similar hand the Lord had dealt her, but she truly prayed that the Worthington family would have better favor.

She carefully located the teakettle's handle and lifted it with the mitt, intent on keeping the kettle level so as not to spill boiling water all over the stove, the floor and her dress. She was concentrating so hard that she didn't notice a strange burning smell until after she'd returned the kettle to the back burner. Her skirts had gotten too close to the hot stove, and she'd scorched the fabric—again. She touched the hot fabric with her fingertips, unhappy with herself for not remembering to check her dress.

The door chose that moment to whisper open. "Don't worry, it's not bad. Just a small spot."

"Thad." She felt foolish fussing over her skirt, and she straightened, knowing her face was flushed.

"What are you doing at the stove?"

"Trying to be useful."

"Seems to me you don't need to be in the kitchen to do that."

There it was, his kindness again. It was harder to confront than all the ways he'd wronged her. A lump formed in her throat. Before she could search for something—anything—to say to break the silence between them, a flurry of steps rang in the stairwell. The girls' voices rose in a clamor. The doctor had come down.

"Guess you'd best get in there." The hinges whispered and silenced.

He had to be holding the door for her. She smoothed down her skirt, set her chin and salvaged what she could of her composure. She would not allow herself to imagine how tall and dark and handsome he looked and the way his steadfast kindness only made him more so.

She breezed through the doorway without a word and did not look back.

The doctor had left, saying he'd done all he could. It was up to Robert now, and up to God, whether he would awaken or if he would not. All anyone could do for him was to wait and to pray. Their reverend had come, and after supper and a sustaining prayer session, he left, too.

The evening had ticked by and midnight was near. Noelle was still dressed—she'd changed into a garment that wasn't scorched—and, alone in the parlor, she worried who would ride for the doctor if Robert needed him. Matilda did not know how to drive, the other girls were too young, and Sadie, the maid, was afraid of horses. With Cook gone home, that only left Henrietta, and heaven knew the woman was too distraught, and rightly so, to do anything.

At loose ends, she settled into her chair by the hearth. The heat was fading and the fire was nearly silent. She tried to open her heart in prayer, but the words didn't come. Only fear did.

Life was a fragile gift, and all it took was one moment in time, one rattlesnake or one poor decision to buy a horse for it to change in a moment and forever. If only Robert had bought a saddle horse as tame as the little old mare he'd gotten Matilda.

That brought her thoughts right around to Thad again. His words had been haunting her all evening long. *I care more than you know,* he'd said with a ring of honesty that confused her.

"Noelle?" A familiar baritone rumbled low and quiet in the midnight stillness, and it was as if she'd dreamed him up. But it was his step coming her way and no dream, echoing in the room and not in her hopes.

"Thad? What are you still doing here? I thought you went home."

"No, I thought I'd stay around and help out. Try to be useful." There was a smile in his words, small, but sure, a warmth she could not deny still lingered somehow, impossibly, between them. "After Aiden fetched the doc and saw to my ma in town, he brought in the mare. I got her settled and then gave the stable a good cleaning. The animals are snug for the night. Thought I'd come in and bank the fires so the house will be safe for the night."

"You've been here the whole time?"

"Yes. Sadie brought a dinner plate out to me while I was working. I'll be staying the night in the stable."

"But it's freezing outside."

"I've got my bedroll, thanks to my brother. I'll be fine."

"You won't be fine." She couldn't say why she was so upset over the image of him bedding down with the horses. "You should stay in the house."

"Nope, I don't feel comfortable with that. I saddled the doc's horse when he left. He said Robert murmured Henrietta's name a few times, so that's hopeful."

"Yes, but it's a bad sign that he still hasn't roused." She thought of the other warnings the doctor had left them with. Robert's condition remained a grave concern. "Henrietta is sitting at his bedside in case he—" Died. She couldn't say the word.

"That's why I'm staying. If you need to send word to the doctor, I'll be here to ride for him."

"Oh, Thad." That was all she could get out, simply his name, when his thoughtfulness meant so much more. Why was she having a hard time telling him that much? She folded her hands tightly together, not moving from her chair. She listened to the fire crackle lazily in the hearth and tried to find safe words—ones that would not leave her vulnerable. "That's a comfort knowing you'll be here. That you're here to help if he needs it."

"Good. I want to make your load lighter. If you're gonna be up, I can feed the fire for you."

"No, I'm about ready to go upstairs. I was just catching my breath." She didn't mention she'd been trying not to think about all that could go wrong for this family she loved.

"It's been a tough day."

"Exactly."

"You won't mind if I bank the embers?"

"Not at all."

The leather of his boots squeaked slightly as he eased down beside her. Over the clank of the fireplace utensils, he spoke. "I've been trying to keep out of your way. That's why I've kept to the stable, for the most part. I know it's gotta be hard having me near."

She couldn't deny it, but she didn't want to say the words, either. She steepled her hands in her lap, feeling raw and worn. "I'm grateful for you. You made a difference for Robert. Matilda said she saw your shadow through the snow this afternoon. She said it was hard to be sure, but it looked as if you were protecting Robert. That you could have been as badly hurt, too."

"An injury like Robert's is serious business. I've seen quite a few in my line of work."

"I imagine you have."

"Not many pull through with a head injury and a bad kick to the chest, but I *have* seen it." There was another click of the shovel against the grate. "How's your aunt holding up?"

"She refuses to leave his side. For all her confidence and bluster, I think she would be lost without him. I'm scared for him. For my family. You know what that's like."

"I do." He'd lost his father more than ten years ago, and Bo McKaslin hadn't been the good, strong father Noelle was used to. The real loss in his life would always be her.

He stood, doing his best to hold in his feelings. "I have a good suspicion that Robert will be all right."

"It's g-good of you to stay."

"It's my pleasure. Good night, Noelle."

"At least let me send some blankets out with you."

"No. Sleeping indoors is treat enough for me. I'm used to bedding down in unheated bunkhouses and on the trail. I can't tell you the number of summer nights a storm rolled in when we were in the high country and I got snowed on."

"Didn't you sleep in a wagon when the weather was bad?"

"What wagon? There was usually the chuck wagon, and that was it. Besides, it wouldn't have been good for a cowboy's reputation to act as if a little bit of snow could trouble him."

"Cowboys are overly concerned about their reputations, are they?"

"The tougher you act, the better cowboy you can fool yourself into thinking you are."

"I suppose you fooled yourself into thinking you were a very fine cowboy?"

"I surely tried." There it was, the hint of a grin in his voice and it warmed her a little in the hopeless places where she felt so cold. "I'll be right enough out there. Don't you worry. If your family needs anything, send word to me."

"Fine." She rose. Her skirts swirled around her ankles as she took a stumbling step. When she was sure she'd put a safe distance between them, she stopped and turned toward the front door, where she supposed he must be. "Tell Sunny good-night from me and to keep warm tonight."

"I surely will. I know he'll be glad to know you wish him well."

Something in Thad's voice made her believe he knew she was speaking not only of the horse. She could feel her heart unraveling string by string. She took another step, careful to skirt the edge of the end table next to Henrietta's favorite sofa. "He's rather a good man for helping out tonight."

"I'll tell him. I know that means a lot to him, that you think he's a great man."

"Good, not great," she was quick to correct.

"Right, I'll let him know that he's got some proving up to do." His voice had a hint of a smile again, warm and wonderful and so substantial it was hard to believe he'd ever let her down.

"Definite proving up." She took one step and realized she was lost.

She'd forgotten to count her steps.

"Good night, Thad." She set her chin, hoping she looked rather as if she meant to stand somewhere in the parlor like a statue.

His steps moved away and the hinges of the front door whispered open. "Good night."

The way he said it sounded more like goodbye. She waited until she heard the knob click shut before she groped her way in the dark. Once she'd found the end post to the staircase she lowered herself onto the bottom stair, feeling alone in the dark. So very lost and alone.

Her heart ached, her spirit ached, her very soul felt cracked apart. She sat a long time in the dark, until the clock struck one, before she went upstairs to check on her aunt.

Chapter Seven

From her uncle's bedside, Noelle heard the faint chime of the downstairs parlor clock marking the early hour—five chimes. She'd been up all night. She thought Henrietta had fallen asleep in the chair on the other side of the bed, but she wasn't sure.

It was hard not to let all the worries in. She had personal ones for her dear uncle, for it had been a blow to her head that had stolen her sight. She prayed harder than she ever had before for him to awaken and be fine.

Exhaustion pulsed through her, and she fought another yawn. She would stay with Henrietta as long as she was needed. The embers popped in the bedroom's hearth, and she thought of Thad. How had he fared in the stable? She wasn't exactly sure why he'd stayed, but she was deeply grateful to him.

Grateful. The hard nugget of emotion—of the thing she hadn't forgiven—hurt like a blister. And it made it easier for her to remember past the hurt of Thad's abandonment to the time before, when she'd been so happy. Happy, because his love had made her that way.

She was no longer the kind of woman who believed

that love was strong enough to build anything on, for it was only a dream. But the girl she'd been, who had believed, remembered and mourned.

"Why, I must have drifted off for a moment there." Henrietta broke the long-standing silence. "Oh, my heart stopped. He's still breathing. I vowed I'd not take my eyes from him, and here I am, drowsing in this chair."

Noelle could feel her aunt's anguish. "It's been a long night for you."

"You would know, as you sat up every moment with me. Unnecessary, dear one, but terribly appreciated." Henrietta's voice broke and she cleared it, but perhaps failing to clear away all the emotion, went on to say nothing at all.

How hard it had to be for a loving wife to fear every ticktock of the clock that passed. The doctor had warned that Robert's head wound was not the most serious of all his injuries. The kick he'd sustained to his ribs had damaged him deep inside. There was no telling if he could heal from that.

"I've been reciting what I can remember from Ecclesiastes." Noelle searched with her fingertips along the bedside table, where she'd put the family Bible for safekeeping, and handed it in her aunt's direction. "Perhaps you ought to resume where I left off."

"Your voice likely needs a rest." The chair creaked as Henrietta took the treasured book. "Relax, dear. I'll read until our reverend arrives. He promised to stop by first thing."

Noelle squirmed in the uncomfortable wooden chair. Her spine burned as if someone had set it afire. She couldn't find a more comfortable position, gave it up as hopeless and set her mind on ignoring her discomfort.

The pages flipped softly. "His color looks to be improving. I'm most certain of it. The doctor said his making it through the night would be telling, and I am sure beyond all doubt that my Rob is going to be fine."

If will alone was strong enough, Noelle knew that her aunt's would be. "His breathing sounds steadier."

"His pulse strengthens, too." The pages stopped ruffling. "For once I am thankful for newfangled ways. The doctor is newly out of medical school back East. Do you suppose he is married?"

Noelle bit her lip, taking comfort in Henrietta's irrepressible concerns. "Don't you think it would be more appropriate to wait until Robert can give his permission before you go marrying off one of your daughters?"

"It's a woman's duty to marry. Would you like me to start quoting passages and verses?"

"You can't fool me, my dear aunt. I know down deep you are a true romantic. That's what's behind all your hopes for your daughters. You want them to know happiness the way you have."

"I'll not admit to such weakness as soft feelings. True love." Henrietta tsked. "Well, perhaps you've caught me at a rare moment of weakness. The greatest gift *is* to be loved as I have been loved. As I love." Her voice trembled and she fell silent.

Noelle fell silent, too. Love was the last thing she wanted to think about. She was glad when Henrietta began reading, in a quiet steady voice. "'To everything there is a season, and a time to every purpose under heaven.'"

She felt Thad's approach like a touch to her spirit, just as she'd used to. Her heart was aware of him long before his familiar gait tapped quietly through the house. He hesitated outside the open doorway, waiting for a break in Henrietta's reading to speak, and her soul leaned toward him, the way a blooming rose faced the sun.

It took Henrietta a moment to notice him, for she was absorbed in her reading. When she did, it was with a gasp. "Oh! Mr. McKaslin. I did not see you standing there."

"Good morning, Noelle. Ma'am. Want me to build up your fire?"

"That will be fine, young man. I take it you've started the fires downstairs?"

"That I have."

The confident, lighthearted jauntiness to his baritone had changed, Noelle realized. This Thad sounded like a seasoned man sure of his worth and capabilities, and through it all he still had his positive humor.

Not that she ought to be noticing so much about him. She sat straighter in the chair and smoothed her skirts with her hands, straightening imaginary wrinkles, since she couldn't see them. It did give her something to do other than to listen to the easy pad of his step and the rustle and whisper of his movements as he knelt down to stir the ashes.

Thad. Why did it feel as if her heart could see him? She wondered if he'd been warm enough or too uncomfortable to sleep; if he had shaved or if a day's growth whiskered his jaw. She could not allow herself to ask.

"Mr. McKaslin?" Henrietta broke the silence. "Might I prevail on you for another favor?"

"Sure, ma'am. What do you need?" His voice lifted higher, and Noelle could feel him towering behind her, his breadth and height and strength undeniable.

"After the house is awake, you come back," Henrietta instructed. "I'm going to need a more comfortable chair if I'm to continue to stay by my husband's side. My back is paining me something terrible, and I must keep up my strength for him."

"That'll be no trouble at all. I'll be back."

When he walked away, he left behind the sweet scent of hay and an impossible longing within Noelle's heart. If only he had been the kind of man she could have counted on.

Henrietta returned to her reading. Noelle struggled to sit straight in her chair and let the Bible's beautiful words comfort her.

As Thad went around the Worthington place doing chores in the stable and later in the house, he couldn't get Noelle out of his thoughts. Seeing her sitting quietly in the hard-backed wooden chair with her hands clasped in her lap, listening patiently while her aunt read from the Bible gave him a new view of her.

It was an image that subdued him as he considered which chair would fit into the space between the Worthington's bulky bed and the bedroom wall. While he considered his options in the parlor, solemn and subdued voices drifted in from the nearby dining room. The Worthington girls were up and taking breakfast, but it was Noelle's quiet alto that he picked out like a melody from the other voices. Her dulcet voice was his most favorite sound in the world.

Once he'd chosen a chair and hefted it up the stairs, his ears strained to keep hearing her. She grew fainter with every step he took and by the time he'd managed to reach the Worthington's bedroom door, he could no longer hear her. Every bit of him seemed to strain, searching for her.

Henrietta looked up from her Bible and squinted at him appraisingly. She looked exhausted and sick from worry.

His heart softened toward her. "Where would you like this?"

"Where my chair is now. You'll have to take the wooden one back down to the dining room."

"Be glad to." He eyed the doorway and angled the chair to wedge it through in one try. The missus seemed to watch him carefully, perhaps she was concerned about him scuffing her fancy woodwork, but she needn't have worried. He set the heavy chair down with as much care as he could and took away the wooden one. "Will that do, ma'am?"

"I'm grateful, Mr. McKaslin."

"No trouble at all, ma'am." He stopped to take a glance at Robert, who lay ashen and motionless against the stark white sheets. "He's been stirring?"

"No." The strong woman who looked as if she could have commanded the army now looked frail.

"I'm sure he'll be rousing soon, ma'am." It was the only kindness he could offer her. "I've seen it before." He backtracked to the door. "You need anything at all, you send word."

"Of that you can be sure."

As he hooked the ladder-back chair over his shoulder and headed down the narrow hallway, he had to admit the Worthington's marriage was clearly based on a deep love. The kind he'd forgotten could exist in this world. The kind he didn't want to admit did exist, because it would make him see how empty his life was.

What did a man do when he'd lost his only chance at a deep, true bond? He knew that whenever he eventually married, it would not be to Noelle. He'd lost his dream. The best he could hope for now was someone sensible and compatible.

The expensive rug at his feet led him to the staircase, where once again he heard Noelle's voice as soft and sweet as lark song. He tried to harden his heart so he didn't have to feel a thing. It was better that way.

He did his best not to look her way the moment he stepped into the fancy dining room. Knickknacks and breakables were just about everywhere, so he moved the ladder-back chair with purpose. He didn't want to lower Henrietta's opinion of him by breaking some of the expensive whatnots. The Worthington girls fell silent. The silence felt painful as he kept his eyes down and slid the chair into place at the foot of the table.

He didn't dawdle, but headed straight for the kitchen door. He had intended to check with the maid to see if any errands needed to be done in town, but he went straight toward the back door. The pressure building so strong in his chest was likely to choke him. He had his hand on the door handle when he heard Noelle padding quietly behind him.

"Thad?"

She looked shadowed and forlorn, and the pressure in his chest detonated like a keg of dynamite in a mountain tunnel. His willpower crumbled along with every bit of his steely self-discipline.

"What can I do for you, darlin'?" He feared she could hear it in his voice.

She took a small step back. "I need someone to tell my piano students I won't be teaching t-today. Most likely for the whole next week."

"You mean you teach piano? But how can you…?"

"Easily." She shrugged simply, unconsciously, gentle

as always. "I don't have to see to hear a bad chord or a wrong note. The keys are always the same whether I can see them or not."

"You've got some lucky students, learning from you."

Her chin dipped. "I'm immune to your compliments, Mr. McKaslin. I'm the lucky one, as I need to make what difference I can in some way and I can't think of a better purpose for me."

"Whoa, there. You need to make a living?"

"Why do you sound so confused about that?" She tensed up some again, as if he'd hit a sore spot with his words. "It doesn't seem to be in God's plan for me to marry, and it's not right I rely too much on my aunt and uncle's generosity. I support myself and I contribute to the household."

"But—" He shook his head and gripped the edge of the counter. "I heard news of your engagement. I'm sorry you lost him, too. In the buggy accident?"

"No, he's alive and well living in town with his wife and newborn son." She let the notes fade to silence, holding her hands still as her heart. "He followed in your footsteps. After my accident, he broke our engagement. He didn't want to marry a blind woman. Or, damaged goods, to use his words."

"*What?* You're not damaged. I—I can't imagine it. I am sorry."

"It wasn't in God's plan for me." She fought the punch of sorrow that would always seize her—not at Shelton's loss but because she'd so wished for a family of her own—something else that could never be. "What about for you?"

"Me? Marriage?" His note of panic was revealing. "Now I'm not sure there is any plan—divine or otherwise—but I'm hoping for a wife one day. Someone who sees life the way I do. You work hard, try to do what's right and at the end of the day rest up for another hard day on the ranch."

"I see." Maybe more than she ever had. "Excuse me, I must get back to my aunt—"

Footsteps thundered down the stairway like cannon fire. Noelle fell silent, icy fear spilling into her veins as she heard the girls at the dining room table cry out in alarm. Henrietta's racking sobs rose above the other noises in the house. The door swung open; Noelle could hear the hinges and feel the breeze the door made against the side of her face.

"Mr. McKaslin! There you are." Sadie was out of breath and panicked sounding. "Quick! Ride for the doctor. Mr. Worthington is awake."

"Awake?" Noelle stumbled over the word, it surprised her so. "He's all right?"

"Has his wits about him, if that's what you mean—" The door thudding open against the wall broke off her words. Thad's boots rang on the wood floor. "Noelle, make a list, and I'll take care of your students when I'm back with the doc."

The door slammed shut before she could answer. He was gone, leaving her wrestling for control of her heart as she hurried upstairs.

After he'd alerted the doc, Thad had pressed Sunny into a brisk pace and nosed him toward home. The long ride and the quiet time in the barn as he rubbed down his horse gave him plenty of time to mull things over. By the time Aiden found him, he pretty nearly had things puzzled out.

"You're home." Aiden stopped in the aisle to give him a grim look. "Didn't see you ride in or I would have come to help you."

"No need. Almost done here." Thad released Sunny's rear hoof and stood. "Just need to fetch him a little water."

"I'll get it." Gruff, Aiden strode away and said nothing more.

Thad scratched the back of his neck. His brother wasn't in the best of moods and probably for good reason. He patted Sunny on the flank before stepping over the gate bar. When he caught sight of Aiden at the back pump, he headed his brother's way.

"Don't blame you for being mad at me," he said by way of an apology.

Aiden turned from the pump and shrugged one big shoulder. "Not mad. I'm concerned."

"Concerned?" That threw him like a wild horse. Thad took the bucket. "Robert woke up this morning. He'll recover from his other injuries."

"Good to know, but that wasn't what I meant." Aiden cleared his throat and pushed the barn door closed once they were through. "You're going to get sweet on that Kramer girl again, and that'll be a mistake."

"No one knows that more than I do." Thad made his way back to Sunny's stall. "I'm helping out is all."

"Fine. Christian duty and all that." Aiden fisted his hands. "How about I take over at the Worthingtons. You hold down the fort here."

"You? At the Worthingtons?" That was almost laughable. "You know there's nothing but women over there? A cook, a maid, those daughters and Mrs. Worthgton?"

"And that Kramer girl." Aiden quirked one eyebrow

as if to give those words special emphasis. "I'm unaffected by her. By any woman. I'd best take over in your stead for a couple of days, at most. I suppose more family are coming to help?"

"Don't know." Thad smiled at Sunny's nicker and poured a quarter of the bucket into the trough. Sunny took a look at that and shook his head in argument. Thad rubbed his nose. "More later, buddy. I'll come back with some warmed mash for you. Is that accepatle?"

Sunny seemed to consider it and dipped his muzzle into the cool, fresh water.

Satisfied his horse was cared for, Thad left the bucket on the aisle floor and turned to face his brother's displeasure. "I'm not going to make old mistakes."

"I'm not so sure."

"Doesn't matter." Thad grabbed his saddle pack from the rail he'd slung it on and hefted it onto his shoulder. "I've got a duty, is all, Aiden. Surely you understand duty."

"What I understand is that look in your eye."

"What look?" Thad shouldered open the side door and barreled out into the harsh weather. He didn't have any look in his eyes. What he had was conviction. He would always do right by Noelle. It was as simple as that.

"Why, Thad!" The lean-to door swung open and there was Ma clutching her shawl closed at her throat and standing in the cold. "You came back. Just when I was starting to worry why we hadn't heard from you."

"Couldn't keep away from the prettiest ma in all of Montana Territory."

She sparkled, despite her worrying paleness. "It's good to have you home, son."

"It's good to be home." He kissed his mother's cheek and followed her into the lean-to.

"I've got a hot pot of coffee on," Ma said as she slipped through the kitchen door, where it was warm and snug. "I've got some cinnamon rolls from yesterday's baking. I'll warm those for you boys, too."

"Thanks, Ma," Thad said.

Aiden, who stepped in behind him, said the same. Not wanting to pick up the conversation they'd been having in the barn, Thad kept his back to his brother and stepped around the morning's supply of stacked wood to fit his boots on the bootjack. "What's the news on Finn?"

Aiden didn't say a single word, but Thad could *hear* his scowl, it was such a strong one.

"That bad, huh?" Thunk, went his boot on the floor. Thad fit his other boot in the jack, his foot slipped out and that boot, too, fell loudly in the awkward silence. He bent to retrieve both and set them against the outside wall. "What? He's still coming home, isn't he?"

"Looks that way." Aiden turned away and thunk, went his boot to the floor. "Ma picked up a letter at the post office yesterday. Finn got himself into some trouble at the prison. A fight of some kind."

Of course. That boy was more trouble. Thad shrugged off his coat and hung it over a peg before he hiked into the kitchen.

Warmth surrounded him. The golden lamplight and the polished shine of the wood floor and table was a welcome sight, but not more than the view of his ma at the stove. She hummed while she worked in a calico work dress and apron. It felt right being back here after all this time. He'd missed her and his home so much.

Heart brimming, he joined his mother at the stove and took the coffeepot out of her hand. "You're not well enough to be waiting on me. You're supposed to wait for Aiden or me to do the cooking. You know that."

"Nonsense! I'm your mother. It's my job." She might argue, but this close, he could see she'd gone from pale to ashen.

"Why don't you sit and let me bring you coffee and rolls?"

"I'm not helpless, young man." Gently said, and lovingly. "But I won't say no to your offer."

"Good." Fixing breakfast had taxed her, he knew. He held out her chair at the table. "You've overdone things, since no one was here to stop you."

"Oh, you know me. I'm not happy unless my hands are busy." Ma settled into her chair. "This illness has been a hardship in many ways, but the hardest seems to be all this idleness."

The door swung open, and Thad went back to the stove. He grabbed three cups by the handles and set them onto the table. By the time he'd returned with the coffeepot, Ma had set the cups in place and Aiden had taken his chair, still scowling.

"How is that nice Kramer girl?" Ma asked, while he poured her cup first.

"Fine enough," he answered, and shot Aiden a warning look. The subject was one that had to stay closed.

He moved on to Aiden's cup, prepared to set his brother straight if he brought up Noelle again. He'd taken all the hurt he could.

He hardened up his heart, fetched the cinnamon rolls from the oven and let his ma take first pick.

This was his life, this was the way it would always be. Fine enough, he supposed, but never as good, never as vibrant, never as meaningful without her.

Chapter Eight

The parlor clock was striking the noon hour as Noelle counted out four of the everyday plates from the kitchen shelves to be carried in to the table. Henrietta and the girls were upstairs by their father's side, and it was as if the house itself had breathed a sigh of relief. Robert was holding his own. She thought of everything Thad had done for her uncle, protecting him from the bucking mare, bandaging him, staying the night. And now, back in the stables at work after delivering notes to her students, according to Sadie.

Thad. His words kept rolling through her mind. *I'm hoping for a wife one day. Someone who sees life the way I do. You work hard, try to do what's right and at the end of the day rest up for another hard day on the ranch.*

"I'm taking a tray up to the missus." Sadie tapped her way closer. "You're a dear to help me, but you needn't do it."

"I'm happy to be useful." She shook all thoughts of Thad from her mind and set the small stack of dishes on the worktable centering the room. She added another plate for him.

"I think he's been out there working with one of those crazy horses." Sadie's voice made clear her opinion on horses that could not be trusted. "Someone needs to take them in hand, I suppose."

Thad. The knot in her chest yanked tighter. She did her best to keep her feelings still and slipped another plate from the shelf. The plates clacked together, Sadie's step retreated to the kitchen door and she was alone again. Her mind was a muddle of stray, troubling thoughts. Exhaustion vibrated through her like a plucked cello string. Sadie's steps faded away, leaving her to think about the one man she should not be thinking about.

When she heard Thad's familiar gait coming from the lean-to, she had only a moment to brace herself before the door opened. She wished that her senses did not focus on him even before he stepped into the room. She knew the brush of his movements, the rhythm of his breathing and the beat he took to pause before he spoke. Again, her spirit turned toward him and her traitorous heart followed.

"Messages delivered," he said with a smile in his voice. "I didn't realize you taught so many students."

"It surprises even me." She couldn't say why she was almost smiling back. She shook her head, gathered up her common sense and blamed her reaction to Thad on the fact that she had yet to sleep after being up all night with Henrietta. "Thanks for delivering my messages."

"I didn't mind, and I got to see more of the countryside." There was a rustle, as if he were taking off his coat and then hanging it on the hooks by the door. "A lot has changed since I've been away."

"A lot has stayed the same, too." She ran her fingertips along the edge of the worktable and followed it to the corner. "Would you like me to get you some coffee? I'd offer you tea, but Cook has commandeered all the kettles for my uncle's medical needs."

"Is that what that awful smell is?" Thad's wry humor made his baritone more intimate and cozy. "I thought a skunk somehow got loose in the house. I was just about to offer to go hunt it down for you."

"How gentlemanly of you, but as you can see, we won't be needing your hunting services." She felt her way along the upper shelf for a cup and found nothing with her fingertips. She went up on tiptoe to search some more. "Is that a yes to coffee? I just helped Cook wash and dry a dishpan of cups. They ought to be here." His steps beat near, and she froze as he came close and then closer. Until she could smell the bite of winter wind and fresh snow on his clothes. Until she could remember what it had been like all the times he'd been this close to her.

Memories stirred up like a kick of wind in dust, limiting her clarity, taking her back in time. How safe she'd felt when her hand was tucked snugly within his larger, work-roughened one. How full her heart and soul had been every time he said her name. How her love for him was as endless as a summer's blue Montana sky.

"Here's one, pushed all the way to the back." His voice rumbled like spring on a late-winter's storm.

Warmly, her heart responded against her will. She took an abrupt step away from him, putting a careful distance between them. Now, if only she could do the same with her feelings. Her throat was tight.

"The rest of the cups are on the drain board, just so you know."

"Y-yes." She knew that somewhere in the dust cloud of her mind, but all she could think of was how she wished more than ever that she could see. Just for one glorious moment, that was all, so she could look at the man who made her spirit stir.

"Am I making you uncomfortable?" His question was blunt, but his words were kind.

Her hands trembled as she turned to the stove. "It's not easy having you so n-near."

"I understand. It's a bad wound between us. It's as simple as that. Nothing in the world is going to change that."

She nodded, unable to agree. Unable to disagree. "Believe me, the last thing I ever want to do—the last thing I would ever do is hurt you, Noelle. I'll eat in the kitchen and keep my distance from you."

She had to fight to keep her feelings still. She had to fight not to let her own honesty show.

There he went again, closing the distance between them, leaning near and then nearer as he took the coffeepot from the stove. Ironware clanged against the trivet and his muscled arm brushed against her shoulder. "I don't want you to burn your pretty dress again."

She blushed. She couldn't help it. Why did she feel so awkward about being near to him? "I don't scorch my skirts every time. Just now and then."

"I imagine being near a stove is tricky for you."

"Yes, tricky."

"Is that your cup on the table? Then I'll fill it, too." He moved away, already speaking over the sound of coffee pouring. "I stopped home and packed my saddlebags for another night's stay."

"Not another night out in that cold barn."

"Only until Robert's out of risk. I wouldn't feel right

about leaving you ladies here by yourselves tonight. If all goes well tomorrow, then I'll head home."

"Th-that's decent of you, Thad." And more than she expected of him.

The coffeepot landed on the trivet with a clang. "Your uncle is going to be bedridden for awhile. Is there any family you can send off to and ask to come help?"

"I'll m-mention it to Henrietta."

"I'll pitch in until then."

No matter how hard she fought against it, she could not keep her emotions still. They rose up like a lump in her throat. She swallowed hard, trying to ignore them, praying they would go back down into the dormant place within her heart. "But aren't you needed at home?"

"It's true, I have obligations." His baritone dipped, low like an invitation to lean and listen.

"What kind of obligations?" The question rolled off her tongue before she could order herself not to ask it.

"I would have thought that you'd heard."

"Heard what?"

"My younger brother's had some trouble with the law."

"Finn? Oh, I didn't know." Noelle choked the words out past the expanding lump in her throat. She swallowed but it refused to budge. "Is it very serious?"

"Serious enough or I would have never come back to help my ma and Aiden out."

Of course. His exciting cowboy life. Impossibly, the emotions tangled up in her throat expanded more, and she could not speak.

"Where do you want your coffee?"

"Oh, I can carry it." She'd never felt so awkward.

"I don't mind. Besides, I filled it awful full."

"The parlor, then."

"Follow me." His steps struck like thunder in the whir of her mind. Somehow she made her feet carry her around the table and through the door, which he held for her.

"I came in to check the wood boxes," he told her, talking uneasily. So, he did feel the awkwardness between them. "Is there anything else that needs doing? I might as well make myself useful as long as I'm here."

Throat aching, heart aching, she could only shake her head once in response. His boots were a slow and sure rhythm in contrast to her own.

She almost forgot to count her steps as she left the corner of the dining room table to make the long path to her armchair by the hearth. The familiar cadence of his gait, his scent of hay and winter and horses, the rustle of his movements and the coziness of his presence all sweetly affected her, and against her will.

"On the table by the chair?" he asked.

"Please." She slipped into her chair.

"There's a Bible on the table, too." His tone dipped with tender understanding. "You must miss being able to read that."

"Very much. The Bible was my mother's, and it's a comfort just to have it near." One of her questions about him rose to the surface like a soap bubble. "I remember you said you're no longer much of a praying man. Why?"

"It's complicated, like most things."

"Yes, faith is complicated. I wrestled with it for a while after the buggy accident."

"I imagine so. It's hard to understand why God would let someone as gentle and kind as you be blind."

Always kind and gentle, that was Thad, too. She hadn't realized how much she'd missed him. "I've learned to accept it."

"Seems to me that would be awful tough."

"It was for a while, but I'm blessed in so many other ways." That was a dark time she tried not to think about. She had learned to accept. "Whatever you're struggling with, you should never let anything come between you and God."

"Don't you go trying to bring me back to my faith. I'll find my way, don't you worry." His footsteps retreated. "Tell the maid I'll be out in the stables if Robert should need the doc again."

"Thad?"

"What is it, darlin'?"

"There is one thing you could do for me. There's a sorrel mare in the corner box stall."

"I know the one. She's a sweet thing. If I don't miss my guess, she'll be foaling in a week or two."

"Would you keep a careful watch on her? Solitude is special to me."

There was a moment of silence. "Then you can count on me."

Was it her imagination or were his words heavy with regret? Or was it sadness? She listened to his steps fade and the kitchen door whisper shut. Even if she sat perfectly still, she could not stop all the ways her heart felt for the man.

And all the ways she didn't.

She reached for her Bible, careful not to disturb the full cup of steaming coffee, and hugged the treasured volume to her. *You can count on me.* Why did Thad's

words trouble her? This wasn't the first time he'd said
something that seemed to have a deeper layer to it.

*The last thing I ever want to do— The last thing I
would ever do is hurt you.* His words puzzled her. She
could not reconcile Thad's sincerity with the man who'd
shattered her heart.

How would a man who had knowingly broken her
heart also be the man who stayed to clean the stable, see
to the horses, chop wood, run errands and ride for the
doctor at a moment's notice? The real truth was that he
had always been hardworking and sincere and caring.
Except for that one terrible point in time.

The fire popped and crackled, and, exhausted, she
laid down her Bible and reached for the bracing cup of
coffee. A wave of chatter floated down from upstairs,
bringing with it notes of measured happiness and hope.

That happiness could not penetrate her deeper sorrow.

Thad put off going into the house as long as he could.
He'd scrubbed the water troughs, washed out the feed
trays, took note of what feed was running low and even
spent some time working with the new mare. She had
a long way to go before she was a reliable horse, but he
had faith in her.

He especially made sure to keep a careful watch on
the expecting mare, as Noelle had requested. He imagined she didn't ride anymore. That was too bad since
she loved horses so much.

As he trudged through the snow to the house, he
couldn't think of anything else. Only her. She still
amazed him. She was more beautiful and as good as ever.

How could love be there all along and he hadn't

known it? Against all common sense, he wanted to take care of her and cherish her. Every fiber of his being longed to protect her with all of his devoted heart.

You are a sorry case, Thaddeus McKaslin, he thought as he beat the snow off the steps. Hadn't Aiden said it? *You're going to get sweet on that Kramer girl again, and that'll be a mistake.*

And what had he told his brother? *No one knows that more than I do.*

It didn't seem as if he knew that now. No, the past and its mistakes and pain seemed to be forgotten whenever he was with Noelle. It was a mistake to let himself care about her again. Plain and simple.

But did that stop the spark of tenderness in his heart when he remembered her in the kitchen with her scorched skirt and determination to be helpful to her family? That flame of tenderness grew until it had warmed his cold winter's heart. He wanted to make her smile again. He wanted to put happiness back into her life. He wanted to love her the right way for every minute of every day to come.

Whoa there, his thoughts were like a wild horse running away with him. He leaned the shovel against the siding. For a moment there in the kitchen, it had been almost like old times. Words had come easily, there had been a zing of emotional connection between them and a moment of understanding that made him hope, just a little, that *maybe*—maybe—she could forgive him.

He knocked the snow from his hat brim and stomped his boots on the back step. His pulse was rattling in his chest, and he felt as if he were about to step in front of a speeding train as he opened the door. The lean-to was chilly but the kitchen was warmer. As he shrugged out

of his winter wraps in the empty room, he had to admit
that he'd been half expecting to see her here, doing what
she could to help out.

That skunk smell had faded some, but not enough
that he wanted to linger in the kitchen. He marched past
the huge worktable, the rows of counters and the wall
of glass shelves, and found himself in the dining room.
It, too, was full of polished wood furniture and shelves
of fancy doodads. But no Noelle.

He didn't spot her until he stepped foot into the
parlor. She was asleep on the couch, stretched out the
length of those stout-looking cushions, her head resting on a throw pillow. Her hands were pressed together
beneath her chin as if in prayer.

An overwhelming lightning bolt of affection hit him.
Left him thunderstruck.

He loved her. Beyond all rhyme and reason, beyond
all good sense and possibility, he loved her.

Quietly, he took the afghan off the back of the couch
and covered her. She didn't stir. He gently tucked the
warm knitted wool around her and stood over her,
watching her sleep. Hopes came to life in his soul—
hopes he could not let himself look at—but they were
there all the same.

No good could come from his feelings and he knew
it. But that did not keep the love in his heart from growing until it was as solid as the Montana Rockies and
just as lasting. Until nothing in this world could alter it.

He resisted the urge to brush away wisps of pure
chestnut from her face. The thick coil of her braid fell
over her shoulder, and she could have been a painting,
framed in the soft spill of the lamplight and the glow

from the fire. His chest cinched with a physical pain as he backed away.

He might be low on faith, but he was starting to believe there was a reason God had led him back to Angel County. Maybe he was meant to be here to help her through this time. Perhaps he was meant to watch over her until her uncle was able to do so again.

And then what? Did he have a chance with her?

As he climbed the stairs in search of the missus, he couldn't rightly see how Noelle was ever going to forgive him for jilting her. He had to be sensible. As much as he wanted her to forgive him, it wasn't likely she would ever trust him again.

His steps were heavy as he headed down the long hallway. He had a lot of work to do before nightfall. Maybe it would be best if he concentrated on that.

The school bell's final tones lingered on the crisp February afternoon as she tried to avoid the deep drifts of snow between the school yard and the road. She didn't want to ruin her new shoes, so she'd hiked her woolen skirts and flannel petticoats up to her ankles. She was in the middle of taking a shockingly unladylike step over the drifts when she heard a familiar chuckle.

"Careful there, you might slip."

Noelle's shoe hit the ice on the street side of the snowdrift, and for one perilous instant she felt the heel of her new shoe slide. If she fell on her backside in front of the handsome Thad McKaslin, she'd have to let Mother send her off to finishing school in Boston, as she'd been threatening to do for the last year, because she could have never faced him again.

Heaven was kind to her because her shoe held, she

heaved herself over the drift and realized Thad had stopped his horse and was standing beside his sleigh. He tipped his hat to her, and a quivering hope sprinkled through her like the snow through the sky.

He held out his gloved hand. "This is my lucky day. I was just in need of some help."

"You need my help?"

"Yep. I just finished building my sleigh, and I need to see how she drives with two passengers."

"I see. You couldn't find anyone else?"

"Who else? I don't see anyone. Only you."

One look at that grin of his, wide and dimpled had her smiling, too. A gaggle of smaller schoolkids went screaming past them, and Noelle didn't tell him the school yard and the street were both crowded with lots of other students.

"I know exactly what you mean," she told him shyly as she placed her hand on his palm. "I don't see anyone else, either."

His fingers closed over hers, and the tenderness she felt in his touch showed in his blue eyes, too. His eyes were blue as her dreams. As blue as forever.

Thad. Noelle woke with a start and a heart full of longing. The fringe edging of an afghan tickled her chin. When she sat up, it slipped to the floor with a swish. The vibrant images of her dream clung to her. The blue sky and brilliant snow and handsome man faded in clarity and color until there was only darkness. Disoriented, she realized where she was by the steady tick of the clock, the lick of the fire in the big fireplace, and the sofa beneath her.

She wasn't sure what had awakened her, but her heart wouldn't stop aching like an open wound that could not heal. She bowed her head, folded her hands and prayed with all of her might. *Please, Father, take the memories of him I can no longer bear.*

There was no answer but a pop of wood in the hearth and the eerie howl of the wind kicking up against the north side of the house. She shivered, although she could not feel the cold wind, and she wished, how she wished that Thad McKaslin had never come back into her steady, placid, safe life.

She had to stop thinking of him. She had to bank that tiny light of caring within her. He was not the right kind of man. He'd *never* been the right kind of man. She—a woman grown and wise to love and life—did not want Thad McKaslin. No, these feelings were coming out of what was past, out of memory of the schoolgirl she used to be, nothing more.

She felt for the heap of the afghan and lifted it off the floor. She stood, holding her heart still, banishing all thoughts of Thad as she briskly folded the length of wool and tossed it somewhere on the couch—she heard it land with a whisper. She couldn't sense much beyond the roiling longing in her heart and the wishes she could not let herself give voice to. How did you stop remembering what had hurt so much? And what had, once, brought her so much joy?

This is not good, Noelle, you must stop this. She felt as if she were suffocating and could not get air, so she headed straight for the door. Careful not to make any noise to wake the house, she grabbed her cloak on her way out the door. Cold air hit her with a bitter force, sapping all her warmth and chilling her feelings like a sudden freeze.

Ice crunched beneath her shoes. The cold moan of

the wind swirled around her and filled in the lonely, empty places where her future and her dreams used to be. She pulled a pair of mittens from her pocket and tugged them on.

The wind was picking up, bringing with it the promise of more snow. Winters were long by tradition in Montana Territory, and she knew it, so why then was she longing for spring? She breathed in the heavy scents of wood smoke and dormant trees and ice. The temperature was falling, and she breathed in the air cold enough to burn the inside of her nose and tingle in her chest. Today the world was especially dark to her, and she sorely missed the colors and look of things and the comfort in them.

The rail was thick with ice and she curled her hands around the thick board. The wind was against her left side, so she knew she faced westerly. The great rim of the Rocky Mountains should be straight ahead of her. She remembered how they speared upward from the prairie's horizon. Night was falling, and the air smelled like falling snow. She knew how the sky would look— thick clouds, white with snow and dark with storm, spiraling together.

What she could not know was the look of this sky at this moment and the exact shade of the mountains as they changed to match it. She hadn't realized how her memory of color was fading with time. Was the sun still out? She strained to feel its cool brush against her cheek and felt none. Had it already sunk behind those oncoming clouds, and what colors had the sun painted them? She tried to imagine it, could not.

Thad. Why was it that when she was with him, she could? She couldn't explain it, so she breathed in the feel of the late afternoon and listened to the near silence of the plains.

Memory took her over in a sudden wash of color and light. A late-winter's afternoon much like this one with the promise of a storm. The sky was a hue of fluffy dove-gray. Every shade of white spread out in the landscape around her. Sunshine glossed the polished miles of snow like a hundred thousand diamonds. Thad had taken her hand to help her into his little red sleigh. At a gentle slap of the leather reins, his gelding carried them forward across the jeweled snow with a twinkle of merry sleigh bells.

She realized that the musical clink of steel shoes on ice wasn't in her thoughts. Someone was riding up to the house from the stables. Thad. If she looked into her heart she could see him, the way his head was down and his eyes low. He always sat his saddle straight and strong.

"Howdy, there." His baritone could warm every sliver of ice away. "Isn't it a little cold for you to be just standing there?"

"It's not any colder out here for me than it is for you."

"Yes, but I have a sheepskin-lined coat."

"My shawl is warm enough for now. You needn't worry about me, Thad."

"Sorry. Can't help myself."

He didn't sound sorry at all, and she ought to be upset about that. She didn't know why she wasn't. "Are you going to town on errands for my aunt?"

"Yep. Got some business at the feed store, and then a stop for a few supplies the doc recommended. Your uncle's looking better."

"Is he? I haven't seen him recently. I must have fallen

asleep on the sofa instead of going upstairs to sit with everyone."

"The way I hear it, you were up all night with Henrietta. Robert's still as gray as ashes, but he's looking better. He ought to be riding green-broke horses in a few weeks' time." The saddle creaked as if he'd shifted in it.

Had he been in the house while she was napping? Had he seen her sleeping? Remembering the afghan and how she'd woken up with thoughts of him in her heart, she knew. He had been the one to cover her up.

A horse nickered, and it sounded like a scolding. She couldn't believe she had forgotten the mustang.

"Sunny, please forgive my manners," she said, feeling her way along the rail. She kept one firm grip on the banister in case she hit an ice patch and moved to a much safer subject. "How are you doing this fine day?"

The horse gave a snort, and his bridle jingled as if he'd nodded his head to say "fine."

"He's looking forward to the long ride to town," Thad answered for his horse. "I promised to give him his head so he can pick the pace."

"You do that often?"

"I'm not lord and master of this horse." He said the words as if there was more, a story behind it, and a question she was supposed to ask.

A question she could not, would not ask. She had to keep Thad at a distance—there was no other choice. She tugged off her mitten and was rewarded with Sunny's warm, velvety muzzle. She rubbed his nose gently. He exhaled into the palm of her hand, tickling her.

Laughter vibrated through her. Making her feel like her old self again. But only for a moment. She fell silent when she felt Thad's gaze like a touch to the side of her face.

Why did a tiny spark of caring quiver to life within her? It was impossible to go back and repair the past like a rip in a seam. It was impossible to forget how he'd shattered her down to the soul. There was nothing to be done but to turn around and head toward the house, which is what she had to do.

"Goodbye, Thad. Have a safe trip," she said over her shoulder.

"I will. You get some more rest, darlin'."

His caring was like a knife cutting deep. With every step she took away from him, the longing for him grew. And for what could have been.

That's all this is, she told herself as she closed the door shut behind her. All that could never be for her. Even if the past did not separate them, even if Thad had not jilted her, she was blind. Having a good husband to love her, her own home and children to look after was not possible for her. She'd accepted that years ago. Why was she upset now? God had chosen this path for her. She had to walk it.

She shrugged out of her cloak and hung it with care on the tree. The warmth of the fire lured her closer and when she was safely in her chair, she held her hands in the direction of the hearth to warm them. Thoughts of Thad came with her, too. It was not easy knowing the best part of her life was behind her—and would always be.

Once her hands were warm, she tucked away her feelings and headed upstairs to check on the family she did have, the people she was deeply thankful for.

Chapter Nine

The days began to blur together as her uncle slowly improved. Life had stood still for the two weeks Robert had been bedridden and in so much pain he could scarcely breathe. Gradually life returned to some normalcy. The girls started back up at school, the minister's visits were more social than serious, the doc was openly optimistic when he'd last driven away, and Noelle's piano lessons resumed.

One thing remained constant. Thad arrived twice a day to care for the horses and tend to other chores. When she was in her music room, she could hear him the best. Sometimes the wind would snatch his voice and carry a snippet to her. Or the rhythmic beat of a horse on a lunge line would interrupt her concentration during a lesson. The scrape of a shovel on the brick walk, the spill of wood into a metal bin, the low rumble of his voice in the kitchen when he returned a tray Sadie had made for him.

It wasn't easy keeping her feelings tucked away. She made sure Sadie packed a few treats for his mother to take with him at the end of the day. A loaf of freshly baked bread. A pan of cinnamon rolls. A plate of oatmeal cookies.

The day Robert took his first few wobbly steps with a cane marked an occasion for celebration. Henrietta ordered a celebratory meal, sending Cook into a flurry. The morning was suddenly in chaos, and no fire had been lit in Noelle's music room.

She pushed through the kitchen door in search of the maid and heard the faint ring of an ax outside the back door. *Thud, thud, thud, chink.* The sound repeated itself like a refrain, over and over in nearly perfect rhythm. Thad was here again.

"Noelle." Sadie's voice came from somewhere near the kitchen hand pump. "I meant to light the fire in the music room, but there was not enough wood. I'll have it done soon enough."

"Thank you, Sadie." Noelle hesitated, drawn by the sounds of the ax. "Hasn't Henrietta hired someone to take care of things yet?"

"I believe she's certain the mister will be fit as a fiddle in a few more days and can do it all himself."

Henrietta, bless her heart, was not thinking clearly. "Robert has several broken ribs and a broken calf bone. He's not going to be able to clean the stable for some time to come."

"Between you and me, you're right. I wonder what the missus is thinking. She refuses to hire anyone. I must tell you all about last night. I caught her and Thad in deep conversation."

Uh-oh. "That cannot be a good thing. She wasn't trying to marry any of us off to him, was she?"

Sadie chuckled. "I wouldn't have been surprised, but she was offering Thad money for his work here, but he wouldn't take a cent." There was a clink of ironware and a rustle as Sadie moved closer. "He said he wasn't the kind of man who stayed on to take advantage of a family in need."

That did not surprise her in the least. That was the man she used to know. "Did he say why?"

"He said as much as he needed a wage, he wasn't helping out for money." There was a clatter and clink of ironware. "Considering the way Thad looks at you, I thought you ought to know."

Emotions swelled in her throat until she could scarcely speak. "How does he look at me?"

"Like you are Sunday morning dawning, all bright and new. Well, now, I've got to get this up to the mister." Sadie breezed on by and left the door swinging in her wake.

The *thud, thud, thud, clink* seemed to echo in the stillness, and the emotions tangled in her throat hurt until her eyes teared. Why was he doing all this? And for no gain for himself? This was the Thad she'd fallen in love with all those years ago.

She forced her feet to carry her forward and down the cool hallway. The north wing felt especially cold this morning. She shivered, but it wasn't the kind of cold a fire could warm. With every step she took, the sound of Thad's ax faded into silence. She was thankful for that.

Leave the past where it belongs, Noelle. She ran her finger along the hallway wall, counting the doorways so she could find her way. Silence seemed to close in around her, bringing with it all the sore, raw edges of the questions she was too afraid to ask. She could no longer deny the hard sheath of anger around her heart, like the tough outer shell of a seed. Anger at him for hurting her. Anger at him for breaking every belief she'd had in him. Anger now at the way he behaved like the man she'd once known him to be.

Although the music room was cold with the chill of the morning, she went straight to her piano. Her fingers yearned for the comfort of the familiar keys. Her heart ached to let music move through her and push away all this bound-up confusion. She settled on the bench, uncovered the keys and let her fingers go.

She amazed him, all right. Thad halted outside the open doorway. That sweet complicated music drifted across the hall, the notes too tangled up for a cowboy like him to figure out, but it was nice. Noelle had always had a hundred pieces of music stored in her memory. At least her blindness did not keep her from playing.

He had a perfect view of her at the piano, the morning sun haloing her like a dream. Lost in her music, she didn't hear his approach. He watched her unguardedly, savoring the sight of her. Her hair was a sleek fall of gleaming cinnamon, held back with a ribbon tied at the crown of her head. The soft locks framed her heart-shaped face. She still had that goodness within her shining up and it was the most beautiful sight.

The lilting sweetness of the music stopped in midnote. She lifted her gaze to meet his, as if she saw him clearly. "Thad?"

"How did you know?"

"The scent of hay and freshly split wood."

"That was mighty good piano playing. Don't stop because I'm here."

Sunshine streamed through the long bank of windows, polishing her with a golden light. She was radiance and everything dear to him as she returned to her playing, caressing beauty from those mysterious white and black keys. He felt gruff and too big and too awkward for her and for this fancy room full of expenve things. Some things, it appeared, hadn't changed a whit.

Her music followed him across the room. Maybe it didn't much matter how many years passed, he would always be able to easily see into her heart. Right now hers was closed up tight to him—and it always would be. He had to face that, too. There was no way to repair the hurt he'd caused her. There would never be a chance she would trust him again. No way he could ever be sorry enough.

That took a piece out of him. His heart, as cracked as it was, broke a little more.

He emptied the wood into the bin, noticing that her playing faltered for a moment. She went on playing, so he knelt at the stone hearth. He drew back the screen and looked around, trying to figure out where the matches were.

The piano playing stopped. As the last notes of the chord faded in the room, she pushed back the bench and breezed toward him. Her skirts and petticoats rustled like the softest music.

"Are you looking for the match tin?" She lifted a box from the shadowed corner of the mantel behind some fancy doodads. Her movements were pure grace as she leaned close, holding the tin in her small hand. "It sounds like it's full. Sometimes the maid gets busy and forgets to fill it."

"I imagine keeping up with Mrs. Worthington's standards is a very demanding task."

"She has overwhelmed more than one maid. It became such a situation that Henrietta couldn't find a single girl to work for her in the whole county."

He whisked the tin from Noelle's hand. "Did she have to advertise outside the territory?"

"She wasn't taking any chances of being without hired help again, so she brought Sadie from back East. She can't go anywhere until she's paid off the cost of her trip out here."

"That's one way to solve the problem." He lit the match and set it to the crumpled paper and dry cedar kindling already in the grate. At Noelle's smile, the tundra of his emotions thawed some. "A fancy house like this should have one of those heaters, what are they called? Furnaces."

"Henrietta doesn't approve of them. She won't allow a single coal heater anywhere in the house." She smiled, looking not as guarded as she spoke of her aunt.

Probably not because she was starting to like him again.

"It's an ongoing discussion of ours." She shrugged as if it was more amusing than anything else. "She believes it's not natural for a house to be so warm. She thinks newfangled inventions make life too easy for us. She is a firm believer that hardship builds character."

"It doesn't hurt it, that's for sure." He watched the paper melt before the flames and the fire lick up through the kindling to snap and pop greedily. He opened the damper. "Is there anything else you need me to do?"

"You've done more than enough." She tilted her head slightly, as if using the sound from the fireplace to orient herself in the room. Her rich chestnut locks shimmered with the movement and drew his gaze.

The woman she was now captivated him. It took all

his inner strength to hold back his heart and the many ways he wanted to care for her. She moved away from him with a swirl of wool skirts, and his self-discipline melted like sun on ice.

He stood and put the match tin back on the mantelpiece. "My ma said she appreciated the baked goods Sadie's been sending home with me, according to your instructions."

"That Sadie was sworn to secrecy." Noelle didn't look too troubled as she felt for her piano bench and settled onto it. She sat so straight and tall and poised the way she always did, it took his breath away.

"You can't get too het up at Sadie." It was tough being smitten, but he did his best to hide it. "She means well. Those cookies and cakes and breads have been a real treat for my mother. For all of us."

She slid her forefinger along the edges of the ivory keys to find the tiny carving to designate middle C.

"I am glad your mother is recovering. She was always kind to me. I remember she was the sweetest lady and had a smile for everyone, whether she knew them well or not. It must have been hard being away when she was so ill."

"It was." He fought the pressure rising in his chest, the pressure of all he wanted to say and everything he could not let himself feel. "I was making a much better wage than I could hope to find in these parts. Better wages helped out more at home, but it left Aiden to shoulder the burdens of the ranch on his own."

"I remember him as a very friendly, outgoing young man. I heard of his loss. They belonged to the other church in town, but I went to the service. It had to be so hard for him to lose his wife in childbirth."

"It changed him forever."

"Understandably." Soft curls fell across her face, hiding her expression as she traced one fingertip along the edges of the piano keys. "How is he doing now?"

"Unable to let go of the past. Like a lot of us."

She nodded and said nothing at all. Her fingertips brushed at the piano keys, drawing out a harmony of music that rose sweetly before fading to silence. "You've sent money home? It must have been hard. Wages never go as far as you need them to."

"Never. I've been sending over half of my pay home since I first went away."

"Truly? All five years?"

He nodded and steeled his chest. He could tell her the truth right now, but at what cost? Her happiness? The high cost of protecting it was taking a big gnawing bite of him.

Best to change the subject. "I've been keeping a careful eye on the mare, like you asked me to. Solitude doesn't have much longer to go."

"Really?" Her reserve fell away. "I've been worried about her after Robert fired the last horseman. Is there a chance that she'll foal before you have to leave us?"

He could not say no to her, hands down. "I'll make sure the mare is all right. I'll be right here, even if your aunt finds someone else to hire or she calls in family from St. Louis to help out. How's that?"

"I'm grateful, Thad." She brightened like dawn. Nothing could be lovelier. "Solitude is such a sweetheart of a mare, and she means so much to me. I can't be around horses the way I used to, but I…" She shrugged, falling silent, as if unable to finish.

"You love them." He understood her. Always had.

Always would. He couldn't stop his feet from carrying him forward. Just as he couldn't stop caring for her. "It's got to be hard, to have given up so much of what you used to love."

"It's just the way life is. I've grown to be terribly practical, I'm afraid."

"Me, too. Hardworking, sensible, no time for fancy. That's me."

"We've grown up, you and me. Time has been kind to you." As if suddenly shy, she bowed her head and her hair fell down to hide her face.

He saw her meaning clearly. The heartache and bitterness battling within him vanished like sun to mist. There was something new in his heart. Not the old tenderness for her he'd always carried within his spirit, but more. A new love for the woman she was now.

He was not practical after all. The hard lessons in life and the rough trails he'd ridden were forgotten when he gazed into her beloved face.

He hated that she'd known hardship. His leaving hadn't spared her from that. The loss of her parents, her broken engagement, an accident that had almost taken her life. It made a man wonder about fate—about God's design for a single life. Was it His intention for Thad to have left the way he did? Or had God meant for them to be together?

If Mr. Kramer hadn't interfered, would they have found happiness? Would he be married to Noelle right now? Would she have been saved from her losses and blindness?

It was a funny thing—a single decision in a man's life could irrevocably change everything else that followed it. He'd lost more than his heart on that September night long ago when he'd been forced out of town. He'd lost his belief in the goodness in people. He'd lost his belief in love and that a simple man could be honest, work hard, do the right thing and it would turn out all right for him.

He was no longer that naive young man but a man full grown who knew how the world worked and the people in it. But being near Noelle, seeing how she was still so good and bright at heart, made him wish he could be the young man he'd once been.

"I'd best get back to the stable." It wasn't the easiest decision to walk away, but it was the right one. "I'd best keep an eye on the mare."

"Yes. You'll keep me informed?"

"Count on it." He left while he could still hold on to his heart. Noelle started playing and her music followed him out into the hall.

It sounded suspiciously, impossibly, like hope.

Noelle hesitated outside her uncle's bedroom and listened. If Robert were napping, she didn't want to wake him. But she heard the creak of the leather chair, so she counted her steps into the room. "Henrietta said you were sitting up."

"And glad to be, too." His voice was stronger. "I didn't know a horse's hooves could pack such a wallop. It's one thing to read about being injured like that. Another entirely to experience it."

"I'm just thankful you are here to tell the tale." Noelle smiled, knowing that comment would please her uncle. "You must be careful not to overtax yourself right now. Do you need me to call for the maid? We can get you lying down again."

"I've done enough of that. Sitting up like this is doing me good."

"All right, then. Henrietta would only take a nap if I promised on my very soul to sit with you every moment and not let you take up your cane and wobble down to the stables."

Robert's chuckle was warm with love. "That wife of mine knows me too well."

"That wife of yours refused to leave your side night and day until she knew you were going to be all right." *That* was love. The right kind of love. The rare kind of love. The kind she'd once dreamed of. She'd seen a glimpse of that dream today.

Don't think of Thad. She cut off her thoughts like a piece of thread.

"I'm a very blessed man, and I know it." Robert paused and the breath he took sounded strained. "I've always known how much, but never more than in the instant when I saw that mare's rear hooves kicking out and I knew I couldn't get away in time. I was in big trouble. That one minute stretched longer than my lifetime, or so it felt, and my last thought was what a fool I'd been, chasing dreams when all I truly wanted was to be with my wife and daughters."

Noelle's heart cinched up tight. He sounded ashamed and regretful. She knew something about those experiences. "Do you mean as the practical bank president who had unerring good sense?"

"That's the man." Robert's voice sounded glad and sad at the same time. He fell silent as the fire in the grate roared and crackled.

Tiny pings against the window glass announced that it was snowing again. Henrietta's words drifted through

Noelle's mind. *The greatest gift is to be loved as I have been loved. As I love.*

It was a while before he broke the silence between them. "There's nothing wrong with dreams and trying to make them come true, Noelle. I might not know what I'm doing when it comes to horses, and I always might make a better banker than a horseman, but at least I got to try. I would be wise to go back to the bank, I suppose."

"Didn't you just say that you decided that it was foolish to chase dreams?"

"That I did. But I just went about it the wrong way. That's all. I wouldn't listen, and that wouldn't be the first time." Robert fell silent. "Thad is the young man your father wrote us about, isn't he? The one you meant to elope with."

"I didn't know Father had contacted you."

"He and Henrietta kept in close touch. Letters every week without fail."

"I remember." There was the lump again, back in the middle of her throat, blocking off every word and every feeling. Noelle groped for the hard-backed chair she knew was nearby and once she'd found it, she collapsed into it. "My father would never have approved of Thad."

"He is not a wealthy man."

"No. And my father thought wealth was important." She thought of Thad working hard to send wages home. "I suppose Henrietta remembers, too?"

"I don't think she's realized that Thad was the man your father disapproved of so strongly. I can still remember the letter he sent us after he'd found out that a poor immigrant's son was beauing his only daughter."

Noelle froze. "Found out? You mean after I told him."

"I only know that Robert was ready to send a posse after him to drive him from the county." Robert sounded sad.

"Drive him from the county?" That made no sense at all. Father didn't know about Thad until that night when she'd been sobbing in her room, jilted. Unless her father had lied to her.

No, not Papa, she thought. But the Thad she'd known had never been a traveler or a wandering spirit, but a steadfast, stay-put brand of man.

He hadn't been chasing dreams, she realized. He'd lost his dreams as surely as she'd lost hers.

"I don't think you should give up wanting a horse ranch." She was surprised how resolute her words were. The lump in her throat had vanished. "You should simply hire someone very good to learn from."

"You wouldn't happen to have someone in mind?"

Was she that obvious? She hadn't realized it until now, but she was starting to get used to having Thad McKaslin underfoot. "He's been doing the work anyhow, and he *is* a gifted horseman."

"As I hear things, he isn't interested in a job or in getting paid for his time here. Something tells me it's because of you."

The cool from the window swirled around her like fog and she shivered, but it wasn't from the cold. She had never seen Thad so clearly.

Chapter Ten

"I'll see you next week, Nellie." Noelle trailed her final student for the day to the front door. "If you stick to practicing your scales for a whole thirty minutes every day, then next week I'll give you something fun to learn to play. Would you like that?"

"Oh, yes!" Nellie Littleton's rush to escape slowed down a bit. "I've been wanting to learn a new hymn."

"Yes, I know." Noelle adored her youngest student. "Now you be sure and practice your scales. I can tell the difference in your playing, so I'll know if you didn't."

"Oh, all-riiiight." The little girl was a doll, even if she did try to get by without practicing the way she should.

Noelle well remembered what it was like to be that age and have piano lessons which were entirely your parents' idea. "I'll see you next week, Nellie."

"Okay. Bye, Miss Kramer!" Her shoes beat a fast rhythm to the front door. Icy wind gusted and then with a quick slam, she was gone. The faint squeak of a wagon wheel told her that Nellie's parents were out-side waiting for her.

Noelle listened to the stillness of the quiet house.

Sadie was out on errands. Henrietta was in town to fetch the girls home from school. Matilda was keeping an eye on her father. The only sounds in the house were from the crackling fire and the faint clatter as Cook went about her work in the kitchen. Robert had been drowsing in his library the last time she'd checked. Perhaps it was time to check on him again.

The quick tap of Thad's step descending the stairs caught her in midstride. She turned toward the archway, listening to the confident pad of Thad's gait.

She wasn't going to examine too closely why she was glad he'd entered her domain. "Hi, stranger."

"Hi there, pretty lady."

With the smile in his voice and the rustle of clothing, she imagined him standing on the landing, hat in hand, looking storm swept from the conditions outside.

She could not explain why that made her heart pitter-patter. "I didn't hear you come in."

"I reckon it was hard to hear me over the sounds of all those wrong piano notes. Even a cowboy like me could tell someone was playing that wrong."

"Nellie is my most promising student *and* my student least likely to practice. I have hopes her attitude will change in time. Are you on your way home?"

"Not quite yet. I'll wait for your aunt to return from town so I can put up her horse. Then I'll go." The boards creaked slightly as his boots knelled closer. "The mare's foal arrived safe and sound."

"Solitude had her baby?" Pleasure warmed her. "Is it a little filly or a colt?"

"A filly. She's deep sorrel like her mother, as shiny as a copper penny in the sunshine."

"She sounds beautiful."

"She surely is. She's a dainty little thing, all long legs and knobby knees. Would you like to visit her?"

"In the stable?"

"I don't think your aunt would want me to bring a horse, baby or not, into the parlor."

"No, you're right about that." She stood, and she looked like a touch of spring in the light pink dress she wore. "As a general rule I keep out of the stable for a few very practical reasons."

"Ah, I think I understand. I promise to look *before* you step."

"I surely appreciate that." Her eyes twinkled.

When she smiled like that, he felt hope trickle into him.

Crystal lamps clattered in his wake, and he felt sort of out of place, like a colt in a glass shop, but she didn't seem to notice, or, he figured, was too nice to comment.

She'd snagged her coat from the wooden tree by the time he reached her and was already shrugging into it. "You're still so independent, I see." He caught the woolen garment by the back of the collar, as he would help any lady. "Let me help a little."

"I suppose."

He didn't miss her playful smile. This close, he could smell the lilac soap she used and see the stray strands that had escaped her braid to curl like tiny gossamers around her face. For the first time in years, it wasn't the past he longed for.

She took a step back, tying her coat around her middle. "It sounds like thunder out there."

"Yep. It's turning out to be some winter storm." He reached for the door. "You want to reconsider coming out with me?"

"Not a chance."

He turned the knob and cold gusted in. The crisp *tap-tap* of snow faded into the howl of the wind. "You used to love storms."

"I still do." She slipped past him onto the covered porch and faced the wind. "I might not be able to watch the force of the storm, but I can hear the symphony of it." Snow bulleted under the porch roof, striking them both. He closed the door against the resisting wind, hardly aware of the boards beneath his feet. All he could see—he feared all he would ever see—was her. "This is wonderful." She held out her hands, palms up, to feel the strike of the blowing snow. "Bitterly cold, but wonderful."

"I get my fair share of weather working outside. It doesn't hold the same wonder for me. Careful now, you keep inching forward like that and you're gonna hit a patch of ice and then where will you be?"

"On my backside?"

"Exactly. You'd best let me help you." His hand engulfed hers.

You will feel nothing, she vowed. Not the past and certainly not an ember of affection.

It took all her strength to keep her heart as if blanketed by a layer of snow. "It works best if I can lay my hand on your arm."

"Sure." He released his grip on her and she slid her gloved hand along the strong plane of his forearm. Even with the thick layer of jacket and sheepskin, she could feel his strength.

That made her wonder more about his life. About all the pieces he hadn't told her. She took a hesitant step forward and he moved with her, nudging her gently to the left and safely down the slick board steps. She felt the softer snow, which meant they were moving over the walking path between the house and the stables.

She found herself asking a question before she had time to think about it first. "Did you like herding cattle?"

"I didn't dislike it. I got to spend time in the saddle. You know how I don't like to be cooped up indoors all the livelong day."

"Yes." That she did remember. She saw the image of Thad in a white shirt and denims working in amber fields beneath an endless, brilliant blue sky. "I suppose you've seen a lot of the West like in those dime western novels you used to read."

"Yep. I've been all over. I've seen the Grand Canyon. The Badlands. The American desert. The prairies so flat and vast you ride for weeks and you think you'll never come to the end of it."

"There's happiness in your voice. You liked traveling."

"I didn't mind it." Thad cleared his throat, trying to bury the truth more deeply. The last thing he wanted was for Noelle to guess it. He made sure to keep between her and the brunt of the gusting wind. "It was an amiable enough lifestyle. I got to sleep under the stars at night. Saw just about everything there is to see in this wide country. Bear and mountain lions and wolves. Flash floods and twisters and blizzard winds so powerful they can freeze a bull's head to the ground."

"Angel Falls must seem very uninspiring by comparison."

"Not at all." It was the only place he wanted to be. Had ever wanted to be. Gazing down at her lovely face, seeing the snowfall clinging to her velvet hat's brim did funny things to his chest. To his heart. To impossible dreams long buried that had come to life again. "It was tough being gone from my family."

"You missed them." She could see that now. "You and your older brother used to be so close."

"Still are. Another good part about being home is that I'm not always having to write a letter. It's better just to walk up to the main house—I'm staying in the old shanty on our place—walk into the kitchen, pull up a chair and share the day's news over a hot pot of tea. I reckon not much in this lifetime has made me happier than coming back to the homestead."

There was the Thad she'd known—had always known. The man Thad had always been. "Then it's a blessing that you're here."

"I'm glad you think so."

Her shoes sank in the deep snowdrifts, and Thad guided her up the slight slope to the stable's double doors. The sweet scent of hay and the warm earthy scent of horse greeted her. The wind-driven snow moved off her face and echoed in the open rafters overhead. She drank in the sounds of the stable, sounds she missed. The movement of the horses shuffling in the stalls. The low-throated nickers of greeting. The rustle of stray bits of straw beneath her shoes.

The steady footsteps at her side were the sweetest sound of all. She could no longer deny it. Not even Solitude's single, gentle whinny could be more welcome.

"The foal is still wobbly on her feet." Thad drew her to his side of the aisle and to a stop. "She's in the corner right now, all folded up in the straw next to her ma."

"I can hear Solitude breathing, but that's all. She's

so quiet." She tried to picture it, the beautiful red horse standing over her newborn foal. Noelle gripped the top rail of the gate. "Hi, girl. I came to say hello to your baby."

The mare exhaled in an expressive whoosh.

"It's hard to say what Solitude meant by that," Thad interpreted over the rustling sounds in the straw and the solid clink of the mare's hooves. "But my best guess is she's saying it's about time. She's torn between coming to see you and staying with her baby."

The storm chose that moment to surge against the northwest side of the stable. The far-off boom of thunder startled the few other horses in the stables, sending them into loud neighs of protest. Robert's unmanageable stallion took to racing around his stall, sounding like a half-dozen stampeding buffalo all by himself.

Suddenly, she felt the mare's hot breath on her face. She put one hand out and Solitude pressed her nose into it, nibbling affectionately.

Thad's arm brushed hers as he reached to stroke the mare. "She knows you pretty well, I see."

"Solitude was my mother's favorite mare. I gave her to Uncle Robert, since I had no need for a horse. Mama understood Robert's horse dreams."

Thad was silent a moment. "What happened to your horse dreams?"

"Life has a way of taking them away." She traced her fingertips along Solitude's velvety nose.

"True, but life also has a way of giving new dreams."

Thad's hand covered hers and nudged her hand higher. "Are you looking for the star? It's right here."

She felt the swirl of fine hair, where Solitude's perfect white star was. How had he known? she wondered.

She tried to imagine the beautiful red horse in her mind. "Dreams. I don't burden myself with make-believe anymore. Just the things that are here and real, and that matter."

"Like this horse. She's the mare your mother once loved."

"Yes." No one had ever seen her so clearly. She'd missed that, too. The straw rustled and four small hooves beat an ungainly rhythm in her direction. "It's the baby."

"Her mane is just like a bristle broom stickin' straight up. Her tail is a red mop. She has her mother's long, long legs." His baritone dipped low as he chuckled warmly. "Whoa, little filly. Those legs keep tangling you up. Slow down."

"I can hear her. Oh, she fell again. Be careful, little girl."

"She's got her front legs crossed, and her hind end is splayed, but she's getting up. She's wobbling, but don't worry. She's going to figure it out."

Noelle listened to the uneven thumps of the foal's ungainly steps. She was aware of Thad moving closer to lean his forearms against the rail. His arm brushed her shoulder. The only thing louder than the cadence of the storm against the roof was her heart. "Has my uncle named her yet?"

"Nope. Not when I was up chatting with him. He's sure looking better day by day. Well, now she's got her front legs straightened out. Here she comes."

"Oh, her whiskers tickle." Noelle's laughter was soft and full of heart. "She's as soft as warm butter. She's lowered her head. I can feel her ear."

"She's got her neck outstretched, giving your skirt ruffle a look. She can see it beneath the hem of your coat."

"She's going to be a sweetheart like her mother."

"Chances are." Although he was no longer looking at the foal, but at the woman Noelle had become, still full of wonder and tenderness.

Now he saw something more. She had a strength that was so subtle he'd almost missed it. He had to look past her beauty and beyond her loveliness to what lay quietly beneath. Now that he saw it, he could not look away.

"Solitude, I didn't mean to ignore you." Warmly, Noelle moved to stroke the mare, and that ruffled skirt hem fluttered with the movement. The foal startled and her long legs splayed in four different directions. Down she went with a skid and a look of puzzlement.

"Is she all right?"

"She looks a little taken aback, but her ma is reassuring her." He watched while the mare checked her foal over and gave her a tender nudge. "It's gotta be tough when everything is brand-new, even your own feet."

"She's back up." Noelle tilted her head slightly, listening carefully to the foal's movements. "Did I startle her?"

"Your skirt ruffle gave her a moment of terror."

"That was exactly Henrietta's reaction when I went to pick up this dress from Miss Sims's shop."

Thad laughed, he couldn't help it. It had been a long time since he'd laughed so readily. "You have quite a protector in your aunt."

"I certainly do. Henrietta is very shielding of me."

"Rightfully so." He reckoned he felt the same way—always had. Always would.

The foal, with her mama watching over her, inched

forward, nose down and neck stretched as far as it would go trying to figure out that scary ruffle.

His heart ached as he watched Noelle hold out her hand slowly, palm up, waiting for the filly she couldn't see to come to her.

He'd given up his dreams and put others aside for later, but it looked to him as if she'd lost all of hers. She had no marriage, no children, no horses she'd gentled and trained, not one of the things they'd talked about long ago.

He would give up all of his goals yet if it could give her what would make her truly happy. The foal gave a nip at her hem ruffle, which she could probably feel judging by the way she smiled. He wished she could see the dainty pretty filly as she braced her four long legs awkwardly.

The mare came close to press against Noelle's hand. "You have a beautiful baby, girl. You did great."

Solitude nickered warmly, a proud mama.

Thad reckoned he would give just about anything in his life or anything yet to come for Noelle to smile for him the way she did the horse. The longing for it was so keen, he felt sliced down to the quick of his soul. He was no longer much of a praying man—he used his prayers for her—but this one time he wanted to spend one prayer on himself and ask that she, just once, look at him with trust and love. The way she used to.

"Thank you, Thad." Her heart rang in those words. "Thank you for seeing the foal safely here. And for... *everything.*"

She smiled at him, and it was tentative and unsure, but he was glad for it all the same.

"No trouble at all." He felt much taller, suddenly, at her side.

After spending the last hour listening to the soft bed of straw rustling and the soothing nickers as the mama spoke to her sleepy baby, Noelle sighed with contentment. She hadn't felt this happy in a long time. Maybe it had something to do with seeing Thad in a new light.

Or, she realized, maybe, because she was now blind, she had to rely on a deeper way of seeing—with her heart. Understanding why he'd left was coming to her as softly as a Brahms's air.

"I suppose it's time to leave Solitude and her baby alone together." She regretted saying those words. She wanted to make this moment last forever.

"You're shivering. You must be getting cold." Thad moved closer with a rustle. "I kept you out too long."

"Not nearly long enough." She wasn't sure if she was talking about the time spent with the horses or the time spent with Thad. Maybe both.

"I can bring you out to see the little filly again."

"That's very generous. I just might accept your offer."

"Then I just might come for you tomorrow about this time."

She let her smile of pleasure be her answer, because she didn't trust her voice. No, her emotions were tangled up like a knot in a skein of yarn.

"Come with me." His intonation was light and friendly.

She reached out and before she realized it, her hand was on his. She could feel the roughness of his skin and the calluses on his palm from years of hard work. His were a man's hands, strong and capable. As he was. It was impossible not to respect that. To respect the man he'd become.

As she let him guide her down the aisle, the symphony of the storm accompanied them. The rise and fall of the low-noted wind played a haunting harmony to the steady, steely beat of the iced snow against the roof. The *chink-chink* of the stallion circling his stall clanged like a melody. The wind moaned in the rafters above. Thad's boot steps added a dependable percussion as he guided her into the storm.

What was she going to do about the man and her suspicions about the past and about her parents? She did not want to think about the past.

The symphony of the storm crescendoed as they stepped out into the yard. Snow hailed like shards of ice stinging her face and pinging against her coat. The wind gusted so hard, it blew her a step backward. Thad was there, his hold strong on her, moving to block the cruelest brunt of the storm.

Yes, she reminded herself, it was respect she felt. Respect that made the spark of caring within her glow a little more brightly. She could feel the change in the air from the lightning strike and the nearly instant strum of thunder. "That was close."

"Too close." His hold tightened on her. "We're out in the open here. We've got to run for it."

"In the snow?"

"Then we've got to lunge for it." He shouted to be heard over another boom of thunder. "Maybe I'd best carry you."

"Try it, and I'll never speak to you again. I'm blind, not incapable."

"I knew you were gonna say that." Standing out in

a storm like this was a dangerous notion, so he tightened his hold on her, the only tenderness he was allowed. "Ready?"

Lightning tore apart the sky, cleaving the dense twilight curtain of snow. Blinding white light sizzled to the right, and an unearthly blast of thunder masked the explosion of the strike. He couldn't see what had been hit, but it had been near enough that he could smell it.

"C'mon." He ran, bringing her along with him. He had a good tight hold on her arms. There wasn't a chance he would let her fall. They ran together, and he bowed his head against the onslaught. How long before the next strike? And how close would it be? The wind swirled, holding them back like an inhuman force.

"We're almost to the house," he shouted above the roar of the storm.

To his surprise, she only stumbled once and then, in a blink, they were on the walkway in the lee of the house. She dropped the hems of her coat and skirts, which swirled at her snowy shoe-tops and swiped at the curls plastered against her face. She turned into the wind and let it batter her. "It's magnificent."

You are magnificent. His pulse slowed. His breathing stalled. A terrible pain traced like lightning through the dark sky and tore apart his hard exterior. It was a change that felt more dangerous than lightning, more powerful than the wind, more life sustaining than the rain.

She was the reason his eyesight blurred. She was the reason his heart stirred to life and why he could not look away. The sight of her filled the empty places in him like the rain pooling on the low places of the earth. He felt whole. He felt healed. He felt at peace with the past. It was like hope and faith creeping back into his soul.

Her smile brightened as the wind kicked up a notch. "I can almost see the angle of the snow."

With the dampness curling the tendrils of her hair and the cold crisping her delicate complexion pink, she looked radiant and rosy. So beautiful it made his teeth ache. It was all he could do to talk past the tight squeeze of his throat. "It's nearly sideways."

"And falling like hail." She closed her eyes as if she were looking inward for the image. "What color of gray are the clouds?"

"Right overhead, they're as dark, and as purple-black as an angry bruise. Can't see much else, as it's nearly a whiteout."

"I hear another boom of thunder. It's definitely moving away. I can't remember the last time we had a storm like this."

I can. He sidestepped closer to her and told himself it was to better shield her from the snow's touch, but that wasn't the only reason. No, not at all. "You're shivering, and the temperature is dropping. I don't want to turn you into an icicle."

"I've been cold before. Besides, I'm having fun."

"That may be, but the last thing I want to do is to get on Henrietta's bad side. That aunt of yours is a fearsome woman."

That made her laugh but it did not make him forget the memory of her and another storm. They'd been at her house in town, standing on the back porch out of sight of any nosy neighbors. They were hand in hand, heart in heart, watching the blizzard blowing down from the mountains and across the prairie like a miracle of white.

Noelle whirled toward the driveway. "Someone's coming. It must be Henrietta back with the girls."

He turned in time to see a dim shadow in the snowfall. Miss Bradshaw broke through and into sight pulling the sleigh. There was no blizzard powerful enough on earth to disguise the stern look on the aunt's proud face—probably one of great disapproval. The girls, back from school, stared wide-eyed in the backseats as Henrietta reined in the mare.

"Inside, girls!" she commanded sharply. "Noelle! I'm shocked at you, risking your health in this way. Why, you're soaked through, by the looks of you, and wearing only a cloak! Not your heavy winter coat. Young man, what are you thinking? No good can come from this. Noelle is very frail. I expect a severe case of pneumonia at the very least."

He realized what she must see, Noelle's hand in his and alone. The hope in his heart withered like a seedling caught in a late frost. He took a gulp of freezing air and reeled in his feelings. For a moment he'd captured a small piece of heaven. For a moment, they were the way they used to be.

He'd almost forgotten that there was the past and the choice he'd made standing between them.

Thad squared his shoulders and met the aunt's gaze straight on. He hadn't thought of Noelle as frail, but he could not argue with the older woman's concern. It was a concern they shared. "Pardon me, ma'am. I was just seeing her inside—"

"Henrietta," Noelle interrupted. "I'm fine. You fret too much. You know I love a good storm."

"You must get your lack of good sense from your mother's side." With what looked like a wink, the older woman climbed out of the sleigh, refusing the offer of his free hand to help her.

If he wasn't mistaken, there was a twinkle in her eyes, a knowing glimmer that made him wonder just how much she'd been able to understand.

Yes, he was serious about Noelle. It ripped his soul in pieces to feel her take her hand from his, to take a step away. Was she remembering what he'd done to her? Seeing a man who'd hurt her?

"I'd best go." His palm felt cold as he stepped away. Lonesomeness set in, beating him like the snow. "Hope I didn't get you in the henhouse."

Her unguarded smile was all the reassurance he needed. "It was worth it. Henrietta's censure isn't enough to go back on your word, right? You'll still take me to see the foal again?"

"I'll see you tomorrow." He tipped his icy hat in the aunt's direction as he took Miss Bradshaw by the bridle bit. "You'd best all get in out of this storm." He paused while another finger of lightning crooked down from the veiled sky. "It's likely to get worse before it gets better."

He turned away so he wouldn't see Henrietta Worthgton and her daughters take Noelle into the fancy house and away from him—where she belonged.

Chapter Eleven

Henrietta barreled through the parlor, the teacup rattling in its saucer with her every step. China knick-knacks and crystal pendants on the lamps clinked and chimed at her approach. "Where you young people get your notions, I shall never know."

Noelle squeezed the damp from her braid with the towel, trying to decide what on earth to say. She opted for silence as she heard the teacup clatter onto the side table and caught a whiff of Henrietta's rose fragrance before the matron marched away and came to a sudden halt. The *thwack-thwacking* sound had her imagining her aunt venting her humor on the innocent sofa pillows.

"If you catch a chill and your death, then I shall know who to blame." Henrietta paused. "A man who has made himself useful around here ought to have realized that much! I hope he is not about to make the same mistake as the last stable hand."

"I can assure you that is not a possibility." Noelle gave her hair a final squeeze and folded the towel.

"Oh, do not be so certain," Angelina commented from the hearth where she was warming up from the long ride from the schoolhouse. "You two looked terribly cozy—scandalously cozy—when we drove up."

"Cozy?" Noelle had to laugh at that, although it wasn't humor she felt. No, any thought of serious feelings between her and Thad only brought up that tangled knot of emotions that hurt more than she wanted to admit. She set the folded towel aside for Sadie to pick up later. "Thad was walking me to the house. He had to be close to guide me. You know that, Angelina."

"Yes, but he's a very handsome man and it didn't look as if being near him was a hardship," Angelina said knowledgeably. "I think he's smitten with you."

Smitten? No. Noelle filled up from toe to top with an aching regret. How could she tell her cousin that it was far too late for that? Any loving feelings Thad had to have once felt for her were long destroyed. They had to be.

Thad was a good man with a good heart. Of course he would always care for her. Her eyes smarted with understanding. It was all starting to make sense. All his kind words and the gentle things he'd said earlier that had made her so angry came clear. How he would always care for her.

And she for him, she realized. Her fingertips felt wooden and clumsy as she inched across the small table, searching for the cup and saucer. Regret and the weight of lost dreams burdened her. No, even if she were not blind, it was too late for a second chance.

Henrietta gave another thwack on the unsuspecting pillows. "I'll have no more talk of this tonight. Robert, are you comfortable? Do I need to help you back upstairs? I shall call Cook to help me—"

"No!" Robert may have been still terribly weak from

his injuries, but his tenor boomed. "No, my dear, I've had enough of that room. I'm quite comfortable here."

"Supper shall be served soon, I'll see you upstairs then." Henrietta sounded as firm as her footsteps on the wood floor. "No argument."

"I thought the man was the lord of his own home?" A small smile warmed her uncle's words.

"Yes, and a woman is the queen, so you will obey me. I'll not take no for an answer." While not a word was said, deep-felt love was there all the same in Henrietta's tone.

An abiding love that made Noelle sigh a little. That she could not know the same love, the kind that grew stronger and richer with the years, would always be a great, lost dream. She inched her fingers in the direction of where she thought the teacup was, and fortunately located the rim of the saucer without upturning the cup or burning her fingertips on the steaming hot tea puddled in the saucer.

"Noelle—" Robert changed the subject "—I wish I'd been up to a trip to the stable. I would have liked to see our newest addition."

"Solitude's foal is adorable." She set the teacup gently into its saucer, aware of Thad's nearness. Although he didn't make a sound, she knew. He was close—in the kitchen perhaps? "Have you named her yet?"

"Not yet. You wouldn't happen to have a suggestion?" Thunder cannoned again. There only seemed one obvious suggestion. Thad's boots tapped a distant rhythm at the far end of the house. She tried to make her voice sound normal and unaffected. "You should name her Stormy."

"Then Stormy she is!" Robert chuckled. He sounded

happy. "I think this horse-raising venture of mine might be taking a turn for the better."

"It could hardly get much worse!" Henrietta commented.

"Ooh, did you see that?" Minnie's words echoed in the dining room's coved ceilings.

Thunder crashed overhead, rattling the windows. Another round of lightning, Noelle realized as she gingerly sipped the hot herbal tea, and the strikes were terribly close. She remembered how Thad had described the storm to her. It was best he stay out of the dangerous weather. "Thad can't ride out in this."

"Sure he can," Henrietta answered. "He has a horse, does he not?"

The tea caught in her throat. She coughed as Angelina answered. "But Mama, it's a lightning storm. He could get struck."

"And he might not. Goodness, Noelle, are you all right?"

Noelle set the cup in the saucer with a splash. "F-fine. I should have kept my thoughts to myself, I see."

"I inquired about the North County McKaslins," Henrietta said by way of an answer. "Your Mr. McKaslin is only a disinherited cousin. Apparently his father was nothing but a disgrace, much like the younger brother is turning out to be."

"So," Angelina teased. "How old is the younger brother?"

"I'll not rise to that bait, missy," Henrietta scolded, although she was struggling not to laugh. "How you test me. Don't think I've forgotten about the incident at school. After dinner, you're to go straight to your room."

"I detest being banished. There's nothing to do upstairs but to read my Bible—"

"Exactly the guidance you need, young lady. Why rumors swirl about you, I'll never know. I'm of half a mind to take you out of that school entirely. How many times must I explain to that teacher that none of my daughters would ever shove over the outhouse?"

"Many a time, Mama." Angelina padded across the parlor as another round of thunder rumbled like cannon fire.

The girls began a discussion, speaking over the top of one another, debating the truth or rumor of Angelina's misdeeds at school, and Noelle took her leave. Keeping careful track of her steps, she made it to the kitchen as quickly as she could.

The moment she pushed open the kitchen door, she heard the maid's quick steps. "Sadie, is there a chance you could set an extra place for Thad?"

"Mr. Worthington has already requested it."

"He did?"

"When you and Mr. McKaslin took off for the stable, miss." Sadie sounded in a hurry as Cook slammed a pot lid down like a crash of cymbals. "Dinner is a bit late tonight. McKaslin is on the back steps, if you got to wondering where he may be."

"Thank you, Sadie." Noelle ran her finger against the far wall, to keep out of Cook's way. The scents of roast beef and simmering gravy hung in the air. Uncle Robert had already thought to invite Thad? Intriguing. Thunder rattled the windowpanes and the crystal teardrops of the lamps as she opened the back door.

Icy wind slammed into her, but she hardly noticed

it. She felt warm and as light as a May day. "Look what rascal has come in out of the storm."

"A rascal?" Thad's chuckle was as warm as hope, as welcome as rediscovered dreams. "I suppose you're right about that." There was a rustle, as if he were hanging up his coat. "Your uncle was kind enough to invite me to dinner with you all."

"Yes, and I think I was the last to know about it."

"That right? I'd thought the invitation had originally come from you."

"It would have, if I had thought of it sooner."

"Is that so?" How about that? Thad felt the hard shell of tension in his chest ease a notch, making it easier to breathe. She breezed past him like warmth and light, and he could not help but follow. Some things like ice and snow and February storms were as inevitable and unstoppable as his affection for her.

He closed the door tight against the pounding weather, glad for the wave of warmth that washed over him. The delicious aroma coming from the stove made his stomach growl. The rare chance of walking at Noelle's side made him feel alive again in his heart and spirit—places he'd thought had been in the dark for too long to survive.

"I can hear Sadie settling the serving bowls on the table," Noelle said over her shoulder as she followed the wall to a closed door. "Prepare yourself for the Worthington inquisition."

"The what?"

Her laughter was a gentle, musical trill as she pushed open the door.

He moved close to help her with it and time seemed to freeze. For an instant, anyway, as he noticed the damp curls of her chestnut hair—she'd unbound her braid and combed out her hair and it fell in a cascade of color and light around her heart-shaped face and past her delicate shoulders. He barely noticed she looked beautiful in the dress of white and gold she'd changed into because the sight of happiness on her face was drawing him more than any beauty.

"Just you wait and see," she said as the door opened fully.

He tried to imagine the entire Worthington family taking his measure with a whole new outlook.

The family was already seated around the elaborately set table. He hardly noticed the room and its blue-and-silver wallpaper, crystal lamps and highly polished woods because of the way the women in the room were studying him, the younger ones with curiosity and the older ones with assessment.

Henrietta, regal at the foot of the table, squinted her eyes at him. Her mouth pursed. "I hear from Robert we owe you yet another thanks. You saw the new foal safely into the world. I hear there was a complication."

"Just had to get her hooves heading the right way, was all." Thad shrugged. "It wasn't anything Robert couldn't have done himself if he'd been up to the task."

Robert nodded in greeting from the head of the table. "You're a humble man, Thad. I can learn a lot from you."

"I've been around horses all my life." Thad took care not to trip on the carpet as he followed Noelle around the table. The whole house was fancy for his tastes, and he felt as discomfited by the surroundings as by the females watching him with unblinking gazes. "I'm a cattleman, mostly."

"Is that so?" Henrietta's gaze narrowed. "Are you done with your wandering all over tarnation? Or is that the life you intend to return to?"

He gulped, a little taken aback. Noelle had stopped at a chair beside the oldest Worthington girl, and he held her chair while she sank into it. "No, ma'am. I've come home to Montana to stay."

Noelle turned toward him, searching his face as if she could see him plainly.

Was that hope he saw? Or sadness? So many uncomfortable emotions were muddying his mind, he couldn't seem to tell up from down.

"Very well then, I suppose that will do." The way Henrietta said it, it didn't sound good at all. Not at all. She gestured toward the empty chair beside her. "I'm determined to get at the truth of your character. You will sit next to me, young man."

Where she could keep a good close eye on him, no doubt. Thad swallowed hard at his murky emotions, but couldn't seem to dislodge them. They were made worse by Noelle and the way her emerald gaze followed the sound of his steps around the table, sparkling with merriment. Good thing she was enjoying this because sweat was starting to bead up on the back of his neck.

As he took his chair at the table, he couldn't shake the notion that Henrietta was out to find his every flaw. She was bound to find quite a few.

"When you went on those cattle drives, did you sleep on the ground with your saddle for a pillow?" the girl directly across from him burst out.

"Y-yep."

"Do you really call the cows little dogies? Did you

tell tall stories around the campfire like in the dime novels?"

"Angelina!" Henrietta looked scandalized. "Those are hardly appropriate questions for a young lady to ask." Henrietta's oblong face looked severe, or maybe it was the tight way she'd pulled her hair back, so that her face looked drawn back, as well.

Well, he should have expected that. He had no illusions. All he had to offer was a savings account that used to be bigger and an old shanty that was three times smaller than the dining room.

Thad shifted again, and the chair wasn't getting any more comfortable. He'd be more at ease sitting in a sticker bush facing down a porcupine bare-handed.

It was a saving grace when Robert spoke. "Lord, bless this food we are about to receive."

Thad realized that hands were folded and heads bowed all around him and he did the same.

"—keep us mindful of our many blessings. Thank you for bringing us together again, as friend and family, and teach us dear Lord to better love one another. Amen."

Thad looked up to a course of "amens" and where did his gaze naturally go? To Noelle.

"So, where did you learn all of this horse knowledge?" Henrietta passed him a bowl of dinner rolls and she gave him a stern look over the crusty tops. "Did you attend some kind of training?"

"Training? No, ma'am." It sure looked as if he'd hit a rocky trail with this woman. He got the notion that the Worthington Inquisition was just getting started. "I learned what I know from growing up on my family's homestead."

"I see. No formal education?"

"Just the local school."

"No academy or college?"

"Begging your pardon, ma'am, but do I look like I've been to college?"

"No, but it was a hope."

He took a dinner roll and passed the bowl to the youngest girl, who looked at him as if he'd turned into a horse right there before her eyes.

Yep, he was feeling mighty uncomfortable. As he accepted the bowl of creamed potatoes from a tight-lipped Henrietta, he caught Noelle's amused expression across the table. She had to know that he was suffering. She didn't seem to mind it at all.

Well, she *had* warned him.

"I got a good look at that mustang you ride." The girl across the table—Angelina?—dumped a spoon of buttered peas on her plate. "Was he once wild? Did you catch him in a roundup? Did you break him?"

"Yes," Robert said from the head of the table. "Tell us about your mustang. A plucky breed, as I understand it."

"Sunny is a mustang?" Noelle asked breathlessly. His pulse ground to a halt. Regret bit him like barbed wire. He forked a helping of roast beef on his plate, knowing what no one else knew at the table. She'd once dreamed of raising her own horses—mustangs, native to this rugged country. It was a dream they'd shared long ago.

"I'd just finished a drive on the Northern Trail and was on my own, heading from Baker City in Oregon to my next job. It was a long haul following the Yellowstone River and there wasn't a town in sight, so I chose a spot near water to camp. Something woke me up around midnight. My horse was nervous, so I got up with my Winchester thinking there was a hungry wolf or mountain lion nearby, but it was an injured colt."

"Was he still a foal or was he more grown-up?" the littlest sister asked, wide-eyed.

"He was probably six months old, I reckon. When I got up to him, he tried to run, but couldn't get up. He'd been shot."

"Shot?" Noelle gasped.

"On purpose?" Angelina burst out.

"Hard to tell but I don't think so. Likely as not he caught a stray bullet from a hunter, since we were far up in the high country. I searched for his mother, too, after I'd patched him up, but there was no telling how far he'd wandered hurt like that. I found out later there was a wild horse roundup a few days before that." He picked up his fork and knife with a slight clink. "I always figured that's how he got separated from his ma."

"It's lucky you found him." She could see the image in her mind, the dark night, the campfire, the caring man and the fragile colt.

"I always figured I was the lucky one." Thad cleared his throat for all the good it did. There was no hiding the fondness in his voice. "I wasn't sure he'd last the night, but he had spirit and surprised me. I named him Sunny because he was a palomino pinto. His coat is as bright as a summer day."

"He took to you like a best friend." Noelle could see that, too.

"Did you break him like a bronco?" Angelina asked again, her voice resonating with excitement. "He was a wild horse, so did it take longer than a tame horse?"

Noelle took a bite of her dinner roll, but her attention remained on Thad and his answer. She suspected she wasn't the only one since the clink of silver slowed around the table. In her heart, she already knew Thad's answer.

"Sunny was and is my best buddy. He's no more wild than I am, and when it comes down to it, breaking a best friend isn't my way of doing things."

"That's how the last horseman Papa hired did it." Angelina ignored her mother's throat clearing. "He got up on the horse's back and stayed on while the stallion kicked and bucked like a bronco. It was exciting."

"Probably not for the horse," Thad pointed out.

How was it that she knew Thad so well, after all? Noelle searched for her glass of water with careful fingers, listening to more questions fired from around the table, including one from Uncle Robert.

The meal progressed as Thad told of how he taught his colt to trust him. He painted a vivid picture of working with the mustang on the journey to his next job, introducing him to kindness and campfire bread and friendship. How he'd worked with Sunny in the fresh, green, wild grasses.

She could see Thad, gentle and patient and dependable, never giving the colt a reason to doubt his kindness. She could picture man and colt together in the rugged mountain wilderness, surrounded by yellow, red and purple wildflowers and crowned by majestic mountains. The honey-gold colt and the dark-haired man painted an image she wanted to believe in.

The lightning storm had passed by the time the maid cleared the dinner plates, and Thad had helped Robert back upstairs, so he'd taken his escape. The mercury had dropped well below freezing as he said his goodbyes and left Noelle with her family. But the way she'd smiled at him, and the hope in his heart stayed with him through the frigid ride home.

As the wind-driven snow battered him, memories of her kept him cozily warm. He couldn't seem to forget how she'd bitten her lower lip in worry as he'd told of Sunny's first cattle drive two weeks later, and how he'd got swept away in a stampede. Likely as not come to a sad end, but the little guy had made it. Thad kept him on a shorter lead rope from then on.

The sigh she'd made of delight wasn't something he could forget, either, when he'd told of the evening, a year later, when he'd been trying to spark a campfire with a flint and looked up at the sound of thunder. It was a herd of wild horses streaking across the plains and there'd been no mistaking the yearning in Sunny's eyes. So Thad had climbed to his feet and slipped off Sunny's halter. The yearling had taken off with an eager whinny, bolting after the herd and out of sight.

How lovely she'd looked, graced by the lamplight, and captivated by his story as he told of standing in the knee-high grass, feeling nothing but lonesome, when a low welcoming whinny sounded in the dark—Sunny had come back to stay with him.

Had he been alone with Noelle when he'd been telling that story, he would have said it had felt like a sign on that lonely night. He'd been traveling too long, miserable living out of his saddle packs and Sunny's return seemed to give him the hope that heaven was watching over him after all. Maybe there were still dreams to be had, and that he shouldn't give up all hope.

But since he hadn't been alone with her, he'd kept those words to himself. They seemed to whisper within the chambers of his heart, in the lonesomeness within that he'd not been able to shake. He'd missed her. He'd been lonely for her these long years, for his best friend, for the woman he'd wanted to marry, for his one true love.

Distant thunder rumbled through the mantle of cloud and snow, but the cold and dark did not feel as bleak as it once had. Thad nosed Sunny toward home.

Noelle shivered in the cold as she knelt in prayer. The storm howled like an angry wolf outside the bedroom window. She ended her nightly prayers as she always did. *I pray that You will watch over Thad, Father. Please see to his happiness. Amen.*

She rose, teeth chattering and dived under the covers. Cold had sunk into the marrow of her bones and the sheets felt as cold as the air in the room. The flatiron at the foot of the bed gave off blessed heat, and she scrunched down to find the warmth with her toes.

"Amen," Matilda whispered. Her teeth chattered, too, and the thwack of the quilt told that she'd covered herself completely beneath the blankets.

The house had quieted. Henrietta's voice came faintly through the walls two rooms down the hall as she wished Minnie good-night. A door shut and then silence.

Surely Thad had made it through the storm safely. So, why was she worried about him? She rolled onto her side to contemplate that. It made no sense because she knew he'd managed to drive cattle and ford dangerous rivers and crest mountain summits for years successfully. Surely he could manage to find his way home through one blustery whiteout.

She had to be honest with herself. It wasn't his safety she was worrying over. It was her feelings for him. For the man he'd made her believe in tonight with his tales of strength and steadfast gentleness.

That was the Thad McKaslin she'd fallen so hard in love with she would have defied her beloved parents and a life of security for the chance at her dream—to love him for all the days of her life.

How could that Thad, the one she'd known so well, have forsaken her? He was not a man who could break a promise, let alone a vow of love and forever. That man was the one she'd glimpsed tonight through his honest, plain stories of befriending a wild colt.

He'd probably meant to tell of his horse-gentling philosophy, but she'd heard something different—a man who was trustworthy and steadfast and committed. The man Thad had always been.

A sharp rustle came from Matilda's side of the room. She must have thrown the covers off her head. "I'm too cold and tired to read tonight. Can I read two passages aloud to you tomorrow?"

"Of course. I'm half asleep as it is, and I hate to trouble you anyway. You know that."

"It's no trouble. I'm just greatly fatigued. I think my mind is overworked from those thrilling stories Mr. McKaslin told at dinner."

"Yes, they were very enjoyable." And for her, personal, although that wasn't something she was about to admit to anyone, even to someone she trusted as much as Tilly. Why, she could hardly admit the truth to herself. "Angelina was enthralled. Do you think she's going to torment your mother with a new desire to run off and herd cattle?"

"Probably. It's Angelina's lot in life to torment poor mama. She ought to be careful or Mama just might make good on her threat to send her to finishing school."

"Think of all the outhouses to overturn there. Angelina will be quite busy."

"True." Matilda chuckled. "He likes you, you know. Really likes you."

"You mean Thad?" Noelle ran her fingertips over the lace edging the pillow slip. "You've told me this before, but I only have f-friendly feelings for Thad."

And there were practical reasons, of course, why she could never risk her heart on him again. Reasons that could not be changed. She groped for the edge of her sheets to pull them up to her chin.

Matilda's mattress ropes squeaked as she leaned to put out the light. "Good night, Noelle."

"Good night, Tilly." She rolled onto her side and closed her eyes, knowing she would dream this night of a wide-shouldered man and his wild horse.

Chapter Twelve

As Thad watched Noelle standing at Solitude's stall alongside her uncle, who was leaning heavily on his stout wooden cane, he tried not to take it as a sign. Of course Robert was feeling strong enough to venture outdoors. It only made sense the first place he'd visit was his horses and had asked Noelle to accompany him.

It didn't mean that she'd changed her mind about *his* offer. That was the story he was trying to sell himself. He wasn't sure it was working. As he patiently waited for the stallion to approach him, he knew one thing—Noelle's face and manner, when she'd greeted him earlier, had been warm and friendly. Not polite and cool, as it had once been.

It didn't hurt to hold out a little hope, did it? "You've done wonders with these spirited horses of mine," Robert praised as he limped closer, leaving Noelle alone at Solitude's stall. "I knew you were helping out with the stable work and heavier chores around here. What I didn't know was that you've been working with these horses."

Thad kept eye contact with the ill-tempered stallion

and kept the apple in his pocket. "I'm only doing what needed to be done."

"But your work with the horses. Triumph is standing still. A first for him, I believe. It's amazing."

"Just a little horse know-how is all." Thad shrugged, keeping his attention on the horse because looking at Noelle would hurt too much. He wasn't sure what risk his heart could afford to take. He'd been up half the night, unable to sleep for working out his plans for the day—his plans for her. "It doesn't much seem like work to me."

"You've made an impressive difference."

"Hate to argue with you about that, sir, but in my view, these horses have a long way to go."

"They'll get there." Robert leaned heavily on his cane, but despite the obvious pain he was in, he was grinning ear to ear. "I'd best get back in before my wife hunts me down and drags me back. She's not keen on this horse-raising venture of mine."

"Do you need help, sir?"

"I'll manage."

There she was, right in his line of sight. Thad gulped hard, and, since Triumph had decided to be a gentleman and stand still without showing his teeth, he palmed him the apple. The stallion took the treat and then lunged back with it, his temper showing as he shook his head like a bull in full charge.

"That stallion does sound more well behaved than he has been." Noelle sparkled with good humor. "He doesn't sound as ornery when he kicks the wall."

"This one has a long row to hoe, but he'd be all right in the end. I'm happy to work with him."

"That's good of you."

"I can't have your uncle getting kicked like that again, not if I can help it." That had her smiling. He loved her smile; he loved everything about her. She tilted her head slightly to one side, as if focusing on the approach of his footsteps, and the soft fall of her hair brushed her face.

"I think we're alone now." She paused to listen. "Yes, we are. There's something I've been wanting to ask you."

"Uh-oh. That sounds plenty serious."

"You have no notion of just how much." She reached out to him, her sensitive fingertips finding first the air, then the edge of his sleeve. "I'm sorry I didn't wait for you to bring me to see Stormy. Robert asked me and he was so excited to be feeling well enough to venture out here. I didn't have the heart to turn him down."

"Sure. I understand that. The question is, do you have the heart to turn me down."

"Turn you down? Why ever would I—" She paused, tilting her head to the side to listen closely. "I hear something. A clink of metal."

"Yep."

"What are you up to, Thad McKaslin?" There was rustling, too.

His chuckle thrummed through her spirit like a harp string. "Guess. It was something you used to love to do. I found this out, and so I asked you for our first—"

"—date," she finished as the *clank-clank* came again. What did he have there? Probably it had something to do with the stables and horses, but for the life of her, the high-noted, pleasant steely sound made her think of one thing. "That can't be ice skates."

They clanked again. "And exactly why is that so impossible? I brought your old pair from home. It seems they were still in the barn where I'd left a few things."

"The skates you'd bought for me." Pleasure filled her up like a warm sip of hot cocoa. "I spent many an hour twirling on one pond or another while you patiently froze on the bank."

"I didn't see it that way. I always figured it was a privilege just to be with you."

"Still a sweet-talker after all this time."

"Hey, it's only the truth, but I'm glad you think so." Was that a smile in his voice? It was, she was sure of it, warm and sweetly handsome. She sighed a little, remembering how captivated she used to be by the sight of his smile—and now, by the sound and feel of it.

"Come take my arm," he offered, his baritone resonant with warmth and promise. "Let me take you out on the ice."

"To skate?" A sweet longing filled her with a sweet force. Longing to be twirling on the ice once again, she told herself firmly—and *not* longing to spend time with Thad.

Or was it?

With his hand firmly on hers, he coaxed her toward the back door. "You used to be a good skater."

"Yes, but I'm likely to fall on my nose. Or worse. It might be a complete disaster."

"I'll keep that from happening, I promise. I'll be right there with you, seeing for you."

How could she keep from caring for Thad now? Every beat of her heart grew stronger because of his words, his presence and the promise that made her feel free again.

"I'll never let you fall." He used that wondrous voice

of his against her, replete with humor and unspoken dreams. Quiet, secret dreams that had her heart opening and her wishes coming to life.

Wishes she could not give life to.

He guided her along the uneven path with a gentle hand—not a domineering one—on her elbow.

"Sit here." His baritone dipped low. With quiet tenrness, he helped her settle on the garden bench.

She hardly noticed the cold trying to seep in through her layers of wool and flannel. The burn of the wind, the twitter of winter birds and the scent of wood smoke on the air faded away. There was only the crunch of snow beneath his boots, the rustle of his clothes as he knelt before her. His scent of hay and horseflesh and leather and his soothing presence was all she could think about. All she could notice.

He lifted her right foot onto his knee, and emotions that had sat like a heavy lump in her chest began to unravel, one aching thread at a time.

She could no longer hold back the question that had been troubling her. "I think I know why you ran off instead of marrying me and why you left me behind." The ice skate slipped from his fingers. "Let's leave the past where it belongs."

"I'm not speaking about the past. I'm talking about this moment. Right now. What's happened between us since you've come back."

"There's no sense in digging up what's done."

"But—"

"Trust me, Noelle. It's for the best if we don't talk about this." He shook the snow off the skate and fit it to her shoe. All he wanted to do was to keep her safe and happy and thriving. It was the only way he was allowed to love her.

And love her he did, with all the broken pieces of his heart and all the lost pieces of his soul. He was more than the nineteen-year-old boy he'd once been, and his love was more now, too. Fuller. Deeper. More everlasting.

More selfless. Which was why he took a long drink of the sight of her, savoring each careful detail. The heart-shape of her lovely face, her high cheekbones and sweetly chiseled chin, her jeweled emerald eyes, her cinnamon hair, her creamy complexion, her delicate features, her small slender hands that felt so dear when he held them in his own.

He reached for the second skate. "I need your other foot."

"You've taken over my uncle's responsibilities around the house and yard." She switched feet, allowing him to take her left foot in his hands. "You've gone beyond your duty as our stableman. You're the kind of man who does the right thing, who works hard, who can always be counted on."

"I take my work seriously, is all."

"No, you are the boy I fell in love with, and you've always been the man you are now. I see you, Thad. All of you."

He squeezed his eyes shut. Her words were an answered prayer. If he'd ever had one for himself, it was this. For her to see that he was the kind of man who would never hurt her, who would always do what he could for her greatest happiness. Without condition. Without end.

He clamped the blade into place on her shoe and

checked to make sure it was on good and tight. He ignored the chill seeping through the knees of his denims and the gnawing of regret.

She reached forward as easily as if she saw him, and her fingertips brushed the collar of his coat, then the scarf at his throat and finally cupped his jaw. "You left me thinking something had happened to you. You left me waiting, stubbornly believing in you. Even after I learned you'd left the county for good, it took me a long time to give up believing that you had to leave for some reason and you would be coming back to me. That's how strongly I believed in you. In noble, good, unfailing you."

My dear, beloved Noelle. He pressed his jaw against the fuzzy sweetness of her gloved hand. Here was the chance he'd always wished for—to tell the truth, to right the wrong and win her back. He gently moved away and climbed to his feet.

There was nothing more precious to him in all the world, and there never would be. Her loveliness was something he would never tire of, the sight that would refresh his weary heart the most. She was everything good and womanly and rare in this world, and the heart of his deepest dream come true. A dream he would not hurt for any reason.

Her happiness was more important than anything he could ever want for himself. Maybe bringing her here, where mist swirled around the frozen pond like lost dreams, hadn't been the best idea. "You might think that breaking my promise to you that night came pretty easy."

"It had once been my impression."

"I can honestly say it was the hardest decision I ever made."

"I understand that now." She held out her hand, confident that he would take it, that he wouldn't leave her sitting alone in her darkness.

He took her hand to guide her. She rose lightly to her feet, balancing easily on her blades, and he tried not to notice the thud of his heart hitting his soul. He loved her more. He'd been a fool to think he had ever stopped loving her. The love he had for her had not vanished. It had simply bided its time, quiet and dormant as the trees in winter, waiting for spring to come.

The dreams he'd given up on were there, alive after all. He swallowed hard against the pressure building in his chest. "I did what I thought was best at the time. I hate that I left you waiting and hoping. I know what I did came at a cost, but I did what I had to do, what I thought was right."

"I know that." Her emerald eyes, her face, her voice, her manner all shone with that truth. "My father forced you out of town, didn't he?"

The blood in his veins stilled. How did she know? Had she guessed? And if she had, if she knew the truth, there was the temptation to tell her the rest of it. But was it the right thing to do? He could not seem to move, although her skirts whispered as she stood, wobbling on the thin blades. He caught hold of her, keeping her steady when he was the unsteady one.

Forgiveness. It shone in her emerald eyes and radiated in her smile. The way she turned to him, the way she trusted him meant more to him than anything in the world. "I know how you loved your folks, Noelle. I can't ruin their memory for you."

"You won't. Whatever they did, they did out of love. That's what you did, too."

She understood. An enormous weight lifted from his soul. His throat closed and he could not speak. The burdens of the past, of the wrongs her father had done to him and his family, and the misery he'd suffered melted away.

She looked like a little drop of heaven—or at least his notion of heaven—full of goodness and mercy and kindness. Mist clung to the gossamer curls caressing her sweet face. "My parents were wrong and misguided and they had no right to interfere, but they're gone now. And if there's something to learn from this, then it's that our time here is so very short. I don't want to waste another moment in heartache. Take me skating, Thad."

She held out her mittened hands, and it felt as if she were offering him a second chance. They'd navigated the short way to the head of the little pond where mist curled over the ice like wishes. "Straight ahead a few steps. That's right."

They toddled together the short distance to the pond's edge. The surface was rippled and uneven. He took the first step and braced himself to help her onto the slick surface. "Easy now."

"Oh, I'm out of practice." Her right blade slid forward, and she wobbled as if losing her sense of balance.

He caught her by the elbows and muscled her around. Her gloved hands fisted in the fabric of his coat as he steadied her. "Are you okay?"

"It's going to take me a moment to get used to this." Her hold on him was a trusting one. "Which way am I facing? So I can get a sense of direction."

"The house is in a straight line behind you. The orchard is to the left."

"That means we have the whole length of the pond ahead of us."

"Yes. Are you ready to take a spin?"

"More ready than you know." She moved to the inside, so she wouldn't catch her blade on any stray branch or stem. She looked fearless.

She was amazing. Thad couldn't take his gaze from her as they took that first sweeping step. She was his perfection. She pushed off into the unknown as if she were not afraid of falling.

"Look! Thad, I'm skating."

"Isn't that stating the obvious?" Her happiness was catching and he wouldn't stop the joy dawning within him even if he wanted to.

She laughed, coming to a shaky stop. "Yes, but I can't believe it. It's just like I remembered it."

"How's that?"

"That it must be close to what a sparrow feels flying across the frozen ground." Her touch on his arm was light. "How long do I have before I run out of pond?"

"Don't worry, I'll turn you before you hit land. Ready?"

"Ready."

They pushed off together, and he was drawn by her—by everything about her. Tiny silken wisps of hair had escaped her braid and curled around her face. Joy shone from her like light from a midnight star, and he felt touched by it. Joy shone into him and there was no stopping the power of it or the truth. They glided together in short sharp bursts, and he nudged her into a curving arc that had them circling to the far side of the pond.

"We're heading back toward the house," he told her, so she could keep her sense of direction.

"I can feel that." She lifted her face into the air. "The wind is coming from the north. It's starting to snow."

"Is it?" He hadn't noticed. He could only see her. But now that she'd pointed it out to him, sure enough, there were the tiniest flakes glinting as they fell. They began to cling to her chestnut hair and the wool of her coat like tiny chips of diamonds.

Maybe it was the love he felt for her seemingly turning the snow to jewels, the ordinary into the rare, but being with her again like this, at her side, taking care of her, *did* feel extraordinary.

"I want to twirl." She shakily nosed her blades into the ice, fighting to keep her balance.

He braced his legs, tensed the muscles in his arms and made sure she stayed upright. "Twirl? I don't see why you can't."

"Me, either." She flung her braid over her shoulder and inched away from him. "I don't want to accidenlly smack you in the jaw."

"Don't worry. I know how to duck."

"You have good reflexes, too, so I don't know why I'm worrying." She couldn't help laughing, she felt so happy. Bliss bubbled out of her. "I should be able to spin and not fall down. That's my theory."

"It's worth testing out. I'll watch over you."

"I know." She held out her arms and glided in a small loop. Hoping she wasn't heading straight into trouble, she hurled herself into the dark and let the skates slice a perfect circle.

She knew when she hit the track of her first revoluon that she'd done it, just as she could feel the air crisping against her face and whispering through her hair. Their movements on the ice were like music; the melody of her quick, light blades and, in counterpoint, the heavier and deeper gait as Thad kept up with her.

She kicked off and for one perfect moment, she was free, gliding into the unknown. She soared over ruts in the ice with the cold wind and tiny snowflakes stinging her face. Never had she thought she would be able to do this again. Joy lifted her up until she wasn't certain if her skates even touched the ice. It felt as if she were gliding on clouds.

"Turn!" Thad called out, and she drew up short. Putting her arms over her head, she gave a little kick with her toe and twirled. Around and around she went, spinning faster and faster. What fun! The sound whirred in her ears and uplifted her heart.

When she stumbled, Thad was there, catching her like her own personal guardian, holding her in his strong arms.

Safe, just as he'd promised.

The world tilted sideways, and she clutched his shoulders, but it wasn't because she'd lost her sense of balance.

No, she was losing her heart.

"You're glowing," Thad said as they left the pond behind, the skates clinking together with his every step.

Noelle practically floated up the path. She was so happy, she had to be doing more than glowing; she felt as though she was radiating joy the way the stars did light. "I haven't had so much fun since—" Her heart gave a squeeze. "Since the last time I was out with you."

"Me, either. And to think I only fell the once."

"You made a loud crash, too." She couldn't help teasing him, just a little.

"I landed so hard on my backside that I'm surprised I didn't crack the ice."

Laughter hadn't come this easily in a long time. She heard the same lightness in Thad's voice and felt it in his touch as he guided her back to the house. "It's been such a perfect afternoon, that there's only one thing wrong with it."

"What's that?"

"It's coming to an end." She sighed, feeling the pathway level out. She knew without needing to ask that the front porch steps weren't far away. "I—I just really liked skating."

"I know just how you feel."

Did he feel this, too? Her knees turned to butter and she was thankful for his strong arm that guided her safely onto the boardwalk. Snow crunched beneath their shoes. Fragile snowflakes brushed against her face and caught in her lashes. She rubbed at them with her free hand, and her eyes burned.

This was not fair. Being with Thad made her feel whole—and not damaged—again. For a length of time out on that ice, she'd felt normal. Unfettered. Free. She knew that when Thad withdrew his arm from her hand and left her, she would be in darkness again.

No, this was not fair, she thought, but it was the way God meant her life to be. As she caught the edge of the rail, she prepared for the icy steps, pulling a little away from Thad, so as to brace herself for the inevitable.

He turned to her outside the front door, his boots shuffling a bit on the pieces of ice and snow. "I won't be around much after tomorrow. Finn's getting out. I've already spoken to Robert about it."

Oh. The air whooshed out of her lungs. She felt deflated. Her heart squeezed. "A-are you leaving us for good, then?"

"You knew I couldn't stay."

She knew. Sadness ribboned through her spirit, taking the joy from the afternoon with it. She straightened her spine and set her chin. Of course, she had to be practical. Thad had a whole life to live and dreams to find.

She counted her steps from the rail to the doorknob and when she reached out, her hand found the china knob perfectly. "I guess this is really goodbye."

"Not a chance, pretty lady. I'll be by when Robert is up for a few lessons on handling horses. And I'll be by to see you, if that's all right?"

To see her? As a friend, she wondered, or as more? She turned the knob and forced her feet to carry her across the threshold and she counted her steps before she turned to face Thad. She lifted the guards around her heart firmly into place. Hurting, yes she was hurting, but she forced a smile onto her face. "I'd like to see you again, Thad. You'll al-always be a friend."

Utter silence. He didn't speak. He didn't move. Not a shuffle or a rasp or an exhale.

"Noelle" came Robert's voice from his chair at the far end of the parlor. "Invite Thad in for a chat, won't you?"

No," Thad answered smoothly, quietly, before she could agree. "I've got to get home. Work to do."

"Work?"

"Aiden's land. We're about done building another barn. Next there's the fences to mend, harnesses to repair, and as soon as the snow melts, we'll be turning sod."

"What about your plans for your own ranch?"

"It doesn't change my obligations to my brothers. Don't look troubled. I don't mind hard work. I figure the Lord set a good example. He worked six days out of seven."

"I thought you were no longer a praying kind of man."

"I guess I'm more of one than I thought."

He took a step back, hating that the time had come to leave. The thud that seemed to rattle his chest was his heart falling even more in love with her.

Friends, she'd said. And that she'd like to see him again. Friends was far more than he'd expected. How about that.

He hesitated on the top step. "I'll be coming back around to see you."

"All right. I won't even pretend not to be home when you do."

She smiled and it was a sight that chased the chill from the air and the snow from the sky.

As he tucked down the brim of his hat and headed out into the increasing snowfall, it seemed as if he walked in sunshine.

Chapter Thirteen

Noelle hadn't realized how much she'd been listening for any sign of Thad until he was gone. Oh, he'd found someone to replace him—although no word of it had been mentioned. A worker had shown up to carry in the morning's wood and tend to the stable work.

After the girls had left for school, Matilda had come in to quietly mention that Thad had sent the youngest brother of the Sims family. But there was no mention of the older boy—Emmett Sims—as Matilda poured a second cup of tea and carried it away to the library with a slight clatter. The mention of the Sims family had upset her.

That's all my fault. Sadness eked into her, dimming the warm touch of the morning's sun through the dining room window. Her well-meaning words in town before Robert's accident haunted her now. She'd meant to protect innocent Matilda, that was all. But as she was listening to the crackle of the fire echoing in the empty room around her, she remembered how it had felt to twirl on the ice and know that Thad was at her side. It had been pure joy.

What had happened to her? On the ice she'd caught a glimpse of the real Noelle—the one who'd once known how to live and love. The one who used her heart, her whole heart.

Noelle reached for the teapot with trembling fingers and found the crest of lid and round of the handle. *You might think that breaking my promise to you that night came pretty easy,* Thad had said. *I can honestly say it was the hardest decision I ever made.* His words troubled her like little teeth taking a bite of her soul.

She'd blamed him, judged him and—for a time— despised him. She'd let those things into her heart, into her soul, and although she'd told herself she'd found forgiveness and had handed her pain up to God, it was not the whole truth. The stain of it, like tarnish on silver, remained, and shame filled her.

She slipped her forefinger against the rim of her teacup and poured with her other hand until she felt the lap of the beverage against the tip of her finger. She set down the pot with care. She'd held all that pain in her heart—without meaning to and in spite of her best intentions—and for what? Thad had done what he'd thought best in leaving her. She knew her parents well enough to see clearly what they had done. Her father, bless his soul, would have used any means to protect her, for that's how he would have viewed it.

She'd been the one to change her heart and her life. She'd been the one to stop believing. To stop living. To stop dreaming. Long before the accident took her sight. She'd decided life and love were about sensible decisions and emotions—nothing else.

She scooped a lump of sugar from the bowl and slipped it into her cup with a plop. The house seemed silent around her. It was best to be steeled to the truth in life. It was best to be practical. She almost said so to Matilda but held back the words.

Once, like her cousin, she'd been young and filling her hope chest with embroidered pillow slips and a girl's dreams. Maybe that was a part of the way life went. Maybe she would be a different woman if she'd been able to hold on to some of those dreams, or at least the belief in them.

But she was a woman without dreams.

She took a sip of tea and turned her mind to her music lessons for the rest of the morning. While there was no sound of Thad—no lazy snap of a training whip, no rhythmic trot of a horse he was working, and no familiar gait in the yard outside—her mind turned to him. Always to him.

If her heart squeezed with caring, then it was an emotion she could not afford to acknowledge. Wherever he was this morning, she hoped the Lord would bless him and hold him safe.

After attending Sunday service, Noelle felt more at peace. Of course, the delicious roasted goose and trimmings for Sunday dinner might have helped, too. Full and content, she sipped at her piping hot cup of tea while Sadie padded around the table, clearing away the dessert plates. She might not have seen Thad for the better part of a week, but he was never far from her thoughts.

The family's cheerful din rose up around her. There was some discussion as to the extent of Angelina's bad behavior earlier in Sunday school. Voices rose and fell in discussion, and Noelle had to wonder. If her parents had not intervened, she would be married to Thad.

Would she have children? Would she and Thad have been happy? Would she still have her sight and her parents? Would she still be the full-hearted girl she'd once been?

"Noelle, are you feeling well, dear?" Henrietta's concern broke into her thoughts. "You look troubled."

Troubled? How could she begin to explain? "I'm fine, truly."

"You were overheated at the dress shop yesterday. It's a wonder you haven't caught your death. A heater in every room is lunacy. What are people thinking nowadays? You ought to lie down for a bit."

"Goodness, no." She couldn't resist teasing her aunt just a little. "I actually feel quite healthy. Perhaps that is due to that overly warm dress shop."

Angelina burst out laughing. "Yes, Mama. We must get a heater in every room. Maybe even a furnace."

"It would be very practical," Minnie chimed in. "We wouldn't have to wear our woolen underwear all the time. It's scratchy."

"Girls." Henrietta did her best to sound shocked at the mention of undergarments, but there was the warmth of amusement in her voice. "Settle down and stop this teasing. We're at the table."

"Where we could use a heater," Minnie pointed out. "I'm always stuck in the drafty corner."

The maid padded from the direction of the kitchen. "Looks as if we have company on the way."

"Company? On Sunday afternoon?" Henrietta's chair scraped against the floor, as if she were standing up to take a peek out the window. "Goodness, it's a horse and sleigh. I don't know that horse. Whoever could it be?"

There were rustles of movement as if everyone were

taking a look. Robert's low chuckle was sheer amusement. "It looks like a caller coming for one of the girls."

"A suitor!" Angelina sounded intrigued. "But Mama won't let us have a beau until we're eighteen."

"Perhaps it's for Matilda," Minnie offered.

"Oh, there would be no one coming for me." Matilda's tone was light.

Noelle wasn't fooled. She didn't know if she was the only one who could hear the quiet despair—or, maybe it was just empathy. Matilda might be without prospects, but she wasn't the only one. She regretted her words to Tilly.

Dear, Lord, she prayed with all her heart. *Please let it be someone for Matilda.*

"I know who that is!" Minnie's voice hit a few high notes of delight. "It's Mr. McKaslin."

Thad? Her teacup hit its saucer with a clatter.

All around her chairs were scraping back, shoes beat away from the table, and Robert chuckled warmly. "I wondered how long it would take that fellow to get up his gumption."

"The gumption for what?" Noelle asked him.

"You'd best get your coat. Looks like he's coming up to the door."

Sure enough, the door was rasping open and Henrietta's voice rose above Angelina's and Minnie's footeps. "Mr. McKaslin! What a pleasure to see you on this fine afternoon. What can I do for you?"

"Is Noelle at home?"

So he'd come for her, just as he'd promised. Noelle tried to ignore the buzzing expectation in the air and everyone's advice. From Matilda's quietly spoken, "Oh, just what I'd been praying for!" to Robert's advice, "Go on, now, go have a nice time," to Angelina's shocking comment, "I'm predicting a May wedding. June at the latest."

She truly hoped Thad had not heard *that*. She was on her feet without realizing it. Matilda had her elbow and guided her to the front door. Henrietta thrust the coat into her hands. And Thad was there, his unmistakable presence had her turning toward him, and she felt his smile with all of her heart.

He thought this was funny, did he? She stepped through the open doorway and let him help her into her coat, aware of her family members' careful and excited scrutiny.

"Goodbye, now!" Henrietta practically sang. "You be back in a couple of hours, Mr. McKaslin."

"Yes, ma'am."

Thad sounded as if he were smothering laughter, and the moment her coat was fastened and he took her hand in his, she could feel the connection between her heart and his. That rare, emotional bond they'd always had was here again, anew, and she felt the strong bright happiness that matched her own.

He'd come for her as a friend, just as he'd said. She let him guide her down the steps and along the path.

She was going to enjoy these moments she had with him because she had learned the hard way in life that nothing lasted. Everything changed. Before she knew it, Thad would be busy with his ranch and his dreams, and she would never see him again.

She waited until the door shut firmly behind them before she apologized. "I don't know what has overcome my aunt, but she has jumped to conclusions."

"So I heard. Everything."

"Angelina's comment, too?"

"Yep."

He was probably not put into a panic at the mention of a wedding the way of men in general—probably because it was a bold impossibility. As surely as the ground was at her feet, there was no way Thad was harboring any wedding thoughts for her.

She knew better than to think it. When he let go of her hand, she stood in darkness, listening hard to hear what he was doing. There was the softest rustling sound—of a lap blanket, perhaps?—and then the prettiest jingle of bells sang out in a short burst. The horse must have shaken his head with impatience.

"Whoa there, boy. Stand still for the pretty lady." Thad's patient voice must have reassured the horse for there was no more shaking of the bells.

Just the ring of appreciation in her heart. "You're taking me for a sleigh ride?"

"Yep, and I'm grateful you've agreed to come along with me. I need the help." His hand found hers again.

"Help? What do you mean?"

"I bought this saddle horse for Finn, and I want to break him to the harness. So I need to take him out for a drive, and I was afraid I'd get lost."

"You need me to help you find your way around the countryside?"

"Don't think I could do it without you."

"Then it's good you came by, although the reason for asking me is going to disappoint Henrietta terribly."

"Funny. I didn't think she liked me much." He took her by the elbow, helping her, always helping her. Tenderness filled him right up. "I've got the riding blankets out of the way, so go ahead and climb on in."

"Do you know what my aunt values in a man more than affluence and social position?"

"Ah, I've got the good sense not to buy a horse that will kick me."

"No." She chuckled; she couldn't hold it back as she settled onto the cushioned seat. "Character."

"Character, huh?" He leaned to tuck the soft fur robes around her. "Then I'm all out of luck."

Oh, she loved his humility. She loved how caring he was with her, and how his sense of humor could make a cold February afternoon seem like a treat. When he had settled in next to her beneath the warm robes and had gathered the reins, she decided not to tell him that ever since her accident she didn't like driving fast.

She took a deep breath and let the icy air tingle in her lungs. The tingling seemed to drive out the last of her uncertainty. She would not allow herself to be anxious, not with Thad driving. He could handle any horse and any situation. She trusted him.

"Why isn't Finn training his own horse?" she asked, because she was curious. "Does that mean that he's not doing well?"

"Oh, he's doing just fine. Finn doesn't have the patience for serious horse work. He's better at other things. We have him putting on the sides of the new barn Aiden and I put up before the last set of storms came in."

"In this weather?"

"We figure it's penance for all that he's putting us through. Work him hard, and maybe he'll get on the straight and narrow."

"What was he in prison for?"

"Stealing a horse. He was lucky he wasn't hung. There's still a lot of vigilante justice in these parts."

Thad's chest closed up. It was hard to talk about, especially to her. The differences between them suddenly felt as wide as the sky and about as impossible to fly across.

"You hurt for him."

Her sympathy touched him. It did more than that, her sweet face was marked with understanding, and it reassured him. "There's no way to measure how hard we all took this. He's smart and talented and he has a good heart."

"Sort of like his older brother?"

Now, that was just what he needed to hear. Snow brushed his cheek like grace, changing his heart, changing his life. Thad took a shaky breath. "Finn's got our pa's weakness for liquor."

"And it's hard for him to resist?" When he didn't answer, she nodded once, as if she understood why without words. "You want him to be stronger than that."

"Yes. That's right."

"I've felt that way about a family member." Her forehead pinched. "My parents. I am sorry for what they did to you. My father was a man who could be very persuasive. What did he say to you?"

"That you wouldn't be happy living a simple life with me."

"And you believed him?"

Her voice, her face, her eyes vibrated with pain. A pain he felt like a dagger sink into his heart. What else could he do but to tell the truth. "I didn't want to. I wouldn't let myself."

"You left me because my father threatened to demand payment on your mortgage, didn't he?"

Thad bit his lip. Hadn't the truth hurt her enough?

"You don't have to answer. I know it's true." She tucked the robe around her more tightly, as if unable to say more. She was hurting, clearly she was hurting.

"It's tough when the people you love aren't the way you want them to be." The cold scorched his face like fiery ice, and yet it was warmer than the pain that settled in him. He was no longer too numb to feel it. Because of her.

"And so you know, my father was wrong," she said. "All I wanted then, all I needed then, was you."

Her words were like coming home. Like Christmas morning and happy New Year and every birthday rolled into one. The beautiful world was all around them, so he began to describe it to her. "The mountains, their faces are hidden in the clouds. The sky is a darker shade of white guarding over the white prairie. The snow is quiet today. Nothing sparkling or glistening. Just a still silent white."

A small smile curved her rosebud lips.

They rode on in silence, gliding over the rise and draw of the rugged plains. They listened to snow whisper and tap, and shared a quiet that felt companionable. Peaceful.

Meant to be.

The sleigh was slowing, and before she could ask why, she heard the waterfall. Angel Falls. She loved the cascading music of the charging water. Even before she lost her sight, it was one of her most favorite sounds. Maybe because she'd built so many dreams around it. It was painfully ironic that she had inherited this property from her father, one of the last investments he had acquired before his death.

"That sounded sad." Thad drew the horse to a stop.

She tilted her head, listening carefully but there was only the snort of the horse, the water falling and the whirl of snow against the dash of the sleigh. "What sounds sad?"

"You. You sighed."

"Did I?" She wasn't aware of it. Then again, it was hard to feel anything. The tangled ball of emotion had returned and expanded like regret in her soul. "Is the water gray like the clouds? Or green from the mountain snowmelt?"

"Green as moss."

She closed her eyes, searching for a visual memory of the falls in winter, but the one that came to her was vivid with color and cheerful wildflowers polka-dotting rich green fields.

"The snowfall is as gray as the clouds," Thad told her. "The snow is white, but it's pure white and gray shadows and a thousand shades between."

She couldn't see it. She couldn't let herself. She struggled to dim the memory in her mind's eye of rainbows the sun made on crystal blue water. And there, on the rise where the meadow met the hills, she used to envision a log house with wide windows glinting in the sunshine and a porch to sit and watch the falls in the evening's light.

A dream. That's what she remembered, and the loss of it thrummed along the broken strings of her heart. The regret swelling in her soul seemed to block out even those colors and that light.

The wind whirring in her ears stilled, as the horse drew the sleigh to a stop.

Thad leaned closer. "We have a lot of memories here.

Remember how we would come here the summer I proposed?"

"I r-remember." Those memories stuck in her throat like sorrow. "You proposed to me on the rise of land, where we would always picnic."

"I would come here on my lunch and you would slip away from your mother's garden parties."

"Yes, I would bring a basket of some of the goodies from the kitchen."

"Cake and cookies. Lemonade and sandwiches. I don't know why I especially remember the ham sandwiches."

"Our cook made excellent ham sandwiches." Suddenly they were laughing together, and the sorrow and the regret lifted away. "It was enough just to be with you," she remembered. "To talk and laugh and walk side by side."

"I remember holding your hand." He took her hand in his, fitting their fingers together with such deliberate care.

Still a perfect fit. As if they were made to be together. Thank heavens. He kept a tight hold on her hand and did not let go.

"You wouldn't happen to be attending Lanna and Joe's wedding?" he asked.

"Yes, as it's the first big social event of the year. We've been preparing for it since the New Year. All the girls need new dresses and bonnets, gloves and shoes. We've kept Miss Sims's dress shop in profits for the last month."

"I thought that might be the case. You're probably going with the Worthingtons?"

"Yes, as I have a difficult time driving to town these

days on my own." She liked that he chuckled, just a little, at her joke. "You'll be there?"

"Count on it. You wouldn't mind saving me a spot on your dance card?"

"I would, but Henrietta does not approve of dancing."

"Then will you save me a minute or two to chat with you?"

"Only a minute. My social card is very full." She smiled, quipping again. She simply felt so…happy. It was Thad. He made her happy. This—being with him, talking with him and laughing with him—was a perfect moment in time.

"I'd rather have a minute with you," he said, "than to have a million minutes without you. I saw your face that night at supper when I told your family about Sunny."

"It was an incredible story."

"I never forgot your dreams, Noelle. They were mine, too." His tone dipped and he paused. In that instant of silence, she could not know how his face looked and what emotion lurked there.

She longed to see him. To know all the little things about his dear face that had changed—and those that had stayed the same.

He broke the stillness between them. "I always wanted to hunt down whoever owned this property and buy it for you. Of course, I was a kid back then. I had no notion of how expensive this land really is."

The wind burned her eyes. Surely it was the wind and not sadness. "I wish I had known that."

"You wanted to build a life here, too, remember?" Did she. The colors filled her mind as love for him did her heart. She couldn't take the pain of it. She curled her fingers around the hem of the robe and felt the icy caress of wind against her face. She could never be a rancher's wife now.

The confusion of her emotions ached within her. "That is a lost dream for me, Thad. A child's dream."

"That's not necessarily so."

She didn't know how to tell him that he was wrong. The swell of wind and snow moved between them like melody and harmony. How did she speak of the remnants of her hopes and the ashes of her future to the one man who knew the value of what she'd lost? Of what she would never have again?

"Some of my hopes have been lost, sure," Thad said with an easy note. "But I've gained some along the way, too. I suppose it's like anything else in life. It doesn't work out the way you want, but sometimes in the end you wind up somewhere better than you expected."

"That sounds awfully optimistic for you."

His chuckle sounded good-natured. "I admit it. You've changed me."

"Oh, I don't think—"

He squeezed her hand to interrupt her. "You've given me dreams again and I thank you for it."

Noelle turned away, letting the concert of snowfall and waterfall fill her senses and create a silence between them. A silence she desperately needed.

"I suppose I'd best turn the horse back. I want to get you home well before suppertime. I don't want to earn Henrietta's wrath. I reckon I'm already walking a fine line as it is."

She managed a weak smile. "I'll have you know that my aunt holds you personally responsible for Angelina deciding to become a mustang wrangler."

"I didn't know proper young ladies from fine families were allowed to be wranglers." He sounded amused.

"They aren't. But when you're sixteen, you have to dream. The world is so full of possibility."

"It still is." There was an unmistakable smile in his voice.

The reins hit the dash, the horse carried them forward, and she listened to the song of the sleigh's runners on the snow. The murmur of the waterfall faded to silence behind them. Thad's hand remained tightly on hers. He did not let go.

Chapter Fourteen

The land office was quiet midweek. Noelle shifted uncomfortably in the hard, ladder-back chair and signed her name on the page where the agent had pointed out for her. The scratch of the pen seemed loud.

There. Done. She handed the ink pen and the legal document to Mr. Dorian on the other side of the desk.

"Are you sure about this, Miss Kramer?"

She hadn't been so certain about anything. This simply felt right. "Yes. You'll contact Mr. McKaslin today?"

"I'll send a message out to him immediately."

"And you won't let him know this land belongs to me?"

"I'll respect our agreement, Miss Kramer, don't you worry. Your father was a good man. He helped me keep my home when times got tough for me, and I owe him. I'll do my best for you."

"Thank you, Mr. Dorian."

Love was complicated, just as people were. She would never understand why her father had pressured Thad so, but maybe she now knew more about what forgiveness truly was. She knew that her father had done the best he could for reasons he thought were very sound. How could she fault his love and her mother's, when they were lost to her now?

Signing this paperwork to sell her father's land, was something she did with love, too. She was finally understanding what it meant to be only human, frail at best, and like all humans complete with shortcomings. Wasn't her blindness, after all, only a shortcoming? It was not a punishment from God, and not something which had damaged her.

If blindness was her price for surviving the accident that should have killed her, then she was grateful to God for sparing her. She was grateful to Him for bringing Thad back into her life.

She rose to her feet and stood a little straighter. "Mr. Dorian, thank you for your time. You'll be in contact?"

"As soon as I have Thad McKaslin's offer for you." The chair across the desk scraped, as, presumably, the land agent stood. He took her hand in a gentle, business-like shake. "Would you like me to see you to the door?"

"No, thank you. I counted my steps when I came in." She withdrew her hand, oriented herself and counted her way to the door. With every step she took, the joy inside her soared a little more, but the sadness did, too, and both together moved through her spirit like melody and harmony.

The moment her shoe touched the slick boardwalk, she took a deep breath of winter air and listened to the chime of ice melting from the rooftops. She tried to imagine Thad's happiness when he received the note from the land office. Finally a good piece of ranch property for sale, he might think, and at the price he could afford. Yes, he would definitely be very happy.

Joy burned within her, balanced by sharpening sorrow. She wanted him to have his dreams and the life he'd always wanted, even though she could not have hers.

"Noelle?" Matilda's gentle alto broke through her thoughts. "We had best start making our way over to the church."

"Yes. Do you have our gifts?"

"They're in the sleigh. Mama will see to it. She's fetching the girls from school first. Here, take my arm. The boardwalks are so slick with all the snow melting off the roofs."

Dear Matilda. She had such a good heart. Sweetness ached through her remembering herself as an innocent, starry-eyed girl who believed in a fairy-tale kind of love.

Dainty footsteps came their way. "Noelle? Matilda? Why aren't you at the church?"

She recognized the dressmaker's soft country cadence. "We are on our way. Would you like to walk with us?"

"What a kind invitation." Miss Cora Sims sounded pleased. "As you know, I'm attending the wedding alone, and I have no one to sit with, as both of my nephews refuse to be anywhere near a wedding. You know how young men can be."

Matilda's grip tightened again. Noelle could not resist asking, "Is Emmett well?"

"Keeping busy enough with his teaming. Oh, there he is. Emmett, yoo-hoo!"

Matilda's grip turned into a stranglehold and she leaned close to whisper. "Mr. Sims is driving his team and wagon over."

There was no excitement. No interest. Not a single note of hope. Just a simple, plainspoken statement. That was all. It was as if the air had drained from the wind.

Noelle winced. Matilda, bless her dearly, had taken her poor advice to heart.

There was no time to speak of it, for suddenly there were the muffled plop of horse hooves in the top layers of the melting snow, the jangle of harness and the low-noted groan of a wagon's axle.

"I've been waiting for you, Aunt Cora." Emmett Sims had a pleasant, quiet voice, and his words held affection for his aunt, not censure.

"I was held up by a last-minute customer. I apologize. Noelle, would you and Matilda like to ride over with me?"

The good Lord had a way of making things right. Noelle did not hesitate, even when Matilda took a step back and started to say, "No thank you—" She spoke right over her cousin. "Yes, Cora, your offer is completely providential. We accept."

"I'm so glad," the seamstress said warmly.

It was a mystery how she had managed to stay a spinster all these years. Noelle felt that was something they had in common, and vowed to ask Cora over for tea and get to know her better.

Boots hit the boardwalk nearby—it must be Emmett climbing down from the wagon. "Let me help you ladies up. You first, miss?"

Was that her imagination, or had his voice dipped a notch, as if he were shy or, perhaps, a little taken with Tilly?

"Oh, yes, thank you." Primly, coolly, Matilda answered.

Noelle imagined the moment when Emmett reached

out with his gloved hand—he was a teamster, he was probably wearing leather driving gloves—and the moment when Matilda smiled up at him. Was this the first time he had noticed her? Did he think her pretty? There was a tap of shoes on the wagon boards, and the springs rasped slightly as Matilda settled on the seat.

Before she knew it, Emmett had kindly but capably helped her up onto the narrow seat, and Cora followed. There was a quiet steadiness to the young man. Later, when they were alone, she would ask Matilda what he looked like, what color his eyes and his hair were.

The reins slapped the dash and the horses clattered to a quick start. Noelle held on tight to the edge of the seat and prayed. If Emmett Sims held a secret caring for Tilly, wouldn't that be perfect? She could not have a happy ending, but she wanted one for her cousin. In fact, she was going to do her best to make sure it happened. She would trust the Lord to guide her.

It was a fast ride to the church with the icy winds blowing against her face and tearing her eyes. The watery touch of the sun did nothing to warm her as she accepted Emmett's hand down to the slick pathway that led to the church door. Merry bells pealed in the steeple above, drowning out the everyday sounds of the horse and foot traffic. She stood disorientated until Cora touched her hand, guiding her out of the crush of those hurrying to the church at the last minute.

"Tell me, Noelle, is your cousin sweet on my nephew?"

"Why are you asking?"

"It's simply wishful thinking. I have never seen him take such care with a young lady." Cora sounded pleased.

Noelle took that as a good sign. Suddenly Matilda

was beside her, a little breathless and unusually quiet. She didn't utter a single word, much less make one sound, as Emmett Sims's boots stomped on the wagon steps—presumably to knock off the slush sticking to them—and called out from above. "Good day, ladies. Miss."

How perfect that they both seemed to be sweet on one another.

Noelle knew he was safely out of sight when Matilda caught her by the hand again and they took careful steps in the slick slush.

"Thad McKaslin is standing in the back of the church," Matilda whispered the moment they'd inched through the vestibule. "He appears to be intently looking for someone."

Joy shivered through her spirit, unbidden and powerful. Her heart squeezed with longing and love for him, and she did her best to quiet those feelings, to stow away those emotions. "Perhaps one of his brothers?"

"No, dear cousin, I think he's waiting for *you*."

The happiness gathering inside her took over with a quiet wonder. She didn't need Matilda to tell her the moment when Thad spotted her in the crowd. Although the organ music and the rumblings of the guests filling the long rows of pews hid the sound of his gait, she could feel him like music in her soul.

"I would like to sit with you," he said simply, kindly, the friend that he was.

The friend which he had to be. They both knew it. She managed what she hoped would pass for a smile. "You would be most welcome, Thad."

Where Matilda and Cora had gone off to, Noelle did not know. She only knew Thad's innocent touch as he led her down the aisle and protected her from the crush of the crowd. He stood so close to her, she could smell the soap on his shirt and the winter wind on his coat. Why she could distinguish the quiet, steady draw and exhale of his breathing in the swell of noise in the sanctuary, she could not explain. Her every sense seemed tuned only to him, to this man who meant much more than a friend to her. And always would.

"I saw you arrive in Emmett Sims's wagon."

What a strange tone in his voice. Noelle took another shuffling step and her hoops bumped against him. "He was taking his aunt to the church and they were kind enough to bring us along."

"Kind enough? He seemed rather happy to be doing so, if you want my humble opinion. I didn't like it."

There it was again, that sharp tone that was unlike Thad. Whatever for? Then realization struck her like the bench post against her toe. Thad was jealous? Why? "It's my suspicion that he's sweet on Matilda. Don't tell me that you are—"

"No-oo. No." Thad's answer came so quick, lightning would be slower. "Oh, your cousin. Sure. They probably went to school together, just like we did."

Noelle inched along the bench, careful not to step on anyone's shoes. "Did you truly think Mr. Sims would possibly be interested in me?"

"Well, I, uh—" He didn't answer.

What was wrong with him, anyhow? Before she could joke with him a little more, a gloved hand caught her by the wrist.

"Noelle!" Henrietta's voice was full of smiles. "I've been saving a place for you. I did not know Mr. McKaslin would be joining us. Robert, scooch down a bit."

"We're awful crowded as it is."

"Scootch!" Henrietta was adamant. "We have plenty of room, Mr. McKaslin. Don't you even dream of going anywhere else. It's a privilege to have you sit with us. Noelle, dear, sit right here."

Noelle let her overly helpful aunt guide her onto the pew, although she hardly needed the help. She was just too amused to think of an argument. What was the matter with everyone today? First Thad, and now Henrietta. It had to be the wedding. It jumbled sensible people's reasoning abilities. Thad worrying that a younger man would be interested in *her,* a blind woman. And now Henrietta.

She was thankful she was not so ill-affected. The music changed; the sanctuary's buzzing and whispering and rustling silenced, and she imagined the minister and the groom had taken their places.

The "ahs" that rose told her that the bride must have swept into sight. Lanna must look lovely, she thought, and happy. Noelle laid her hand on Thad's arm and whispered in his ear. "Tell me how beautiful she looks."

"She can't hold a candle to you."

With those words, he'd won a little bit more of her heart. Noelle said nothing more. It was wisest not to.

"Why is a lovely lady like you sitting alone in the corner?"

Thad and his sense of humor—*he* had been the one to leave her. Noelle drew herself up straighter on the chair, brushed a stray curl out of her eyes and shook her head once, very slowly. She hoped she was giving him her best schoolmarm look. "The man I was with left me here all alone so he could get some punch."

"His loss is my gain." The chair creaked softly beside her as he settled into it. "Sorry I took such a long spell. Your uncle caught me in line for punch and started jawing my ear off. Sounds like he's happy with the younger Sims boy."

"I believe so. And so far, the young man has not made any show of interest in one of my cousins."

"I bet your aunt is ecstatic that her daughters are safe. I'm toeing a narrow line as it is." He caught her hand.

The small glass cup was icy against her palm and the sweet scent of lemons and limes tickled her nose. "Can't you tell that she likes you?"

"She has been unusually glad to see me with you. You think she'd be concerned about your reputation."

"My reputation?"

"Hanging out with a cowboy who doesn't have a wealthy family or social connections."

While his tone was light, there was something in his voice. Something serious. Her pulse skipped a beat. Could he be serious about her? She took a sip of the tart punch. No, she was reading too much into things. Perhaps it was her heart, wishing that he at least loved her, too, a little.

Because she loved him. Very much. She could no longer deny it. She cherished this man. She honored him. She wanted nothing more than to love him for the rest of her days.

"I think my reputation would be greatly improved being seen with you tonight." She kept her words as light, but they were honest, too. "Do you see your family anywhere?"

"I haven't seen hide nor hair of them. I know Aiden was planning on bringing Ma, but I didn't see them in the church. Of course, it was crowded. Half the town must have been there."

"And here, by the sound of it. That must mean your mother's health is still improving?"

"She's holding her own. She ought to do better once the warm weather decides to show up. That could be June, knowing this part of the country."

"And your younger brother?"

"We made him stay home tonight. We didn't want him getting into any trouble here."

"By trouble you mean…?"

"Getting his hands on some alcohol. Maybe thinking about joyriding with someone's horse tethered up outside. We were hoping jail would have straightened him up. Shown him that life is a serious matter."

"It didn't?"

"No. He's bitter. He's full of hatred. It's not a good situation."

"And he's your little brother." Sympathy marked her face, making her all the more comely. The dress she wore was the color of lilac blossoms and made her look like a princess. "You must want so much for him to live well and be happy."

"That's what I want." Thad swallowed against the hard emotion. The helplessness of it nibbled at him. "I can't make a grown man's decisions for him. Aiden and I are doing our best, but we're both here tonight."

"And he's home alone?"

"If we're lucky, he is." His throat stung. "The thing is, I could have gone down that path myself."

"You?" She looked at him as if she saw him perfectly, the man he was, down to the soul. "No, not you."

His Noelle, so beautiful and unguarded, she made

his spirit soar. She looked at him as if he were ten feet tall. Admitting the truth, well, it was tough, but she may as well know everything. "After I had to make the decision to ride away from Angel Falls, I knew what I'd done to you. It about broke me. You were my dream, Noelle, and all I saw was a future without you. A life without you. You were about all that I'd ever thought of living for."

Her eyes brightened with tears and she turned away so he could not see the emotion on her face.

He would always be able to see into her heart. "I was hurting bad. Very bad. After a long hard day in the saddle when the cattle were down for the night we'd all gather around the campfire. Whiskey would get passed around and it h-helped. I didn't feel anything for a long time, and that was all right by me."

"Oh, Thad." She kept her face turned away. She set her cup aside and then folded her empty hands.

"Once I realized what I was doing, I haven't had a swallow since. I'm not the sort of man who will follow my father's path in life. But I can see how easy it might be for someone else to. I know Finn doesn't think he has much to live for. He's just existing. Spending his days one at a time."

"I've been guilty of that, too."

"You?" That surprised him. The woman who'd made the most of her life in spite of her blindness. The woman who could have any man in the room proposing to her, judging by the looks she was getting from several of them. The woman who still chose to be with him.

When she straightened, her eyes were bright with unshed tears. "I'm so sorry for your brother. It's easy to fall into the habit of walking through life. It's safer.

Because you don't have to risk as much. You don't have to really feel."

Yep, he was standing on that spot himself. He'd been afraid to move a step forward. He couldn't see how this would work for them. He didn't know if Noelle still had the same dreams. He didn't know if she would want him for a husband.

Still, he had to try to find out. He was already so far in love with her that he couldn't see straight. His every breath was because of her. He took her folded hands in his. "Come. Walk with me."

"You don't want to listen to Chopin?" she teased, although she stood as quickly as he did.

"To who?"

"Haven't you noticed the piano music coming from the ballroom?"

"It's tough for me to notice anything when you're nearby. Any man of good sense would be as muddled in the presence of such a beautiful woman." Thad's gait fell in rhythm with hers. "Did I say something wrong?"

"No, not at all, if your intent was to perjure yourself."

"I was only telling the truth, Noelle. You'll always be the loveliest woman in any room to me."

"Oh, Thad." Her poor heart couldn't endure any more of this. The moment they stepped onto the front porch, the icy air swept over her, cutting through her, and she prayed for the cold to numb her clear to her soul. It didn't. She was left with her impossible love for him.

"You must stop saying such kind things to me. You'll spoil me."

"That's my hope, darlin'." Still sounding light-hearted, he accompanied her to the rail, where the great silence of the night stretched out before them.

The streets were quiet, the town settling down for suppertime, and the noise of the party was behind them.

She tried to imagine the sky. Was it velvety dark with white sparkles of stars? Or one depthless stretch of black? Wondering about the sky was far easier than thinking of the man at her side. She shivered; she'd fortten her cloak.

"Here. I can't have you freezing to death." There was a rustle of fabric and then the weight of his coat on her shoulders. "Your aunt wouldn't like it if I let you catch a chill. She might not let me in the house the next time I came calling."

Calling. Why had he chosen that word? Her entire soul squeezed with longing for what could not be. Surely he was making a small quip, that was all. There was no way Thad McKaslin was coming to court her. It didn't matter how deeply she wished for it to be so.

She tucked away her sadness and lifted her chin a notch. "After what you've done for our family, Henrietta would welcome you with open arms no matter what."

"Then I guess I don't have a single worry. I'm planning on taking you for another sleigh ride this Sunday afternoon."

"Oh, and you're simply assuming that I will agree to go with you?" she teased, hoping it would chase away her doubts.

His warm, wonderful rumble of laughter did that for her. He moved one step closer. Then another. "I'm hoping that I'm the one man you can't say no to."

"Maybe. Maybe not. You will simply have to wait and see."

"I don't have to wait. I think I already have my answer." His hands cupped her chin, such a tender gesture.

Surely, it was one of friendship. It had to be one of friendship, right? She couldn't help pressing her cheek against his callused palm. "You are a tad sure of yourself. Perhaps I intend to say no."

"What? And miss your chance to drive a real mustang?"

"You'll be bringing Sunny?"

"Yep, and there's no reason why I can't let you take the reins for a spell."

"No reason?" Oh, it felt like an answered prayer to laugh with him again. "Other than the reason that I can't see where I'm going, you mean?"

"Well, I'm sure I'll keep an eye on your driving."

"Yes, that would be prudent, although I'm sure Sunny is smart enough not to let me drive him into a tree or a fence post."

"If this warmer weather lasts, we might have to go horseback riding instead of driving."

It was not the past she saw, but a future. Riding beside him, laughing in the summer sunshine, so happy and in love. It was a future she could not have. "Now you're using my lost dreams against me."

"Not against you. Never that." His voice dipped tenderly, gently.

With the sift of snow blowing in from beneath the eaves and the wish filling her soul, she thought for one breathless, sweet moment that he was going to kiss her. Really, truly, lovingly kiss her. Her soul sighed with longing. Her spirit ached with the wish.

Then a hush of a footstep told her they weren't alone. "Thad?" A woman's gentle voice spoke. "There you are. They're serving dinner. Oh, is that Noelle?"

Thad's mother. Embarrassment burned her face to

the roots of her hair, and Thad's touch fell away from her face, but he did not step away. No, he remained solidly at her side. His hand crept around hers.

Noelle felt her face heat. "H-hello, Mrs. McKaslin."

"Noelle, dear, call me Ida. Aiden is holding a small table for us. Will you join us?"

"I would love to." What could it hurt? Come tomorrow, he would receive the land agent's news, and, God willing, he would be starting to work on his dreams.

Dreams she could not share with him. No, that would be the privilege of some other lucky woman, one who could see, one who could do what she, Noelle, could not.

For tonight, she would treasure simply being with him.

Hand in hand, and heart to heart, she let Thad lead her out of the cold night and into the hotel's warmth.

Chapter Fifteen

It was late evening by the time dessert was served and finished in the hotel's finest room, and later still, Thad thought with a yawn, as he made his way to the coatroom. Plenty of Angel Falls's finest gentlemen were gathered outside the back door, in the shelter of the porch. He thanked the young gal at the counter and slung the small pile of coats over the crook of his arm.

"Thad McKaslin!" Abe Dorian emerged through the smoky doorway. "I hadn't thought you would be here tonight. Don't know as to why."

"I went to school with Joe and Lanna."

"Of course you did. Got too much on my mind, I guess." Affable, Dorian gave a shrug. "If you were at the wedding, then you weren't home this afternoon to get my note."

"Your note?" Could it be? Thad didn't dare get his hopes up. "A good piece of ranch land didn't come up for sale, did it?"

"Good? My son, it is prime property. The owner is asking a reasonable price, too. She's inherited it some time ago and decided to sell only this morning."

Dorian's dark eyes twinkled. "I thought of you right away."

And of a sure sale, if what he said of the land was true, Thad thought. "Which piece is it? Is it close to town?"

"It's the northeast quarter section right at the falls."

His pulse skipped five beats. He almost dropped the coats. Had he heard that right? "Did you say at the falls, not below it?"

"That's what I said, son. Prime land and it's at the price you want."

Noelle. He could see her through the crowded room. His gaze went to her as inexorably as snow to winter and the stars to the night. Emotion closed up his throat so tight, he couldn't speak for a spell.

"I gave you first crack at it." Dorian hitched up his fine black suspenders. "Do you need time to think it over?"

"No. That's one piece of land I've always wanted to own. Never thought I could." His heart full, he didn't lift his gaze from her, from his Noelle.

If he could have one dream, why not another? "Then stop by the office first thing tomorrow and we'll make it legal. You have yourself a good evening, son." Dorian, sounding pleased with himself, returned to the back porch.

Thad stood stock-still, unable to move, unable to blink. She was at their small table, interested in something Ma was saying to her. There were so many things he wanted to remember about her on this fateful night. The way lamplight shone like liquid red satin against the highlights in her hair. The curve of her face was delicate perfection, and the slope of her dainty nose just right.

She made him believe that real love was enough. That in the end good happened if a man worked hard enough.

I'm gonna marry her. He felt the decision with all of his soul's might. He didn't remember walking down the hallway or crossing the room. He only knew that he was suddenly at her side, where his heart had led him.

"We were just talking about you." She turned toward him, a smile shaping her lovely mouth and happiness alight on her sweet face. "I was telling Ida and Aiden about how you've managed to almost tame the two impossible horses my uncle bought."

If he blushed to the tips of his ears, he wasn't going to admit it. "It wasn't much. Glad to help."

"It proves you have a great gift with horses, Thad." Her soft, slim hand found his arm and rested there so naturally. For one brief tender moment, she betrayed her feelings for him. "I know this time your dreams are going to work out. You wait and see."

"I was just speaking to Mr. Dorian." Wrestling to keep his emotions under control, he handed his ma her coat, and then Aiden his. "He said there's a piece of land along Angel River for sale."

Aiden cheered up at that. "Which parcel?"

"It's near the falls." Thad came back around to Noelle's chair and settled his hand on her shoulder. There it was, the connection between them, so binding and infinite that he could feel his spirit turn around her like stars around the North Pole.

"What luck." Aiden's voice came muffled, as if from very far away. "That's prime land. I can't remember the last time anything upriver from the falls has been for sale."

"No one deserves it more than Thad," Noelle said quietly, sincerely.

She captured his heart all over again. Yep, he was in a bad situation, loving her as he did. His soul hurt with the strength of it.

"I'm grateful for this chance." His tone was raw and real, betraying his feelings. That embarrassed him because he wasn't talking about the land.

Noelle leaned toward him, as if she were unaware of his turmoil and his adoration. "It looks as if you will be able to have your horse ranch, just as you've always dreamed."

He prayed it wasn't only the land she meant, for she was part of his dreams. He carefully shook out the folds of her wool coat. "Think your uncle will let me see you home?"

"Maybe." There was that mischievous smile again, the one he loved so well. "But there you go, assuming I'll want to go with you."

"Darlin', I know what you want." Yes, he could see that clearly, too. He helped her slide back her chair and then into her coat, tenderness filling him up so there was hardly any room left to breathe. Hope could do that to a man.

The whisper of the falls came quietly at first through the soft music of the night, a quiet whir above the low-noted air whizzing past her ears, hardly noticeable at all. Then rising in volume until it was the dominating sound. It was a solemn chorus of water and snow and hope against the steady *chink-chink* of Sunny's shoes upon the ice.

It had been a perfect evening. The excellent meal was improved with excellent company; there seemed to be no one more dear than Thad's gentle mother. And to have spent the entire evening in Thad's presence, at his side, sharing simple conversation, had uplifted her. She still felt as light as the airy, spun-sugar snowflakes dancing lazily against her cheeks and eyelashes.

She knew where they were without a single word from him. It wasn't the sound of the waterfall alone, but Thad's wistful sigh. "Are you planning on going into the land office tomorrow morning?"

"You know I'll be there well before they open. Just trying not to let myself get too excited." The amused notes in his voice told her he was grinning ear to ear. "I'll try to be dignified for your sake."

"For my sake? I'm not Henrietta. As much as I love her, I do not think reputation and decorum are everything." She smoothed the buffalo robes covering her skirts, to give her hand something to do. Many secrets lay inside her heart. It would not do to give him a single hint of them.

"Then I can let out a whoop?"

Now she was grinning ear to ear. "I have no objections."

"I'd better not. Best not to scare any fellow traveler up ahead. They may take out their rifle, thinkin' I'm a wolf. And considering how I look, who could blame them?"

She felt the laughter bubbling up. Oh, no one could bring summer to her life the way he could. She could tell he was slowing the sleigh, for Sunny's gait slowed. Taking a long hopeful look at the land? At his land? She hoped he was not only grinning ear to ear but glowing with happiness from the bottom of his soul. "What's the first thing you're going to do with the land?"

"The first thing?" He fell silent a moment, and the crash of the falls began to ebb a tad. "I ought to fence it, but seeing as Aiden, Finn and I have been repairing fence for the past month, I'm not too keen on starting out digging one hundred and sixty acres of fence posts."

"If not the fence first, then what will you do? The stable?"

"No. I'll start on a house."

A home. Her chest wrenched. How could she be ecstatically happy and deeply sorrowful all in the same moment? "T-tell me about it."

"It'll be two stories. Not big, I can't afford something grand, but a nice-size parlor to spend winters cozy by the fireplace without feeling cramped and still have plenty of room for all the bookshelves I intend to build."

Exactly what she herself would have wanted. "W-with big windows and a porch for quiet summer evenings?"

"Yessiree. With a roomy kitchen for my wife."

"W-wife?" Agony filled her. She clamped her lips together, set her chin and braced herself for the sorrow.

As much as she longed to be the woman who could marry him, his happy future mattered more. Her sadness faded away like one last long note, leaving only peace in her soul. "You are ready to settle down. You must have someone in mind."

"I've got my eye on a real nice lady." His baritone warmed gently. Perhaps he was worrying he was hurting her feelings.

Her love for him shone so strongly within her that she felt as if she were glowing, too. Happy for him, deeply and truly happy, she leaned back in the seat, sure, so completely sure, that God would bless Thad in this new part of his life. "Do I know her?"

"I think you do. Maybe you might offer your opinion on the plans for this house. I want her to have a roomy place to do all the kitchen work easily and not so close that she catches her skirts on fire on the stove."

"Very easy to do," Noelle agreed.

"And a sunny spot for the kitchen table, a place where you just want to sit over a cup of tea and spend time jawin'."

"I can imagine it. A lot of cabinets and a roomy pantry—you could spend some of your winter months making them for her. A round table between the corner windows and a place for boots and coats to dry." The future she could see might have once been her dream, but it felt right sharing it with him. "There will be children one day who will need a place to come in from playing in the snow and warm up."

"Children." His baritone dipped intimately. When he spoke next, his voice vibrated with emotion. "Now, I hadn't quite got that far. Except for four upstairs bedrooms."

"Four sounds like a nice number."

"It surely does." His heart was full to bursting as he nosed Sunny off the main road. "I've been thinking about building a little cottage behind the main house for my ma. Aiden's taken care of her all this time, and I feel as if it's my duty now. What do you think of that?"

"As long as she would want to move. She has her own house."

"Yep, and with both of my brothers there, too. It's my hope Aiden will come to marry again one day, and then she'll be feeling in the way again." He gripped the reins more tightly. He could feel his dearest hopes ready to come true, and it was so much to lose. "I would like

her close. I've missed her, and she can feel good helping to take care of things at my place. She likes taking
care of the people she loves."

"Then it sounds like a good solution. She would be
closer to any future grandchildren."

There she went, mentioning children again. Thad
couldn't say what that did to his heart, but he was fairly
sure it would never beat normally again.

"As long as she got along well with your wife," Noelle pointed out sweetly, "it sounds perfect to me. Does
this mean there will be another wedding soon?"

"I'm praying that's the truth."

"Praying? Does this mean you're a praying man
again?"

"Maybe. You never know." The Worthington manor
came into sight, windows ablaze with golden lamplight.
It looked like the family was already home. "About this
wedding of mine. Think you'd like to attend?"

"Absolutely beyond a doubt. It's what I've been praying for."

How about that. Thad reined Sunny to a stop outside the porch. He climbed out from beneath the snug
buffalo robe and circled around the sleigh to help Noelle out. Powerful love for her broke him wide-open,
and it was greater than anything he'd ever known. Incapable of speech, he simply took her hand in his, and
led her with care up the porch steps. Joy lifted him so
far up, he couldn't feel the boards beneath his boots,
for there was only her. Just her. In his thoughts, in his
heart, in his soul.

She broke the silence between them when they
reached the door. "You will let me know how tomorrow goes with the land agent?"

"I will. The moment the land is mine, you will be the first one I tell." He acted on impulse and again cradled her face in both his hands with all the tenderss in his soul. He wanted more than anything to tell her he would take care of her, that he would do his best for her, and how great his love was for her.

As if she realized that he intended to kiss her, she tipped toward him an infinitesimal amount. Her eyes widened with such honesty, and they were the color of his dreams. Her smile was every last piece of his heart.

"Good night, Mr. McKaslin." The serene notes of her voice blew through his spirit like the rarest of joys.

He opened the door for her. "Good night, Miss Kramer. I'll talk to you tomorrow."

"Good." Her smile was the last thing he saw as he tipped his hat to her and left her in the care of her aunt, who was in the act of charging toward the door.

Maybe it wasn't so polite to run off, he thought, as he took the steps two at a time, but he wasn't a parlor-sitting kind of man. And he wanted to end the evening when it was perfect. Just perfect.

The snow fell soft and airy as an answered prayer. His boots sank up to his ankles in the new blanket of snowfall and he rubbed Sunny's nose before he slogged back to the sleigh. Funny how it did feel as though God had been watching out for him in the end. That He hadn't forgotten a simple hardworking man after all.

Thad settled on the seat, pulled the robes tight and gathered the reins in his gloved hands. Snow tapped on his hat brim and slapped his cheek as he turned Sunny in a lazy half circle, nosing him away from the bright lights of the Worthington home and into the cloying darkness.

Maybe things just take time to work out for His good; that's all. Maybe that's what he'd lost sight of when he was so far from home and everyone he loved, his heart dashed. Faith had been a painful thing for a long spell, and now it was hurting in a whole new way.

The wind kicked up, cold and shrill, so he knuckled down his hat against the stinging snowflakes. That pain seemed to spread through his chest like wildfire. For whatever reason, he was being given a second chance with Noelle. What he didn't know was that gratitude could hurt, too.

Noelle's words tonight came back to him. *It's easy to fall into the habit of walking through life. It's safer. Because you don't have to risk as much. You don't have to really feel.* Maybe that had been his problem more than he'd realized. He'd gotten awfully used to walking through his life instead of feeling it. That made it tough to know anything much of value, including God's presence.

You didn't give up on me and I thank You for it.

Thad gave Sunny more rein, but the mustang already knew where he was going, heading toward the falls, toward home.

In the bedroom she shared with Matilda, Noelle carefully poured the pitcher of warm water and measured the rise of the water level in the porcelain basin. The pitcher clinked gently onto the stand, and she felt the curls of heat from the water's surface against her face.

Happiness still strummed through her, and it was a good feeling, and a welcome change. She splashed water on her face and reached for the bottle of soft soap she liked so well. The lilac scent always reminded her of late spring, when the earth was warm and the sun's warmth a welcome friend.

She lathered and scrubbed and rinsed, going over the evening's events in her mind. Whatever God's purpose in all of this—her blindness, Thad's coming back to Angel Falls, his plans for a ranch and a home and a family starting to come to fruition—she could not know. She could only trust that He was bringing them both to the greatest good for their separate lives.

She patted her face dry in the soft towel and rehung it on the bar. Footsteps marched down the hall like a division of soldiers coming closer.

"Angelina!" Henrietta's voice echoed above the strike of her shoes. "I am shocked. Simply beside myself with agitation at what I've only just heard from your father."

And what shocking behavior would it be this time? Noelle wondered as she sprinkled tooth powder onto her toothbrush. Knowing Angelina, it was bound to be most entertaining.

Robert's cane tapped after Henrietta. "Now, now, dear, it's not as bad as all that—"

"Not that bad?" Henrietta's outrage echoed in the corridor. "Caught smoking behind the outhouses! I cannot think of why Clarissa Bell would accuse you of such a thing!"

Poor Henrietta, Noelle thought in turn, for it was not easy being a general in charge of such troops. It took a lot of internal fortitude to stay in denial about Angelina's rebellion, which was not acceptable for a Worthington.

Matilda's steps padded a little heavier than usual down the hallways. "Uh, I don't know why Mama is going on about Miss Bell. You know that Angelina was smoking behind the outhouses. The more Mama refuses to see it, the more outrageous she behaves."

Noelle heard a muted clunk, realizing that Tilly was carrying the warmed flatirons for their beds. She rinsed and dropped her toothbrush into her cup by the basin. "Henrietta loves her daughters so much, she cannot find a single flaw in any of you."

How she wished she still had her own mother to do the same.

"Mama made comments all through dinner how she thought my wedding should be, much grander, of course, than Lanna's." The bedclothes rustled and snapped. "Who does she think I'm going to marry? No one has ever come calling. I'm not exactly pretty like my sisters are."

"You are lovely in your own way."

"That's another way of saying that I'm plain." She sighed deeply.

"No, dear heart, not at all." Poor Matilda. Noelle rembered when she had been that naive and young—it had been like walking with her heart wide-open. Fairy-tale love could lift a girl right out of her shoes. She might have walked on thin air for the better part of her courtship with Thad—and probably had for half of this evening, too.

"I'm just starting to fear I'll have to live with my mother forever." Tilly sighed again.

Noelle listened to the rustle and chink as the flat-irons clinked into place. "I know what it is like to have a heart full of love to share and no one to give it to."

"Perhaps we shall be old maids together. I'll read to you at night, and study from the Bible as we do now. I'll take care of you."

"I would not wish such a fate for you, to take care of me. You deserve a good man to love you truly." She went to her bedside table. "I owe you an apology, Tilly."

"Whatever for?"

"I gave you some bad advice about Emmett Sims." She pulled open the drawer and felt for her button-hook. "I should have told you that I hope he feels the same way about you, and if he does, to hold on to that love and protect it from all things."

"But I thought—"

"I told you that love is frail and not to place all your hopes on it, but there is nothing greater than love. The Bible tells us so. I think I'm finally understanding. God's love for us is not trifling or fleeting or simple. It is the greatest strength, the greatest loyalty, and it is complex. Love is the only thing strong enough to put your hope on."

"Is that what you did once? With Thad?"

She had thought it was love—and Thad—at fault, but that was not true. As she unhooked one button and then the next, she thought of all that had happened, all that she had lost.

Oh, Papa, how could you have done such a thing? Her father's intervention and his stubborn will had changed her life. He had destroyed her one real chance at loving Thad. Now it would be forever too late. Thad was going on with his life. She had to go on with hers. Maybe Matilda would have a better experience.

"Don't give up hope, Tilly." She started loosening her other shoe. "Perhaps we ought to have our next dress purchases delivered. What do you think?"

"Oh, Mama would not approve of that."

"Spring is almost here. You might need a few new

dresses and bonnets. I can arrange it when I'm in town next."

"Oh, I would be too embarrassed. As much as I wish for it, I don't think Emmett Sims is interested in me." Matilda, the dear she was, didn't sound sad, only wistful. Her bed ropes squeaked as if she had sat down on the edge of her mattress. "A few more years, and I'll be on the shelf. I'm never going to get married."

I know the feeling. Noelle ached for her younger cousin. "I would hold out hope, if I were you. Something tells me that Mr. Emmett Sims might have noticed you."

Tilly remained quiet, but there was hope in the air. The floorboard outside the door gave a tiny squeak. Was it Angelina? Noelle wondered, as bare feet padded quietly into the room.

"Angelina!" Tilly scolded in a low voice. "You are not supposed to be out of bed. Didn't Mama just hand down a punishment?"

"Yes, but she's helping Papa, so she won't know that I'm out of bed unless you tell her." Angelina's whisper floated closer.

Noelle felt the foot of her bed dip and turned toward her troublesome cousin. "Do you really think it's wise to smoke cigarettes? It's a poor choice for you for many reasons."

"I know, but I was bored. I told Mama I didn't want to wear that frilly lacy dress. I looked like I was about to go to a convent. Or get *married*." It took no imagition at all to see Angelina rolling her eyes. "She's really planning them, you know."

"Planning what?" Matilda asked.

"Our weddings. Meredith and Lydia aren't home

from finishing school yet, and she's almost planned a seven-course meal for each of them. And a string quartet, but not for dancing. She started to ask what I wanted, and that's when I needed a bit of fresh air."

"You mean smoky air." Noelle couldn't help jesting.

"Ha-ha." Angelina was probably rolling her eyes again. "Noelle, you'll be the next to marry, anyhow."

"*Me?* Why would you say such a thing?" She tugged off one shoe and then the other. "I'm the last woman any man would marry. Men are looking for a helpmate, not someone they have to steer around the parlor."

She set the buttonhook inside the drawer, careful to keep a smile on her face. "Matilda's will be next."

"Oh, I don't know." Tilly's voice sparkled with humor. "We all thought Mr. McKaslin was rather devoted to you throughout the evening."

"Devoted?" Angelina sounded equally as amused. "Now tell the truth, Tilly. That handsome cowboy of Noelle's isn't merely devoted. He is utterly in love with her. He is a courting man. Valentine's Day is tomorrow. I would bet—"

"Don't bet, Ange," Tilly argued.

"I would *bet,*" Angelina emphasized, her rebellious streak showing, "that he proposes before tomorrow is done."

Noelle's jaw dropped and she sputtered for air. Thad, propose to her? For one brief instant, joy flooded her soul. Then drained away, leaving her in shadows.

No, he would need a wife who could help him with his dreams and not keep her from them. She rememred his plans for a wife, a wife who could cook, a wife who could tend children and, she figured, who could work alongside him with the horses.

It hurt, she couldn't say it didn't.

Somehow, she kept the smile on her face. "What an outrageous thing to say, Angelina. *This* is how you get into so much trouble."

"What? I'm telling the truth. The way he looked at you wasn't like anything I have ever seen before. Tell her, Tilly."

Matilda sighed. "I didn't want to mention it. I know it will make you sad. But it's true. All through the wedding ceremony and the dinner at the hotel, his gaze never faltered. He adores you, Noelle, and in the right way. The real way. The loving way that lasts forever and nothing can break."

Noelle opened her mouth to argue.

Angelina was already talking. "He doesn't seem to mind that you can't see. Something like that doesn't stop true love."

"What am I going to do with you two?" She could only shake her head, doing her best to hold down the sorrow that was hers alone. She was no longer an idealistic girl seeing romance and fanciful possibilities instead of practical, real life.

Somewhere deep inside her she wished she could. "I hear voices, Matilda and Noelle!" Henrietta called from down the hall. "It's well past your bedtimes. In my day, a young lady was asleep before nine or it wasn't proper!"

"We'll say our prayers now, Mama," Matilda promised earnestly over the nearly imperceptible pad and rustle of Angelina tiptoeing from the room.

Noelle pulled her nightgown from her bureau drawer, listening to the squeak of floorboards as Matilda knelt down to pray. There was a damp chill in the cold that crept through the walls and she shivered as she unbuttoned her bodice. She wondered if a change in the weather was coming.

Good. The sooner this snow melted, the quicker Thad could start building his dreams. For that was her most cherished dream, she realized as she stepped out of her dress and untied her petticoats. Her only dreams were now for him.

She was starting to see that life, like music, was a careful balance of melody and harmony, of sweeter notes and deeper ones. As she slipped her nightgown over her head and knelt beside her bed, she thanked the good Lord for both.

Chapter Sixteen

This had to be the best day of his life, family problems aside. His troubles at home seemed manageable from his current outlook, Thad thought as he dismounted in front of the Worthington stables. The sun was shining, he was the proud owner of a real fine spread and was carrying an engagement ring in his shirt pocket. Knowing that she would say yes just made it easier to feel on top of the world.

"Howdy there, McKaslin!" Eli Sims came through the open stable doorway to take Sunny's reins. "Good seein' ya. Looks like you beat the storm here."

Thad hadn't noticed the dark clouds overhead. He was in too good a mood to let them trouble him now. "Guess so. How's things going for you here?"

"I can't thank you enough for finding me this job."

"I'm glad it suits you." Thad grabbed a package from his saddlebag before Eli could take Sunny in out of the cold. "How's that stallion treating you?"

"He's an ornery one. You come to work him some?"

Thad glanced up at the house, where wide windows

glinted with lamplight. "Maybe in a bit. Has Noelle's last student of the day left yet?"

"Yep. Left a while back," the young man called over his shoulder before he disappeared with Sunny into the shadowed aisle.

Nerves kicked his stomach. Slushy snow squished and skidded beneath his boots. He clutched the package, going over all the decisions he'd come to. He'd already run it past his ma. Normally he took Aiden into his confidence, but he suspected his older brother was still sour on love and marriage. Best to figure out how this was all going to work on his own.

Ma seemed to think moving into a little cottage next door to him was a fine idea. In fact, there had been no way she could have disguised her happiness at his plans. He knew she was unfulfilled with only gruff Aiden and independent Finn to mother. Hadn't she been spoiling him too much since he'd come home?

Surely Noelle wouldn't mind some of that spoiling. The nerves in his gut took another hard kick. At least, that's what he was hoping. Hadn't she liked the notion when they'd talked on the ride home last night?

Stop worrying, man. His pulse beat like a runaway train down a steep track with such force, he began to wheeze as he headed up the walkway. The brick stones were wet from snowmelt, as were the steps of the porch.

Noelle. He saw her through the window. She was sitting in an armchair near the hearth with sewing on her lap. Her chestnut hair was loose, framing her lovely face and tumbling over her shoulders. She was beauty itself in a rose-pink dress, looking like spring had come early to this hard land.

His spring.

First off, he had to stop wheezing so hard. He stood on the top step and drew in a calm breath. Now all he had to do was raise his fist and knock on the door and lay his heart, his pride, his dignity and his future on the line. Not a fearsome prospect at all, right?

Just knock. He did it, one knock was all he could manage. He waited, hoping—praying—someone had heard it. He took a step back and tried to buck up his courage for the next difficult event. One thing was for sure, he'd be feeling a whole passel better once she'd said yes and he could relax.

The door swung open and instead of the maid looking up at him, it was his Noelle. "Thad, is that you?"

"How did you know?"

"I recognized your gait and your knock." She opened the door wider, waltzing backward a few steps, her rose-pink skirts swirling around her ankles. "Come in. My aunt took the girls to town, and Robert is out with Matilda for her first driving lesson."

He managed to force his feet forward and into the warmth of the house, surprised his watery knees could hold him up so well. "You're here all alone?"

"Not exactly alone. Sadie's upstairs cleaning and Cook's in the kitchen. Would you like some tea? I'll call Sadie—"

"No." Had she gotten lovelier overnight? He had never seen her so beautiful, but then he was biased. "No need to go to any fuss. I came to talk to you—"

"About the land sale." Her smile dazzled him. "Come, sit and warm yourself by the fire and tell me everything."

"It was good luck mostly." He closed the door and followed her to the hearth. She moved with grace, as she always did, walking almost as if she saw where she was going. She caught the edge of the chair's arm with her fingertips and settled into it, waiting for his story expectantly.

He sank down into the chair opposite her. His damp boots squeaked once on the wood floor. Heat radiated over him like his dazzling love for her. His chest cinched so with powerful affection for her, he didn't see how he was going to be able to get the words out.

Maybe it was best to talk about the land sale, as she'd asked. "It's a stroke of luck that this section came up for sale. I've signed papers too fancy for me to read, and I still don't believe it."

"It's not luck." She said it with confidence. "That land was intended for you."

Faith wasn't what he'd come to talk about, but it was the truth. It had to be the truth. The hard journey of the past five years had led him here, to this shining, shimmering hope. God had been watching over him after all. Knowing that gave him courage.

"I have something for you." He placed the wrapped package into her hand. "It's for Valentine's Day."

"*What?* No, this can't be—"

"It's for you." She sure looked surprised. "Go on. Open it."

"But, Thad I—"

"No arguments." He was out of words, so he knelt before her. "Aren't you curious about your present?"

"All right." Her fingertips inched across the spine of the volume. "Is it a *book?*"

Thad lifted it for her, because it was heavy. "You're thinking, this is an odd gift since you can't see to read, am I right?"

"I can have Matilda read it to me." She unfolded the paper to reveal the black leather cover.

"No need for that." He opened the thick vellum pages with care and slid the book onto her knees. "This is one book you can read. It's raised print. Go on, you can feel the title."

"It's the Book of Psalms." She turned toward him and it wasn't only tears that stood in her eyes. He saw her heart and her soul, all she was, all wrapped up in surprise and joy. "I love the psalms."

"You always did." It did him good to see her so happy. He loved her without end. He would do anything for her. The need to cherish and protect her left him iron-strong. Now all he had to do was ask the question, and she would be his. His intended, his fiancée for all the world to see, and soon enough, his wife.

His *wife.* That would have brought him to his knees, if he wasn't there already. "I remember how much you used to love to read, especially your Bible."

"This is extremely thoughtful. And expensive."

He brushed the tendrils away from her sweet face. "Go on, give it a try."

Her sensitive fingertips skimmed over the top of the page and found the raised numeral. Her face brightened until all her heart shone sweetly. "It's the twenty-third psalm. I can feel the letters. Why, I can read them. 'The Lord is my shepherd; I shall not want.'"

"How does it feel to be reading again?"

"It's an answered prayer." Happiness filled her cometely. "'He maketh me to lie down in green pastures; He leadeth me beside the still waters. He restoreth my soul.'"

"Glad you like it."

"Like it? This is—" She looked at him with tears in her eyes. "I don't know what it is. It's—just. Thank you."

Those tears broke him open completely.

God, if you're listening, a little guidance would be a help. Thad swallowed, not expecting to be heard for he knew the Lord was busy, but he asked anyway. He covered her hands with his, psalm book and all.

Noelle leaned closer to him, her unspoken question on her face. The soft gray daylight kissed her sweetly, or maybe it was his own love for her making her seem so dear, so perfect in all the ways that mattered.

"Noelle, some things have changed an awful lot in the five years since I've been gone. Surely both of us have." He had to take a pause because his heart was beating as though he was running on a steep uphill slope.

"Thad, you sound so serious."

"That's because I've never been more serious or more sure." Nothing had mattered so much before this moment. He gathered up his strength and kept going. "I want the job of making you happy for our lifetimes to come. I want to be with you in those green pastures. Marry me."

"What? What did you say?"

"Marry me, Noelle." His tone was complete love and pure wonder. "Be my wife."

"Wife?" She repeated the word blankly. Her mind was like a midnight fog. Nothing seemed to penetrate it. "You want to m-marry me?"

"You needn't sound quite so horrified," he quipped. "This shouldn't come as a surprise. Isn't that what we talked about last night?"

"What talk?" Panic crept up her spine like hungry ants at a picnic. Noelle vaguely felt the book slide off her knee and heard the distant thunk as it hit the floor at her feet, but it was hard to notice anything beyond her fears. "Do you mean our talk on the sleigh ride home?"

"That would be the one." His hands were comforting, his voice soothing. "I don't want you to be so disaught, sweetheart."

"I—I—" She couldn't make any words come. The panic was crawling into her throat now, and a horrible sorrow taking root in her chest. A dark, agonizing sorrow.

"I love you." His baritone broke through the sorrow. "Surely you know that I do."

His love for her made it worse. She could hear Shelton's words echoing in the chambers of her mind. *You're damaged goods, now. What use are you?* Henrietta's loving reassurances after she'd woken up from the buggy accident. *I'll take care of you now. I'll never consider you a burden.* Well-intended words, but even Henrietta, her own father's sister, had used the word *burden.*

"I was hoping," Thad was saying, "that you'd come to love me, too."

Love him? Love was too pale a word for the deep abiding devotion she held for him. "Y-you are supposed to marry someone else. Someone b-better."

"Who could be better than you?" He said those words as if he could not see the problem.

Her dear, sweet, good-hearted Thad. Did he truly not understand? What did she say? She longed to throw caution and her very real concerns to the wind. She wanted to wrap her arms around him, accept his proposal and spend the rest of her life as his wife.

His wife. Her soul soared at that very notion. Having the privilege to love and cherish and honor him day by day, year by year for the rest of her life felt like her heaven on earth. Sweet longing filled her with such force, it threatened to lift her right out of the chair.

And what about what Thad wanted? Her joy faded. Her longing vanished. She had to keep her feet on the floor and tight hold of her common sense. A marriage between them would never work. Not if he wanted to realize his dream of running a ranch. She could not help him with that, not the way she once could.

That's what he hadn't realized, she thought. He was acting on his past feelings for her. He still viewed her as he did five long years ago when the world seemed full of possibilities and their love unshakable.

She knew better now. She was wiser. If her heart cracked into a million pieces, she had to ignore the pain of it. She had to do the right thing. The best thing for Thad.

And, yes, for her.

He broke the silence. "It shouldn't take you this long to say yes to marrying me. Not if you want me."

She withdrew her hands from his—and her heart, too.

"You do love me, darlin'. Don't you?"

"Love isn't the question, Thad." She sat very still, gathering up every bit of might she had and yet it wasn't enough.

"Then what is the question, darlin'?" So tender his words. So loving.

Sorrow dripped through her. "I c-can't marry you."

"You sound so sure about that. Why not?"

Because I won't trade my dreams for yours, she ached to say. Because I don't want to be a burden to the one man I love beyond all else on this earth.

Her soul squeezed with pain, making every inch of her ache. She covered her face with her hands, unable to say the truth. Unable to bare herself so fully.

Not even Thad would understand. He would say all the right things, about how her blindness didn't matter to him, and that was not the truth. It couldn't be the truth.

She swallowed hard against the burn in her throat. He hadn't seen her real limitations yet. She had worked extremely hard to adapt to the constraints of her blindness, but he didn't know that. He only saw what she could do and not what she couldn't. She had to do the right thing for them both.

"Noelle? Are you crying?"

"N-no." She would make that the truth. She set her chin and blinked hard against the heat behind her eyes. "I don't know what else to say to you, Thad. I c-can't marry you."

"You haven't told me why, darlin'."

His tenderness tore her apart. Fear left her helpless. Truly in the dark, she reached out in prayer. *Help me, Lord. Don't let my words hurt him.*

There was no answer, not one in her heart, not one in the darkness. Outside the house another gust of wind slammed against the house, rattling the windowpanes, jarring her soul.

"Tell me, sweetheart, just tell me the truth."

"Which truth?" She squeezed her eyes shut. Torn, so torn. Saying no to him was like ripping out her soul.

"We're simply not suited, Thad. Not anymore. You said it yourself. You've changed. I've changed. It's too l-late."

"No. No, it's not. I won't believe it."

"Please, I—I can't marry you."

"But this is our second chance."

Her eyes were luminous and her face filled with such sweet longing that for one blissful moment he thought she was going to say yes. To tell him that she loved him truly and forever, as he loved her.

He knew he'd thought wrong when she seemed to withdraw from him. The longing slid from her face, her lovely expressive face that would always be so dear to him.

"No." Her rejection came quietly. Tenderly. She bent forward and her hair fell in a curtain to hide her face and her emotions.

They were not secret to him.

The psalm book lay on its back on the floor between them. He lifted it carefully, dusted it off so it was as good as new and laid it on the small table beside her chair. Although she'd said no to him, the great abiding love he had for her did not fade.

It would never fade.

"Guess I'd best get going, then." While he didn't say it as a question, he meant it as one. He watched her carefully. She nodded once, that was all, as if trying to shield her heart from his.

He climbed to his feet, holding his soul still against the pain he knew was coming. Like a lethal blow, there was no pain at first, just the shock filtering through him like cracked ice in his veins. He took a step backward, waiting, hoping, praying she would reach out to him. That she would stop him before he made it to the door.

She didn't. He opened the door and forced his feet across the threshold. It took all his self-restraint to keep from looking back at her one last time. To keep from reaching out to her when he knew she was hurting, too.

How had this all gone so wrong? He closed the door with a click and let the wind batter him. Snow lashed at him like a boxer's glove, and still he could not move off the porch. He'd left his heart behind in that room, and he couldn't leave without her.

What was he gonna do? Stand here forever? He had to get moving before the shock wore off. Before the pain set in and the sorrow with it. It was bound to be bad—he'd experienced this before. He'd ridden away from her once, and he knew the emptiness of living his life without her love. How was he going to manage it a second time?

He started down the stairs, and her words stuck with him. *We're simply not suited, Thad. Not anymore.* Not suited? And what did that mean, anyhow? His boots crunched in the slush and snow on the walkway. Big, fat flakes fell from a gray sky as he crossed the yard to the stable. *You said it yourself. You've changed. I've changed.*

I haven't changed that much. He stopped stock-still between the house and the stable, realizing that wasn't true. Not true at all. How about that? The hardness from years of unhappiness and a tough life on the trail had fallen away somewhere, sloughed off him like a too-large, worn-out coat.

He was no longer bitter and unbelieving. He was no longer thinking God had stopped noticing the troubles

of an average man. He no longer believed life was about
hard work and that relationships ought to be, too. He'd
found himself again—the man he used to be—because
of Noelle. Because of her love and God's grace.

Why had she said no? Why had she turned him
down? He'd thought she'd loved him. He'd thought she
wanted him to love her.

"Hey, Thad!" Eli called above the rush of the storm.
"I saw you comin'. I've got Sunny for you."

"Thanks, Sims." Thad seized the reins from the
younger man, nodding. "You'd best get inside before
this gets much worse."

"Will do. Looks like we're in for a hard blow." Eli
waved his hand and took off.

Sunny wheeled around, eager to get home and out
of the weather. Thad grabbed the saddle horn, ready
to mount up, and realized the house was in his view
again. There she was, standing in the window, veiled
by the bleak snow. His heart turned over. His soul filled
with longing.

It's too late, she'd said. Too late.

Swift pain like a dagger's tip to his heart stole his
breath and weakened his knees. He took a stumbling
step, leaning on the horse's shoulder for support, and
somehow he scrambled into the saddle.

The wind gusted, driving cold that hit like bullets.
The snow had turned to rain, soaking him down to the
bone. She'd said no to him. He had to respect that, although it tore out his heart.

"C'mon, Sunny. Take us home."

The mustang obliged, heading swiftly down the road.
Lucky thing, since the sorrow was setting in. It wasn't
easy riding away from his dreams a second time.

* * *

Noelle listened to the rain sing against the parlor window. The wind lifted and fell like a cello's haunting tones. The limbs of the hawthorn tree outside the window rubbed against the eaves with a tuba's low notes. The fire in the hearth crackled in counterpoint to the gusts of wind and beat of rain. It was a haunting symphony, one that spoke of sorrow and regret.

Regret for the lost years between them. Regret that she never had a voice in Thad's decision to leave. Regret at the years she'd wasted. Regret that there would be only wasted years ahead without real love.

She swiped the last of her tears from her eyes. She knew for certain that she would love only Thad forever. *I'm hoping for a wife one day. Someone who sees life the way I do. You work hard, try to do what's right and at the end of the day rest up for another hard day on the ranch.* Her blindness separated them more successfully than her parents' had. There was no solution to that.

She heard her cousin's hurried gait well before the door opened on a chorus of wind.

"That rain is cold." Matilda shut the door behind her, dripping water on the floor. There was a rustle as if she were shedding her sodden wraps and her shoes squished wetly on the floor coming closer. "I need to sit by the fire and warm up. Papa said maybe we're in for a spot of good luck. This could be a warming spell that brings us an early spring."

"I hope so." Noelle prayed her voice sounded normal and feared that it didn't. "Then you can take me for rides in the buggy. How did your driving lesson go?"

"Fine. We rode up to the waterfall and back. It's roaring with all the snowmelt and rain."

"The waterfall has never frozen in the winter, not in my memory." Her love for Thad was like that, she realized, never ending, always replenished. Alive in her heart when it was the last thing she needed or wanted. "Would you like me to bring you some tea?"

"Please. I can't remember the last time I've been this cold."

Tea. Yes, that sounded like something soothing to do. She rose from her chair, ignoring the ache that burned her eyes and tightened her throat. She didn't want to talk to anyone, not even to Matilda, about Thad's proposal. They would pity her, and that was the last thing she wanted. The last thing she needed.

She skirted the end table and headed across the parlor. Grief lodged so tightly within her she could hardly function. Her pulse thudded in her ears so loudly that the strike of her shoe on the floor muted. There was Thad at the edges of her memory and glued to her soul.

Who could be better than you? he'd said with complete sincerity. *I love you,* he'd said with utter honesty. *This is our second chance.* His tender plea filled her mind again and again. This is our second chance.

If only it could be. She had to stop thinking about this. About the tender love in his voice, even when she turned him down. And the defeated cadence to his gait as he walked away from her. What she could not think about was the future without Thad in it. Without a prospering ranch, and happiness, buckets of happiness. She could almost see it, vivid, so vivid, those fields of green dotted with grazing horses. The two-story house where drying laundry snapped on a clothesline and children played in the yard—

She froze in midstep, confused. Where was she?

She'd forgotten to count her steps. She didn't know if she was about to walk into the window or if she was on a collision course with her aunt's whatnot shelf.

"Where did you get that book?" Tilly broke the silence.

"I-it was a gift." Outside the symphony of the rain crescendoed to a roar, confusing the sounds in the room, confusing her.

"From whom?"

She turned toward Matilda's voice, using it like a compass. "Just someone."

"Thad came by, didn't he? Angelina was right. Too bad he didn't propose, too. Wouldn't that have been something?"

A rush filled her ears. The sound of her heart breaking all over again. She spun on her heel, careful to keep track of her orientation. She guessed how many steps would take her through the archway and into the dining room.

"Noelle?" Tilly called out. "He really didn't propose, did he?"

Her step faltered right along with her heartbeat. She reached out a hand to catch the corner of the dining table and caught air.

"Noelle? Are you all right?"

Two more steps and she tried again. There it was, the beveled, polished edge. She gripped it with relief. Her knees were wobbling so she lowered herself into the nearest chair, glad that her cousin hadn't noticed how lost she'd been.

How lost she would be from this day on.

Chapter Seventeen

In the warmth of the town's dress shop, Noelle ran her fingertips across the skein of fine crochet thread. Her mind should have been on deciding if the yarn had the right weight and feel for the lace tablecloth she wanted to make for Matilda's hope chest. But when she heard the name "McKaslin," she couldn't seem to concentrate on anything other than what the shop owner was telling Aunt Henrietta.

"—should have been helping his brothers with the spring planting," Cora Sims was saying over the *thump, thump* of fabric being pulled off the bolt to be measured. "That boy is trouble waiting to happen. He's on a bad path for sure."

"It's all in the upbringing." Henrietta's voice echoed across the length of the shop. "I haven't had one bit of trouble with my children. I've taken a firm hand right from the start and made it clear there were standards to be upheld."

Noelle bit her bottom lip, remembering the uproar at last night's dinner table when Angelina had announced she wasn't going to finishing school like her sisters and wanted to take to the cattle trails instead. Since she heard Matilda choking as she struggled not to laugh, she wasn't the only one amused by wonderful Henrietta.

"This is the color I want," Tilly said when she was able. "Light blue."

"A light blue tablecloth sounds lovely to me. We need ten skeins."

"I'll count them out," Matilda said eagerly. "Mama's busy with Miss Sims."

"Is she ordering more spring dresses for your sisters?"

"Yes. She's taken charge as usual and I don't think Angelina is going to be very happy. Mama's chosen two different pink fabrics for her."

"Pink for Angelina? That's wishful thinking on your mother's part." Noelle tried to imagine the shop full of new spring fabrics so soft and bright and pretty, but her imagination was not the same these days. Nothing was, not one thing, since she'd let Thad walk out of her life over a week ago.

Thad. The thought of him still hurt in the broken places of her soul, where she'd banished her love for him, although it still lived.

The noise of the rain on the roof, the shop conversations and the background din from the streets outside faded away. Regret filled her until she was brimming over. Thoughts of him carried her away to the steadfast comfort of his hand on hers as she swirled over the ice of the pond at Thad's side. Once again, she heard the deep rumble of his cozy chuckle in the stable with the new foal nipping at her skirt ruffles. Once again she felt the bright dreams of lush fields and grazing horses standing at Thad's side.

It's not possible. Stop thinking of him. She squeezed her eyes closed, but that did not begin to stop the colors of her heart. Her heart did not see reason. Nor did it understand that there could come a day when Thad realized he had made a mistake. That the dreams they'd once shared were not something she could give to him as his wife.

Is that the real reason? a logical, sensible voice asked at the back of her mind. It was a question she could not let herself answer.

"Did you want to get that, Noelle, dear?" Henrietta bustled her way to take the basket of goods. "I'll be glad to get this totaled up, if you and Matilda want to go browse at the cobbler's."

"Yes, thank you."

Although she kept a good memory of the shop, she was glad when Matilda guided her around a new fabric display and on toward the door. The bell jangled overhead as they scooted outside into the cool spring air. The damp stung her face as she bundled up against the rain.

"Oh!" Matilda squeaked with surprise. "There he is." Thad? Noelle turned toward the sounds of the street, wondering where he was, if he was well, if he looked happy, if he had all that he'd wanted. Love blazed up from the locked-away chambers of her heart, and she longed for him the way gray skies longed for blue.

"He tipped his hat to me!" Matilda's whisper was tremulous. "Oh, he smiled at me from the street, where he sat on his wagon seat, and as his horses drew him past, he reached up with his hand and tipped his hat brim. He was smiling just a little, nothing flashy or bold, just *polite*. Oh!"

Her pulse turned hollow. Emmett Sims, not Thad. Disappointment weighed her down like a blacksmith's anvil. And it made no sense whatsoever because it wasn't as if she were holding out a single hope that— No, not one single hope that there was any way Thad would love her enough—

No, it's not what you want for him, Noelle. She kept her spine straight, gathered up her resolve and smiled at her cousin's joy. "Perhaps Mr. Sims fancies you more than you've thought."

"Perhaps. We shall have to wait and see is all."

"I'm not fooled, you know, by your reserve. Inside you are floating like a cloud."

"How did you know?"

"I've felt that way myself." She tucked away that memory, too, not of being young and in love, but of all the ways she loved Thad more now. And always would. "I've lost count. Where are we on the boardwalk? Is that the bakery?"

"Yes. I can smell the cinnamon buns."

"I think we need to celebrate, don't you? Henrietta needs to go to the post office before she catches up with us. We have plenty of time. We'll have iced cinnamon rolls and tea, which ought to put us in a much better mood for shoe shopping."

"I think you're right." Matilda took a better grip on her arm. "Come with me."

As Noelle turned on her heel to let her cousin guide her to the door, she thought she felt a feather brush against her soul like a touch from heaven. But there were no other footsteps squishing anywhere close by on the rain-soaked boardwalk. Just the sucking of mud at horse hooves and wagon wheels and the concerto of the rain falling.

Strange. Shrugging, she followed her cousin into the shelter of the bakery.

"Thad?"

He ignored his older brother's voice as he watched Noelle step inside the bakery across the street. Affection tied him up in knots, for he could still see her through the gray sheets of rain and the street traffic and the bakery's window. She was feeling her way for a curving chair back and, after three tries, found it and, with care, settled onto the seat.

"You and Finn are both useless," Aiden quipped from the row filled with buckets of nails. "Both of you aren't doing a thing to help me. I should have left you two at home."

"Don't go tossing me into the same stall as Finn." Thad couldn't seem to rip his gaze away from the bakery shop window. "I'm not the lazy one."

"Hey!" Finn's voice rose up from the back corner of the store. "Watch who you're calling lazy!"

Aiden came close to peer through the window, too. "You've been watching her since you spotted her enter the dress shop. Tell me again how you think her saying no was for the best."

A dagger through his gut wouldn't hurt as much as Noelle's rejection. No, nothing in this life could hurt him like that. But it was a private pain. "Between Finn, helping you with the ranch and working on mine, I haven't had a whole lot of time to ponder it."

"Perhaps you'd best start right now, since you've got

time to stand idle at the window." Aiden strode off, hiding a small smile.

Think about it? He'd been doing nothing else but going over the last two months in his mind. He was sure he had won her back. He was sure she'd felt the same way. She loved him. He knew that. She hadn't bothered to deny it. Yet something worried at him that he could not shake and could not look at because it hurt too much.

He hadn't given up on her. He would never give up. Seeing her again hurt enough to bring him to his knees, and yet, could he look away? No. He could not turn his back and walk away from even the sight of her.

She looked subdued, without the joy he'd seen in her when they'd been together. Across the street, the bakery owner was serving a pot of tea. Two plates of enormous cinnamon rolls were on the table. Noelle was exchanging pleasantries, smiling sweetly to the older woman who ran the place. Her fingers nimbly searching for the flatware and the sugar bowl, unaware that as she spooned sugar into her cup half of it landed on the tablecloth.

He remembered, too, how Matilda had guided her along the boardwalk with care, and earlier, in the shop, helped her around the displays in the dress shop. Her words came back to him, haunting him, always haunting him. *You've changed. I've changed. It's too l-late.*

Now he heard a different meaning. When he'd feared that she had meant they were no longer suited, that she no longer wanted a life as a simple rancher's wife, perhaps that wasn't what she'd meant at all. No, maybe she'd been speaking of something else entirely.

Oh, Noelle. His heart crumpled with love for her.

Tender affection swept through his soul like a flash flood, leaving him sure. Absolutely sure. His vision blurred for a moment as he watched her take a sip from her teacup and then lower it into its saucer by touch.

Understanding rained through him like a March squall. The last years of his life, so tough and lonely, suddenly made sense to him. He knew now where the good Lord had been leading him all along—home to his precious Noelle.

"Thad!" Aiden called from the front counter. "Are you coming or not?"

"Coming." He tucked his heart back into his chest, went to collect Finn and followed his older brother out the door.

"I am insulted. That's what I am." Aunt Henrietta bored through the parlor like a runaway train on a mountain grade. Crystal lamp shades clinked and chattered as if in fear. "The nerve of the territorial governor! Suggesting that I perhaps tend to my realm of home and children instead of complaining about modern progress!"

"Clearly the governor is in error." Noelle's fingers stilled. She counted the stitches of her new project—a patchwork quilt—with her fingertips. "You've spent a lot of time composing letters trying to make a difference for us all."

"I hardly expected them to listen to a woman, but I did not expect being insulted." There was a *thwack, thwack* as Henrietta beat one of the decorative pillows on her best sofa before dropping onto it. "For the first time in my life I think it's a pity that woman do not have the vote. If I did, I would vote such a man out of office."

"Well, you should," Noelle said as kindly as she could. She recognized the touch of drama in her aunt's tirade. "He clearly does not appreciate a woman with good sense."

Across the hearth, Noelle heard Matilda struggling to hold back a chuckle.

"Precisely. It gives me pause. I may have to admit those suffrage women in town have a good argument." There was a clicking of steel needles—Henrietta, gathing up her knitting.

Matilda apparently could not hold back her amusement any longer. "But Mama, you don't approve of women wanting to vote."

"I don't. But in light of this uncomplimentary letter, I do not know what the world is coming to. Perhaps I should give an ear to their cause. Clarissa Bell is in my prayer group. I shall speak to her today. Yes, that is exactly what I shall do."

Noelle carefully slipped her needle into the quilt block she was sewing. It was hard to be certain above the music of the spring storm, but she thought she heard a horse in the driveway. Perhaps it was Cora Sims arriving early for an afternoon of sewing. With any luck, maybe her nephew, Emmett, had driven her.

She slid her work into the basket at her feet. "Is Robert still in the stables?"

Henrietta humphed. "Out working with that mare the way Mr. McKaslin taught him. He refuses to give up on that animal. If he gets hurt again—"

Noelle rose from her chair, thinking of Thad. Her spirit lifted as it always did. Always would. "If Thad says so, then Robert should keep the mare and work with her. It will be all right."

"Mr. McKaslin has not been coming up to the house lately." Henrietta's voice turned thoughtful over the ambitious *click-click* of her knitting needles. "And here I had believed him to be most enraptured with you, the poor man. Utterly besotted. Did you see it, too, Matilda?"

"Yes. He's very sweet on you."

Sweet on her? Her heart broke all over again. She headed straight for the door before anyone could guess at her feelings. Or her failures. "Me, marry? I'm on the shelf and have been for long enough to gather dust. Far too long to try to tidy me up and marry me off now."

"You're young and as lovely as could be." Henrietta rose to her defense. "Mr. McKaslin is a man of character, and so he is deserving of you. He ought to propose to you and consider himself blessed with you for his wife."

Dear Henrietta, so loyal and true. She could not understand. Noelle lifted her cloak from the tree, fighting the sorrow. Grief suffocated her. She slipped the wool fabric around her shoulders. "I'm too set in my ways to adjust to marriage. I rather like being a prickly spinster."

"That you could never be!" Henrietta sounded deeply amused. "Trust me when I tell you Thad could not take his eyes off you."

Suddenly Matilda was at her side. Noelle startled. She had been too upset to hear her cousin's approach. Everything was wrong, everything was amiss, since Thad had asked her to marry him.

Since she'd had to say no to him.

It was for the best. She tied her hood snug beneath her chin and opened the door with determination. She'd done the only thing she could do, and it was the right thing.

But her life without him was dark. It was like being blind all over again.

Outside on the doorstep, the wind gusted with a spray of wet. Raindrops fell like striking lead, ricocheting off the earth, making it hard to hear the horse's progress up the road. Bleakness washed over her like the heart of the storm. She gripped the porch rail, letting the rain strike her. Would Thad be working in this gale anyway? Would he be working on that house of his? Or in the fields turning sod with his brothers?

Wherever he was, she hoped he was happy. She would gladly give all of her happiness through her lifetime to him.

Matilda joined her at the rail. "If you married Thad, I could help you. It's not far at all to his new place at the falls, and I can drive now."

"Oh, Tilly. You're like a sister to me. I don't want that life for you, always having to help."

Noelle hung her head, letting the rain batter her. Why wasn't Matilda's offer reassuring her? Why did it only make her feel more panicked?

Because your blindness isn't the only reason you can't marry Thad. She swiped the wet from her face with trembling fingers. She no longer felt safe, no longer sheltered. The storm turned angry, beating against her so hard, it was a surprise it didn't blow away her fears like last autumn's leaves.

"It looks as if it won't last long. It's starting to break up to the west." Matilda moved away from the rail. "Oh, there's someone at the stables."

"Mr. Sims, I hope, coming to bring Cora to visit." The ache in her soul beat at her like the storm.

"I don't think it's the Sims. There's no buggy. Just one horse and his rider."

Thad. With him came the sweetness of hope. She fought against it, but there was her great love for him and the slide of her heart forever falling. She steeled her spine and reminded herself she could not let herself love this man any more than she already did. She would not.

And then he said her name.

Chapter Eighteen

"Noelle."

When she held out her hand to him, wet from the rain, feelings came to life within his poor heart unlike anything he'd felt before. True devotion as soft and warm as a prayer lit him up until he felt as hopeful as a spring dawn. He wanted her. Just her.

Only her.

"Th-thad. What are you doing here?"

"It's your worst fears come true, darlin'." He wasn't hurting anymore. He was no longer alone. He was sure beyond all doubt. Rain slanted beneath the porch roof, striking him, and he moved to shadow her from it. Out of the corner of his eye he saw the cousin slip into the house and close the door to leave them alone. "I've come to change your mind."

"About m-marrying you?" Her heart showed on her face, all of her pure longing and sweet love for him so revealed to him. His heart wrenched with hope. Then she turned away, and sorrow crumpled her face. "Thad, you have to leave. I can't go through this again. It hurts t-too m-much."

"I can see that." He laid her hand over his heart. "I can feel how much it hurts you."

"Then why are you here? You have to go."

"No." He stood resolute. "Your pain is my pain. That's the way it is. I'm not going to walk away from you this time."

Her chin shot up, and there, revealed on her lovely face was the truth. He could see it, he could see the hurt and want and other precious emotions on her face. But she could not see his.

So he lifted her hand to his chin, her fingertips to his cheek. "I want you to feel what's on my face, since you won't look in my heart."

"Thad, just leave this be. Please." Tears stood in her eyes, as if refusing to fall. "I told you. You can't turn back time. Not even God can do that. It's too late."

"That's where you're wrong, darlin'." He pressed a brief kiss to her fingertips. Tenderness took him over, and it made him stronger. Better. "It's never too late for God's greatest blessing. So, you can't turn down my proposal over it. It's because I left you once, and you're afraid I'll do it again. Isn't it?"

"Why didn't you come to me instead?" Rain trickled down her forehead. "You didn't love me enough, that's why. You cared for me, I know that, but I loved you more."

"Not a chance, darlin'. Everything has changed these past five years except one thing. My enduring love for you. That's something that will not end." Another drop of rain trailed down her forehead. The tears standing in her eyes still did not fall.

His heart was breaking for both of them, but this had to be said. So he said it. "I didn't realize why I left without a word, even with your father's threats, until years later. But you've gotta understand. I was young and down deep, I was afraid your father was right."

"Right that you didn't love me enough?"

"No, darlin'." Tenderness, unmistakable tenderness, made those words intimate and sincere. "I was afraid that one day down the road, the shining way you looked at me would dim. Life is tough, and hardship might rub off that shine. You might get tired of long days of working this hard land just to try to prosper."

"You think I cared about those things?"

"No. Fear isn't rational. You just don't know what's up ahead in your life, or which way the weather will blow. Down deep, I was afraid things might not work out. That we'd be scraping by just like my parents had, running short and losing hope. And that would be the day you would look at me as a failure."

"You think I would have stopped loving you?"

"Maybe. I didn't know. What if I was the reason you wound up losing all of your dreams? What if that day came and the comfort of your parents' fancy home and privileged lifestyle would lure you away from me?" He stopped, his voice raw with emotion. "I can see how the thought of losing you that way hurt more than leaving you for good before you had more of my heart. I don't know if you can understand that, darlin'."

"A little." Tears fell in a slow hot roll down her cheek. "A lot."

"But I promise you this. I've matured. I've been out in the world. I've earned my experience the hard way, and I know my worth." Truth rang in his voice, was granite-solid on his face. "I'll stand by you no matter what. I'll never stop trying for you, never let you down and never stop loving you. If only you will give me this chance. This one precious chance to marry you. Please, don't say no."

"I h-have to." She choked on a sob. "You look at the past when you see me. You're trying to fix what hurt you so much. I understand that. But look at me now, Thad. I can't be a rancher's wife. I can't be what you need."

"You *are* what I need. Why can't you see that?" His honest words tempted her. How they tempted her. Another sob wrenched up from her soul. His face was warm against her fingers. She could feel the faint rasp of his day's growth of beard along his jaw and the set of his jawbone. He meant what he said. At least, he *thought* he did.

If only she could make him understand. She struggled for air and still she could not speak the truth—she had to say the whole and terrible truth. "Can't you see I'm afraid now? Love just isn't enough. Can't you see that?"

"Real love is always enough, darlin'."

"I'm not the woman I was. I can't do most of the work around a ranch house by myself. I'm not whole. I don't want the day to come when you look at me and see a burden. You'll realize all that I've cost you. You'll stop loving me."

A muscle jumped along his cheek. He breathed in air with one long inhale. She trembled in the cold and the uncertainty.

At last he broke the silence. "Fine. Let's say you're right. You say yes to me. We get married. Down the road, I'm working with a new horse and I get kicked hard, just like your uncle did. Let's say I don't wake up right away, but when I do, I can't move my legs. Are you going to stop loving me?"

Tears burned as they spilled down her face. A sob

ripped up from her chest. There was only one truth. One bright shining truth. "No. Never. I would only love you more."

"Well now, that's how I feel about you, darlin'." His hands cupped her face tenderly, sweetly. "You are my dream. Marry me. Please. Don't make me live in the dark without you."

She felt the heart of the girl she used to be, the young woman who believed in love and fairy-tale wishes. Her future stood before her, the man who was rubbing away her tears with the pads of his thumbs and pressing chaste kisses where her tears had been.

She felt whole, she felt healed, she felt renewed. She covered Thad's hands with her own, her precious Thad. She could feel the smile changing her face and his love changing her life. "You want me to marry you pretty badly, it seems. Perhaps I *could* be persuaded."

"Maybe you'd best tell me what it'll take to persuade you fully."

"A kiss."

"Darlin', now that's something I'd be happy to do." When his lips touched hers, it was perfection. Her soul sighed. Her hopes lifted. Every dream within her was renewed.

The front door burst open with a clatter. "Young man! I do not permit such behavior unless you are engaged! Now unless you're—" Henrietta stopped. "Oh, you are! Noelle, I can tell by that smile on your face. My prayers are answered. You two come in. We've got celebrating to do."

The rain chose that moment to stop. Noelle didn't need to ask Thad if the storm had broken. Warm, soft sunlight spilled over her like grace.

Epilogue

August

Noelle felt a tug at the hem of her skirt as she passed by the corral fence and laughed. She'd been laughing a lot lately; she couldn't help it. She was blissfully happy. "Stormy, are you trying to eat my ruffle again?"

"Yep," Thad answered at her side, always by her side. "That pretty green dress you're wearing obviously looks as tasty as grass to her."

Noelle laughed again, letting her fingertips ruffle the growing filly's mane. Solitude nickered gently, patiently watching over her baby. Both had been a wedding gift from Robert.

"Let go, sweet thing." Thad's low baritone rumbled with happiness and humor, too. "That's right. We'll come see you later, after our ride."

"Yes, we don't want to be late. Henrietta likes supper at six o'clock sharp."

"We'd best get a move on if we want to ride the trail along the river." His hand cupping her elbow was gentle, guiding her down the aisle to where Sunny and Sky, a mustang Thad had bought for her, stood saddled and patiently waiting.

Sunshine kissed her warmly, and the fragrant breezes ruffled the sweet grasses at her feet. It was a beautiful day.

A beautiful life.

Sky nickered and sidled over to nudge Noelle's free hand. Warm breath puffed across her face. Fine whiskers tickled her palm. The mare gently leaned against her, pure affection. Her own horse. Noelle feared she might burst from joy.

Thad's arms slipped around her waist, drawing her against his chest. His voice rumbled cozily. "You're looking mighty happy, Mrs. McKaslin. Care to tell me why?"

"Well, let's see." She let her fingertips trail up the placket of his muslin shirt. "I have a mustang that I love. A ranch I love. A house I love."

"What about me?" There was only pure tenderness in his tone. Only devotion in his words. "What about the husband who adores you?"

She laid her hand on his chest over the beat of his heart. Deep, abiding love welled up from her soul. "My husband?"

"What? You're forgetting about me already?" He was chuckling. His kiss grazed her forehead. "What about your husband?"

"There are no words to say how endlessly I love him." She lifted her face to his. "No number big enough to measure all the ways I love him."

"What a coincidence." His kiss brushed the very tip of her nose. "For that's exactly the way I love you, Noelle. Without condition. Without end."

She knew. Her heart ached with happiness. The past was healed and now there was only the beauty of their lives together. After a shockingly short engagement, according to Henrietta, they had married in May. Three perfect months of marriage had passed, with each day better than the last.

And now there was a new dream to come true. Thad's hand slipped to her tummy, which was still flat, but that would change soon enough.

His lips slanted over hers in a tender, loving kiss. Sweetness filled her heart. Joy left her dizzy. Hope lived in her soul. Yes, theirs was a love that would last forever.

"Henrietta's gonna be mad at me now." He stole one more kiss. "We're definitely going to be late for supper."

"Perhaps she'll forgive us once we announce our good news." It was her turn to steal one last kiss. "She'll be too ecstatic to be really mad at us."

"I know how that feels. I'm ecstatic, too."

She laid her hand on his, and it was the future she saw. Those four upstairs bedrooms full, the house pleasantly loud with children's footsteps and laughter and play. Ida would be watching over them all, sweet and loving. The evenings would be best of all. She would spend them on the front porch beside her husband, hand in hand, heart to heart.

Yes, it was easy to see her dreams these days. Thad was right. Love *was* enough. And when dreams came true, it was called happiness.

"Are you ready?" he asked.

She grabbed hold of the saddle horn and suddenly she was airborne, lifted by Thad's strong arms. She slipped into the saddle and she smoothed her skirts, while Sky stood patiently. The wind ruffled her hair, and she pulled at the strings of her hat, which was hanging down her back. The Stetson slid up into place and its wide brim shaded her face from the sun's heat. "Are you settled okay?" Thad asked, handing her the reins.

She nodded, and while he mounted up with a creak of the saddle, her heart brimmed with gratitude for this wonderful life full of blessings. She knew that God had brought her and Thad together again. The good Lord had blessed her with the privilege of being Thad's wife.

She would be forever thankful to Him. "Ready, darlin'?"

"Ready." She gathered the sun-warmed reins.

They started out together. Side by side they rode into the rays of the sun and through green pastures.

* * * * *

The author of more than fifty novels with more than two million copies sold, **Catherine Palmer** is a Christy Award winner for outstanding Christian romance fiction. Catherine's numerous awards include Best Historical Romance, Best Contemporary Romance, Best of Romance from Southwest Writers Workshop and Most Exotic Historical Romance Novel from *RT Book Reviews*. She is also an *RT Book Reviews* Career Achievement Award winner.

Catherine grew up in Bangladesh and Kenya, and she now makes her home in Georgia. She and her husband have two sons. A graduate of Southwest Baptist University, she also holds a master's degree from Baylor University.

Books by Catherine Palmer

Love Inspired Historical

The Briton
The Maverick's Bride
The Outlaw's Bride
The Gunman's Bride

Steeple Hill Single Title

That Christmas Feeling
Love's Haven
Leaves of Hope
A Merry Little Christmas
The Heart's Treasure
Thread of Deceit
Fatal Harvest
Stranger in the Night

Visit the Author Profile page at Harlequin.com.

THE BRITON

Catherine Palmer

For Mary Edstrom Robitschek,
my dear friend, encourager and prayer warrior.
Thank you for loving and supporting me
all the way back to Rosslyn Academy in Kenya,
and for helping me survive seventh grade math.

Acknowledgments

My great thanks to four special people.

To my agent, Karen Solem, for representing me with such love and care. To my editor, Joan Golan, for believing in *The Briton* twenty-three years after I wrote it. To Mary Robitschek, for transcribing all 694 pages of the manuscript from hard copy to disk.

To Tim Palmer, for seeing the potential in the first book I ever wrote and for reading and editing its 694 pages more times than either of us likes to remember. May God bless you all.

You are all children of God through faith in Christ Jesus.... There is no longer Jew or Gentile, slave or free, male or female. For you are all Christians—you are one in Christ Jesus.

—Galatians 3: 26–28

Chapter One

December 1152
Amounderness in northeast England

Like some relic of a half-forgotten age, the Viking longboat sliced through the icy waters of the natural harbor. Its once brightly painted bow was scarcely visible through a thick coating of barnacles and algae. The sails hung limp and tattered.

A soft dipping of oars drifted through the mist toward an ancient walled keep, where a thin shaft of light from an open window glimmered on the water. An anchor suddenly splashed into the water, shattering the light.

The dark-haired young woman at the window of the keep watched as a small boat, heavily laden with armed men, left the longboat and made its way to shore. A burly old Viking lord stepped from the boat and waded to the beach. Then, with a shout that echoed into the marrow of the woman's bones, he called his men to follow him across the hard sand toward the stronghold.

"The barbarian has come," the woman whispered as she barred the wooden shutter.

* * *

She turned to find her younger sister looking at her with a petulant expression. "Do leave off peering into the night, Bronwen. I want no gloomy tidings on the eve of our winter feast. Just look how Enit has arranged my tunic. Please come and drape it properly."

A chill ran through Bronwen as she hurried from the window across the rush-covered wooden floor toward her sister, who stood by a fire built on a stone hearth in the center of the room. The warm flicker of the flames served only to intensify Bronwen's discontent. And the smoke, drifting upward to the vents in the roof, filled her nostrils with an acrid tang.

How could her father invite the Viking to their feast? To her, the barbarian stood for everything evil that her people, the Briton tribe, had worked so hard and so long to defeat. Vikings! Raiders of villages, ravishers of women, pillagers of the countryside. Why would her father, with the Viking threat all but over, extend the arm of friendship to this barbarian now? Bronwen shook her head in dismay.

But she was forced to smile as she caught sight of Gildan fussing over the folds of her tunic with the nursemaid.

"Sister, you look lovely just as you are," Bronwen admonished. "Let me help you with your gown, and then I shall plait your hair. Most of the guests have arrived, and Father will be growing impatient."

"Yes, only to have us make an appearance and then send us back up to our rooms again so the entertainments may begin." Gildan pouted as her sister arranged a golden gown over her tunic. "I do think this waist is too long, Enit. And just look how pointed the sleeves are!"

The old nurse clucked at her charges. "You two sisters are even fussier than your mother, may she rest in peace. But you do look pretty. As they say, 'Fine feathers make fine birds.'"

Taking an ivory comb, Bronwen divided and began to weave Gildan's hair into two long golden braids. Her sister was entirely lovely, Bronwen realized. Though she had been a sickly child most of her life, tonight Gildan's pale skin glowed rosily and her blue eyes shone. She would make some man a lovely bride to carry on the great line of Edgard the Briton, their ancestor.

At the thought of marriage, Bronwen gazed into the fire. As her fingers continued nimbly in the familiar braiding pattern, Bronwen imagined she could see in the coals a dark shape. A man's black eyes flickered, and in the wraithlike fire his raven hair floated above his temples. Bronwen sensed a strength in his determined jaw, a gentleness in the curve of his lips and a high intelligence in the smooth planes of his forehead.

Sighing, she turned away from the vision she had conjured more than once in the flames. Her father would never link her with such a man. She must wed the one he selected, and his choices were few indeed. He must betroth her to one of the remaining Briton landholders in the area, for her veins coursed with blood of the most ancient tribe still dwelling on the great island of Britain.

"Bronwen, just look at what you've done!" Gildan's voice broke into her sister's reverie. "You have wrapped this ribbon backward. Do stop your daydreaming and help me with my mantle."

Bronwen gathered the soft woolen cloak and laid it over her sister's shoulders. She placed her own mantle on the heavy green gown she wore and arranged her thick black braids over its folds. Kneeling on a pillow, she waited patiently as Enit veiled Gildan and set a circlet of gold on the younger woman's head.

"Bronwen, you do look fine," Enit remarked as she arranged Bronwen's veil. "Let me rub a bit of fat into those dry fingers. You've worked far too hard on this feast. You must learn to let things go a bit, child. And do stop worrying over your father's choice of guests. Edgard is a wise man."

The young woman looked up into Enit's bright eyes. The old nurse had cared for her since Gildan's birth had resulted in their mother's death. Enit's skin hung in thin folds beneath her chin, and tiny lines ran randomly across her face. But when she grinned, as she did now, showing her three good front teeth, each line fell into its accustomed place with ease.

"That's better." Enit chuckled as Bronwen's expression softened. "Now hurry down to the great hall, you two imps, before your father sends up the guard. And, Gildan, remember, 'Silence is golden.'"

"Oh, Enit! Come Bronwen, you carry the rush light, and I shall carry your mantle down the stair."

"Enjoy the feast!" Enit called after them.

Bronwen shook her head in contradiction of the nurse's words. With barbarians in the keep and little to anticipate in the coming year, she felt the evening's feast must be far less than enjoyable. But at last she lifted her head, slipped her arm around her sister and set a smile upon her lips.

As Bronwen followed Gildan down the stone stairs, she breathed deeply the fresh scent of newly laid rushes on the floor. She had worked hard to prepare for the feast, just as she labored at every endeavor. Since her mother's death, she had been mistress of the hall. She had, on occasion, even managed the entire holding while her father was away at battle.

Standing in the light of the entrance to the great hall, the sisters surveyed the merry scene before them. Guests, all of whom were men, stood around the room discussing the latest news from the south. Bronwen recognized most of them. Some were her father's close friends, and others came only because they were loyal to the Briton cause. Few of the men held much land, and many served Norman conquerors.

"Look, Bronwen. Those swinish Vikings are already inside the hall. How vulgar their tongue sounds!" Gildan crossed her arms in contempt.

Bronwen spotted the Viking party in one corner, where they had gathered to tell bawdy stories and laugh raucously. She identified the leader standing in their midst. A heavy old man he was, probably boasting of his battle prowess. He owned Warbreck Castle and its surrounding lands—a holding that adjoined her father's. Thanks be to the gods, he had never threatened Rossall nor made any attempt to seize it. Indeed, he had allied himself with Edgard against the Norman invaders. But a Viking in their halls? A Norse barbarian? She sighed in frustration.

"Look!" Gildan broke in on Bronwen's thoughts. "The minstrels are beginning to play. It's time we made our appearance. I wonder if Aeschby will have come."

"Of course he will. Father has invited all our neighbors."

"How lovely the hall appears tonight!" Gildan said as they made their way toward the dais. Sounds of music—

lutes, harps, dulcimers and pipes—drifted down from
the gallery at the far end of the hall. Beneath it stood a
high table draped in white linen and a green overcloth.
Metal tankards and goblets were scattered across its surface and down the two long side tables next to the walls.

Cupbearers bustled from one man to another offering
drinks. Servitors removed platters, pitchers and spoons
from the cupboard and laid them on the tables.

As the sisters made their way through the crowded
hall, Gildan admired aloud the sheaves of wheat deco-
rating the tables, and the green ivy, holly and mistletoe
hanging from the torches. "Father is looking well tonight," she whispered. "Is that Aeschby he stands with?
What a fine red tunic he wears."

Bronwen spotted the tall blond man across the room.
He stood well above their father in height. Because of
the tract of land he held across the Wyre River to the
east, and because of his Briton bloodline, Aeschby often
had been mentioned as a possible husband for Bronwen,
even though they were cousins.

But Bronwen had never cared for Aeschby. The times
they had met as children, he had played cruel tricks
on her and Gildan. And once he had dropped a kitten
to its death from the battlements just to see if it could
land on its feet.

"Indeed, Aeschby appears in good spirits tonight,"
Bronwen had to acknowledge. "But look, the piper has
seen us, and now the feasting begins."

As she spoke, trumpets sounded and each man
moved to his appointed place, according to his rank.
The sisters stepped onto the dais and waited beside
their father's chair. Bronwen looked fondly at the heavy,
aged man as he lumbered to his place. His long white

mustaches hung far down into his beard. And though the top of his head was bald, thick locks of snowy hair fell to his shoulders. He had always been a proud man, Edgard the Briton, and he stood tall before his guests.

"Welcome, welcome one and all. The house of Edgard enjoins all friends of the great Briton kingdom of this isle to share in our winter feast."

He lifted his golden cup high over his head, and a mighty cheer rose from the crowd.

"Now let us eat in fellowship. And when my daughters are gone to bed, we shall enjoy an even greater merriment!" At that all the men burst into laughter. Bronwen glanced over to see Gildan blushing. "But before they are gone, Edgard the Briton will make an announcement of great import to all gathered here. And now, let the feasting begin!"

Bronwen sank into her chair. An announcement of great import? What could her father mean? Perhaps he had some news of the civil war between the Norman king, Stephen, and his cousin, the Empress Matilda, both of whom claimed the throne of England. Yet Bronwen felt quite certain the news was something closer to herself. She knew it must be the announcement of her betrothal in marriage, for her father had been hinting of an arrangement for many months now.

But to whom? Edgard had called Bronwen to his side upon her last birthday. She remembered thinking how old and withered he looked. Though his body was still strong, he had put on much weight, and he often complained of aches in his joints. Bronwen recalled how he had placed his arm around her shoulders, a sign of affection he had not displayed since she was a child. "Bronwen, you have eighteen years, now." His voice had been filled with emotion. "You are well into womanhood. For too long I have depended on you for the management of my household. You remind me so of your mother when she arrived from Wales to become my wife."

Her father had stopped speaking for a moment and gazed at his thick fingers, entwined in his sash. Though the marriage had been arranged by their fathers, Bronwen knew he had truly cared for her mother.

"Now it is time that you had a husband. Though we are dwindled in number, there are some men remaining who sympathize with our cause. Bronwen, I want you to know I have been negotiating for your marriage, that you may prepare yourself for what lies ahead."

Was this to be the night she learned of his plan? Bronwen looked at her father. He was talking with Gildan and admiring her long golden braids and the bright ribbons binding them. Yes, Bronwen was certain her father meant to announce her marriage betrothal.

How paltry all her dreams seemed in the harsh light of this reality. She felt foolish at the memory of the man she had so often imagined in the fire. Indeed, she had to smile at the childish imagination that had led her to believe she someday might wed such a one.

As the servitors poured into the hall bearing food and drink, a commotion near the door drew Bronwen's attention. A small band of strangers dressed in heavy woolen mantles had entered the great hall. At their head stood a tall figure whose hood concealed his features from the curious crowd.

"Edgard the Briton," the man spoke through the fold of cloth as he approached the dais. "We weary travelers request your kindness upon us this night. We ask to sup with you before we resume our journey."

Edgard studied the visitors before replying. "This is our winter feast. Who are you, and whom do you serve?"

"We are merely wanderers, sir."

"Sup with us, then, and be welcome. But take heed… we are men of strength and power. We tolerate no deceit."

The robed man bowed slightly in acknowledgment and led his companions to a table among the guards lowest in rank. Bronwen watched as he began his meal without removing his hood.

"Father, why do you speak of deceit?" she asked. "And why will this stranger not reveal himself to us?"

Edgard looked grim. "There have been rumors for many months now that the Empress Matilda's son, Henry Plantagenet, is spying out our land. He hopes to make it his own one day. Of course, King Stephen will never allow it as long as he lives. Though we have not chosen sides in this war between Stephen and Matilda, I do not like the idea of spies on our land."

"And you think this man could be a spy? Is that the announcement of which you spoke, Father?"

Edgard squeezed his daughter's hand and shook his head. "Bronwen, leave these matters to men. Look now! Aeschby has risen to pay homage to me. Let us hear him and dismiss this weighty talk."

Edgard took his knife to a hunk of spicy meat as Aeschby strode to the dais. Gildan, obviously enjoying herself, picked up a tart. She was unconcerned by her father's announcement, Bronwen realized. Probably, Gildan assumed it was purely political in nature.

Bronwen cut a sliver of omelet, but its strong onion smell displeased her. She stared down from the dais at

Aeschby in his bright red tunic. Was he the one chosen for her? She had a sizable dowry—all her father's land, upon his death, would go to Bronwen's husband, according to Briton custom. And this acreage, together with Aeschby's, would reunite the old lands and make a fine large holding.

He was looking now at the dais, his white teeth gleaming in a proud smile. Bronwen had heard that Aeschby was a cruel and harsh master to his serfs, and he had been known to fly into rages.

But at this moment, he appeared serene as he gazed—not at Bronwen—but at her sister. Gildan had blossomed into womanhood, and she was beautiful. Though the younger woman had no land dowry, Bronwen was certain her father would provide much gold to the man she would wed.

Gildan hardly needed gold to draw the attention of a man. Aeschby could not keep his eyes from her. And Bronwen noticed Gildan glancing at him from time to time with a coy smile upon her lips.

Perhaps there was some true affection between the two. Bronwen dreaded the thought of marriage to a man who desired her sister.

Aeschby now signaled one of his retainers. The man carried a black box from his position at a table below the salt container. Together they stepped up to the dais, and Aeschby lifted the box from the hands of his kneeling servant.

"Take this heirloom, my lord," he addressed Edgard, "as a sign of my loyalty to you, and of my fealty to our Briton cause."

A loud cheer rose from the crowd as Aeschby lifted a golden neck-ring from the box and held it high over his head. It was a truly magnificent work, hand-wrought many generations ago for some unknown king.

Edgard received the ring and thanked Aeschby. "This young lord shows himself to be a treasure-giver worthy of his noble heritage," he said. "I accept this ring as a father accepts a gift from his son."

At that, another roar went up, drowning the sound of the minstrels as they announced the second course of the feast. Bronwen was impressed with the gift her father had been given, but she was startled to hear him address Aeschby as "son." Perhaps there was truth in her speculation that their betrothal would be announced that evening.

The next courses came and went, but to Bronwen the meal seemed a blur. According to her plan, mince pies, dilled veal balls, baked lamprey eels, swan-neck pudding, giblet custard pie, currant tart and elderberry funnel cake marched out of the kitchen one after the other. Men rose and gave one another treasures, as at all feasts, and speeches of thanks and boasting followed. Bronwen sampled little of the foods set before her, but her father and Gildan ate with relish.

"Father, Bronwen has been deep in thought all evening," Gildan said over the din. "Perhaps we should have a song to waken her." Gildan looked at her sister with teasing eyes.

Edgard laughed. "Always the pensive one, Bronwen. Indeed, it is time for the boar's head now!" He called the musicians. "Let us sing to the boar's head on this night of feasting."

As the marshal entered the hall bearing a large platter, all the company stood and began to sing. Bronwen noticed that the tall stranger had risen, but a hood still covered his features.

"The boar's head in hand bear I," the feasters sang. "Bedecked with bays and rosemary, and I pray you my masters, be merry!"

As the song ended, the marshal knelt before Edgard and offered the platter to him. "And now may the gods bless all noble sons of Britain," Edgard said. "May the coming year bring prosperity to one and all."

The carver sliced the meat, and the servers passed it from one guest to another. As feasters cut into the delicacy, Bronwen tried to believe this was to be a happy evening after all. There was no need to dwell on gloomy things. Even if she were to marry Aeschby, she could return often to her beloved home to visit Gildan and her father. These were her people, the Briton men, and she must—indeed she wished to—carry on their lineage.

Then a movement caught her eye, and she turned to see the old Viking leader rise from his seat. "I salute you noble Edgard the Briton, ring-giver and sword-wielder," he said in a strong voice.

Bronwen noted that the other men quieted as the barbarian spoke, some glancing darkly at the Viking. It was clear to her that this man was resented at the feast, though Edgard appeared pleased with the salutation. It was strange to hear her father addressed as *ring-giver,* for he had awarded few treasures in recent years. No battles had been won or glories deserved.

"A feasting so fine as this," the man continued, "we Vikings have never before seen. We commend the food-provider and the hall-adorner for this pleasure."

Bronwen wanted to laugh at the odd way his Norse tongue spoke their language. It was an outrage against decency to have him here. Yet the barbarian was making some effort to be civilized. She scrutinized the heavy brown woolen tunic he wore, so out of place in the brightly decorated hall. As he lumbered forward, Bronwen wondered what his gift would be. The barbarian was an old man, nearly the age of her father. Though his hair and beard were still the color of saffron, his face was crisscrossed with lines and his walk was pained.

"I, Olaf Lothbrok," he intoned, "who have done many brave deeds, who have crossed the salt sea and borne hardship on the waves, I, who have wrestled with the whale-fishes and battled mighty monsters, I come gladly into the hall of the strong and generous Edgard. Before this one filled with manly courage, this battle-brave ring-giver and treasure-lord, I present this cross."

Bronwen gasped. The cross he now held before her father was a work of immeasurable value. Almost as long as his arm from elbow to hand, the piece was wrought in fine gold and set with rubies and sapphires. It was obviously a relic stolen from some Norman church the barbarian or his father had raided. Though Bronwen knew little about this religion that had been brought to Britain by wanderers known as Christians, she believed all sacred objects should be respected. How could such a gift—a plundered holy symbol—be accepted? Yet here was her father now, holding the cross and admiring its workmanship.

"Olaf Lothbrok," Edgard addressed the man, "this generous gift I receive from the hand of a neighbor and friend. Though our people were once at war, now—in these difficult times—we are allies."

A murmur arose from the men, and Bronwen noticed the hooded stranger at the far end of the room speaking with great animation to his companions. She was appalled. It was bad enough to invite the Viking to the feast—a move Bronwen had protested vehemently—but for Edgard the Briton to claim him as a friend and ally? Surely her father had lost his wits. Bronwen turned to Gildan and saw her staring open-mouthed at the Viking as he returned to his table.

It was too much! Bronwen wanted to bolt from the room, escape the house and run down to the beach, where she could sit alone and ponder what her father's actions could mean. The Britons had tried to keep themselves a pure race, never to be allied with such a people as this old Viking and his Norse companions. Blood pounding through her head, Bronwen forced a deep breath as she watched her father step back onto the dais and lay the cross on the table.

"Fellow Britons," her father said loudly, "at the start of the feast, I spoke to you of a great announcement. As you know, I am possessed of two fine treasures. Stand, Bronwen! Stand, Gildan!"

Bronwen rose shakily to her feet, and the men began to cheer. Gildan had turned pale and appeared also to be short of breath.

"Though I have no sons to continue the line of my forefathers, I have two daughters, both now of marriageable age. They are fine women, and through long negotiations, I have found worthy husbands for both."

So it was to be Gildan, too, Bronwen realized. Poor Gildan. For so long she had dreamed of a husband, and now that her betrothal was to be announced, she stood ashen and shivering. Bronwen longed to go and take her sister's hand as she had done when they were children.

"My elder daughter, Bronwen," Edgard continued,

"the child who seems almost the spirit of her mother, so nearly do they look alike—I now betroth to Olaf Lothbrok."

At the name, Bronwen gasped aloud, incredulous at her father's words. Gildan cried out, and all the company of men began to murmur at once.

"Silence please," Edgard spoke up. "Allow me to continue. My daughter Gildan I betroth to Aeschby Godwinson. Gildan brings to her marriage one fourth of all my gold and treasure, and upon my death I will her to receive one fourth more."

Half! At this news, the men cheered wildly. Bronwen saw that bright spots of pink had flowed back into Gildan's cheeks, and her sister was smiling again. Aeschby moved to the dais and stood proudly beside his betrothed.

Edgard spoke above the roar. "Bronwen brings to her marriage one half of all my gold and treasure." He stretched out his hands, motioning for silence. "Now you must listen carefully, Britons. Hear my will to my daughter Bronwen upon my death."

The men in the room fell silent, and even the servitors stopped to listen. Bronwen knotted her fingers together as her father continued to speak.

"When I die, Bronwen will receive *all* my lands and this Rossall Hall into her own hands. They will not pass under the governance of her husband, Olaf Lothbrok, as is the Briton custom. I shall not permit my possessions to slip from the hands of my tribe. If my daughter Bronwen gives birth to a son by this Viking, then the inheritance will fall to the son upon his coming of age. If she has a daughter or no child, at her death these lands will pass to Aeschby and his lineage through my daughter Gildan."

Edgard stopped speaking for a moment and looked long at his stunned guests. Then he began to recite the many brave deeds of his forefathers, those beloved tales Bronwen knew so well. As the Briton talked, Olaf Lothbrok moved from his bench and came to stand beside her. Bronwen drew back from the touch of his woolen tunic as it grazed her hand. She could not bear to look at this man or meet the hard gaze of the silent Briton company.

Instead, she found herself staring down at her own slippers, intricately crafted of gold threads and purple embroidery. Edgard had brought them for her from the market fair in Preston, and she had saved them for this special feast. Her eyes wandered to the large leather boots of the Viking. They were caked with mud and sand, and small bits of seaweed clung to their thick crossed bindings.

Could she ever learn to care for the man who wore those boots? Would she one day look forward to the heavy sound of their entrance into her chamber? Would there be a time when her eyes grew accustomed to their presence beside her own thin slippers at the foot of their marriage bed?

Bronwen shook her head, then shuddered as she felt the barbarian's huge hand close around her own. Why had her father done this? She could make no sense of his plans. At last she lifted her chin as the Viking beside her raised their hands high above their heads.

"And so the continuation of the great line of Briton nobles is assured," her father was saying. "I have accomplished this by the favorable marriages of my two daughters to these worthy men."

For a moment, the room was silent. Slowly one or two guests began to applaud, then several others pounded their mugs upon the tables. At last the entire company broke into a thunderous roar of cheering and shouting.

Bronwen looked up in time to see the group of travelers rise and move toward the door. Their tall leader bowed toward the dais, then stepped out of the great hall. Bronwen gave their departure little thought, for the eyes of the Briton guests burned into her. She dared not look into any man's face, for she knew she would find it filled with questioning, doubt and pity.

As Edgard finished speaking, he turned to Bronwen and wrapped his arms around her, though she knew no warmth from the embrace. Then he grasped Olaf Lothbrok by the shoulders and congratulated him heartily. Finally he turned to embrace Gildan and Aeschby, and Bronwen knew she was at last free to go.

Without another look around the hall she had worked so hard to prepare, she pulled her hand from the grip of the Viking and stepped down from the dais. As she hurried toward the door, she felt a hand catch hold of her skirt.

"Welcome to the family, Briton," one of Olaf's men said in a mocking voice. "We look forward to the presence of a woman at our hall."

Bronwen grasped her tunic and yanked it from the Viking's thick fingers. As she stepped away from the table, she heard the drunken laughter of the barbarians behind her.

Running down the stone steps toward the heavy oak door that led outside from the keep, Bronwen gathered her mantle about her. She ordered the doorman to open the door, and he did so reluctantly, pressing her to carry a torch. But Bronwen pushed past him and fled into the darkness.

Dashing down the steep, pebbled hill toward the beach, she felt the frozen ground give way to sand. She threw off her veil and circlet and kicked away her shoes and mantle. The sand was cold on her feet as she raced alongside the pounding surf, and hot tears of anger and shame welled up and streamed down her cheeks. Unable to think beyond her humiliation, Bronwen ran—her long braids streaming behind her, falling loose, drifting like a tattered black flag.

Blinded with weeping, she did not see the dark form that sprang up in her path. Iron arms circled her, and a heavy cloak threatened suffocation.

"Release me!" she cried. "Guard! Guard, help me."

"Hush, my lady." A deep voice emanated from the darkness. The man spoke her tongue, though his accent was neither Norman French nor any other that she recognized. "I mean you no harm. What demon drives you to run through the night without fear for your safety?"

"Set me free at once! I demand it!"

"I shall hold you until you calm yourself. We had heard there were witches in Amounderness, but I had not thought to meet one this night."

Still bound by the man's arms, Bronwen drew back and peered up at the hooded figure. "You! You and your band of wastrels spied on our feast. Unhand me, or I shall call the guard upon you."

The man chuckled at this and turned toward his companions, who stood in a group nearby. Bronwen caught hold of the back of his hood and jerked it down to reveal a head of glossy raven curls. But the man's face was shrouded in darkness yet, and as he looked at her, she could not read his expression.

"So, you are the blessed bride-to-be." He returned the hood to his head. "Your father has paired you in an interesting manner."

Relieved that her captor did not appear to be a highwayman, she pushed away from him and sagged onto the wet sand. "Please leave me here alone. I need peace to think. Go on your way."

The tall stranger shrugged off his outer mantle and wrapped it around her shoulders. "Why did your father betroth you to the aged Viking?" he asked.

"For one purported to be a spy, you know precious little about Amounderness. But I shall tell you, as it is all common knowledge."

Despite her wariness of the man, she pulled his cloak about her, reveling in its warmth. "This land, known as Amounderness, has always been Briton territory. Olaf Lothbrok, my betrothed, came here as a youth when the Viking invasions had nearly subsided. He conquered the Briton lord of the holding directly to the south of Rossall Hall, where he now makes his home. Then the vile Normans came, and Amounderness was pillaged by William the Conqueror's army."

The man squatted on the sand beside Bronwen. He listened with obvious interest as she continued. "When William took an account of Amounderness in his Domesday Book, he recorded no remaining lords and few people at all. Some say it was because our marshy land was too difficult for his census-takers to penetrate. Perhaps so. But our tales insist that the Britons had hidden in caves and secret places of the forest."

"And when the Normans retreated?"

"We crept out of hiding and returned to our halls. My father's family reoccupied Rossall Hall, our ancient stronghold. And there we live, as we should, watching over our serfs as they fish and grow their meager crops. Indeed, there is not much here for the greedy Normans to covet, if they are the ones for whom you spy."

Unable to continue speaking when her heart was so heavy, Bronwen stood and turned toward the sea. Rising beside her, the traveler touched her arm. "Olaf Lothbrok's lands—together with your father's—will reunite most of Amounderness under the rule of the son you are beholden to bear. A clever plan. Your sister's future husband holds the rest of the adjoining lands, I understand."

"You've done your work, sir. Your lord will be pleased. Who is he—some land-hungry Scottish baron? Or have you forgotten that King Stephen gave Amounderness to the Scots, as a trade for their support in his war with Matilda? I certainly hope your lord is not a Norman. He would be so disappointed to learn he has no legal rights here. Now, if you will excuse me, I shall return to Rossall."

"Amounderness is Scottish by law," the man said, stopping her short. "Would you be so sorry to see it returned to Norman hands?"

"*Returned* to the Normans? Amounderness belongs to the Briton tribe. Neither Stephen nor David of Scotland has deigned to set foot here. We are a pawn in their game. As far as I am concerned, it matters not who believes himself to own our land—so long as he does not bring troops or build fortresses here. Tell your lord that any man who aspired to that folly would find a mighty battle on his hands. We Britons do not intend to forfeit our holding."

Bronwen turned and began walking back along the beach toward Rossall Hall. She felt better for her run, and having explained her father's plan to the stranger, it didn't seem so far-fetched anymore. Distant lights twinkled through the fog rolling in from the west, and she suddenly realized what a long way she had come.

"My lady," the man's voice called out behind her.

Bronwen kept walking, unwilling to speak to him again. She didn't care what he reported to his master. She wanted only to return to the warmth of her chamber and feel the softness of Enit's hands plaiting her hair before she dropped off to sleep.

"My lady, you have quite a walk ahead of you." The traveler strode to her side. "I shall accompany you to your destination."

"You leave me no choice in the matter."

"I am not one to compromise myself, dear lady. I follow the path God has set before me and none other."

"And just who are you?"

"I am called Jacques Le Brun."

"French?" Given his accent, she had not expected this. "Then you are a Norman."

The man chuckled. "Not nearly as Norman as you are Briton."

As they approached the fortress, Bronwen could see that the guests had not yet begun to disperse. Perhaps no one had missed her, and she could slip quietly into bed beside Gildan.

She turned to go, but Le Brun took her arm and studied her face in the moonlight. Then, gently, he drew her into the folds of his hooded cloak. "Perhaps the bride would like the memory of a younger man's embrace to warm her," he whispered.

Astonished, Bronwen attempted to remove his arms from around her waist. But she could not escape his lips as they found her own. The kiss was soft and warm, melting away her resistance like the sun upon the snow. Before she had time to react, he was striding back down the beach.

Bronwen stood stunned for a moment, clutching his woolen mantle about her. Suddenly she cried out, "Wait, Le Brun! Your mantle!"

The dark one turned to her. "Keep it for now," he shouted into the wind. "I shall ask for it when we meet again."

Chapter Two

"Bronwen! Bronwen!" A thin high voice drifted through the mist. Bronwen turned from the shadow of the retreating man and looked toward the keep. Enit was searching for her.

Hurrying along the wet sand, Bronwen cried out, "Enit! I'm here!"

"Silly girl," the nursemaid scolded as she scurried down the hill. At the bottom she picked up Bronwen's slippers and waved them in the air. "You'll catch your death in this cold, and I cannot say I shall be sorry to be rid of you. Hurry up, hurry up, foolish girl!"

Bronwen laughed in spite of herself. "A fool's head never whitens, Enit," she chirped, throwing one of the nursemaid's favorite proverbs back at her.

Enit stopped, exasperated. "You'll see I'm right. You'll be sick before tomorrow. Time trieth truth."

Bronwen slipped her arm around her old nursemaid as they made their way up the incline. "I'm to marry the Viking, Enit," she said softly.

"I have heard." They walked on in silence for a moment. "Your sister is pleased with her match. You must try to share her joy."

As they passed into the courtyard and climbed the stairs, Bronwen noticed the old woman was trembling. This must be a sad day for Enit, too. Her charges soon would leave the hall and travel to new homes. The women crossed the entrance to the great hall, but Bronwen did not look inside. She could hear the throaty laughter of the men and the music of the pipers.

Soon the guests would listen to tales from the scop and gawk at the jugglers and tumblers she had hired. But Bronwen desired only to slip under the heavy warm blankets of her bed.

As she and Enit entered the sleeping chamber, Gildan rushed toward them, face aglow. "Oh, Bronwen! Where have you been? Such a day! I'm to marry Aeschby!" She whirled about the room. "I'm so happy! Did you see his face when Father said—"

Gildan stopped short when she noticed Bronwen's wind-tangled hair and tattered gown. "Have you been on the beach? Whatever for? Oh dear sister, I'm such a fool. You aren't happy at all."

"I'm not happy at the moment," Bronwen said. "That is true. But I'm not sad either. Our fate is in the hands of the gods, is it not? Now let me remove these damp tunics, and you must tell me everything Aeschby said to you."

Enit pushed Bronwen toward the fire, then bustled about stripping off the damp gowns and rubbing the girl down with heavy linen cloths. Gildan, too excited to sympathize long with Bronwen's situation, chatted joyfully as she combed the tangles from her sister's hair.

Soon Enit ordered her charges to bed and took her

own place on the cot outside their door. While Gildan slept, Bronwen lay staring up at the dark ceiling, too troubled to sleep despite her exhaustion. She had been betrothed to the old Viking—and then the dark stranger had taken her in his arms. But one memory weighed even more heavily than the other. Why had she not resisted the Norman's embrace? She had been taught to despise his breed—and truly she did. Yet, why did the warmth of his kiss still linger on her lips? And what of his parting words? Certainly their paths would never cross again.

And yet...

Bronwen reached for the woolen mantle she had pushed under a blanket so no one would notice it. She held it to her cheek and recalled her wild run down the beach. A faintly spicy scent still clung to the folds of the garment, evoking the presence of the raven-haired traveler.

A girl must marry for the good of her family, Bronwen reminded herself as she closed her eyes and stroked the rough black wool. Everyone knew that.

Yet, was it possible that the gods who inhabited the trees and the stones and the driving seas that surrounded Amounderness had another destiny in store for her?

The morning dawned under threatening skies, and Bronwen awoke to Gildan's fervent tugging.

"It worked! It worked, Bronwen," Gildan cried. "I dreamt of my future husband. I put one shoe on either side of the bed, as Enit told me. Then I put rosemary in one and thyme in the other. I slept on my back all night. And I did dream of the one I'm to marry—Aeschby!"

Gildan danced around the room, her gowns flying. "Get up, silly goose! We must make haste to welcome the day. Hurry."

At the commotion, Enit entered the room and began to take the sisters' tunics from a wooden chest.

"My red one, Enit," Gildan commanded. "And for my sister, the purple."

Bronwen struggled from the bed and quickly opened another chest to hide the mantle Le Brun had wrapped around her the night before. As she combed out her long hair, Enit dressed her. Then Bronwen plaited her hair and slipped on her shoes.

"Are you well, Bronwen?" Enit asked.

"Quite," Bronwen replied.

"Good, then listen closely to what I tell you now." Enit spoke in a low voice. "The Viking fears that a large storm is gathering and will hinder his sea passage, making his land vulnerable to attack during his absence. He insists that your marriage ceremony take place tomorrow."

Bronwen was too stunned to reply. She had thought the wedding was weeks or even months away. Before she could question Enit further, Gildan pulled her down the stairs into the hall. It was crowded with men, some still sleeping and others conversing quietly. Servants carried about jugs of frumenty and chamomile tea. Bronwen accepted a bowl of the hot, spicy frumenty and took a spoonful. The milky concoction laden with raisins warmed her stomach.

"Your appetite has returned, daughter," Edgard said, coming up behind her. Despite the night's revelries, her father looked hale and wore a broad grin. "I know the announcement of your betrothal was unexpected. Yet,

I hope not too unpleasant. Lothbrok is a good man, and he will treat you fairly."

"But, Father, must the wedding take place so soon? Surely it is not our custom nor the Vikings' to have a wedding follow an engagement by two short days!"

Edgard frowned. "I worry more about the reaction to my will than I do about this hasty wedding to a Norseman."

Bronwen knew by his tone of voice that arguing was futile. "I believe all will be well. Enit told me there was much excitement in the kitchen last night."

Edgard nodded. "It is a novel idea, but I saw no better way to preserve our holdings. After lengthy negotiation, Lothbrok agreed. Come with me, daughter. I must show you something."

Bronwen followed her father from the hall toward the chamber built below ground many generations before. As they made their way through the darkness, she heard him fumbling with his keys. At length, they reached the door that Bronwen knew led into the treasure room. Her father unlocked the door and beckoned her inside.

The chamber was filled with wooden chests, one stacked upon another, and all locked and sealed. Once, as a child, when she and Gildan had been exploring the keep and its grounds, they had come upon this room. Bronwen had to smile at the memories of her adventures with her reluctant sister. Scaling the timber palisade that surrounded the keep, getting lost in the forest, stumbling upon the entrance to a secret tunnel and following it from outside the walls to a trapdoor ending somewhere deep beneath the fortress—all were a part of the childhood she soon would leave behind forever.

"These treasures one day will be yours," Edgard

said, interrupting her thoughts. "Some will go to Gildan, of course. Gold coins and bars fill the chests. Several contain jewels. When I am gone, Bronwen, you must see that this room is well guarded."

"Yes, Father," Bronwen answered, conscious of the great responsibility he placed upon her.

"But this small chest contains the greatest treasure of all." Edgard lifted an ornate gold box to the torchlight. "It is my will—set down in writing. As you well know, in declaring that you will inherit my domain upon my death, I have broken a long Briton tradition. Some of our countrymen may see fit to overlook or disregard the pronouncement. But beyond providing us with a reliable ally in Lothbrok, this document does two important things."

"What are they, Father?"

"It keeps these holdings in Briton hands. Though they be the hands of a woman, you are capable of managing them. Of this I am confident. And this will encourages you to bear a son soon or to remarry quickly should Lothbrok die. Though the lands will be yours, you *must* remarry in order to provide a reliable caretaker."

"Why Lothbrok?" Bronwen asked. "Aeschby is the stronger ally."

"I had to give you to the weaker. If Gildan were to wed Olaf, nothing would prevent his changing loyalties upon an invasion. He could simply conquer Rossall for himself under the authority of King Stephen or Matilda. But with you as Olaf's wife, Bronwen, he has hope of securing our lands through a child. The Viking will defend all lands destined for his future heirs."

Bronwen knew her father spoke the truth. And like

him, she felt confident that she was as well trained to oversee the land and serfs as a son would have been. Indeed, she had been left in charge several times when her father had gone away to battle or to meet with other lords. Yet the law of inheritance remained, and she accepted that it was right for a man to be the primary caretaker of an estate and all its assets.

"The will inside this box," Edgard told her as he drew a golden key from his cloak and inserted it into the lock, "was inscribed by the same scholar who came from Preston to teach you and Gildan to speak the French tongue of Britain's Norman invaders."

When her father lifted the lid, Bronwen saw a folded parchment imprinted with her father's seal. He touched it with his fingertips as he spoke. "Whether written in my native tongue or in French, I cannot read this document to know what was written. But my marshal assured me the scribe was an honest man. And he taught you well, did he not?"

Bronwen recalled the months the balding man had spent instructing her and Gildan in the cramped room behind the great hall. She had objected to having to learn Norman French. After all, why should they compromise themselves to speak that hated tongue?

"Times are changing, daughter," Edgard spoke up. "You do not know half of what happens now in England. There is much turmoil, and our dream of reuniting this island under Briton rule grows ever more dim. Though I send out my spies and discuss such matters with other Briton landholders, even I am unaware of many things. But this I know—the written oath will prove more convincing than the spoken."

"Can this be possible, Father?" Bronwen asked.

"Among the Britons, a man's word must be true. The history of our people is known only through the stories and ballads of the scops and bards. Few Britons can read and write more than their names. Indeed, I believe Gildan and I may be the only speakers of Norman French in all Amounderness."

"This is a new world, daughter," Edgard said in a low voice. "And not a good one. Promise me you will guard this box, Bronwen. Keep the key always about your neck. *Never* take it off!"

"Of course, and may the gods protect it." She took the golden key and slipped it onto the chain about her neck. By the urgency of her father's speech, she understood that his strange deed was important. More than once he had consulted with those deep forest-dwellers who could foresee the future, and his plans had served their family.

"Father, I thank you for leaving me your lands. Though I cannot desire a union with the Viking Lothbrok, I understand its purpose. I shall obey you, as I always have. My desire is to bear a son soon, that you may know our Briton line continues."

Edgard smiled. "Your obedience pleases me, Bronwen. When you depart Rossall, carry this box with you unobserved. No one must suspect its contents. Come let us return now to the hall, for we must prepare to see you wed."

As they climbed the stairs and approached the great hall again, Bronwen spotted a young man with flaming red hair. He sat with his back against the wall, a desolate expression on his face. Concerned as always for her people, she tucked the golden will box under her cloak, left her father's side and went to him.

"You are troubled," she declared.

"Seasick," he corrected her, speaking their tongue in the crude fashion of Briton peasants. "All night. I never felt worse in me life. I'm the serf of them brutish Vikings, you see. Now morning comes, and I'm hungry as a wolf. Poor Wag, I says to meself, sick and hungry. But all the food is gone—not even a trencher to be had."

"I shall see you are given something to eat, Wag," she told him. "But first—tell me something of your lord. He is to be my husband."

The peasant scrambled to his feet and made an awkward bow. "Be you the bride then? The daughter of Edgard?"

She smiled. "Indeed I am."

"Much obliged for your kindness, my lady. The Viking is a good master, though his men can be cruel at times. I fear you will see little of your new husband, for he follows the ways of his forefathers and is often gone to sea in his horrid, creaky boat."

This came as glad news on a day of unhappy and confusing surprises. Bronwen thought of questioning Wag further, but she decided against it.

"Go into the kitchen and tell cook that the lord's black-haired daughter promised you a large bowl of frumenty, with plenty of raisins."

"Thank you, ma'am. And best wishes in your marriage."

In her bedchamber, Bronwen found Gildan in a flurry of excitement. The younger woman had learned that her wedding, too, would take place the next day—a decision Aeschby had made on learning of the Viking's plans. Bronwen pursed her lips as her sister thrust three tunics into her arms and bade her decide which was the loveliest.

"I adore the red," Gildan said with a pout, "but silly old Enit keeps saying, 'Married in red, you'll wish yourself dead.' And I do so admire this green woolen, but 'Married in green, ashamed to be seen!' I am attached to the red, but Enit says blue is good luck. 'Married in blue, love ever true.'"

"Does she now? Then blue it must be."

"But this is such a dull, common tunic!"

Gildan appeared so distressed that Bronwen had to suppress a chuckle. "Come, sister. You must have the golden ribbon that was brought to me from the last fair at Preston. We shall stitch it down the front of this blue woolen, and you can trim the sleeves with that ermine skin you have had for years."

"Oh, Bronwen, you are so clever!" Gildan embraced her sister. "Indeed, it will be the loveliest gown Aeschby has ever seen. Is my lord not a handsome man? And powerful! And rich! The gods have smiled on me indeed."

Realizing she must begin to think of her own nuptials, Bronwen went to the chest where she kept her most elegant tunics. But as she lifted the lid, the mantle given her the night before by the stranger slid onto the floor. Hastily, lest anyone notice, she swept it up. As she began folding it into the chest again, her attention fell on the garment's lining. It was a peacock-blue silk, startling in its contrast to the plain black wool of the outer fabric. Even more stunning was the insignia embroidered upon the lining near the hood. A crest had been worked in pure gold threads, and centered within the crest were three golden balls.

The elegance of the fabric and the nobility of the crest gave evidence of a wealthy owner of some influence and power. *Jacques Le Brun*. Who could he be, and why did the mere thought of the man stir her blood?

Bronwen pressed the mantle deeply into the corner of the chest and took out several tunics. "What do you think of these, Gildan?" she asked, forcing a light tone to her voice. "Which do you like best?"

Gildan took the garments and fluttered about the room, busy with her plans. But Bronwen's thoughts had left the warm, smoky chamber to center upon a dark traveler with raven curls and a kiss that could not be forgotten.

As the day passed, it was decided that Enit would go to live with Bronwen at the holding of the Viking— Warbreck Castle. Gildan protested, but she was silenced with Enit's stubborn insistence that this was how it must be. She could not be divided in half, could she? By custom, the older girl should retain her. Pleased at the knowledge that her faithful companion would share the future with her, Bronwen tried to shake the sense of impending doom that hung over her.

During the day, Bronwen worked to fit and embroider the wedding gowns. In the hall below, Edgard's men stacked the girls' dowry chests along with heavy trunks of their clothing and personal belongings. But Bronwen slid the small gold box containing Edgard's will into the chatelaine purse she would hook to a chain that hung at her waist.

Toward evening, the hall filled once again with the

sounds and smells of a feast. Rather than joining yet another meal with her future husband, Bronwen bade Enit walk with her in silence along the shore as the sun sank below the horizon. Looking up at Rossall Hall, Bronwen pondered her past and the years to come. She must accept the inevitable. At Warbreck Castle, there would be no pleasure in the nearness of the sea, no joy in the comforts of a familiar hall, no satisfaction in the embrace of a husband.

Surely for Gildan, marriage might someday become a source of joy in the arms of one who cared for her. But for Bronwen, only the heavy belly and grizzled face of an old man awaited. As she imagined her wedding night, Bronwen again reflected on the traveler who had held her. Though she tried to contain her emotion, she sniffled, and tears began to roll down her cheeks.

"Fare you well, Bronwen?" the old woman asked.

"Dearest Enit," she burst out. "I cannot bear this fate! Why do the gods punish me? What ill have I done?"

She threw herself on the old woman's shoulder and began to sob. But instead of the expected tender caress, Bronwen felt her head jerked back in the tight grip of the nurse's gnarled hands.

"Bronwen, hold your tongue!" Enit snapped. "Be strong. Look!"

Bronwen followed the pointed direction of the long, crooked finger, and she saw the fearsome profile of her future husband's Viking ship. It was a longship bedecked for war—a Viking *snekkar*—and it floated unmoving, like a serpent awaiting its prey.

"Enit, we must hurry home." Bronwen spoke against her nursemaid's ear. She must not be met on the beach by Olaf Lothbrok's men. They would question her and perhaps accuse her of trying to escape. Now she had no choice but to return to her chamber and make final preparations for her wedding. When Lothbrok saw her the following morning, she would be wearing her wedding tunic, having prepared herself to become a wife.

At their request, the two brides ate the evening meal alone in their room, though Bronwen could hardly swallow a bite. "Gildan," she said as they sat on a low bench beside the fire. "I hope you will be happy with Aeschby. I shall miss you."

At that, Gildan began to weep softly. "And I shall miss you. You must come to see me soon in my new home."

She flung her arms around her sister, and the two clung to each other for a long moment. Bronwen felt as though she had never been more as one with her sister...or more apart. Gildan looked so young and frail. If only Bronwen could be certain that Aeschby would treat his wife well, the parting might come more easily.

"I smell a storm coming across the sea," Gildan whispered. "Let us send Enit out and go to bed. I have had more than my fill of her predictions and proverbs about weddings. Truly, I am not sad she goes with you. She can grow so tiresome."

"You will miss her, sister. She's the only mother you have known."

Gildan's face softened as she rose from the fireside and climbed into the bed the young women had shared almost from birth. "Just think...from now on it will be Aeschby sleeping beside me, Bronwen. How strange. How wonderful!"

Bronwen dismissed Enit for the evening and set the

bowls and spoons into a bucket beside the door. Then she banked the fire and pulled the rope hanging from the louvered shutters in the ceiling. Now the smoke could still make its way out, but the cold night wind would be blocked from blowing into the chamber.

Shivering slightly, Bronwen slipped under the coverlet beside her sister. For one brief moment, she pictured herself on the beach again, wrapped in Le Brun's mantle. She imagined the silken lining of the hood caressing her cheek and tried to smell again the faintly spicy scent clinging to the woolen folds. As she recalled the embrace of the man who had worn it, a pain filled her heart. Unable to bear it, she forced away the memory, and hid it in a dark, secret place—just as she had done the mantle.

The two weddings had been set for midmorning, to be followed by a feast, and perhaps even a day or two of celebration. Gildan flew about the chamber like a mad hen, refusing to allow Bronwen a moment to herself. Both women had chosen to wear white woolen undertunics. Enit laced up the tight sleeves of the fitted dresses. Gildan hurried to slip on her beautifully embroidered and fur-trimmed blue frock.

"Bronwen!" She laughed as Enit combed the shining golden waves of her hair. "Such a happy day! Hurry and put on your gown."

Bronwen had chosen a light gray tunic embroidered with red and silver threads. It hung loose to her ankles, and she sashed it with a silver girdle. Then she clasped about her waist the chain that held her purse with the will box hidden inside. After carefully plaiting her long braids, she stepped into a pair of thin kidskin slippers.

"I am quite sure I shall freeze during the ceremony," Gildan was protesting.

Enit, already in a sour mood from being ordered about since dawn, glowered at her. "Your mantle will keep you warm, girl. Now put it on and stop fussing. It's almost time."

On an impulse born of a sleepless night and a heart full of fear, sorrow and anguish, Bronwen lifted the lid of her wooden clothing chest and drew out the dark mantle Le Brun had given her. Wrapping it over her bridal tunic, she followed her sister out into the day.

The sun was barely visible behind a thick curtain of snow that sifted down like flour as the young women stepped into the great hall. Bronwen spotted her beaming father. The two bridegrooms stood beside him.

With a grim expression written across his face, Olaf Lothbrok stared at Bronwen as she took her place beside him. He wore a heavy bearskin cloak that fell to his leather boots. His hair was uncovered, and his thick beard spread across his chest.

A druidic priest began the ceremony by burning sacred woods and leaves, then chanting ritual petitions for health, safety and fertility. Before Bronwen could fully absorb the significance of the man's words, the wedding was ended. As if with the snap of a finger or the crash of a wave upon the shore, she became a wife. She had stood beside this aged and heavy Norseman who had once been her people's enemy, and now she was wedded to him forever.

Clinging to the edges of the black mantle around her shoulders, Bronwen joined the wedding party as it left the great hall. The snowstorm had worsened, and she lifted the hood over her head as pebbles of sleet stung her cheeks and slanted across the keep's muddy yard. A heavy gray fog obscured the horizon to the west across the water.

Lothbrok surveyed the sky and turned to Edgard. Speaking in his broken Briton tongue, he told Bronwen's father of his decision. "I must set sail at once. The weather comes bad across the seas."

Edgard scowled. "The wedding feast is being prepared in the kitchens. There is yet time for a celebration. Stay longer here, Lothbrok—at least allow your new wife time to eat and refresh herself before the journey."

A shiver ran down her spine as Bronwen stood on the steps and watched her new husband in animated discussion with her father. They must be nearly the same age, she surmised. Together, they looked like a pair of old bears, scarred and spent with years of battle.

As Olaf finished speaking and stomped down the stairs toward the waiting ship, Edgard turned to his elder daughter. "Bronwen, the Viking insists he must return to Warbreck at once. He has been sent a message that a village near his holding was burned. Whether it was the work of Normans or Scots he cannot tell, but he fears the coming storm could hold him several days here. You must depart with him at once."

"But what of the feast? Has he no respect for our traditions?"

"Daughter, you must remember that this man's ways are not our ways. You sail at once."

Bronwen ran to her sister's side and embraced Gildan. And so this was how it must be. A wedding. A ship. A new life far from home and family. Bronwen held her sister for a moment, then pulled away.

"We must part," she said. "My love goes with you. Be happy, Gildan."

Without a final glance at her beloved home, Bronwen stepped into the biting gale. In the distance, a small boat moved toward the shore. She saw that her chests and trunks were being loaded in another.

Edgard followed his daughter down the steep hill toward the water's edge. He took her arm and drew her close. "Do you have the golden key?" he whispered. "And the will box?"

"Yes, Father. I have them both." She drew back the mantle that he might see the outline of the box inside her chatelaine purse.

Edgard nodded with satisfaction. "Keep them with you always lest they fall into the wrong hands. Never let Lothbrok know of the will. He would not understand that in this new world of Norman kings and knights, the written word holds great power. And now, farewell, my beloved daughter. You, who are nearest to my heart, go farthest away. You will dwell with a strange people and an aged husband, but you must never forget that you are a Briton and that Rossall is your true home. When I die, return here and join my lands to those of your husband."

Bronwen slipped her arms around her father and held him close for a moment. Then she turned and hurried toward the waiting boat. As she was rowed across the bay toward the *snekkar,* Bronwen buried her head in the folds of the dark woolen cloak and wept bitter tears.

When the small boat bumped against the bow of the Viking ship, she looked up to see the head of a dragon rising above her, and higher still, a purple sail painted with a black crow billowed in the buffeting wind. But once aboard the *snekkar,* she turned her face away from the land, away from her father and from her sister and her home. She looked out into the darkening fog and tried to summon her courage. Fate had laid out this path, and she had no choice but to walk it.

As the *snekkar* inched its way southward, icy rain began to fall more heavily. Bronwen huddled under the thick mantle and covered her head with the hood that once had concealed the features of a man she must no longer remember. Enit, shivering beside Bronwen on the cold, hard deck, held up a soggy blanket to shield her head from the pelting sleet.

The sky grew black as heavy fog rolled over them from the Irish Sea. The mouth of the Warbreck River lay only ten or twelve miles south along the coast, but darkness fell before it came into sight. Wind whipped and tore at the sails and sent waves crashing into the seamen who tried to keep the ship upright with their twin rows of countless oars. At the front of the ship, Lothbrok stood peering out into the fog, now and then pointing east or west.

Bronwen hugged her knees tightly to her chest, and the hard edges of the small gold box pressed against her legs. Thinking of her father's earnest lecture about the power of the written word, she tried to erase from her mind the image of the boat, herself, and the box sinking to the bottom of the sea, lost forever.

As the night deepened, the storm continued raging until at last Bronwen heard shouts from the crewmen. Rather than continuing south, the ship began to turn eastward. Peering out from under the hood, she saw a pinprick of light in the distance. When the ship drew close enough to shore to weigh anchor, Lothbrok hurried his bride and her nursemaid into a small boat. Giving no instruction, he turned his back on them as crewmen hurriedly lowered the boat toward the water.

"Wait!" Bronwen shouted at her husband. "Lothbrok, where do you send us?"

The Norseman peered down at them. "See that light? Go ashore and find shelter. I cannot abandon my *snek-kar* in such a storm."

"Yet you would send your wife away with only her nursemaid for protection?"

"My man will stay with you. Go now!"

"Whisht," Enit muttered, elbowing Bronwen. "Speak no more. Keep your thoughts to yourself, girl."

Two crewmen rowed the women toward the fog-shrouded shore. As soon as the boat scraped bottom, the men helped them out and dragged them through the icy surf. Her clothing heavy with seawater, Bronwen struggled across the wet sand toward the light. While one of Lothbrok's men rowed back to the *snekkar,* the other accompanied them along the beach.

The light in the distance proved to be that of a candle burning inside a small wattle hut along the edge of the forest that met the beach. Lothbrok's man hammered on the door, which opened to reveal a tall, fair-haired man. To Bronwen's surprise, he did not ask their identity or loyalties, but warmly bade them enter. Around the fire, a small group of travelers took their rest.

When Bronwen approached, one of their number rose and withdrew silently to a darkened corner. Bronwen's heart stumbled at the sight—for as the man pulled his hood over his face, the hem of his black mantle fell aside to reveal a peacock-blue lining.

Chapter Three

His visage protected by shadow and the hood of his cloak, Jacques Le Brun studied the party his friend was now ushering toward the fire. One man. Two women. And unless his eyes failed him in the dim light, the taller lady was the daughter of Edgard the Briton.

"Thank you for welcoming us." The man spoke the Briton tongue poorly, and he was no Norman. A Viking, then. A rough, barbaric breed. Jacques felt for his sword and knife as the boorish fellow stepped in front of the two women and took a place in the circle around the crackling flame.

"We were caught up in the storm at sea," he told the others. "I protect the women while my father keeps charge of his ship. I am called Haakon, a Viking of Warbreck and the son of Olaf Lothbrok."

Edgard's daughter gasped aloud to learn that her escort was Olaf's son. Clearly they had not yet been introduced. Jacques couldn't imagine what had compelled the lady to leave her father's hearth in this weather and so soon after her betrothal to the old Viking. Jacques knew a Briton wedding would never take place until the spring or summer, when conditions were optimum for their pagan marriage rites. For a maiden to reside with a man unwed was unseemly. Yet the Britons—an ancient race that sought out witches for their charms and seers for their supposed foresight—were hardly more civilized than the Norsemen. Perhaps the woman's father had made this arrangement for some ulterior purpose.

"Hail to you in the name of our Lord, my friend. I am called Martin." The tall, scrawny man who had opened the door to these vagabonds now held out a hand toward the fire in the center of the hut. Jacques realized his companion's ability to converse with them was good, for he had been brought up not far from this place. This would be a help in days to come.

"Greetings all three," Martin said. "Ladies, I beg you to remove your wet cloaks and take places beside the blaze."

"Thank you, sir," the younger woman said. "You are good."

As she removed her mantle, Jacques knew for certain that this was the woman who had mesmerized him during the feast at Rossall Hall. And it was she to whom he had given his first kiss in many a long year.

"Only God is truly good," Martin replied with a smile as the other men made room for the women to seat themselves on a low bench. "So you are from Warbreck? We passed through that village this very day."

Jacques grimaced. Leave it to Martin to welcome total strangers without removing their weapons and to disclose information they hadn't even requested. Jacques must speak to his friend about this on the morrow, though he feared it would do little good.

When Edgard's daughter turned her face into the

light of the fire, Jacques could no longer keep his thoughts focused on Martin's latest faux pas. The woman again captured him—her dark beauty smiting him with misty memories of days he could hardly recall and fancies he had rarely permitted himself to imagine.

She was beautiful—truly, the most beautiful creature he had ever beheld. Long black braids reached down past her shoulders, and her brown eyes danced in the flames. Yet, despite the woman's loveliness, Jacques knew from their prior encounter that she had a sharp tongue and strong opinions.

"I am Bronwen, daughter of Edgard the Briton," she stated in her own language. "This is my nurse, Enit. We hail from Rossall Hall."

"Not Warbreck?" Martin registered confusion. "But Rossall is a fine keep, too, I understand. We have just roasted a small deer, and here on the fire, you see I am baking bread and warming drink. I hope you'll join us for dinner. You must be hungry after such a journey."

"I confess I am half-starved," Bronwen acknowledged. "I'm sure we all would enjoy a hot meal."

After speaking, she glanced directly at Jacques, who had kept to his station in the corner of the room. Clearly, she had noted his presence. But had she recognized him? From beneath his hood, he stared at her. What was it about the woman that drew him so? And why had he been so foolish, so recklessly impulsive, as to kiss her that night on the beach? Even now he could hardly countenance what he had done—yet the memory of that moment haunted him like nothing else.

The men cordially welcomed their guests and resumed their muted conversations. As expected, none drew attention to their master's presence in the room.

Jacques had trained them well. Bronwen the Briton, however, peered at him now and again—often enough that he began to suspect she had recognized him.

In the warmth of the fire, she and her nurse spread their skirts to dry. Their once ashen faces began to regain color, and they smiled as they whispered to each other—their good spirits obviously restored. As the maiden unbraided her wet hair, her nurse produced an ivory comb and set to work on the tangled knots in her charge's black tresses.

Martin began to slice the meat as the company watched in anticipation. Earlier, he had wrapped a few wild turnips and onions in wet leaves and placed them among the coals. The scent of roasted deer, steamed vegetables and baking bread began to fill the hut, and Jacques acknowledged his own hunger. He did not wish to reveal himself to the women, yet how could he resist the opportunity to fill his belly after his long journey?

"I'm sure I shall never be completely warm again," the nurse said with a small laugh. "Such waves and wind! It's cold enough to starve an otter to death in wintertime, as they say."

"That it is," Martin concurred. "I don't envy your master on the high seas in the midst of it. Here now, Enit, put this dry blanket about you. I'll have some hot drink for you in a moment."

Jacques shook his head in bemusement at this act of kindness toward a servant. That Martin had chosen such a deferential path in life perplexed him still. The tall man placed a thick blanket around Enit's shoulders, and Bronwen accepted a cup of the steaming brew that bubbled in a pot on the coals.

When Martin announced that the meal was ready,

he called those in the room to rise. Jacques remained in the shadows, yet he stood as Martin lifted his hands and began to pray. "Bless us, oh God. Bless these gifts which we receive from Your bosom, and make us truly thankful. In the name of our Savior we pray. Amen."

As Bronwen seated herself again, she addressed Martin. "Good sir, may I ask which god you serve? Or do you make prayers to all of them?"

Martin smiled at her as he began to pass around slices of the dripping meat. "I am a follower of the one true God. I serve His only Son, my Lord Jesus Christ."

"Christ?" she said. "Then you are a Christian?"

"Indeed I am. This party travels to London, that I may join believers in obedience to His Spirit through service to Jesus. Those who live at the monastery make it our mission to preach the good news of the Kingdom of God."

"Strange words," Bronwen said. "I have heard tales of Christians. Is it true you worship only this one God and give no homage to the spirits of the trees and mountains?"

Martin smiled. "God fashioned the earth and all that dwells upon it. We choose to worship the Creator rather than His creation."

"But surely your God has a dwelling place?"

"He abides in the heart of every true believer."

"Only in the heart of man? Why should this Spirit not also wish to inhabit the rest of His creation? Surely man is not solely blessed with the presence of the gods."

As the two spoke, one of Jacques's men rose and carried a slab of venison to him. Without pausing in the conversation, Bronwen turned and peered into the corner where he sat. She was opening her mouth to speak when Martin handed her a bowl filled with chunks of meat and steaming vegetables. He gave her a brief nod and then turned to Enit with another bowl.

"Putting the feast on the board is the best invitation," the older woman cackled.

Bronwen smiled at her nurse before returning to Martin. "The venison is tender and succulent, while the turnips and onions melted away like butter. I daresay I have never tasted such a fine meal or been so warm. Again, sir, we thank you for sharing your dinner with us."

"I am honored to be of service, my lady," Martin replied.

Haakon, the Norseman who had been consuming his portion in silence, tossed an onion over his shoulder before speaking up. "Tell me, holy man, where did you slay this deer?"

Martin and the others stopped their eating to eye the Viking. Jacques stiffened. Setting his meal aside, he again touched his knife. Clearly Martin's generosity meant nothing. Haakon wanted to know if the deer had been poached from his father's land.

"Where Christopher bought his coat, as they say, sir," Martin answered.

Haakon glowered at him. "I asked you a question, man. I expect an answer."

"We got the deer where 'twas to be had."

The burly Viking stood and pointed a thick forefinger at Martin. "You play games with me, do you? That deer belonged to the lands of Olaf Lothbrok, and you—"

"And you have kindly fed his wife and her attendant," Bronwen cut in. "We appreciate your generos-

ity, Martin. Do we not, Haakon? You, too, have filled
your belly. Would you now turn against your provider?"

Wife? Jacques could hardly believe he had heard
aright. Was it possible she had wed the old man already? Teeth clenched, he drew his knife from its scabbard and rose on one knee.

Haakon was glaring at Bronwen, as she stood to address him across the fire. "I am your mistress now, and
I command you to apologize to this gentleman."

"I obey no command given by a woman," Haakon
snarled. "I protect my father and his possessions, and I
comply only with his requests."

The woman lifted her chin. "I am the chattel of Olaf
Lothbrok—not only his possession but his chosen wife.
Obey me now, as you will in the future. I insist upon it."

Jacques understood the deep significance of this con-
frontation. Though the custom of both Briton and Viking gave authority to men, Bronwen had chosen to
assert her own station as Haakon's superior. She must
not relent. Failing to defend her claim would put her
forever under the man's domination and control.

"Apologize, Haakon," she repeated. "I command
you."

The Viking started to speak, but he held his tongue
as he glared at Bronwen. She maintained her cold,
steady gaze. Finally, he turned to Martin and muttered,
"As this woman commands, I apologize for questioning you about the animal."

Martin nodded. "No offense taken."

Bronwen did not acknowledge Haakon's obedience.
Instead, she bent down to help the old nursemaid to her
feet. As the young woman gathered their now-dried
woolen cloaks, she cast a glance at Jacques, who still

crouched in deep shadow. Though he fully expected her to confront him with as much fervor as she had the Viking, she took Enit by the elbow, stepped to another corner of the small room and began arranging a sleeping pallet.

Jacques sheathed his knife again and picked up his dinner. In time, his men finished their meal and began to settle around the room. He was glad they had found this shelter near the beach, for all were weary from the day's journey. Jacques watched as Haakon took a place near the door and cast a final hostile glance at Bronwen. She turned her back on him and lay down beside her nurse, who soon was snoring softly.

Exhausted, Jacques leaned his head against the wall. He was tired, but he would not sleep. Though silence had fallen over the gathering, he knew that darkness often brought misdeed.

Unable to sleep, Bronwen considered the fate of the ship that had brought her to this place. Vikings were legendary seamen and rarely lost a vessel. She had no doubt that Lothbrok would return for his wife and son—perhaps even by morning. Was he as brash and spiteful as his son? The thought sent a curl of dread through her stomach.

As the icy rainfall quieted from a roar to a gentle patter, Bronwen turned her thoughts to Martin and his kindness toward her and Enit. What was the nature of this God he served, and what powers could He offer to faithful worshippers? Did Martin tremble at the power of his God, or was this God the cause of his smiles and humility?

Recalling the festivals, rituals and sacrifices of her

people, Bronwen considered the questions that filled her mind. As the hours passed, she came to realize that she didn't know enough to pass judgment. It was a mystery—but one she wished to explore.

And the man in the corner? Could he truly be Jacques Le Brun? She had studied him in the firelight, but she couldn't be certain. It seemed impossible that they should meet again so soon. And if he recognized her, why not identify himself? No, it could not be the man. Yet as dearly as she wished to wash away her memories of Le Brun, she was powerless.

Late in the night, the rain ceased, leaving only the soft sound of waves breaking on the beach. Unable to rest her mind or even stretch her legs in the cramped, smoky hut, Bronwen decided to walk down to the sea. Perhaps she would see the Viking *snekkar* in time to steel herself for another meeting with her new husband. Rising, she slipped the mantle over her shoulders. The man in the corner dozed with his head against the wall. And Haakon, lying next to the hut's door, was snoring as she edged past him and stepped out into the night.

The dense bank of clouds had rolled back, leaving a cover of newly washed stars. Bronwen dug her bare toes into the wet sand and shook out her long hair as she wandered toward the water's edge. Some years ago, her father had employed a tutor, a man who once had been steward to a Norman family in the town of Preston. He had taught Bronwen and Gildan to speak French, to learn how their enemy viewed the world, and to understand some sense of the characteristics of the Christian God.

Much of what the tutor had told the girls was either laughable or revolting, but his explanation of the natural world fascinated Bronwen. On this night, she could see that nature was in balance again. Earth, fire, water, air—the four elements making up everything on the earth—must always remain in harmony, the tutor had said. When one asserted itself, the others brought it back into order.

So it was with kings, lords and serfs. It would take a mighty king indeed to subdue all of England and bring it under control. Bronwen had heard that Matilda had such a man in mind—her son Henry Plantagenet—to rule England if she prevailed against King Stephen in their civil war. But Henry was a Norman to the core, and Bronwen doubted he had any interest in the island to the north of his French homeland. She didn't care what the Normans did anyway. As long as they kept their distance from Amounderness and Rossall Hall.

As she strolled, Bronwen came upon a log washed up by the storm. But as she sat, her eye caught a movement down the beach near the hut. If she had wakened Haakon as she'd left the hut, he could have revenge in mind. Heart pounding, she slipped behind the log, hoping its shadow would conceal her.

As she watched the figure draw nearer, Bronwen saw it was Haakon. She closed her eyes and prayed to the gods—even to Martin's one God—that she might be spared. How foolish she had been to leave the hut unarmed. Yet, even if she had a weapon, she could never hope to physically overcome a strong, well-trained warrior. Would the man be so foolish as to harm his father's wife? Of course. He could kill her and slip back into the hut. All would believe him innocent.

She heard the Viking's footsteps crunching the sand near the log, and then he stopped. "So, Bronwen the

Briton, we meet again in the dark of night. Is it your
habit to wander beaches alone and without protection?"

With a gasp, she sat up. "Le Brun? But I thought you
were...someone else."

"Your Viking protector? But you have no fear of that
man, do you? At dinner you were quite impressive."

"And you—crouching in the corner like a mouse?
Do you fear him?"

"I fear only God."

"So, you follow your friend to London to pay homage to this God so favored by Normans. Or are you still
spying out Amounderness?"

The man chuckled but made no answer. "You must
call me Jacques. We know each other too well for for-
malities. And I see you have put my mantle to good
use. I'm glad of that. Now perhaps you'll tell me why
you attempt to hide when the stars illuminate everything on this beach."

Bronwen stood and unclasped the cloak. "Stars reveal the future and the present. But they don't show
your face, sir. You are the one who hides, not I. Here—
take your mantle. I want nothing to do with a scoun-
drel and a spy."

Jacques caught the hood of the cloak before it could
slip to the ground. "Keep it, my lady. I beg you."

"No, I—"

"Please honor my request." He drew the garment
around Bronwen's shoulders again and fastened the
clasp at her neck. "I am not ready to collect it just yet.
We are met untimely."

His fingers lingered for a moment at the clasp as he
looked into her eyes. Then he drew away, took a place
on the log and stretched out his long legs. Reaching up,

he grasped Bronwen's hand and gently pulled her down beside him. She settled herself at some distance, wary of the Norman yet grateful for the warmth of his mantle.

"Your husband is at sea," he said. His voice was deep, and his eyes searched the horizon as he spoke. "When were you married?"

"This morning. Soon after the rite, we left Rossall Hall in haste because of the storm."

"Little good it did. And now you spend your wedding night sitting on a wet log."

"It is of no consequence to me. My husband and I have never spoken a single word. Our vow is all that unites us."

"A vow has great power, Bronwen." He glanced at her. "May I call you by name?"

"As you wish. It matters not, for I don't imagine we shall meet again after this night."

Jacques leaned back against a twisted branch and folded his arms across his chest. "You were imprudent to leave the safety of the hut. You have no protection."

"I assumed the men were sleeping. Clearly I was mistaken."

"A leader of men is never fully at rest, even in his own home. When I saw you leave, I feared for your safety."

Bronwen clasped her hands together, uncomfortable at his words. "You are leader of your party, then. But who do you serve—Matilda? Stephen? Or perhaps the Scot, David, who presumes to claim Amounderness by virtue of Stephen's treaty."

"You know more of politics than a woman should, madam. Perhaps you had best tend to your new home and leave such intrigues to your husband."

Annoyed, Bronwen stood. "A wise woman knows as much of politics as any man. You will recall that my father willed his landholdings to me—not to my husband. He prepared me well for that responsibility, and I should like to know who spies out our lands and for what lord?"

"I am no spy, Bronwen." Jacques rose to face her. "I serve Henry Plantagenet, the son of Matilda Empress, who has battled King Stephen these many years. Henry is wise and learned beyond his eighteen years. Already he is heir to Anjou and Normandy in France. Many in England support him."

Bronwen squared her shoulders. "We Britons will not serve any Norman king—and you have my permission to report that to your beloved Henry Plantagenet. Our men will fight to the death to protect Rossall from Norman rule."

"You're already a pawn of King Stephen." Jacques shook his head. "Don't be so foolish as to think you rule yourselves. Stephen has given your lands to Scotland by treaty. Would you not rather have a fair and just king like Henry Plantagenet? I assure you, he would treat your people well in his dealings with other landowners in this country."

"I know nothing of this young Plantagenet. Neither Stephen nor David of Scotland has made his presence felt in Amounderness—and for that I am grateful. Certainly Plantagenet has never come our way. Our lands have been Briton since time began, and they will remain so."

As Bronwen fought the frustration and vulnerability that shackled her, Le Brun reached out and covered her hands with his own. Warm and strong, his fingers stroked her wrists, and his thumbs pressed against her palms. Startled, she shrank back, but he held her firmly.

"Have you been so sheltered that you tremble at a man's touch?" he asked. "I mean you no harm, my lady. We speak from our hearts. Though we differ, the honesty in our words is good. Forgive me if I've dismayed you."

"You do dismay me, sir. And more than that."

Bronwen drew her hands from his and attempted to tame her hair into some semblance of order. But again, Jacques caught them.

"Leave your hair," he said, drawing her hands to his chest. "It's beautiful blowing in the wind as it does now."

At his words, Bronwen felt the blood rush to her face, and she turned her focus to the ground. She had been told she was plain, especially compared with Gildan, the golden one. Often while standing beside her sister, Bronwen pictured herself—a thin, angular, olive-skinned creature. No one, not even Enit, had ever called her beautiful.

Jacques reached out and lifted her chin. "So shy? A moment ago, you would have run me through had you carried a sword. My lady, you are indeed most lovely and desirable. You may recall I held you in my arms on such a night. And I kissed your lips."

His fingers trailed from her chin, down the side of her neck to a wisp of hair that snaked between the folds of the mantle. Bronwen shivered as he traced its course to the soft skin of her throat.

Her thoughts reeled as he wove his fingers through her hair. Craving again the kiss of this man, she struggled for air. This must not be. She belonged to another man. A husband who had never spoken her name.

"How I am drawn to you, Bronwen the Briton." Jacques's breath was ragged on Bronwen's cheek. "Though we have met only twice, you beckon me as no woman ever has."

She lifted her eyes to his shadowed face. "Sir, you are wrong to hold me in this manner."

"If I sin, then you sin, too—for I feel your desire as strongly as I do my own."

"No," Bronwen whispered. "I am another man's wife. I know nothing of such wickedness."

"All are sinners," he said. "Even you, my lovely Bronwen. But your words return me to my senses. You are wed. I cannot ignore a vow made before God."

"Indeed, I must return to the hut."

"Stay with me a little longer—on the beach, where we can be alone."

"I dare not." Bronwen backed away from him. "It is unseemly. And you...you are a Norman. My enemy."

"I am not your enemy. My blood is that of a man, and yours is that of a woman. On this night, we are neither Norman nor Briton."

"Blood can never lie," she said. "I go."

Turning from him, she pulled the mantle tightly about her. The sand felt cold beneath her feet as she started toward the hut. Dizzy with emotion, she brushed a strand of hair from her cheek. How could she have allowed this to happen? And how would she bear his memory now?

"My dearest lady." Jacques's long stride brought him to her side. "What troubles you?"

"*You* trouble me!" Bronwen cried out. "You know

I am a married woman. You know I am a Briton, and you a Norman. Yet your words belie those facts. What is it you want of me, sir?"

Jacques fell silent for a moment. Bronwen sensed his presence beside her as they walked, but she could not bring herself to look at him. "Your question is well asked," he said at last. "I don't know what I want of you."

She halted. "Then why do you pursue me? Why do you behave as a knave?"

"I am not a knave. I am a knight. And I cannot say why my training in chivalry has deserted me. I know only that I have never met a woman like you—a woman of such fire, such wit, such dark beauty. When I saw you in the great hall at Rossall, I felt my heart drawn to you. Yet I sat in silence as your father betrothed you to the Viking. You obey him in every way, do you not?"

"Of course," Bronwen said. "He is my father."

"But when we met later on the beach, and when I took you in my arms—though it was wrong to have done so by my code of knightly honor—"

"Indeed it was. It was wrong."

"But I am more than a knight. More than a Norman. I am a man. And since that night, my thoughts have been consumed by you. Can you deny what passed between us then— and now?"

Bronwen looked away. "I must deny it. There was nothing between us, and there is nothing now. You say you are a man—more than a knight and a Norman. Are you a Christian, too, Jacques? Do you follow any guide that holds power over your passion? I do. More than woman, I am a Briton and a wife. We have met, as you predicted, but we shall not meet again. So when you chance to think on me again, know this—I am a Briton above all else."

"And a stubborn one."

"If you had taken a vow that pledges you to the future awaiting me, you would understand that stubbornness must be your fortress."

"Don't let it blind you to the stirrings of your heart, Bronwen."

"What place can the heart have in the life of a lord's wife, sir? As a knight, you should know that my work is to tend to my husband's castle and his holdings. I must bear him sons to succeed him—and daughters to wed the sons of his allies."

"Such cold determination to duty." He ran his fingertips down her arm. "But this is not the way of noblewomen in France, my lady. In France—"

"In France? My lord, look about you. This is hardly France. We stand on the shore of Amounderness—the most rugged and desolate land in England. Here we fight to survive. We have no time for Norman luxuries of the heart."

"I disagree. It is in the cruelest of lands that one needs the warmest solace."

Bronwen clutched his mantle about her shoulders. "It matters not to me what you think, Jacques the Norman. Go on about your French ways, then. Go back to Normandy where you belong, and leave us in peace. Our lives are difficult enough without your interference."

As she stepped past the man, he caught her shoulder and swung her around. "I shall not forget you, Bronwen. When we meet again, I believe our lives will be changed."

"You speak with certainty," she said. "I am certain

only that I go to my husband's castle. Tell your Henry Plantagenet we shall never give over to him."

With that, she turned away and hurried down the beach to the hut. The tall knight was left standing in the starlight and looking far out to sea.

The remainder of the night passed slowly for Bronwen. Her breast was filled with a tumult of new emotions, and her mind whirled with thoughts. In a moment of time, her life had changed inexorably. Though she knew almost nothing of the man with whom she had argued so fiercely, and who had kissed her so passionately, she sensed that he had thrown open a door before her. And she knew she had stepped through it. For the rest of her life, this Jacques Le Brun would live within her.

She had never felt so fully alive as when she was with him. Never had she known a man to hold a woman in high esteem. He had encouraged her to speak her opinion. He had freely praised her. Certainly Bronwen knew men desired women. But to speak of their beauty? To openly express feelings of admiration? Never.

Britons married by arrangement, often never having seen their spouse before the ceremony. The pair contemplated contentment with children and a sense of partnership in the venture of life. As for desire—women never felt such strong emotion for their husbands. And men were far too involved with daily business to show tenderness toward their wives.

Confused and restless, Bronwen knew only that her loyalty must remain with her father. Though she ached for the touch of this Jacques Le Brun, it could not be. She must face forward and carry on.

The sun had not yet risen when Enit began to stir. The old woman yawned and stretched, scratching her grizzled head. In a moment, she nudged Bronwen.

"I'm awake," Bronwen said softly. She had watched the door all night, but Jacques had not returned to the hut.

"Girl, you look as though you have not slept at all," Enit clucked as she surveyed her charge with dismay.

"I daresay she has not," Haakon remarked gruffly, stepping out of the hut.

Bronwen started at his words, fearful that he knew she had been out in the night with Le Brun. If he did, he must suspect all manner of evil about her, and he might use his knowledge to disgrace her. But as she considered this, Bronwen realized that Haakon's word would be weighed against hers. She held a powerful position as his father's wife, and she would not let him forget it.

Martin was bent over the fire, his blond hair tousled from sleep. He was stirring a mixture of oats and honey he had taken from his bag. Enit began combing and plaiting her charge's dark braids as the other men went about strapping on their swords and traveling gear. Bronwen was fastening Le Brun's mantle at her throat when the door fell open and the man himself strode into the hut.

"The day is clear and the sea has calmed," he announced. "Haakon, your father's ship has not returned. You should journey to the Warbreck Wash by foot. He will have weighed anchor there, knowing you would meet in time."

The Viking's eyes narrowed as he studied Jacques. "What do you know of the ways of Olaf Lothbrok? You are a Norman dog."

"Even a dog has the sense to take shelter from a storm."

"And who are you, good sir?" Enit asked Jacques. "You are a stranger to us. Do you journey to London with these men?"

"I am Jacques Le Brun, their leader. We take our brother Martin to a monastery in London. I must see he is well settled."

Enit smiled. "Well now, I suppose you do have a godly brow, Martin. Listen sir—beware of those other Christian men. Not all are as pure as you might wish. As we say in Amounderness, 'He who is near the church is often far from God.'"

"I shall be as wary as a fox," Martin assured her. With a grin, he went about collecting the empty mugs. Jacques had gone back outside, and Bronwen could hear the men saddling their horses. She felt for the key around her neck and the will box inside the chatelaine purse that hung at her waist. Again reminding herself of her duty to her father and countrymen, she determined that she must not look at Jacques again. Even a meeting of their eyes might weaken her resolve, she realized as she helped Enit into her cloak and mantle.

As the sun peeked over the distant mountains behind them, the company stepped out of the hut. Bronwen breathed deeply of the clean sea air. Though tired, she longed to be on her way from this place.

"Thank you for your generosity," Enit was saying to Martin as she readied her bag for the journey.

"You are most welcome. And you, Haakon, may we part as friends? I wish no enmity between us."

Bronwen turned in time to see the Viking walk away from the proffered hand. "I feel no enmity for you, Norman," Haakon spoke over his shoulder. "I desire no friendship either. Come, women. The sun rises."

Bronwen set out after the Viking, but she stopped when a familiar deep voice spoke her name.

"Bronwen the Briton," Jacques said from his horse. "I wish you well in your new life. Please tell your lord I look forward to our meeting."

Bronwen turned to him, her heart thundering again. "Sir, my husband will welcome neither you nor your lord Henry Plantagenet, I assure you. Nevertheless, I wish you safety and godspeed."

At this she turned away and rejoined her companions, never looking back.

Chapter Four

The sun was fully risen when Bronwen's party arrived at the mouth of the Warbreck Wash, a swampland where the Warbreck River met the sea. Jacques had been wrong. The Viking *snekkar* was not moored there. Despite exhaustion and hunger, Bronwen's spirits lifted. She was grateful for the reprieve, even though she knew that unless the gods had altered her fate, Olaf Lothbrok would soon return. In his absence she could take time to accustom herself to her new role in life.

At the river's edge stood a small village, busy with the day's activities. Men readied boats for fishing, while half-naked children poked into the sand with sticks and looked for cockles. Haakon shouted at them in his Norse tongue, and three of the youngsters scurried toward the nearby buildings.

Bronwen was appalled by the filthy condition of this seaside village—far worse than those of Rossall's holding. Enit muttered her disgust as they lifted their skirts over the wet places in the streets. When they came to the river—afloat with rotted vegetables and rags—two men waited with a small fishing boat. Once they were settled, the men set to with their oars.

The gentle rocking of the boat as it pulled upstream against the sluggish current lulled Bronwen's body and soothed her troubled mind. Before long she fell asleep on Enit's shoulder and stirred only when the boat bumped against a wooden pier at their journey's end.

Rubbing her eyes, she looked up into a sky filled with towering gray clouds. Outlined against them stood the imposing battlements of Warbreck Castle. The dizzying height of the keep that rose behind the stone wall took her breath away.

"Look, child!" Enit cried out. "Rooms built one on top of another.

"Imagine that." Bronwen's private chambers at Rossall had been on a higher level than that of the hall, but certainly not on top of it. She had never thought such a thing possible.

"Welcome, Haakon, son of Olaf Lothbrok." A mail-clad guard saluted as the party approached the keep. When he spoke, Bronwen realized that Viking warriors must have intermarried with their conquered Briton populace some generations ago. Though their tongue was different from her own in many ways, she understood it well enough.

"Where is my lord?" the guard asked. "And the *snekkar?*"

Haakon related the details of the storm and its consequences. "And this," he said, pointing a thumb at Bronwen, "is the bride."

To her satisfaction, the guard knelt before her. She bade him rise and lead her to the keep.

"Such a great number of men," Enit said under her

breath as they passed through the wall's gate into the courtyard. "Look at 'em standing at post and walking about the perimeters of the wall. They're everywhere."

"This holding is far more heavily guarded than Rossall," Bronwen returned in a low voice. "I fear we are surrounded."

Ahead of them, Haakon pushed open the heavy oaken door of the great hall and led them inside. Though a large log blazed in the center of the room, its high stone walls were cold and desolate.

"They have a dais," Bronwen whispered to Enit.

"But no musicians' gallery above it. Perhaps these barbarians don't even have music."

Bronwen elbowed her nurse to silence as Haakon pointed out the servitors gathered before her. "These are your personal attendants," he said. "Most speak some form of your vulgar tongue."

Bronwen pasted on a smile as she studied the motley group, though she wondered dismally if they would be as difficult as Haakon. A small woman with flaming red hair and ruddy skin beckoned, leading Bronwen out of the hall and up a steep flight of stone stairs. Enit puffed along behind, muttering good riddance to Haakon, boats and stormy seas.

At the top of the stairs a guardroom was filled with spears, swords, bows and arrows. In its center, coals from the night's fire glowed, while a heap of blankets and furs indicated that this was also a sleeping room.

"So many weapons, Enit," Bronwen murmured as they picked their way across the room.

To her surprise, the red-haired woman responded. "Your husband's lands are hard pressed by Normans to the south and by Scotsmen to the northeast. He often travels to aid his neighboring allies and strengthen his borders."

The women crossed the guardroom to a door on the far wall. It opened into a small chamber with a sagging wooden bed in one corner and a narrow slit for a window. Thick layers of rotting rushes on the floor sent up a dank musty odor. "Your chamber, my lady."

Bronwen turned to Enit, who stood aghast. "This?" Enit muttered. "This room is fit only for pigs."

"Enough," Bronwen snapped. "Our trunks are aboard the *snekkar,* and I need a clean, dry tunic. See what you can find." She turned to the other woman. "I must have a fire, and send at once for the rush strewers. I'll not sleep this night in such an odor."

"We have no fresh rushes, madam. It is our custom to gather them once before winter, and not again until spring."

Bronwen shook her head in disbelief. "Upon the morrow I insist that fresh rushes be gathered and set to dry."

The servitor nodded and followed Enit from the room. Alone in the foul chamber, Bronwen stepped to the bed and ran her hand over the pile of furs. These at least were clean. The narrow arrow-loop window allowed only a slit of light, and she peered out it into the gathering gloom. A village lay far below, and in the distance the wide expanse of woodland was broken now and again by a glint of setting sun reflected on the river.

Was Jacques Le Brun traveling those woods even now? Bronwen at last permitted herself to reflect on the man who had held her twice in the darkness. Did he truly travel toward London and a house for holy men? Or did he journey to meet his lord, Henry Plantagenet?

What were those Normans scheming for Amounderness? Haakon had referred to Jacques as a dog, and Bronwen's father insisted the French conquerors were the scourge of England. If Normans were so vile, why did Jacques speak to her with such kindness? Why was his touch so gentle? And how would she ever forget that man?

"You are too much like your mother, child," Enit said to Bronwen as they ate together the following day. "She was dismayed at the state of Rossall when she first arrived with your father. But soon she put it right and let everyone know she was mistress. You'll do the same."

Heavyhearted over Jacques's departure and uncertain what had become of Olaf's ship, Bronwen had spent the morning surveying her new home. The kitchen was well stocked. Dried herbs and onions hung in bundles from the beams; strips of salted fish lay in baskets, and a freshly dressed boar roasted over the fire. But when Bronwen had run her fingers through a bag of dried beans, tiny black bugs had scurried across her hand.

The cook had dismissed the pests as if they were of little consequence. She was more interested in telling her new mistress about the nuts that could be gathered in the nearby forest. Fruits, too, were plentiful. Apples, pears and plums were harvested in season.

Bronwen sighed as she handed Enit a slice of cheese. "They grow no flowers here. Did you know that?"

"What, none?" Enit's brow furrowed. "At Rossall we had roses, violets, primroses, all manner of blossoms. I loved to sugar the petals and eat them."

"As did I."

"But shall we have no petals to scent the water for

hand washing and to flavor our sweets? Do they have bees then? And honey?"

"I don't know." Unable to hold back the tide of emotion any longer, Bronwen covered her face with her hands. "Oh Enit, I feel so far from home. I miss my father and Gildan."

"Hush, my girl," Enit soothed her. "Continue your duties, and each morning as it comes will look brighter."

The thought of Enit faithfully lying in her blankets by the door reassured her. And indeed, as the nursemaid had predicted, the next days passed peacefully enough. With no word of the *snekkar's* fate, Bronwen had little choice but to take on management of the holding, just as she had done when her father was away from Rossall.

Each morning she rose early and washed from head to toe in warm water. After breakfast she inspected the house and set the servitors to work cleaning and strewing fresh rushes on the floors. Outside, the kitchen gardens had been planted in haphazard rows and were dried out and weedy. Bronwen ordered them plowed under, even though the ground was almost frozen.

A walk through the village of Warbreck disclosed that it subsisted in the same state of filth and disrepair as the coastal town. A week after her arrival at the castle, Bronwen was discussing the deplorable situation with Enit when a tumult arose from the grounds. The nursemaid scurried to the window of the chamber.

"Bah!" she exclaimed. "This window is too narrow. Come girl, let's go down to the hall."

Bronwen considered for a moment. "No, Enit, that would be unseemly. You go down first and see if the mistress of Warbreck Castle is required."

Enit nodded approval and set off. Despite all intentions to remain calm, Bronwen's heart began to flutter. But she didn't have to wait long before Enit burst through the door.

"It's him, Bronwen! Your husband is returned. The old boat ran aground, but most of his men escaped with their lives. They're in the hall now, demanding food and drink. Such confusion—shouting orders at the servitors. They've the biggest mouths I ever saw clapped under a lip!"

"And my husband? Does he ask for me?"

"He's too busy ordering a feast for his men," Enit spat in disgust. "Never have I heard so loud a roar nor seen such mayhem."

Confused, Bronwen sat down on the bed. So Lothbrok had not even asked about her welfare. She was pondering the significance of the news when a company of servitors brought the clothing chests upstairs. Enit busied herself unpacking, but as hours passed with no word from below, Bronwen began to grow ever more dismayed.

What could it mean that Olaf had ignored her? Surely the man had not forgotten his wedding day. He must know that his young bride awaited his bidding. Did he mean to consummate their union this night? The thought of acting upon her vows with the old Viking filled Bronwen with trepidation. Yet, she was not the first woman wedded to a stranger, and she wouldn't be the last. Duty to ancestry and protection of land came above all else. Bronwen had no intention of shirking her responsibility.

But when night fell and still no summons had come from below, Bronwen stood. "Enit, lay out my purple

gown," she said. "I shall wear it over the crimson un-
dertunic."

"You mean to go down? Uninvited?"

"I do."

The nursemaid clucked as she helped Bronwen dress,
wove red ribbons into the long black plaits and placed
a golden circlet over her veil. "But do you really wish
to go among them now, girl?" she asked. "They'll be
drunk, you know, and he hasn't called for you. It is unseemly."

Bronwen held up a hand to silence Enit, who drew
a soft white woolen mantle over the shoulders of her
charge. "Light a torch. I go alone."

Muttering, Enit lit one of the rushlights that stood
by the door and gave it to her mistress. As Bronwen
started through the guardroom, she breathed deeply,
trying to gain control of her trembling hands. She did
not know what her reception would be in the hall, but
she was determined to make known her presence as the
woman of the household and the wife of Olaf Lothbrok.

At the bottom of the stairs, Bronwen heard the raucous sounds from the hall. Summoning her courage,
she pushed open the heavy door, entered the room and
stood in silence. One by one, the men ceased their rev-
elry and turned toward her. Lifting her chin, Bronwen
began to make her way between the tables to the dais
where Olaf sat.

"Aha, my wife is come!" the man said on spying
her. Unwashed from his journey, Olaf looked older and
heavier than she remembered. He shoved one of his
men aside and indicated a place next to him on the
bench. Lifting his hands, he cried out, "Fellow Vikings,

I present my bride—Bronwen, daughter of Edgard the Briton."

Bronwen could not help but wonder if her presence was a surprise—her existence a sudden afterthought—to her husband. His men applauded the announcement but soon resumed their laughter and feasting. When Olaf called a servitor to fetch the woman a slab of meat and a flagon of drink, Bronwen used the moment to assess her husband.

Olaf's aging skin was leathered from the sun, and his belly protruded over his belt as he seated himself beside his wife. The thick brown tunic he wore smelled of salt and sea and dried fish, and his beard hung tangled and matted across his chest. He tore off a bite of mutton, then wiped his mouth on his sleeve before addressing her.

"So, you had a safe journey," he said. His tongue, thick with the ale he had drunk, slurred over the words. "Haakon is a good guide. I trust him well."

Bronwen tipped her head. "He is your son?"

"The child of my first wife." With a stubby finger he pointed out the sandy-haired man at the end of their table. "Haakon is my only offspring. His mother has not been long dead—five or six years perhaps."

As Bronwen struggled to make sense of such a dismissive statement, a servitor set a large trencher of greasy roast mutton before her. With no ewer to wash her hands and no linen to dry them, she had little choice but to pick up a knife and cut into the meat.

"How fares your longboat?" she asked, hoping to have some conversation with the man her father had chosen.

Olaf grunted. "Badly damaged. We struck a reef near the Irish coast. Six men died at sea."

"I'm sorry," she said softly. "Sorry for your loss."

With a quizzical expression on his face, Olaf chewed for a moment. Then he shrugged. "Why be sorry? We can repair the *snekkar,* and death brings glory to ourselves and honor to the gods."

Bronwen reflected on the Celtic deities of her forefathers. Then she recalled the man she had met in the seaside hut, Martin, and his lifetime devotion to Jesus.

"Which are your gods?" she asked.

"Baal, god of the sun, of course. And Odin, Thor, Frey, Balder, Aegir—"

"What of the Christian God?"

"A God who allows Himself to be killed?" Olaf scoffed. "Yet I suppose each deity—weak or strong—has some purpose. Our great joy is to die in battle, for no man can go to Valhalla of the gods if he dies not by the sword."

"But surely illness or disease takes many men."

"No Viking male may die except by the sword. We do not permit it."

Bronwen was taken aback at this information, but her husband returned to his meal as if indifferent to such a barbaric practice. Unable to eat, she listened as Olaf's men rose and began to tell battle tales—one gruesome, horrific and bloody story after another. The drunken narratives were difficult to understand, but Bronwen was able to make out awful accounts of severed heads and men torn apart, their entrails drawn from their bodies while they were still alive. Soon she had no doubt she had been united to the most vile and despicable race on the earth.

At the tale of the Viking practice of slicing open a man's chest and pulling out his pulsing lungs, she could endure no more. Standing, she excused herself. Olaf acknowledged his wife with a nod but made no move to stop her. Feeling ill, Bronwen hurried from the hall to the staircase that led to her bedchamber.

"They are animals," she told Enit as she entered the room. "Worse than animals. They glory in torture, suffering, murder. They kill without thought. Their swords swing heedless of a man's age or station in life. My husband tells me that every man must die by the sword if he wishes an afterlife. *Every* man!"

Enit reached to soothe the young woman, but Bronwen brushed her aside and went to the window. "How can I stay here?" she cried clutching the rough stone sill. "They worship gods I do not know and welcome death with every breath. Enit, how can I bear the filth, the barbarity, the bloodshed? Tomorrow I shall send word to my father. He must allow me to return to Rossall and end the marriage."

"Impossible, Bronwen. You made a vow."

She pursed her lips. "I cannot allow that man to touch me. Do you hear what I say, Enit? You must bar the door against him tonight."

"La, child, stop talking nonsense." Enit took Bronwen's shoulder and turned her from the window. "You are his wedded wife, and you will perform your duty. Take off your tunic now and put on this gown. You must make ready for your husband."

Bronwen fought tears as her nurse slipped a cotton gown over her head. "It was horrible, Enit," she said. "They told stories of what they had done to their enemies. Dreadful, wicked things. And at all this, they laugh!"

"Ask the gods to help you forget the tales and forgive the ones who spoke them." Enit took Bronwen's arm and ushered her to the bed. "You cannot return to Rossall. Your home is here."

Buried under the furs, Bronwen lay awake listening to Enit bank the fire. Tonight the old nurse would go to new quarters in the keep and no longer sleep outside her charge's room. The bride must await her husband.

Bronwen woke with a start and sat straight up in bed. She had been dreaming of a great crow. Its flapping wings had begun to envelop and suffocate her when at once they changed into the heaving, bloody lungs of a dying man.

With a shudder, she left her bed and went to the window. The sun was risen, but no one had awakened her. And Olaf had not come.

"Enit?" Bronwen called out. "Enit, are you there?"

The old woman hurried into the room bearing a tray of bread and steaming porridge. "The servitors tell me he never entered the room, child," she said as she arranged the tunic Bronwen had selected. "Can this be true?"

"I never saw him after I left the feast."

Shaking her head in consternation, Enit combed and plaited her mistress's hair. While Bronwen ate, the women discussed the coming day, but neither again mentioned the fact that she had slept alone.

Fearing that she had shamed herself and disappointed the entire household in failing to lure her husband to bed, Bronwen decided she must find the man and make an attempt at forming some sort of bond between them. Slipping the black mantle with its peacock lining over her shoulders, she crossed the guardroom and hurried down the stone steps.

On entering the hall, she saw men lying about in deep sleep. It was a lucky thing they had no battles to fight today, she thought, picking her way through the tangle of arms and legs. At last she made her way past the dais to the small partition at the far end of the hall where the lord typically slept.

Flat on his stomach in a knot of blankets, Olaf snored loudly. Bronwen approached and touched his arm. The Viking did not budge.

"Husband," she said. "I am come to you. Bronwen—your wife."

Olaf's eyes fluttered open, and he gazed at her for a moment before rolling away onto his side. "Leave me be," he growled. "My head thunders!"

Before she could take a step away, he was snoring again. Disgusted and frustrated, Bronwen left the hall and summoned Enit. "My husband sleeps off his drunkenness. He has dismissed me—and so I shall go."

"Go where? You cannot return to Rossall, Bronwen!"

"I'll not stay here to face that man's surly disposition and his servitors' stares. I mean to leave the castle and walk upriver."

"Alone?"

"Of course. I always wandered the woodlands around our keep at Rossall. Why should this place be different? If the Viking wakes, tell him his wife will return by nightfall."

"But Bronwen—"

Unwilling to listen to Enit's warnings or her own

conscience, Bronwen left the hall. She made her way across the courtyard, through the gate and down to the Warbreck River. As she followed it, the green mosses growing along the banks lifted her spirits. Even in winter, life thrived. Envisioning the primroses, cowslips and bellflowers that would bloom in spring along the water's edge, she imagined the trees thickly leaved, their branches laden with fruit or nuts.

One day she would be happy here, she determined as she strolled along the river's edge. She would bear children and teach them to love the land and revere their Briton forebears. Her husband would learn to admire her. His son would accept her. The servitors must respect and obey their mistress, and in time she would make the castle her home—a clean, warm, proud place where visitors would be welcomed and where everything thrived.

The sun rose and then began its downward journey while Bronwen walked, and finally decided she must turn back. Her heart, though still heavy, had calmed. As soon as she reached her chamber, she had decided, she would send for messengers. Her father would want to know she was safely at Warbreck. And Gildan—oh, how Bronwen missed her sister! A message must go to her, too. Gildan would be happy in Aeschby's arms, and Bronwen must celebrate her sister's happiness with tender words.

As shadows crept along the path, the sound of horses' hooves in the distance rang out. Bronwen caught her breath, at once aware of her precarious position. At Rossall, she had given little thought to dangers, for she was never far from a cottage or a hut. But—on Viking land—she now admitted she had been careless not to heed Enit's warnings.

Electing to hide until the possible threat was past, Bronwen started for the darkened woods. But as she stepped from the path, she heard her name called out.

"Bronwen, wife of Olaf Lothbrok!" The man himself spurred his horse forward from the midst of a group of mounted comrades not far from where she stood. His long beard lifted in the wind as his steed thundered toward her. "Halt in the name of Thor, woman, or I'll flay the skin from your back!"

Stiffening, she squared her shoulders. "Here I stand," she told her husband. "I await your bidding."

He reined his horse and surveyed her coldly. "Wife, what mischief have you played today?" he barked out. "Do you not know the dangers of this forest? We have not only wild beasts, but also wild men, thieves and witches here. If you had been killed or taken, I would have a war with your father at my northern borders—to add to the conflicts on my southern and eastern flanks."

"I am well enough, sir, as you see." She stared back at him. "And I do not fear beasts or witches. Or men."

Her value to her husband was purely strategic, Bronwen realized, nothing more. But her brazen straying from his protection was enough to set the Viking's rage aboil.

"You, woman!" He pointed his finger at her. "You will never again leave my keep. Do you think you are a queen who may rule her own husband? Upon my honor, you are my chattel. My possession. I command your obedience. Do I have it?"

"Of course, sir." She bowed her head. "I am your wife."

Turning his horse, Olaf called out to his men. "Return her to the castle."

Before Bronwen could react, Haakon rode out from the others. Grasping her by the arm, he jerked her off her feet and threw her across his horse like a sack of meal. The ride back to the keep was excruciating and Bronwen's humiliation grew with every thud of the horses' hooves. In leaving the castle grounds, she had sought peace and reflection, but her action had only brought her shame. A chattel, he had called her. And she was. A sack of meal, indeed.

When the horses reached the inner courtyard, Haakon pushed her to the ground and dismounted. Lightheaded and queasy, Bronwen sank to her knees as the men stalked away toward the hall. For a moment, she could do nothing but try to suck down breath. Her ribs ached and her arm felt as if it had been pulled from its socket.

Aware of the stares from those around her and trying not to weep, she was struggling to her feet when a man approached.

"My lady, may I have a word with you?"

He spoke her tongue with a Norman French accent, and Bronwen lifted her head in sudden hope. But this was no dark, hooded knight come to her rescue. The man was short of stature, and his blue eyes warily scanned the castle courtyard.

"Speak, sir," she told him.

"Are you Bronwen the Briton?"

She recognized the address as the one Jacques Le Brun had given her. Though she knew this was not the man himself, her heart flooded. "I am Bronwen the Briton," she affirmed.

The courier tipped his head in a sign of respect. "My lady, I have been given a message for you."

"And what is this message?"

Rather than answering, he drew a small box from beneath his mantle. Carved of a deep red wood she had never seen, the chest bore swirling mother-of-pearl and gold inlays. An exotic fragrance filled her nostrils as she took it from him.

"Thank you, sir," she said. "But who gave you this? Where is the one who sent the message?"

"That man is my lord, madam. A traveler from afar."

"And his name?"

"He said you would know." The courier again gave her a slight bow and then turned away.

"But, sir—"

Bronwen could see she would not hold him. Indeed, he was already slipping through the gate in the wall. With a mixture of hope and trepidation, she studied the seal on the chest's clasp. But the wax had not been imprinted—it was blank. Breaking it, she slid apart the clasp and lifted the lid. The chest was filled with white eiderdown.

Bronwen shook her head in confusion. Feathers? Who would send her feathers? What message could they signify? The sun was almost set as she reached into the soft bed and felt about. Her fingers closed on a solid round object, and she removed it. Against the waning light, she held aloft a small golden ball.

Again, she dipped her hand into the box and brought out a second ball. And then a third. Three gold balls in a nest of soft down?

Bronwen weighed the box in her hand. She felt certain it could not have come from her father. Her dowry had already been brought to Warbreck, and it was more than sufficient. Gildan would never have sent the three gold balls. The wealth-hungry Aeschby must surely prevent such a treasure from leaving his premises. Besides, the gift signified nothing between the two sisters. What did these orbs mean, and what was she meant to do with them? Most important, who had sent them?

She had hoped, even prayed, that she might meet with Jacques Le Brun again. But he had not come, and she could identify no reason to tie him to the orbs.

Was the chest itself intended as a message? A gift? Again Bronwen searched the box for a crest, an identifying color, a sign. She could decipher nothing.

Lest her husband begin to search for her again, she dropped the three spheres back into their downy bed, shut the chest and slid the hasp. As she placed it under her arm, her black wool mantle fell over it. And in the corner of the cloak, she caught a glimpse of an embroidered crest on the peacock-blue lining. The crest bore upon it three gold balls.

Chapter Five

"Your husband requests your presence at his table this night," Enit said on entering Bronwen's bedchamber. "You must ready yourself and go down to him."

Bronwen sat in silence on the clothing chest where she had hidden the box with its secret golden message. Humiliated and in pain, she could think of nothing but Jacques Le Brun. Perhaps he awaited her outside the castle wall. Or maybe he had sent the gift as a way for her to buy her freedom. With the gold, she could purchase passage on a ship to London. Maybe she could find him and his retinue at Martin's monastery. But it was all impossible. All nonsense. She could never escape her fate here, and she could not even be certain the Norman had sent the gift. Even worse—Le Brun was her enemy. A Norman dog. A conqueror of her homeland.

No, she must be faithful to her father, her forebears and their land. She had no choice but to obey her husband…her master. But now that he had shown his domination of her, must he display her disgrace before the entire household?

Bronwen closed her eyes and tried to block out the

memory of Olaf's face, flushed with fury and indignation. How she dreaded and feared him. How he disgusted her. Yet she knew that any further defiance of the man was useless.

"I shall go," she declared, rising from her place on the old trunk. "Find something clean for me to wear, Enit. Anything will do. Quickly now."

Bronwen smoothed her hair with an ivory comb. Enit helped her into a yellow tunic and laced the tight sleeves of the undergown. Bronwen draped her veil while her nursemaid settled the golden circlet in place.

"Give me the black mantle I wore today, Enit," Bronwen ordered.

"But it's covered in dust and caked with dry mud. You cannot go before your husband and his men wearing this!"

"It warms me." Bronwen took the mantle and shook it out. She drew it over her shoulders, felt for the key at her neck and the purse that contained her father's will box. Then she lifted her chin to fasten the mantle's clasp.

"Where did you get the cloak, Bronwen? You wear it always—yet we did not stitch it, nor did I see it in the items purchased for you at last summer's fair in Preston. Who gave it to you?"

Bronwen turned away. "It was a wedding gift, and I do not mean to part with it."

As she dipped a rushlight into the fire and saw it catch, Bronwen took a deep breath. She did not know how she would face her husband again, but she was determined to do all in her power to quell his wrath.

Leaving Enit, she went down to the hall and was pleased to find that fewer men attended this night's meal. Yet as before, the general mumble ceased when she entered, and once again every eye fell upon her as she stepped to the dais. Olaf stood by while Bronwen seated herself beside him. Haakon sat at her other elbow.

Servitors carried out the trenchers—a meal of roast suckling pig, breads and cheeses, and finally baked lamprey eel with herbed beets. Bronwen managed to eat, but she said nothing to the men on either side of her. They, in turn, were focused on their dinner, feeding themselves with much lip smacking and belching. They threw bones and other leavings over their shoulders to the floor, where the dogs that roamed the castle snarled and fought over them.

"So you went on a journey today," Haakon spoke up as the final course was carried away. "And what did you find?"

"The mossy bank of the Warbreck River," Bronwen replied. "That is all."

"Nothing more? Not even a tall, black-hooded knight, perhaps? A Norman on his way to London?" At that, the man rolled back his lips and let out a hearty guffaw.

"Keep quiet, son," Olaf growled. "You know not when to shut your mouth."

Haakon continued to snicker as Bronwen rose from the table. She knew that all color had drained from her face. Trembling, she bowed before Olaf. "My meal is complete. If you will excuse me, husband, I bid you good evening."

Olaf started to say something, then he gruffly acknowledged her departure. Bronwen stepped down and hurried from the hall to the stair. Mortified, she entered her chamber to discover that her nurse had already gone for the night. As she undressed and slipped into her bed gown, her mind spun. Olaf's anger was more than justified, she realized. Not only had she left his protection without permission, but Haakon had whispered evils against her into his father's ear.

She drew back the furs and crept into bed. What would Olaf do to her this night? Would he seek vengeance? Would he treat their first union with total disregard for her, or might he even torture her? She had heard tales of such atrocities against disobedient wives, and she and Gildan had clutched hands at night in the fear of such violence ever happening to either of them.

Closing her eyes, Bronwen prayed to gods the druids had taught her to honor and worship in her youth. Then she offered petitions to her husband's Norse gods. Perhaps they would intervene on her behalf. She was beginning a desperate prayer to the last deity she could recall—the Christian God of Martin and Le Brun—when the door to her room fell open.

Peering over the edge of a blanket of brown bear pelts, she saw Olaf Lothbrok step into the room. He kicked the door shut behind him and approached. Quaking, Bronwen could do nothing but silently utter the name of Jacques Le Brun's one God. Oh, dear Jesus... Jesus... Jesus...

"You boldly leave my castle without protection," Olaf addressed her, standing wide-legged and planting his fists at his hips. "Your behavior flouts my authority. And today my son tells me you have been a false wife. Like a harlot, you shamelessly slept with another man on the night of our wedding. A Norman and a stranger. Yet now, I find you shivering in your bed—a mouse worthy of nothing but a snap of the neck."

Bronwen tried to reply but words would not come. She gripped the fur, her fingers tight and her body quivering. Olaf took another step toward her, and she shut her eyes, waiting for it to begin.

"Well?" he barked. "What have you to say for yourself, wife?"

"Me?" Her eyes flew open. "You wish me to speak?"

The Viking stood outlined against the fire. "Defend yourself, if you can."

Confusion and incredulity filling her, Bronwen gazed at him. "But…but what do you mean, sir?"

"Are you dim-witted as well as disloyal? Surely you know that when a person is charged with an offense, we consider him innocent until his peers decide his fate. It is our custom to allow a person to testify on his own behalf. So speak for yourself if you have any justification for your deeds."

Bronwen had never heard of such a thing as this. A Briton lord always decided guilt or innocence based on hearsay or tests of honor. But Olaf Lothbrok—full of ire and thrice as strong as she—was permitting her to testify to her own blamelessness.

With this unexpected hope, she summoned courage. "I went to your bedside this morning," she said. "You were sleeping. I woke you, but you sent me away. I felt certain you did not require my presence."

Olaf's brow furrowed. "You did come to me. I recall it now. But surely I gave you no permission to leave this stronghold, to wander the woods without a guard."

"No, sir. You did not. But I beg you to understand that at Rossall, it was my custom to walk the countryside alone in order to clear my thoughts. I never meant to alarm you, my lord, yet I confess, I did leave this castle. Of that I am guilty. My intent was innocent, however, and such a thing will never happen again."

"Continue," he said. "Explain this tale of Haakon's. He swore to me that he witnessed your misdeed with his own eyes. I cannot imagine you untarnished in the event."

Bronwen swallowed. "When you put your son, my nursemaid and me ashore on the night of the storm, we discovered a hut on the beach. It was already occupied by a band of wanderers. They shared a deer they had killed, for they saw we were hungry. Haakon ate his fill—and then accused the men of poaching the deer from your lands."

"Ate first and then laid blame?" Olaf fingered his beard. "Haakon would do such a thing, I fear. He is… young. Brash. Continue, wife."

"I predicted conflict, my lord. The strangers outnumbered us, and they were well armed. We were but two women and your son. Sir, the men had been respectful to us. More than polite, they were welcoming. As your wife, I chose to reprimand Haakon. After much dispute with me, he apologized. Now I believe he takes his revenge by spreading evil rumors to disgrace me in your eyes."

"Then you deny that you were on the beach with a Norman? A member of the wandering band you had found in the hut?"

"I do not deny it, my lord," Bronwen said, meeting her husband's blue eyes. "I could not sleep for I wondered how you fared in the storm, and I was dismayed over Haakon's behavior. Just as I foolishly did today, that night I left the hut to walk alone and put my thoughts in order."

"Again this *walking* nonsense?" Olaf said, shaking his head. "Perhaps it is a Briton custom. No Viking wife would be so unwise. And the Norman? Surely he was not putting his thoughts in order, too."

"He came to warn me of the danger in my action." She hung her head, realizing how rash she had been on both occasions. "We spoke, it is true. Nothing untoward passed between us. I thanked him for his caution and returned to the hut, where I slept the rest of the night at my nursemaid's side. I am innocent of disloyalty to you, my husband. Indeed, I am yet a maiden and as chaste as the day of my birth. You will discover the truth this night when you test my purity yourself."

Without response, Olaf squatted by the fire and held his hands over it. He fell silent, and Bronwen knew he must be weighing her words against those of his son. More time passed than she imagined possible in such a situation. The man appeared to be hovering on the verge of his decision, testing it, forming a verdict. Some inner struggle ate at him as he rubbed his forehead and drew his fingers through his beard. At last, he stood.

"I accept your word as truth, wife," he said, meeting her eyes. "You speak well and honestly."

"Thank you, my lord," Bronwen replied. Relief flooded through her. "I await you humbly now."

His lips tightened as he studied her. "Tomorrow I return to Warbreck Wash where my men and I will repair the *snekkar*. From thence, I survey my borders. While I was at your father's holding, word came to Warbreck that an army of Scots has attacked my neighbor to the east. My spies report that his hall is under siege. The lord requests my aid, and he is my ally. At dawn, I leave with my men."

At the news of Scottish aggression, Bronwen's ire rose. Pushing back the furs, she left the bed and joined her husband at the fire. "Those coarse and hostile Scots believe this is their land now," she said. "If I could have that Norman king in my power for one moment, husband, I would send him to London's white tower and order his head lopped off. With his foolish treaty he has lost the best part of his kingdom to our northern enemy."

"You know of the land grant King Stephen gave to Henry of Scotland?" Olaf asked.

"The grant that includes both Rossall and Warbreck? My father told me about it, of course. It's an intolerable situation."

Rolling a few strands of his beard between thumb and forefinger, Olaf gave a low chuckle. "You astonish me, wife. A woman innocent of personal danger, yet well informed of politics? This is a wonder."

"I am to hold Rossall one day, sir, and I am prepared for the task." She turned to him, aware that seeing her in the bed gown must surely encourage her husband to set aside his consternation about his bride, his son and his lands. If she were to win an alliance with the man, she must ensure that their union this night was pleasurable to him.

She touched his arm. "Your hurry to aid a neighbor betrays the seriousness of these Scottish raids. While you're away, I shall see to the keep, my lord. You'll find it secure on your return."

Nostrils flaring and breath labored, Olaf jerked his arm from her touch and stepped away. "I must sleep. Tomorrow will be a long day."

Bronwen indicated the bed. "Very well, husband. Come now and take your satisfaction."

"Another night," he said and turned from her.

Before she could speak again, he was gone. The

sound of the door closing behind him echoed through the stone chamber. Breathless, Bronwen stared at the blank wall. Then she looked at the fire. And last, she gazed down at her bare feet on the icy floor.

"May the gods go with you, my husband," she murmured.

The following morning Enit could hardly wait to tell Bronwen of the excitement among the servitors. Even the guards seemed happier this day, for Olaf had gone to his wife's chamber at last.

"La, my good girl!" Enit clucked. "Everyone will be looking for signs of a child now! You must be certain to tell me if you start to feel ill. I'm sure it won't take long for the old man to do his work in you. Your mother was bearing you only two months after she married Edgard."

Bronwen looked away from Enit. "I will thank you to leave this matter to me. Stop your gossip, I beg you, and see to my day's garments."

Enit nodded and set about her work, but Bronwen could not help noticing the smile that played about her nursemaid's lips. Bronwen thought of the heavy, aged man who was her husband. The night before, she had offered herself to Olaf exactly as she had been taught. To her satisfaction, he had declared her innocent of wrongdoing, chuckled at her wit and expressed admiration of her knowledge. Truly, he had seemed to admire her. But then he had left the room without touching her.

Why had he gone away? What had she done wrong? Did Norse women have some other way of welcoming their husbands or had Olaf truly preferred to sleep in preparation for his journey? Or, Bronwen wondered, was her appearance unpleasant to him?

Without intending it, she drifted back to the night on the beach when she had first spoken with Jacques Le Brun. How her heart ached for the stranger who had held her in his arms. She had known by his voice and by his touch that he was a man of strength and honor. And he had called her beautiful...desirable.

Now, in the light of Olaf's rejection, Le Brun's words began to ring false. Surely she was not desirable. Surely she was not beautiful at all.

"Are you in pain?" Enit was asking. "Your face is pale and your expression troubled. I have herbs to ease your tenderness, child. Trust me, each night with your husband will be better than the last. Some women even learn to enjoy—"

"Olaf will not be at Warbreck tonight," Bronwen cut in. "He and his men left at dawn to begin repairs on the *snekkar.* After the ship is seaworthy, he will survey his borders. An ally is besieged by Scots, and my husband plans to render aid."

Enit's face fell. "But he may be away for weeks!"

"Or months. I am to remain at the keep with the retinue of guards he has left to defend me. My obligation now is to protect and improve my husband's holding. But first, I wish to send messages to my father and Gildan. Enit, send for two couriers to meet me in the great hall. I have tarried too long in this duty."

Bronwen settled down to her breakfast with an uneasy heart. Olaf had left his bride chaste. Haakon must surely despise his father's wife all the more. Far away, Edgard would be tending to his own affairs at Rossall. And Gildan was surely at peace in Aeschby's arms. Bronwen felt abandoned and forgotten.

Worse yet, Jacques Le Brun must be approaching

London. He would soon put her out of his mind. Certainly she must set her memories of the Norman aside. All she would have of him was the black mantle with its peacock-blue lining. That, and a small box containing three gold balls.

Once it became clear that Bronwen was not carrying Olaf's child, Enit and the rest of Warbreck's staff registered great disappointment. But as winter's chill began to subside, Bronwen threw herself into the tasks at hand.

Inside the castle, the rotting rushes gathered up from the floor were burned and new ones were strewn across the freshly swept and washed floors. Servitors scrubbed down the table boards in the hall to remove layers of greasy fat and spilled mead. Several women set about to make new overcloths for the tables, and Bronwen instructed Enit to embroider one with the great black crow that festooned the sails of the *snekkar*. Though the bird seemed evil to Bronwen, she sensed it would please Olaf.

"Do you know the symbol of the crow?" she asked a cook one afternoon while they cleaned stones and insects from the lentils.

The woman explained. "If in battle a crow flies by with flapping wings, victory is certain. But if it glides with motionless wings, defeat will soon follow."

Pondering the many differences between two peoples so closely connected by land, Bronwen wondered if these disparities had something to do with Olaf's rejection. Perhaps she had broken some Viking custom. She could only hope the cause would become clear to her before his return.

Outside, Bronwen ordered a large garden staked out and tilled near the kitchen. Workmen brought marl from the fields and turned the lime-rich soil into the ground. She selected seeds from all manner of vegetables and legumes to be saved for spring planting. The sad condition of the few tattered basket beehives made her wonder how any of the valuable honey and wax was retrieved. Thus she set several women to begin weaving new hives at once, and she instructed the herders to be on the lookout for wild swarms with which to replenish the depleted stock.

Several dead fruit and nut trees were chopped down and burned while dairymaids scrubbed the buttery from top to bottom. Most of the cheeses that had gone blue during the winter were tossed away, though a few were saved to place on sores and wounds for their healing powers. It was well known that a piece of moldy cheese placed on an open infection usually healed it within a week.

Two light snowfalls ushered in the busy days of February, and several stormy days marked the beginning of March. One morning late in that month, Bronwen espied a red-haired man carrying dung to the kitchen garden, and she recognized him as the peasant who had been so seasick at Rossall.

"Good morrow, my lady," he greeted her.

"You are called Wag." She smiled at his obvious amazement. "I see you made your way back to Warbreck."

"Indeed. And you—have you found the place to your liking?"

"It pleases me well enough."

The redhead wiped his hands on the apron at his waist. "May I ask the health of your sister? Are things improved with her husband?"

"You speak of Gildan and Aeschby?" Bronwen

stepped forward. "How could they be better? What do you mean by this question?"

The man swallowed and looked away. "Never you mind, madam. I must be about my work now."

"Stop at once." Bronwen lifted her skirts and strode toward him. "Do you have news of my sister? I demand to hear it."

He chewed his lower lip for a moment. "'Tis said there is trouble in the marriage, madam. But that is only a rumor, and I put no great stock in such talk."

Rooted to the garden soil, Bronwen numbly watched the fellow shrug and go his way. Was something wrong with Gildan? Trouble in the marriage? But she had been so happy at her wedding. What could have happened?

Knowing she could not leave Warbreck to go to her sister, Bronwen later spoke to Enit about her encounter with Wag.

But the nursemaid reinforced the peasant's nonchalance. "People love to gossip, child," she reminded her mistress. "They want nothing more than to imagine intrigues for their lords and ladies. It enlivens their own dreary days."

Deeply troubled, Bronwen decided to send another courier to her sister. These riders reported messages by word of mouth, and too often the information got muddled along the way. By the time they returned, news they brought might be old or distorted. But as Bronwen was forbidden to leave Warbreck, she had no choice. When the courier arrived from Aeschby's keep, he brought no reply from Gildan. He said he had not even seen the woman. Indeed, weeks passed with no word from Rossall Hall, nothing from Gildan, and utter silence from Olaf Lothbrok.

As the days of April bloomed brightly one after the other, Bronwen tried to convince herself that all was well. May slipped by and then lapsed into the warm, brilliant month of June when the hardest field work began. Bronwen ordered the sheep washed in the streams and shorn of their thick white wool. Men mowed the long meadow grass and stored the hay for winter feed. In the early mornings they plowed and planted the fields, and later they cleaned and greased their carts. The mistress of Warbreck ordered new hog sheds built to shelter the piglets, and hovels erected to store peas and other dried vegetables.

A swarm of bees had been captured in late May, and now the hives were flowing with honey. But Bronwen gathered few combs, for she wanted the colonies to grow strong and healthy. With the days and nights so warm again, there was no need for mantles or thick woolen undertunics. But she found herself unable to pack the silk-lined mantle in her chest. It was the stuff of which dreams were woven—and she needed her dreams.

The Midsummer's Day celebration arrived with great excitement among the villagers, but duty called Bronwen to spend the hours riding from one hut to another, collecting the steep rents on her husband's behalf. The sun was dipping low in the west when she rode through the castle gate to behold the courtyard swarming with armed men, who shouted as they hoisted tankards of drink. Here and there lay groups of wounded being tended by village women.

Olaf, she understood, had returned at last.

Inside the great hall, Bronwen made her way past piles of dull and dirty shields, bloodied swords, bows and spears as she headed toward the dais. When she approached, Olaf's men stood aside.

"Good husband," she said, dipping a deep curtsy before him. "I welcome your return."

"Ah, wife. You are a pleasant sight for weary eyes."

Keeping her head low to ensure he recalled her subservient position, she spoke again. "How fares the *snekkar?* I hope she is restored to good service, sir."

"The ship has been repaired and is seaworthy. We took her out for two days and felt that the gods had given us back our home."

"The sea is your home?" She looked up, aware for the first time that to the Vikings, Warbreck was only a stone castle and not a warm, longed-for sanctuary.

"Our conquest of the sea enables us to possess the land," Olaf said. "It is our way."

Bronwen tried to respond, but the shock of her husband's appearance swept all polite repartee from her mind. Barely able to accept that this was the same man who had left her in late winter, she saw that Olaf looked much thinner, and his face appeared older than ever.

"What has happened?" she asked him. "I fear you are not well, my lord."

Olaf drew a shaking hand through his long beard. "Our journey to aid my eastern ally brought hardship. At first, we routed the Scots and entered the hall in victory. But a second army joined by remnants of the first surrounded us. We have been held in siege these many months."

"Besieged? Had I but known, I should have come to your aid."

A weary smile crossed his face. "A woman fending

off her husband's foes? I see you have not forgotten how to astound me, wife."

"But you defeated the Scots, did you not?"

"They tried to starve us—and nearly succeeded. The winter stores ran out, and my ally was unprepared to feed so great a number. We fought boldly, but each time, we were driven back into the hall. At last we devised a plan. In one great body, we drove through the gates and fought our way across their lines. Feigning retreat, we hid in the forest nearby. When they rushed into the hall, we turned back upon them and set fire to the place."

Bronwen held her breath as Olaf continued. "We could not have succeeded, but the Scots taunted us that a great Norman army was marching toward Warbreck. Our fury and dread led us to victory. Yet now my ally's hall is burned, and so, in the end, the Scots had their way."

"But is this rumor true?" Bronwen asked. "Do enemies approach us?"

"Indeed," Olaf replied. "We expected to find them here already. The gods spared us, but we have little time to ready our weapons. If you are the worthy wife I hoped to find on my return, you will assist me."

"Of course, my husband. As you wish."

"My soldiers must rest. I have ordered the village children to clean and polish our weapons and armor. The women will carry sacks of cheeses, dried meats, beans and flour into the keep's storehouses against the threat of siege. The men must groom the horses and repair weak places in our walls."

"My father is wary of the Normans," Bronwen told Olaf, "but he refuses to fear them. He believes Amounderness protects itself. The great wet forests, marshy ground, wild moors and windy fells are not easily tamed. The woods are difficult to cross and the rivers, ponds and shallow meres make travel almost impossible. You must have no doubt about your strength, husband. The Normans are not nearly as strong as the Scots, are they? I have heard they grow soft and tame like King Stephen. My father believes they soon will lose the country."

"Your father forgets that the Normans are descended from Vikings," Olaf grunted. "Their line comes directly from Norsemen who raided France and settled in the northern region they called Normandy. Their first duke was Rollo—a Dane. No, wife, Normans are not soft men. They hunger for land and power. They desire England not so much for herself as for the influence it gives them in France. King Stephen is a mere duke in France. But here, he is king. Many English knights owe him homage, and this makes him a mighty force against the French king."

"You teach me more of politics than even my father did," Bronwen said. "But do you know anything about the one who comes to Warbreck?"

"My spies tell me he is of mixed heritage. Half his blood runs Norman, and half is of some eastern race— Jew, Turk, Moor or another such breed."

Bronwen frowned at this news. "Then he can have no religion, no traditions, no worthy lineage. His men will not be loyal—you may be assured of that. I have no dread of the Norman, for your men will easily defeat him."

Olaf took her hand and rubbed his thumb over it for a moment. "You are a good wife," he murmured. "Your father was too generous with me."

Her cheeks growing warm at this earnest tribute, Bronwen realized that for the first time since meeting

Olaf Lothbrok, she knew a sense of kinship with him. Perhaps their marriage would be a good one after all. Maybe, in time, they would even learn to care deeply for each other.

"I must go to the kitchen," she said. "I will order a fine meal for you and your men. And I must oversee the women as they stock the storage rooms."

Olaf gave her a last look and then turned to speak to a guard. Bronwen left the dais and was hurrying across the great hall when she passed Haakon. Amid a group of his peers, he stood with his arm around a woman greatly swollen with child.

"Greetings, Briton," he called out as Bronwen passed. "I see you are not as fortunate as my wife. Soon I'll name my son, but your womb is sure to dry like a grape forgotten on the vine."

He guffawed as the group around him snickered in amusement. Pretending she had not heard the untoward remark, Bronwen pushed open the door and left the hall.

As she expected, Bronwen heard her husband's footsteps outside her door that night. He entered her chamber, and she was pleased to see that he wore one of the many tunics she and her ladies had sewn for him during his absence.

"You appear refreshed," she said, turning from the narrow window through which she had been studying the stars. "I trust your meal was satisfactory."

"Delicious." He walked to the fire. "You have been busy in the past months. I'm told you ordered so many tasks that my servitors now lie exhausted in their beds."

Bronwen smiled. "I have looked after the keep—as I promised."

"This honors me. You join the ranks of treasure-givers. You are my keep-protector, my respected wife."

Bronwen dipped her head. "Thank you, my lord. I take pride in my position as your life companion."

"Good," he said. "Come and stand with me here in the warmth of the flame."

Obeying, Bronwen noted that her dread of the man had lessened. She would welcome him into her bed this night. Unless Haakon knew something about his father of which she was unaware, before long she would be bearing Olaf's heir—the one who would someday unite both Warbreck and Rossall.

"I had not realized your son was wed," she said. "His wife is due to give birth."

"That woman—" Olaf stopped himself. "The woman is not Haakon's chosen wife. I will never acknowledge the child, and my son knows it. He must marry the lady of my choosing—a good and virtuous wife. That wanton wastrel is a scrap of refuse Haakon met in the village at Warbreck Wash. She has no dowry, no lineage, no land, nothing."

Bronwen studied the man as he spoke. She felt that somehow she was looking into an ancient face, the face of Thor, perhaps, or Odin. It was the craggy, wrinkled face of the past, of centuries gone by—years filled with bloodshed and darkness and many gods. The face of a time that was passing and would not return.

Olaf met her eyes. "You are honorable, and I fear I am…" He sighed. "I'm not worthy of you."

"My father believed differently. He trusted you with my life."

"Oh, woman," Olaf groaned, his arms drawing her into his embrace. "You are strong and noble. And this makes you...difficult. Everything is now so difficult. Much more than I expected or planned."

Bronwen rested her cheek against his shoulder. "You had a wife once. Can it be so difficult to have another?"

Olaf trembled as he took her shoulders and set her away. "You must try to understand. Try to accept."

"Accept what, husband?"

He turned from her and strode to the door. "Accept *this*."

The door shut behind him and Bronwen knotted her fists in frustration. Not again! Why did he not take her as his wife? Sinking onto a bench by the fire, she buried her face in her hands.

The next morning Bronwen woke to the sounds of a melee—shouts, cries, metal clanging, horses whinnying.

"They come, they come!" Enit cried, bursting into the chamber. "A great throng of horsemen rides out of the forest and surrounds the keep walls. Get up, child. Get up at once."

"Normans? Are they here so soon? But we are unprepared!"

Throwing back her blankets, Bronwen dressed in the first gown she could find and cast her black mantle about her shoulders. As she left her chamber and stepped into the guardroom, she saw several men standing at the windows, their longbows drawn and their arrows at hand.

"Permit me to look," she ordered one of them. Around the stone outer wall, the Norman forces took up posts just beyond arrow range. She observed that few of them carried the longbows common among Olaf's men. Instead, the attackers bore short crossbows, which they held cocked and aimed at the parapets.

Olaf's men stood in defense positions, their spears and broadswords at the ready. The courtyard echoed with panicked villagers rushing to seek shelter within the keep—a scene of utter chaos.

"Oh, Enit," Bronwen whispered as her nurse slipped to her side. "Look, the Norman leader rides out—and there stands my husband on the parapet."

A mail-clad, helmeted knight astride a large gray steed approached the gate. His horse and shield bore a red ground, with a golden lion on hind legs facing to the side. Looking up at the Viking, the man shouted his challenge. "I come in service of Henry Plantagenet, known as CurtMantle, FitzEmpress, and the Lion of Justice. Will you give homage to the rightful king of England?"

Henry Plantagenet? Bronwen pressed her hands against the rough stone wall. This Norman served the same man as Jacques Le Brun. Could it be? But no— the warlord's crest was nothing like the one on her mantle—golden balls on a blue field.

Now Olaf leaned forward to respond. Beside him, Haakon held his family's great purple standard emblazoned with a black crow.

"I am Olaf Lothbrok, lord and master of Warbreck. I serve no man but myself! Never will you take my keep, Norman dog!"

At that, Olaf's men sent up a mighty cheer and with it a sally of arrows. But the Normans rode forward, sending a return volley. The guard beside Bronwen pushed her from the window and raised his bow to launch an arrow.

Chapter Six

"La, child," Enit pleaded. "You must return to your room quickly. They're upon us! Even now the Normans are upon us!"

"Calm yourself, Enit. We are safe within the walls."

"Do you see their number? Oh, they're a fearsome lot!"

As the guard reached for another arrow, Bronwen touched his arm. "What will happen, good man? Has my husband spoken a plan?"

"In a short time, we'll know whether the Normans plan to storm the castle or lay siege to it." The guard fitted the arrow to his longbow. "My master will never allow a siege, madam. We are unready. He must force a battle."

"But we have food! We can endure a blockade of supplies, I'm sure of it."

"Our men are too few to hold back the Normans. Many of us were injured in the battle with the Scots, and the rest are too weak to endure a siege. We must attack with what strength we still have. Madam, your husband would wish you to return to the protection of your chamber. Have you food? The kitchens are busy boiling oil for Norman heads."

Enit squawked in dismay. "I'll try to find some bread and an apple or two, child. Go now, stay in your room."

Bronwen spoke to the guard again. "Is it safe for my nurse to cross the courtyard?"

"For the time," he said. "Few arrows fall inside the yard—the Normans are not close enough yet."

"Then I shall go to my husband."

"Bronwen!" Enit wailed. "Come back!"

But she would not be deterred. If Norman forces took this castle, she would not perish without a battle of her own. Hurrying down the stair, she passed women and children struggling to push their way up to the protection of the highest point in the keep. Soon she broke out into the courtyard and paused to scan the parapets for Olaf.

"I'm happy to see you care so little for your own peril," a voice said at her shoulder. She turned to find Haakon sneering at her. "If the gods will it, a Norman arrow will find your Briton heart."

Hardly able to bear the sight of the man, with his thick lips and huge hands, Bronwen glared at him. "Leave me in peace, Haakon. I search for my husband."

"But does he search for you? Does he rush to your side to protect you from the Norman threat? I think not."

"My husband is busy with—"

"My *husband,* my *husband...*" Haakon mocked. "Olaf Lothbrok is not your husband."

"What do you mean? Of course he is. You saw us wed."

Haakon leaned against her, his sour breath heating her cheek. "My father has never bedded you. Nor will he. You are a maiden. Do I not speak the truth, Briton?"

Clutching the edges of her mantle, Bronwen took a step backward. "What is this? My husband cares for me. I know he does. Why do you say these things, fool?"

"You are the fool," he snarled. "Have you not discerned our plan? My father will never come to your bed—for you must not be allowed to bear his child. From the beginning we have planned that Rossall is to be mine. *Mine!* I am my father's only heir. You will never see Rossall again."

"You lie!" Bronwen said. "Your father is a good man. He and my father arranged the marriage to benefit—"

"To benefit *me!* I am the only son of Olaf Lothbrok. I am his heir. Why would he endow his holding to anyone else? No, loyal wife, you are a pawn in this game we play. Your father bartered you to win control of Warbreck for the Britons. My father took you, and will keep you barren, until Edgard of Rossall is dead—at which time that land will become mine."

With instinct born of fear, Bronwen touched the small will box she carried always in the chatelaine purse at her side. "Upon my honor, I remind you that Rossall is to be mine and my son's. That was the agreement between our fathers."

"Rossall will belong to my son—the child my wife carries even now."

"Your father said you are unwed. He told me he intends to arrange a marriage for you."

"Olaf Lothbrok is not my master," Haakon said. "I married Astrid, and she bears my heir. Heir to Warbreck and Rossall. My father might choose another woman for me, but I'll not have her. He knows full well I'm wed to Astrid. She brings nothing to the union—nothing but beauty, pleasure and satisfaction. Those are all I need of a wife."

For a moment, Bronwen was unable to speak. The chaos inside the courtyard and the battle outside the wall seemed to fill her mind, echoing its pandemonium, confusion, turmoil. Could Haakon's words be true? Was it possible that she and her father had been betrayed to such an extent?

"Why do you tell me this now?" she demanded of Haakon. "Your father lives, as does mine. I, too, am alive and can testify to this outrageous tale you've spun. Olaf took my word over yours once—why should he not do so again?"

"If you go to my father with your accusations, he will lie to you again. He knows the plan we made, and his absence from your bed proves I speak the truth. Now the Normans come, playing perfectly into my game. Before this battle is out, I will hold Warbreck and Rossall."

Haakon called for an armor-bearer and selected a sword. Holding it menacingly in Bronwen's face, he laughed. "Watch and see, Briton. My Viking blood conquers all."

Running up the stairs to her chamber, Bronwen felt the first touches of fear and uncertainty. Had Haakon's words been true? As much as she longed to deny them, he had been right about his father. Even now she could hear Olaf's words as he turned away from her. *You are strong and noble. And this makes you…difficult. Everything is now so difficult. Much more than I expected or planned… You must try to understand. Try to accept.*

Haakon had called this *plan* a game of treachery. Was she blind, and had her father been so deceived by his ally? Surely not. For all his barbaric ways, Olaf had become a man she honored and was determined to please. But now it appeared both men detested her presence in the castle. She was an obstruction, a barrier to their goal of taking Rossall. Indeed, her very life was in danger.

If Olaf held his stronghold against the Normans, would he continue to protect her? Or did Haakon mean to use the battle as a shield behind which to kill her?

And if by chance the Normans prevailed, would they let her leave? Could she return to Rossall and her father's hall? How very far that dearly loved place seemed now.

She found Enit huddled beside the fire in her room. For the first time in her life, Bronwen recognized fear in the old woman's eyes. "I have found a piece of dried cod, some cheese and a little black bread," Enit told her. "Eat, child."

"I cannot," Bronwen said, pushing away the trencher as she seated herself next to her nurse. "I feel ill."

"Did you find your husband? Can you tell me what he plans?"

"I know nothing of that man. As for his plans, they intend only evil toward me. When the battle is over, you and I must return to Rossall. My father will have the marriage agreement terminated. In truth, it never was a marriage."

"Dissolve the union? But this defies your father's will. And what if you are with child?"

Bronwen looked into her nurse's worried eyes. "Enit, you heard my father's will for me. He intended me to inherit Rossall. I shall be obedient to him above all others. That land is the future of my people. It is our only hope."

Enit sighed and stirred the fire. "Great hopes are often quickly dashed."

"But if I have no hope, then I have nothing." Bronwen felt a lump thicken in her throat. "Enit, I must have my dreams or I might as well die."

In the chamber where Bronwen and Enit sat, they could just make out the muffled roar of battle below. The narrow window provided little information, and no one had come to report on the conflict. By late afternoon, Bronwen could endure no more. Despite her nurse's protests, she took Enit's arm and left the protection of the room.

The moment they stepped into the crowded guardroom, Bronwen heard the sounds of horses neighing in fear and the swift hiss of arrows. She located the guard she had spoken to earlier. He stood at his post near the window.

"What news, good man?" she asked.

He glanced her way. "Madam, the Norman army has set up pavilions along the river and in the forest. Their men remain positioned around our walls."

Bronwen peered around him. "Their arrows fall well within the courtyard now. Yet ours miss their mark. How can this be?"

The guard stepped away from the narrow window and leaned heavily against the wall. "They have a new bow, my lady. Their crossbow shoots much farther than our longbow. Already we have lost many—while they have lost few. Their lord is an able warrior who leads his men with bravery and wisdom. We are told he prepares secret weapons in the woods."

"Who brings this news?"

"Our spies have ways of leaving and entering the walls undetected. But also we have watched the Normans felling trees and gathering great stones."

"And what of Olaf? Why does he allow them time to build? Why not go out to meet them on the battlefield?"

The guard let out a deep breath. "Madam, we have few men, and our weapons are no longer adequate. We must hold our ground until they bring out this new armament. Then we shall try to burn it and overcome them as they approach. We have no other choice."

"Carry on, then. I wish you well."

As Bronwen left his side, she saw two men carrying a wounded comrade into the guardroom. An arrow protruded from his leather breastplate, and blood foamed from his mouth. He groaned in agony as he tried in vain to pull out the arrow.

Dismayed, she took Enit's hand and hurried down the stairs into the main hall where the cries and wails of the wounded echoed to the high ceiling. Sprawled about the floor lay the injured and the dead—far more men than Bronwen could have imagined. Two women moved from one to the next, attempting to administer care and ease pain.

"Where are the others?" Bronwen demanded of one exhausted lady. "Why does no one assist you?"

Looking up at her mistress with great ghostlike eyes, she wiped her fingers on an apron. "Most women labor in the kitchens or repair weapons. Many are yet in the village, for the Normans came so quickly that few were able to get inside the walls."

"Enit," Bronwen said. "Return to the chamber and gather your medicine bags and herbs. We are needed here."

The hours crept toward sunset as the women removed arrows, bound wounds and dragged the dead into a corner. Bronwen set a pot of mallow root to boil for bathing injuries. A second pot of chamomile tea would help the men to sleep. She and Enit taught the other women how to make poultices of goldenseal and slippery-elm bark, which stopped the bleeding for many of the deep punctures.

In all her life, Bronwen had never seen such horror. Her anger at Olaf diminished as she gazed into the pain-filled eyes of the wounded. When the sky grew dark and the battle ended for the day, warriors poured into the hall in search of food. Their women brought dried meats and bread, and the men fell to their meal, seated among their moaning comrades but saying little.

Enit nestled beside her mistress on the cold floor where they shared a small green apple and a piece of salty pork. As she rested her head upon the stone wall, Bronwen's focus fell on Olaf. The old man stood at some distance across the hall. He leaned heavily upon his sword and looked at her with tired blue eyes.

"Stay here, Enit," she murmured. "I must speak to Olaf. Keep close watch on his son—there by the fire. Haakon is my enemy."

Before Enit could question her, Bronwen crossed to the Viking and asked to speak to him in private. Nodding, he led her to the curtained alcove where he slept. "What do you need of me, wife?" he asked. "I have little to give at this hour, but what I have is yours."

"I need answers, sir." She crossed her arms, as if that might defend her against the agonizing truth. "Today, Haakon told me of your plan. He said you intend to keep me childless so that your only son will inherit Rossall. You deceived my father and me."

Olaf held up a hand. "Wait. I must sit."

But as he sank onto his bed, Bronwen could no longer hold her tongue. "Haakon ridiculed me as a fool for not perceiving your scheme. Since my wedding day, I have been his greatest threat. He fears I will lure you to my bed, and his dreams will be lost. But he has little to dread, because you join him in this mockery of our vows. You would have your household believe I am barren."

"Madam, please—"

"Do not suppose I am without power and influence, Olaf Lothbrok. Despite the Norman attack, I shall escape both you and your wicked son."

Olaf sat silently before her, his face as pale as ivory. Bronwen waited for him to speak, but when he said nothing, she poured out her heart. "I thought you were kind. Indeed, held a measure of affection for you. I had learned to accept your people's strange ways, and I had all but come to call this place my home. But now I see you as an evil, heartless man and our marriage as a sham."

Staring down at his interlaced fingers, Olaf shook his head. "I can say nothing in my own defense. Haakon spoke the truth—but, believe me, our treachery was woven before I knew you." He looked up at her. "My son has reason to fear. Given time, I would not be able to resist you. You are a woman like no other…and I am the fool."

At that the old man pushed himself up from the bed, lifted his sword and lumbered from the alcove.

As Bronwen stepped into the hall again, she spotted Enit fast asleep on the floor. Her heart softening, she decided they should return to the silence and safety of the upper chamber. They needed to rest, and Bronwen had much to consider.

But as she lifted her tunic and stepped over the legs of a wounded man, she saw Olaf beckon her. He stood near the door, again leaning on his sword, as he spoke with a peasant who wore the garb of a woodsman.

"Come, wife," Olaf said. "Before we hear this man speak, I must tell you that when I heard the Normans were approaching, I summoned my spies for word of an ally who might assist us. This man has just arrived. He brings news from the north."

"North?" Bronwen's heart stumbled. "Have you been to Rossall Hall? Do you have word of my father? Surely he will come to our aid!"

The man dropped to one knee before her. "Madam, I bear unwelcome tidings. Edgard the Briton has died."

"Died?" Bronwen cried out, pulling the man to his feet. "You lie! This cannot be true."

Olaf gently drew her back. "Tell us what has passed at Rossall, man."

"Edgard was taken ill in early summer, but he insisted he would recover. Indeed all believed it must be so. He would allow none to go to his daughters lest they be alarmed for no good cause. For the same reason, I did not inform you, my lord. But a fortnight ago, Edgard died in the night. He has been buried. I was journeying to Warbreck with that news when I received your summons."

"No, no, no," Bronwen moaned as hot tears welled in her eyes and spilled down her cheeks. "It cannot be."

"What of Rossall?" Olaf asked. "Who holds it now?"

"My lord, the Briton had not been buried a week

before Aeschby Godwinson—husband of Edgard's younger daughter and holder of the land across the Wyre River to the east—rode into Rossall and declared himself its lord."

"Aeschby?" Olaf grabbed the messenger's tunic by the neck. "Is this true? Did you see the man himself, or have you only a rumor?"

"With my own eyes, I saw Aeschby, his men and his entire household take possession of the keep. At that, I departed for Warbreck at once."

"You did well." Olaf clapped a hand on the man's shoulder. "Take your rest now."

As the Viking ordered a servitor to find his son, Bronwen stood numb. It was impossible. Unthinkable. Her father was dead? Rossall taken by Aeschby? No.

"I must go home," she murmured as she tried to stem her tears. "My father... My sister..."

"You forget we have a battle outside our walls. When the time comes, I'll send Haakon to Rossall."

"Haakon? No—"

"Go to your chamber, woman. Bar the door, mourn your father and wait in silence. When the castle is safe again, I shall come to you."

Bronwen covered her face with her hands and wept in the dark emptiness of her bed. In clear memory, she saw Edgard's dear face before her. His warm arms seemed almost within reach.

"I have lost my father," she sobbed to Enit who lay on a pallet beside the bed. "I have lost Rossall. My husband has deceived me. And what of Gildan? Is she at Rossall? Does she assist her husband in betraying our father? Oh, Enit, I fear I shall never see my home again. The Norman dogs will rip us to shreds or carry us away as captives."

"Whisht, child," Enit murmured. "Sleep if you can. The morrow will bring trouble enough of its own."

As Bronwen closed her eyes, a distant voice emerged. *Take the box,* her father whispered as he passed the small chest to his daughter in secret. *Try not to let him know of it. He would not understand.*

Bronwen's breath went shallow at the recollection of that moment. Her father had not completely trusted Olaf after all. Perhaps he had even suspected Aeschby of duplicity. Wiser than she could comprehend, Edgard had ordered a scribe to set down his will. Words, he insisted, held sway with Norman conquerors. In their courts of law, the pen would always defeat the sword.

Heart slamming against her chest, Bronwen slipped from the bed and located the chatelaine purse she had always kept chained at her waist. As she removed her father's will box, she grasped the key at her neck. She inserted it into the tiny lock, and the lid lifted. For a moment, she stroked her fingers across the parchment. *This* was power? But the fragment would vanish in flame or water. It seemed impossible that anyone could care what had been marked down with inky nicks of a goose's quill. Surely such an object could have no influence.

But Edgard the Briton had entrusted his daughter with it, and she had nothing else of him. His health was broken and his life lost, his older daughter betrayed, and his land and keep usurped. Bronwen knew she must protect the box, but she could no longer carry it. By morning, she might be a prisoner of the Normans. If Olaf triumphed and she survived, the written will would mean nothing to him or his son. But somehow, some way, it must survive.

"Why do you slip about in the dark, girl?" Enit whispered. "Did I not beg you to sleep?"

Bronwen knelt at the old woman's side. "Enit, on the night of my betrothal, my father declared his will for Rossall. Do you remember?"

"Of course I do. He broke with Briton tradition by leaving management of his holding to you."

She held up the chest. "Inside lies a document on which Edgard the Briton's will was inked in words."

Enit propped herself up on one elbow and peered at the box in the firelight. "Bronwen, your father was wise, but I fear that both of you are bewitched to believe that squirrel scratches on rolled parchment have any meaning or worth. The document may declare you to be mistress of Rossall, but it will have no power against the might of Aeschby's men or the force of Olaf and his son."

"Nevertheless, I am honor-bound to protect it. I must hide it in a safe place until I can return to Rossall."

"Hide it *here?*"

"Where else? I'm not an eagle to soar off to a far mountain, Enit. Here I am, and here the box must stay. If I'm released or can escape, it will go with me. But the Norman dogs outside this castle must never have it."

Grumbling, the nursemaid clambered up from her pallet. "You try me, child. I lie in fear of my death, and you bid me conceal a box of ink blotches." Padding across the room, she spoke in a low voice. "When we laid new rushes, I noted that this floor is made of wood instead of stone. More easily burned, true, yet a good hiding place."

Bronwen knelt and swept back a thick layer of rushes. The women used a knife to pry up two boards, and then Bronwen set the will box into a space directly below the window. As they replaced the slats and redistributed the rushes, Enit heaved a sigh.

"*Now* may we rest?" she asked.

"Promise me you'll never forget where this box is hidden," Bronwen said.

"You have my vow."

Bronwen kissed Enit's cheek and both returned to their beds. But the younger lay awake for many hours. She decided that at dawn, she would find Olaf's spy and offer him one of her three gold balls to reveal a way through the castle wall. She must escape, for she could rely on no one now. Every man she knew—Olaf, Haakon, Aeschby—had proven treacherous. There was but one who had treated her with honor, but Jacques Le Brun was far away in London with his beloved Henry Plantagenet.

A hammering at her door woke Bronwen the following morning. "Madam," a deep voice cried out. "The Normans approach with their machines! My lord sends word that you must stay in your chamber."

Throwing her mantle over the tunic in which she had slept, Bronwen ran to the door and lifted the bar. The guard she had spoken with before stepped into her chamber. "The new weapons may threaten all our lives," he told her. "You are not to go down to the hall."

"But the wounded—they need our help!"

"Leave them to the gods, madam. You can do nothing more now."

"What are these terrible new weapons, then?"

"First comes a wooden tower on high wheels. Norman warriors cover their heads with shields as they roll it toward us. Behind the tower comes a catapult, madam. It has a long arm on which rests a great bowl. They will use it to launch stones at our outer wall. Once the catapult breaches the fortification, the tower will be rolled forward so that the Normans can climb over and attack us."

"We must burn the weapons! Surely it can be done."

"The Norman leader on his gray steed directs all the action on the field. He's shrewd and clever. Your husband is… He is uncertain how to respond."

Even as he spoke the words, a stone missile struck the wall around the castle. The fortress shuddered from the impact, and Bronwen could hear rocks tumbling to the ground below. Enit screeched in terror as the guardsman bolted from the chamber to return to his post.

Unwilling to lock herself into a doomed chamber, Bronwen followed the man. Through his window, she saw hordes of Normans racing past the catapult, swarming up the wheeled tower and climbing onto the crumbling parapet of Warbreck Castle. The catapult flung another stone and knocked away a second section of the wall's top. The lower wall began to weaken and collapse as well.

As one band of Norman warriors worked the catapult and a second climbed the rolling tower, a third regiment bore down on the gate with a massive iron-tipped battering log. Though shields covered their heads, the assailants were turned back when Olaf's men poured boiling oil on them from the battlements. But at once another group took their place.

Bronwen left the window and ran back to her chamber. "Enit!" she cried, bursting through the door. "The Norman army overpowers us, and I fear they mean to kill us all. Their leader thirsts for Viking blood. These warriors live to die by the sword!"

"They live to die for their honor, child." Enit had covered herself in Bronwen's furs as if somehow they might cushion her from the falling walls. "This is the way of men, and we cannot hope to understand it. Sit down with me and await your fate, for this is the way of women."

"Last night I spoke with one of Olaf's spies." Bronwen knelt beside her nurse. "He can lead us to safety. We must find him and escape this place. My father is dead, and I will not lose you, too. Take my hand and follow me."

Enit shook her head. "If you find a way out, return for me. Either way, I am ready to meet my destiny."

Nearly bursting with fear and frustration, Bronwen left the chamber again and hurried through the guard-room. As she passed a window, she looked out to discover that the Normans had already overrun the outer wall. Within the castle courtyard, men wielded sword, shield, spear and mace in fierce hand-to-hand combat. Many of the Norman troops had ridden their horses through the battered gate that now hung splintered and broken on its hinges. These men held a clear advantage over their unmounted Viking foes, who fell beneath the heavy blows of Norman swords.

But the Vikings fought on. In their wild eyes and bared teeth, Bronwen saw a bloodlust not present in the calculated strikes of the Normans. She recalled Olaf's words—to Vikings, death by sword was the only death. Only then might men walk in Valhalla with the gods.

As she scanned the throng for Olaf, Bronwen realized that some of the Vikings had turned upon their own men. They killed each other rather than face capture and lose the glory of death by sword.

A loud thud below told Bronwen the Normans had moved their battering ram to the wooden door of the castle itself. Panic rising in her throat, Bronwen tried to think what to do. In a moment the enemy would be inside. She was too late to escape! And how could she protect Enit?

She had started up to her chamber for the nursemaid when she heard a great splintering crack and the crash of the huge keep door falling open. Shouts of victory flooded the hall and echoed up the stairway. Running for her chamber, she felt the heavy pounding of footsteps behind her—and a massive, mail-clad warrior threw her to the floor. Just as a sea of blackness swam before her eyes, the Norman jerked her to her feet.

"Release me!" she cried, pushing at him. "I am the wife of Olaf Lothbrok!"

"So we know," the knight replied brokenly in her tongue. "Our orders are to take you to our lord."

Surrounded, Bronwen saw she had no choice but to go with them. She spotted Enit standing ashen in the door of the chamber as the men ushered her forward.

"I walk alone," Bronwen told them, speaking the Norman French the tutor had taught her. "Release my arms."

The knights halted in surprise. "She speaks our language."

"Yes, and you will treat me well. Now unhand me."

The men set her free, and Bronwen smoothed out her tunic and straightened her mantle. Just as they reached the bottom of the stair, four Viking men carried the blood-soaked body of their lord through the broken door. With a cry, Bronwen pushed between the knights escorting her and ran to Olaf's side.

The Vikings placed the old man on the floor and Bronwen knelt beside him. His face was gray and blood-spattered, and the tired blue eyes were half-closed. Bronwen saw that Olaf's mail had been hewn across the arm, leg and chest. The gaping wounds bled freely.

"Olaf," she whispered. "It is I, your wife."

At her words, the parchment-thin eyelids slid back, and Bronwen looked into his eyes. In that moment, her ears closed out the sounds of groaning men and the sight of armored knights around her. All she saw was the man she had tried so hard to please and had longed to understand.

"Bronwen," he murmured, his lips barely moving.

Taking Olaf's wrinkled hand in hers, she held it to her cheek. This was not the father of Haakon, the deceitful betrayer of Edgard the Briton or the overmatched warrior who lacked a strategy. He was her wedded husband. She remembered the night in her room when he had taken her in his arms and spoken words of admiration.

"You... You have been good to me," he rasped. He rested for a moment, and then he lifted his focus to her again. "Yet I betrayed you."

Bronwen shook her head. "It is all past now. I hold nothing against you."

"Then I go happy to Valhalla of the gods."

Bronwen bent and kissed her dying husband's hand and rested her lips there as she tried to accept the dim certainty of her own fate.

"What a hovel this is," a loud voice called out behind her. "It can hardly be called a castle. Are we certain we want the place now that we have won it?"

Laughter followed the remark as another voice spoke up. "I would call it the cesspool of England. We should return it to the barbarians."

As Bronwen listened to the cutting remarks and harsh amusement, a sudden rage coursed through her. These men cursed the land they had taken from her husband. Here he lay—dying from his wounds—and they mocked the holding he had given his life for. And she had taken pride in her work here. This *hovel* was the product of her own hand as well. Bronwen glanced to one side and she saw Olaf's great sword lying blood-stained on the stone floor.

She could not allow this sacrilege. Enit had said that battle was men's work. Now none remained to defy their foes. But she remained, and she would take down one Norman to pay for Olaf's life.

Bronwen reached out, grasped the hilt of the old weapon with both hands and leaped to her feet. She lunged forward and whirled the sword in a wide arc.

"Villains!" she shouted. "Death to you all!"

Her first pass sent the knights around her stumbling backward. Behind them the enemy leader in his bloodied mail and gray helm approached. With all her strength, Bronwen swung the heavy sword at his neck.

"Norman dog!" Bronwen shouted. "Pay for your crime!"

As the weapon made its way toward the mark, the knight raised his own sword to block the blow. The ringing clash of weapons sent a shock down Bronwen's arm. Olaf's sword flew from her hand and clattered on the stone floor.

Her fury unabated, she rushed at the Norman, hammering his ironclad chest with her fists. Ignoring the rain of blows, he grasped her arms in his gloved hands and pinned them to her side.

"You are the hated one," she spat in his own tongue. "Take Warbreck then. I shall stay no longer in your presence—heathen!"

At her last word, the man released his grip. The knights surrounding them stared agape at the woman who dared curse their lord. The Norman warrior reached up and lifted his helm from his head.

Bronwen's heart stumbled as she fixed her gaze on the man's face. His eyes were deep and gentle. His hair, darker than her own, curled long and loose about his neck. His skin was bronze.

"Bronwen the Briton." The man addressed her with a low bow. "Permit me to introduce myself. I am Jacques Le Brun. I believe we have met before."

Chapter Seven

"I express my regret at your husband's passing," Jacques said, facing the woman whose memory had refused to flee him in the months since their last meeting. "But you are mistaken in assuming my guilt. One of his own men was responsible for the death of Olaf Lothbrok."

"'Tis true, my lady," a voice spoke up from behind the throng of knights. A red-haired peasant shoved through to the forefront. He stopped in front of Bronwen and fell to his knees. "This Norman speaks the truth about your husband's death, madam. 'Twas not the Normans that did the old man in. 'Twas his son."

"Haakon?" The bright flush of color drained from her cheeks. "But—but where is he now?"

"My men tell me he escaped into the forest," Jacques told her. "Madam, I intended to capture your husband and transport him to London. I had no plan to kill him, though perhaps it would have come to that in the heat of battle."

Jacques studied Bronwen as she looked down at the still figure of her husband. Had she learned to love the man in the months following their wedding? It was hard to imagine the old man winning the heart of such a beauty. But the actions of Bronwen the Briton had never ceased to intrigue him.

Aware of his men standing around him, Jacques addressed the woman. "Your attempt on my life was justified," he said. "You defended yourself. But as to your accusations against me, I take exception."

In her dark eyes a flicker of smoldering anger lingered as she looked into his face. "What have I said that you did not deserve, sir? My husband is dead, my home is taken, and I am your captive."

"True on all counts," he acknowledged. "But you labeled me a heathen, and I am not."

"No? I have heard otherwise. Defend yourself, then."

"With pleasure. My father is a Norman baron who journeyed with Robert, Duke of Normandy, on the First Crusade to the Holy Land in 1096. When Robert returned, my father elected to remain in the East to build a shipping enterprise in Antioch. He acquired land and became a wealthy merchant. There he met and married a Christian woman, by whom he had six children—of whom I am the second son. My mother's lineage can be traced to the earliest followers of Jesus Christ, for the first church ever established was at Antioch."

"Your Christian heritage is one of bloodshed and tyranny. Your God demands carnage. In your blood mingles the impurities of many races." She lifted her chin. "I am a Briton—pure and unpolluted. My gods are worshipped in the trees, stones and waterfalls of this holy land on which you dare to tread. Let us make no mistake, sir. You may have captured me, but you will never conquer my spirit."

"What of your heart?" Jacques asked. "Does it remain free? Or are you bound forever to the Norseman? I fear, madam, you have failed to discern that your own father was less interested in the purity of your children's blood than in the preservation of his land."

Her dark eyes suddenly welled with tears. "My father is dead. My husband is dead. In what other way will you mock my pain, sir?"

Feeling the rapier tip of the remark, Jacques turned to his men. "Bring in the wounded and see that the kitchens cease their boiling of oil and begin turning out food fit for hungry warriors. We must eat, rest and begin our true labor. We have much work to do here before we can call this a stronghold of Henry Plantagenet."

When he looked around again, Jacques saw that the woman had again fallen to her knees beside her husband. The Viking's ragged breathing had ceased, and his body lay still. The mask of death had already transformed his face. As Bronwen passed a blood-caked hand over her eyes, Jacques could not prevent himself from going to her.

"Madam," he said in a low voice. "Are you well? You are bloodied, and your gown is torn. Did one of my men—"

"No. I'm not injured." Drawing her cloak about her, she stood. Her fire was gone now, and her lip trembled. "I have been tending the wounded."

"I see you wear my mantle. Perhaps then you do remember me?"

At his words, a soft pink suffused her cheeks. "The mantle is…warm," she said. "You told me you would ask for it when we met again. I had not thought it to be under these circumstances."

She reached to unclasp it, but he stepped forward and covered her hand with his. "Please. Keep the mantle. Did you receive my gift? A small chest containing—"

"Three golden orbs." Her eyes searched his face. "I did, but why? Why did you send them?"

"I had hoped you would see the crest on my mantle and know that my emblem is the three golden balls of St. Nicholas. He is my patron."

"But why?" Bronwen asked. "Why would you honor the patron saint of virgins?" Though the Britons were pagans, she had heard some of the saints' tales, including Saint Nicholas.

"St. Nicholas is also the patron of sailors. As a boy, I dreamed of becoming an adventurer."

"And so you have. Now you're lord of a beautiful and valuable holding."

"Indeed I am. I sent the gift because I wanted you to know I remembered you. And that I was coming—as I had promised."

She looked down. "I thought you were in London."

"I went…and returned with my army."

"The victor," she murmured.

"Tell me of your father, I beg you. And your lands—bequeathed to you upon your betrothal."

"You intended to take *my* holding, too?" Bronwen shook her head. "My father is dead. Aeschby—my sister's husband—has taken my lands. I must go to Rossall."

A touch on Jacques's arm drew his attention before he could reply. The red-haired man who had told his mistress the truth about Olaf's death knelt at his feet.

"Sir Norman," he said. "What is to be done with the body of Olaf Lothbrok? It is the Viking custom to carry a lord to the sea and set him aboard the *snekkar*. The ship must be set afire and sent into deep waters."

"You have my permission to follow the tradition of Lothbrok's people. See to it, good man."

The peasant nodded. "Madam, your nursemaid awaits you beside the broken gate. She has readied horses and sends me to say she wishes to depart before sunset."

"Thank you, Wag," Bronwen said. She turned to Jacques. "May I have your permission to leave the castle, sir?"

"I had not thought to lose you so soon upon finding you again. Why not stay in the castle until I can organize a proper escort for your journey? I'll ensure your safety and comfort. You have my word of honor on it."

At his offer of shelter, protection and ease, she seemed to shrink into herself. "My lord—"

"Jacques is my name."

"Jacques, please forgive my attempt to...to harm you."

"Harm me?" He couldn't hold back a laugh. "You intended to lop off my head!"

She glanced away, but when she faced him again, a faint smile tickled her lips. "Indeed I did. One day I'll take lessons in swordsmanship, so that the next time my aim will be more exact."

"I'm an able swordsman. Stay here, and I'll teach you."

She sobered. "I hear your kindness, but please now, forgive me and let me go. I must do my father's bidding."

"Your father is dead."

"But his dream is alive in me, sir. I must go."

Jacques weighed his sword, studying the fine blade.

He knew he could keep her if he chose. As conqueror, it was his prerogative. But the plea in her eyes was too much to bear, and if he forced her to stay, she would despise him all the more. He considered all options but knew he could take only one path. Drawing a dagger from its sheath on his belt, he held it out before her.

"Take this then," he said. "My sword would hamper you, or I would gladly offer it. This blade was given to my father by Robert, Duke of Normandy. It served him on his crusade, and it has served me well to gain these lands for Henry Plantagenet. Now you have your own crusade."

The woman's hands trembled as he laid the dagger across her palms. It was a magnificent piece with a hilt of brilliant sapphires and a gleaming razor-edged blade. Though he had little else with which to remember his father, he was glad to give it to her.

"Thank you," she whispered. "Thank you, Jacques Le Brun, lord of Warbreck Castle."

"May the dagger protect your life and bring us together again in better days."

His heart thundered as she stepped away from him and hurried toward the gate. All his being cried out to prevent her leaving. He had thought of this woman, dreamed of her, even prayed for her in the months of separation.

As he and Henry Plantagenet had gathered a force of armed men in support of this cause, Jacques knew his loyalties were torn. Without doubt, he believed in Henry's right to claim the throne of England. But with even greater assurance, he knew that the black-haired woman who had stood beside her father on a chilly winter night in Amounderness was meant to be his.

* * *

Darkness slipped like a thief across the sky to the sea as Bronwen and Enit made their way up the final steep hill to Rossall Hall. The journey had taken two full days—two days of traveling across hard sandy beaches under a burning summer sun, of waiting for tides to recede, of sleeping under the stars, until at last they saw the faint outlines of huts in the village. The timber keep, salt encrusted and weatherworn, stood over the village like an old shepherd guarding his flock. And there was the old gate through which the young girl had run many times to the sea. Bronwen turned and looked over the water as the last rays of the sun spangled the waves and cast glorious golds and oranges into the deep sky.

"I look forward to seeing Gildan," she said softly. "But it is hard to think of Rossall without my father."

Enit nodded. "The greater pity lies in the fact that Aeschby now holds Edgard's hall."

Bronwen knew both women were reflecting on the terrible truth that in the turmoil of the Norman attack, neither had remembered the will box. The only proof of Edgard's will was hidden beneath the floor at Warbreck.

"Your business now is Aeschby," Enit said. "Leave your father's memory buried for a while."

Bronwen looked at the wise woman. It was true that she must try to concentrate on her struggle with Aeschby. But the memory of Jacques Le Brun drew her. How could she forget the muscle in his jaw tightening as he'd handed her his father's precious dagger? The fine planes of his smooth skin had been lit by the sun. His raven curls had shone a blue-black.

She had openly attacked and then reviled him. In return, he had offered his protection, spoken words of affection and support, and then allowed her to leave. What interwoven threads of destiny had created such a man? Both warrior and peacemaker, he confused and beckoned her. While his sword dealt destruction, his eyes spoke gentility and tenderness.

He had given her the dagger with the hope that they might meet again. But now he was lord of a castle in need of repair and lands that still held enemies loyal to Olaf Lothbrok. She could not imagine he would have time to think of her. And she would not permit herself to dwell on him.

As she and Enit reached the gate, a guard stepped out of the darkness. "Who approaches the gate of Rossall Hall?"

Bronwen did not recognize the man, and she wondered what had become of her father's gatekeeper. "I am Bronwen, widow of Olaf Lothbrok, daughter and heiress of Edgard the Briton," she said. "Stand by that I may enter."

The guard frowned. "Await Lord Aeschby's bidding, madam." He opened a door in the wall, went through it and left Bronwen standing outside.

"Aeschby has faithful forces here, child," Enit said. "Much as I love this land, the offer of the Norman lord tempts me to turn back to Warbreck."

"This is where I belong, Enit. We must stay."

They had not waited long before the guard returned. "My lord sends this message. 'I do not know you. Return to Warbreck from whence you came.'"

Bronwen stiffened at the rebuff. "Tell your lord that I have come a long journey and I will speak to him at once. Go and tell him now."

The guard vanished again, and a renewed determination flooded her. She would have this place. She must wrest it from Aeschby whatever the cost.

"Lord Aeschby requests your presence in his hall." The guard opened the door as he spoke. "Enter, madam. Your maid must wait."

Bronwen opened her mouth to protest, but Enit touched her elbow. "I'll stay with the horses, child. Come to me when it's safe."

"Guard, protect this woman with your life," Bronwen told him. "She raised your master's wife from the cradle."

At the look of alarm on the man's face, Bronwen knew that fear would prevent him from harming Enit. She stepped into the courtyard, and the sight of the familiar old keep with its timber-and-wattle kitchen at one side, and its comfortable sagging benches by the door made her heart swell. Rossall was indeed her home.

Led by another guard, she crossed the yard and entered the hall. The aroma of a pig roasting over the fire filled the room. Tables had been erected around the dais, on which sat the fair-haired Aeschby. A look of disdain flared his nostrils and turned down the corners of his mouth as he rose to meet her.

Before he spoke, Bronwen took a moment to look at her sister. The sight stopped her in horror. Gildan's skin was sickly pale. Her eyes, two sunken hollows, bore blackened bruises about them. The once-glorious golden hair now hung limp, unbraided and tangled. Her lips trembled, two thin white lines.

"Gildan?" Bronwen mouthed.

But Aeschby spoke up. "So you have come to my hall, Bronwen of Warbreck. I understand from my new advisor that you are now a widow."

Bronwen focused on the slouching form behind Aeschby's chair. *Haakon.*

"Welcome home," the Viking said with a laugh.

Eyes narrowing, she gripped the dagger beneath her black mantle. "I have come to speak with Aeschby."

"Speak then," the Briton lord commanded. "What can you say that would warrant my attention?"

"I have returned to take possession of Rossall Hall and the entirety of my father's holdings—as he wished me to do upon his death. You know I speak the truth, Aeschby, for you were present at the winter feast when my father announced his will. Your wife can affirm my words."

Aeschby sneered. "Your sister is a pretty package with nothing inside. She cannot affirm anything."

As he spoke, Bronwen ascertained two things at once. He had taken more drink than was prudent on this night. And Gildan was in agony.

"Your father," Aeschby went on, "would never leave his holdings in the hands of a woman. Rossall belongs to me—the Briton husband of his daughter. On hearing of Edgard's death, I dutifully occupied his lands and united them with mine to form one great Briton holding."

"Upon my honor, I vow that you heard my father's will," she flung back at him. "Everyone heard it. Sister, you were there. What did Father say?"

Gildan sat silent, her face gone whiter than death. Suddenly she bolted from her chair. "Bronwen, help me!" she wailed. "Don't let him touch me again!"

Flinging herself at her sister, Gildan began sobbing. But Aeschby left the dais, shoved the two women apart and drew his sword. Grasping Gildan by the hair, he threw her to the stone floor. Then he pointed his blade at Bronwen.

"You will die, woman," Aeschby snarled.

Clutching the slender dagger, Bronwen stepped back warily. She was outmatched, but she would have her say. "I am mistress of Rossall Hall. I shall—"

"No, Bronwen!" Gildan screamed. "He'll kill you, I swear it. Run, sister! I beg you—run!"

Aeschby thrust his sword at Bronwen. His drunkenness threw off his aim and spared her, but she knew she must flee or die. As she ran through the door, she glanced back to see Haakon standing over Gildan, his foot resting on her neck.

"Never return to Rossall!" Aeschby shouted behind her as Bronwen took the steps two at a time and dashed across the courtyard. "I'll kill you the next time I lay eyes on you!"

As Bronwen darted through the gate, she heard Haakon's raucous laughter ringing in her ears.

Once outside, Bronwen grabbed Enit's hand and hurried her toward the protection of the forest. "Enit, we must leave at once," she gasped as they stood in the darkness. "Aeschby means to take my life. And Gildan… Gildan is—"

"Speak, child."

"Oh, Enit, she is very ill. Aeschby beats her! I saw him throw her down. I cannot leave her here, but how can I rescue her?"

Hidden in a thicket of trees above the village, Enit drew the younger woman into her embrace. "Whist, Bronwen," she whispered. "Let us go to the hut of

Ogden, your father's butler. His wife, Ebba, was my friend, and he'll be loyal to your cause."

"But my presence would endanger him, Enit."

"Ogden will gladly give his life for you, child."

"Very well," she said. It was a great risk to turn back to the village. Yet, she could not leave Rossall without Gildan. Her sister had begged for help.

They made their way to the edge of the Wyre estuary. While Bronwen tethered the horses, Enit knocked on the door of a small hut nearby.

"Great cockles, woman! What do you here?" Ebba flung open the door and hugged her friend. "And who's this? Bronwen, Edgard's daughter! But you wed the old Viking."

"My husband is killed and his land taken by Normans, Ebba. I've come to claim my rightful place at Rossall."

"Ach, you'll not get a stone from Aeschby," Ebba spat as she ushered the women inside and barred the door.

"Ogden!" Bronwen exclaimed at the sight of the butler's familiar face. "How glad I am to see you."

"Madam, welcome," he greeted her with a bow. "Your father is greatly mourned in the village. Such a time we've had since that devil usurped Rossall."

"Aeschby means to see me dead. You risk your life by hiding us here. Say the word and we'll depart."

"Never. You honor us with your presence. Please— sit you down."

Still shaken from her narrow escape, Bronwen sank onto the rickety bench beside Enit. As Ebba handed out bowls of hot stew, Ogden spoke.

"Madam, the whole village opposes Aeschby. We would rise up against the man if only we had weapons."

"Serfs rising against their lord?" Bronwen said in disbelief. The idea was unthinkable. "Something must be done, Ogden. Even if I'm unable to take back the land, I cannot abandon my sister."

"Let my husband go to Gildan," Ebba suggested.

"I've seen what that man has done to the poor girl," Ogden concurred. "I'll take her the garments of a peasant. Clad in such a way, she can escape with me here."

"But if Aeschby learns of this deed," Bronwen protested, "he will kill you. The man has no conscience."

"Madam, I am the butler. I know the secrets of your father's keep—doors, tunnels, hidden passages. Your sister will be gone long before Aeschby discovers her missing, and he will never learn how she escaped."

Bronwen could hardly argue with the man. It was the only plan at all possible. Without allowing dissent, Ogden took a bundle of his wife's clothing and slipped through the door into the darkness. Bronwen closed her eyes, leaned her head against Enit's shoulder and tried to sort out her thoughts.

The golden box hidden under the floor at Warbreck was all but useless in light of Aeschby's claims. Her mind wandered to the tall Norman with his head of dark curls and his firm jaw. How easy it would be to go back to him. Jacques had asked her to stay and told her he would protect her. And yet, he was a Norman. Bronwen shuddered at the thought of her father's words if she were to accept the man's protection. To Edgard, a land-hungry Norman was the devil incarnate.

But Aeschby was a Briton, and his treacherous actions far outweighed those of the Norman and Viking men whose lives had twined with Bronwen's. If she could not return to Rossall or Warbreck, what was to become of her?

As Enit and Ebba ate, Bronwen realized that her only treasures were three gold balls and a jeweled dagger—all gifts from Jacques Le Brun. Even with that wealth, where could she live? Any lord who discovered the daughter of an enemy on his land would banish her. Not even her father's Briton allies would welcome the woman Aeschby had vowed to kill.

A tapping at the door brought Bronwen to her feet. Ebba lifted the heavy wood bar. "Ogden is returned," she told the others. The butler slipped into the house and assessed its safety. Then he drew a slender figure through the door. Two pale hands pulled back the hood of a brown cloak, and Gildan's golden head emerged.

"Sister!" Bronwen cried. She threw her arms about Gildan's thin shoulders. In an instant, Enit was embracing the pair, hugging and kissing them both.

"La, Gildan!" Enit cried, wiping tears from her wrinkled cheeks. "You're as thin as a comb. What are these marks on your face? I vow, if I could get my hands on that man for one moment, I'd tear him limb from limb."

Gildan clapped a hand over Enit's mouth. "Silence, I beg you. He'll kill you all if he finds me here. It cannot be long before Aeschby knows I've fled."

As the woman began to weep, Bronwen drew her sister close and kissed her golden head. "Gildan, where will he think you've gone?"

"To you. I've told him many times I would find you if I ever escaped him."

"He'll know we could not return to Warbreck. He must think we journeyed down the coast to Preston, for it can be our only haven. We must take a different path then. With a boat, we can follow the Wyre as far as possible—and then go overland."

Gildan's eyes shone. "At Preston, we'll find a place of Christian worship. Our tutor told us that churches offer sanctuary, and there we shall take refuge from Aeschby."

Bronwen stood beside a small boat bobbing at the edge of the River Wyre. Filled with blankets, cheeses, dried fish and black bread, it had been provided by a fisherman and other villagers still loyal to Edgard and his daughters. The women began to board, but a rustle in the bushes halted them. Bronwen put a hand on her dagger.

"Halt, travelers," a stocky man called, his sword drawn. "Who crosses the land of Aeschby of Rossall?"

Bronwen's heart skipped a beat. "We're merely travelers. Let us pass, guard, for we bear you no malice."

"And I bear you no malice, madam. I served your father well when he was lord of Rossall Hall." He grinned at the surprise on her face. "I should take you to my lord on penalty of death, but I know how ill he treats his wife—and his own men. Nay, I'll tell him nothing. Indeed, you must have my bow and arrows."

The guard shrugged off his quiver and handed it and the bow to Bronwen. Then he knelt before her. "I do swear to protect the true heir to Rossall with my life. If you seek to claim your rights, madam, you'll have my loyalty."

Bronwen touched his shoulder. "Rise, sir. You are a good man. God be with you."

The women stepped into the boat and set to with the oars, taking turns rowing and resting until dawn began to spread across the sky. By midmorning, the river had narrowed at last, and Bronwen knew they were almost out of the estuary and into the river proper.

Shedding her mantle, she folded it and tucked it beside her. She wiped the beads of sweat from her brow and pulled at the oars. Gildan sat in the stern of the boat, her golden hair long and tangled, and her bruises blue-black. One cheek had turned a livid purple.

Noting that Enit snored, Bronwen spoke to her sister in a low voice. "Gildan, what happened between you and Aeschby? At our wedding, you were overjoyed to marry him."

"He is not what he seemed," she said. "You're lucky your husband was killed. Surely you despised that old man. If I had known what marriage was like, I sooner would have had myself baptized a Christian and become a nun."

Bronwen had to smile. "Come, Gildan. You could never live like a nun, hiding in a cell and praying all day."

"Indeed I could. As bad as Normans are, they cannot be worse than my husband."

"On what grounds can your marriage possibly be terminated? The agreement between our father and Aeschby was spoken aloud and witnessed by many."

"Edgard of Rossall is dead, Bronwen. Even if he were alive, his word would hold no power over anyone except the Britons of Amounderness. Everywhere else, the Christian church judges matters of ritual and faith, while the king enforces civil law."

"If so, perhaps your marriage never really existed. You may be free already."

"Not in Aeschby's eyes. I'll need a greater authority than you to enforce an end to the union."

With a nod, Bronwen had to acknowledge that her sister was right in this. "But how does your marriage violate church or civil law?"

"Do you recall the tutor our father employed to teach us how to speak Norman French?" Gildan asked. "It was he who told us tales of the Christian God—His birth, miracles and death. He spoke of strange customs that Christians practice."

"I remember stories of Easter and a God risen from the dead. I know Christians hold certain holy men and women in high esteem. Saints, they call them. Nicholas who saved three virgins, Paul who wrote much of the holy book—"

"But think of their *laws*," Gildan cut in. "We Britons marry our cousins in order to increase the family's holdings. But our tutor said the Christian church forbids marriage between close relatives. Aeschby and I are cousins, Bronwen. By church decree, our union is illegal. I shall have it violated on the grounds of consanguinity."

Gildan was no fool, Bronwen knew. "Sister, I believe you may be right. You have given this much thought."

"Oh, Bronwen, I had little to do these past months but deliberate how I might escape that man," she confessed in a wavering voice. "My marriage bed was unbearable agony. Aeschby is determined that I bear him an heir. He knows it's the only way he can keep his own holding and claim Rossall, too. Every day and every night he forced me to submit to him. If I begged for respite or tried to flee, he beat me into submission."

Gildan's voice faltered as she continued. "Often he

locked me in my chamber—once for nearly a week. I tried desperately to conceive. I used charms and potions, and I said all manner of prayers and spells. But as each month passed without a sign of a child, he would punish me for my failure. I don't know why I'm barren, Bronwen. I tried to be a good wife. Truly I did."

Bronwen stopped rowing and put her arms around her weeping sister. "Gildan," she whispered. "You were only married six months. That is hardly a sign of barrenness."

"He… He said he would bring in a village woman and get her with child. And he would make me raise that son as my own—as his heir."

"No!"

"Yes, and when Father died, he revealed the plan he had meant to follow all along—to take Rossall. I fought him over that, Bronwen! I kicked him and tore his flesh with my nails. I hate that man, and I'll never return to him. I shall do everything in my power to see that he is destroyed and Rossall returned to our line."

Bronwen resumed rowing. "Very well," she said at last. "At Preston we must take refuge in the church. We shall speak to the priests there about your plight."

"I intend to become a Christian," Gildan announced. "You should do it, too. Why not?"

Reflecting on the spirits of earth, sky, fire and water that she had worshipped since childhood, Bronwen had no answer for her sister. Was the Christian God simply another deity to add to this list? Or might He be different altogether?

"My aim is to set you free of your suffering, Gildan," she said. "I hope the priests will hear your argument against Aeschby and agree to dissolve the marriage.

But what we might do after that, I cannot say. We are two women without husband, protector, treasure, land or home."

"We must join a nunnery. Then all will be well, you'll see. We'll never have to think about Normans or Vikings or men ever again."

Unable to hold back a tired smile, Bronwen felt sure their lives never would be quite as tidy as her sister imagined.

Damp, muggy days made the journey exhausting, and chilly nights brought scant relief. The boat mired often in the sticky black mud, and roots and brambles choked the water. When the river flattened out into wild moorland covered with heather and gorse, it became so shallow in places that it resembled a series of large puddles.

After more than a week of exhausting travel, the women left the water and set out by land. At dawn one day, they met a peasant leading an ox-drawn cart filled with woolen fabrics. Bronwen greeted the sturdy fellow, who introduced himself as Rodan.

"How far is it to Preston, good man?" she asked him.

"Not far," he said. "I go to market there. Come, seat yourselves in my wagon and take your rest."

Grateful, the women climbed in and settled among the man's bolts of woven cloth. "What is Preston like?" Gildan asked. "We've never seen a town."

He laughed. "Never seen a town? There's a church, of course, and our lord's manor home is nearby. The market lies near the edge of the Ribble River."

"Is your lord a Norman?"

"Can there be any other? He's a good man. He

doesn't tax us too greatly, though we feel the burden. He supports Matilda's choice for the crown—Henry Plantagenet."

The familiar name prickled Bronwen's attention. "We are Britons and have heard little of Henry Plantagenet."

"Who could not know of that man? You must have come from the upper wastelands. I heard there were a few bands of ancient tribes there—though I never believed it."

"Ancient tribes?" Gildan retorted.

"Tell us more of Henry," Bronwen spoke up.

"He's the son of Matilda Empress, and the great grandson of William the Conqueror. He is but nineteen years old. Matilda wants Henry to be king after Stephen—but Stephen wants his own son, Eustace, to take his place."

As the peasant spoke, Bronwen realized that nearly all the nobility in England must now be Norman. How odd to think that a great civil war had raged while she and Gildan had been tucked away at Rossall, believing that their father's Briton dreams posed a real threat to Norman rule.

"Two months ago, Henry made himself a fine marriage," Rodan continued. "He wed Eleanor of Aquitaine, wife to the king of France for fourteen years. She never bore a son."

"She was barren," Gildan said, glancing at Bronwen.

"No, there was a daughter who now causes much ado in the south of England. She believes men should honor, respect and do battle for women. I'm told she holds court, where she judges cases of *amour*—passionate love between men and women."

"What nonsense," Enit muttered. "Foolish Normans."

"Perhaps, but if Henry becomes king, those odd French ideas will make their way to England. Eleanor is a powerful woman. She had her marriage with the French king annulled, and then—before a decent waiting time was up—she wed Henry Plantagenet."

"An old woman with such a young man," Enit marveled.

"To this marriage, Eleanor brought Aquitaine—a large part of France—and added it to Henry's inheritance. He now holds more than half of France. If he wears England's crown, he'll be more powerful than the French king."

"Do people here truly support a Norman as their king?" Bronwen asked in wonderment. "The French can have no idea how deeply we love this isle, how far into the past our roots go—beyond Arthur to that shrouded mystical time when the world began."

"Most of us in the north support Henry, for Stephen is allied with the Scots. Farther south, the battle lines are evenly drawn."

"But the Normans who've ruled England never cared to spend much time here," Bronwen reminded him. "They use their kingship to extort taxes and build armies in order to support their interests in Europe and the Holy Land."

As she spoke, Bronwen reflected on Jacques Le Brun. He could be no better than any other power-hungry Frenchman. Even now, she pictured him seated on the dais at Warbreck. She could almost see the way his hair curled at the nape of his neck, hear his deep voice as it whispered in her ear. Jacques had offered his protection, but she had refused. She knew she had done right. He was a Norman, after all.

As the sun rose, Bronwen marveled at the dusty road now lined with carts and wagons bound for Preston. When the wagon crested a small hill, the sight below took her breath away. Crowded along both banks of a narrow river stood more houses than she had ever seen. These were timber structures, and many had generous gardens. In the distance, the square tower of a large stone church rose above the sea of thatched roofs.

At the women's cries of amazement, Rodan chuckled. "This is but a small town, ladies. I've been to Chester, and it is far bigger. London must be larger still."

"What does everyone do?" Gildan asked.

"Many things," Rodan said as the cart bumped along. "In the villages a man's entire family works to survive, but here one man catches and sells fish, another sells eggs and cheese, another cloth, and another leather goods. A craftsman trades his wares for other items he needs. Some people use money, but I don't trust it myself."

Bronwen agreed with Rodan. It was foolish to trade goods for coins. Proof of the fact was the hoard of gold and silver pieces gathering dust in the treasure room at Rossall. Other ancients had tried to make such a system succeed, but common people always returned to the simpler, more reliable method of trade and barter.

As Bronwen surveyed the bustling town, her attention narrowed at the city gate. A robust man with yellow hair and armed men accompanying him stood near the wall. He was speaking earnestly to a town guardsman. As the wagon approached, Bronwen gasped and grabbed Gildan's hand.

"Aeschby!" she cried. "He is here in Preston."

"Oh, sister! How did he know?"

"Rodan," Bronwen whispered. "Our father's enemy waits at the gate. We must find another way into town."

The fellow frowned. "You did not tell me you were pursued. This is the only entry other than the watergate."

"We must go there," Gildan pleaded. "He'll kill us."

"The watergate is only for boats," Rodan told them. "Hide yourselves under my fabric. I'll take you to the protection of the church. He cannot touch you there."

Bronwen held her breath as the rickety cart jolted through the gate without incident. But Gildan chose that moment to push a bolt of fabric aside and sit up for a peek out the back of the cart. Bronwen heard her gasp, and then an angry shout sounded from behind them.

"There!" Aeschby cried out. "My wife. Follow her."

"Down, Gildan!" Bronwen grabbed her sister's sleeve and tugged her under cover again. As Rodan goaded his ox into the market, the pursuing horsemen were slowed by crowds of shoppers. The stone church loomed at the end of the square, and the cart at last creaked to a halt before it. Falling over each other, the three women called out their thanks as they fled the cart and ran for the steps.

Following Gildan and Enit toward the upper portico, Bronwen felt herself swept from her feet and borne upward to the church door.

"Bronwen the Briton," a deep voice said above her. "You embrace trouble."

"Trouble embraces me," she gasped out. "And its name is Jacques Le Brun."

Chapter Eight

Jacques carried Bronwen into the cool shadows of the church and set her on her feet. He slammed the door behind them, then dropped the bar. Only a moment later, heavy thuds sounded on the door. Lifting her into his arms again, he strode down the nave into a small dark room in which a young priest sat at a table copying a manuscript. There, Jacques set Bronwen on her feet beside her sister, who was shivering and sobbing in their nursemaid's arms.

"Who pursues you?" the priest asked. "You must tell me at once, or I cannot grant sanctuary."

"Allow me to make introductions," Jacques spoke up. He gestured at Bronwen, who was staring at him as if seeing an apparition. "This is Bronwen, widow of Olaf Lothbrok, lately of Warbreck Castle. This is her sister, Gildan. And this woman, I believe, is their nursemaid."

"And who are you?" the priest inquired.

"I am Jacques Le Brun, lord of Warbreck, bound in service to God and to the rightful king of England, Henry Plantagenet."

"Who's outside? Who defies the sanctity of the church by pounding on our door?"

"It is my husband," Gildan choked out. "He used me ill, sir. To save my life, my sister helped me escape, and I take haven in the church. I come to you now, pleading that you terminate my marriage."

"Wait here," the priest told them. "Bolt this door after I leave. Sanctuary is easy to grant but often hard to enforce."

When he was gone, Bronwen pinned Jacques with a dark look. "Why are you here?" she demanded. "What has brought an armed Norman to Preston—to this church? I left you at Warbreck, but now I see you wear battle mail—and today your crest is not that of Plantagenet."

"No, indeed, this is my own." He glanced at the peacock-blue symbol with three gold balls engraved on his sword's scabbard. "Yet all I do is in behalf of my lord."

Pleased to see she had lost none of her fire, Jacques was hard-pressed to hold back a smile. "I came to rescue you," he said. "I learned that Aeschby had gone in pursuit of his fugitive wife. When I heard what had occurred between you and that man at Rossall, I knew trouble was afoot. So I followed."

"I have no need of rescue, sir," Bronwen told him. "You see with your own eyes that we are safely inside this sanctuary."

"Bronwen," her sister interrupted. "Aeschby wants *you* more than me. He fears you. I saw the look on his face when he heard your claim. He believes you'll try to take Rossall. I am no more to him than a womb with the proper bloodline. But you are a threat to his lands and wealth."

The old nurse nodded. "It's you Aeschby pursues, Bronwen."

At a knock on the door, Jacques drew his sword and lifted the bar. Two priests entered the room, the young one and his elder.

"Which of you is called Gildan of Rossall?" the more senior priest asked.

The tattered blonde lifted her hand. "I, sir."

"Come with us, madam. We shall hear your argument against your husband."

"Where is that man?" Jacques asked, stepping in front of her. "I believe he means great harm to these women."

"Aeschby of Rossall waits in the chancel."

"I won't go!" Gildan cried. "He'll take me away. He is not a Christian and has no respect for church law."

"Let me go with her," Bronwen said, starting forward. "I am her sister."

Jacques took Bronwen's arm, tucked the spirited creature behind him and held her there while he addressed the priests. "I must accompany these women. They are in danger of their lives."

The priest weighed his words, then beckoned. "Very well. All may come."

Jacques insisted on leading the entire group into the church, a stone building with high walls supported by great pillars arching overhead. Rows of wooden benches filled either side of the long aisle. Despite the peril ahead of them, he welcomed the familiar scent of the place—the smell of years passing, of people sweating out their sins, of incense carrying prayers to God, of melted candle wax burned in honor of the saints. The church he had attended in Antioch was much older than this one, but the holy sense of God's presence was in both places.

As the group made their way across the rush-strewn floor, Jacques spotted Aeschby standing near a carved wooden screen. Unlike himself, the man had been disarmed and was waiting in the gloom between two more priests. Close by his side stood the Viking, Haakon, who had fled Warbreck not long after it had fallen to the Plantagenet cause.

The elder priest now called on Jacques's party to remove their weapons. With reluctance, he set his sword to one side and was surprised to note that Bronwen removed the dagger he had given her. He had fully expected her to argue with the command. Perhaps her lack of respect for the Christian faith was not as great as he had assumed.

"Aeschby of Rossall," the old priest began. "Is this woman, called Gildan, your wife?"

"She is," he barked out, "and I mean to have her back."

"Why did she leave you? What caused her to run away?"

"Her sister—that woman there—stole my wife in the night."

At the heat of Aeschby's words, Jacques heard Bronwen suck in a deep breath. Her backward step brought her against his chest. He took her cold hand and closed his own over it, preventing her from moving away again.

"Is this man your husband, Gildan of Rossall?" the priest asked.

"Yes—and he knows very well why I left him. He married me because he had made a treacherous plot against my father, Edgard of Rossall. Father willed all his lands to my sister, but Aeschby planned to get me with child and claim the lands for himself and his heir. When my father died, he waited not a day before taking Rossall himself."

The priest turned. "Is this true, woman? Did your father will his lands to you and your heirs?"

"He did," Bronwen confirmed.

"I can attest to that," Jacques spoke up. "I was at the betrothal where Edgard of Rossall made his will known."

"The old man had lost his mind," Aeschby blurted. "Anyone will tell you that. A woman could never manage and protect so large a holding as Rossall. Edgard was mad. He believed that Britons could conquer Normans one day."

Jacques gripped Bronwen's hand more tightly. Leaning forward, he whispered into her ear. "This man is determined to work you great evil. Allow me to intervene."

At the touch of his mouth against her hair, she stiffened. "Your offer is kind, but my head tells me you are like every other Norman. Hungry for land and power."

"What does your heart tell you?" Though he kept his eyes on the others in the church, Jacques felt dizzied at the nearness of the woman. The soft skin of her cheek mesmerized him, and the turn of her ear beckoned for his touch.

His lips brushed it as he spoke again. "When I saw you the night of your betrothal—standing beside the old Viking—I pitied you. But when we met on the beach, when I kissed your lips, I knew it was no longer pity that moved me, my lady."

"I beg you to refrain from addressing me in such a manner," Bronwen murmured, her cheeks flushing pink. "I have no cause to trust you. You took my husband's lands just as Aeschby has taken mine. Are you so much better than he that you presume to offer me protection?"

Before he could answer, she withdrew her hand and stepped into Gildan's side. "May I speak plainly?" she asked the priest. "My father and my husband are both dead, and I have no ability to dispute Aeschby's claim to Rossall. But this man has beaten my sister and used her ill. She wishes to have the marriage invalidated. What say you to that, sir?"

The man looked her over. "Are you and your sisters Christians, madam? If not, the church has no authority over you."

"I wish to become a Christian at once," Gildan told him. "By any means necessary, make haste to convert me and then dissolve my marriage."

"The church does not annul a holy union simply because the two parties are not agreeably matched," the priest told her. "God ordained marriage for the procreation of children. Although your husband's motives and behavior may be questionable, your primary task in life is to bear him sons and heirs. I see no grounds for annulment."

"But there *are* grounds," Gildan cried out as Aeschby made a move for her. "My husband and I are cousins. Our marriage is consanguineous. My grandfather and his were brothers, sons of Ulfcetel of Rossall."

The priest's brow furrowed. "Is this true?"

"You cannot deny it, Aeschby," Gildan said. "You know it is so. The line runs through your mother."

Bronwen spoke up. "The union was arranged because Aeschby is a Briton and had agreed to allow me to inherit Rossall. But he broke his vow to shield and care for my sister."

The priest faced Aeschby. "What is your mother's name, sir?"

"Edina," Aeschby muttered.

"And your grandfather's?"

"Alfred of Preesall."

"And your great grandfather's?"

"Ulfcetel of Rossall."

Jacques knew that consanguinity would doom Aeschby's marriage to Gildan in the eyes of the church. Yet, he could never deny the facts of his blood lineage, or he would have no claim whatsoever to Rossall.

"And your father's name?" the priest asked Gildan.

"Edgard of Rossall."

"Your granfather's?"

"Sigeric the Briton, of Rossall."

"And your great grandfather's?"

"Ulfcetel of Rossall."

After a moment's deliberation among the priests, the eldest spoke again. "The woman has chosen to convert to Christianity, an act that will put her under the authority of the church. But I myself do not have the power to annul a marriage. One or both of you must take the issue before the church court in Canterbury. This is an expensive undertaking, and I cannot see how it will be accomplished without substantial funds. In light of the confession of consanguinity, however, I must declare that any cohabitation between these two is fornication and a sin before God."

As the priest finished, Aeschby spat on the church floor and started down the aisle, followed by Haakon.

"Madam," the priest said to Gildan, "you must join

me and the other priests if you wish to convert. There is much to be done before such a rite may take place."

"Oh, never mind that now," Gildan snapped at the man. "I shall do it in London."

The priest frowned as Gildan called after her husband. "Do not rest too peacefully in your stolen hall, Aeschby! Bronwen and I are going to become nuns, and we shall pray every hour for God to send his wrath down upon you for your treachery."

The Briton whirled around and sneered at her. "You have no skill to please a man, Gildan—how will you ever please God? The next you hear of me, I shall be lord over all Amounderness. I'll get me an heir easily enough, but you will stay my wife, for you'll never have the wealth to divorce me."

Gildan stood in the church aisle, her fists knotted, as Aeschby stepped through the door and into the sunlight. Observing from the shadows, Jacques leaned one shoulder against a stone pillar. Such delicate, gentle-looking women, these two Briton sisters, he thought. Yet the moment they opened their mouths, they transformed from butterflies into dragons. But where Gildan was frail and drew from her sister's strength, Bronwen was the boldest, most outspoken, and certainly the loveliest woman upon whom he had ever laid eyes.

"Jacques," she said now, approaching him with an appropriately meek expression written on her face. "I beg you to forgive me for shouting at you earlier. Also for questioning your intentions here. And for speaking ill of your people. You have been kind."

"I see," he said, hoping to provoke a continuation of this fascinating charade of humility.

"Thank you for following Aeschby to Preston," she

went on. "And for being here to offer your protection. But now, as you can see, the event is ended and we must speak with the priest about a nunnery."

Jacques knew he had been brushed off in exactly the same manner as she had rid herself of him each time they met. "You truly wish to enter the church, Bronwen?" he asked, attempting to conceal his amusement at the very idea of this outspoken hothead in a houseful of silent nuns. "It seems you have much life ahead of you. The nunnery is but an early grave for one of your intelligence and beauty."

She looked down for just a moment, and he realized that at last her emotions were genuine. "What life have I ahead of me, sir?" she asked. "My husband is dead. You hold Warbreck. Aeschby holds Rossall. I have no home, no family, no wealth. For Gildan and me, the nunnery is more a chance of life than it is an untimely death."

"You will adopt Christianity as your faith, then?"

This clearly gave her pause. "I suppose I must," she told him. "Yes, I shall."

"Then you believe that there is but one God. That His son Jesus Christ was born of a virgin girl—"

"A virgin?" she cut in. "How can that be?"

"Aeschby thinks I cannot become a nun," Gildan said storming up the aisle. "But I'll show him I can. I'm just like that woman Rodan told us about—Eleanor of Aquitaine, who is wife to Henry Plantagenet. She got rid of her French husband, even though he was a king."

"Gildan," Bronwen chided. "Save your boasting for another time and place. Aeschby is right about one thing. You can never afford to go before the church court. Neither of us has any hope for revenge against the man. Now stop your foolish chatter and let us make plans."

Gildan stopped before the altar, her hands on her hips. "I have a plan, Bronwen." She looked at the priests. "Sirs, where may we find a nunnery—a large and wealthy one with all the comforts of a fine home? The ladies there will know how to convert me to Christianity, and I shall convince them to assist me in paying for my annulment at Canterbury."

The oldest of the priests cleared his throat. "Madam, a nunnery is a place to serve God, not to seek revenge and certainly not to gain wealth. Most nuns are widows or maidens who have chosen a life of chastity and prayer above marriage and children. They're humble women searching for God's truth while serving the sick and the poor. I am not at all certain that a nunnery would suit you."

"Then you do not know me well enough. You paint such a pious picture—but I cannot believe what you say. What woman would welcome such a life? Surely these nuns wear fine gowns and jewels. They eat tasty foods, and spend their days strolling through gardens singing and playing harps. This is the sort of nun I plan to be."

"You'll not find a nunnery like that in the north of England. Now if you will excuse us, we have the Lord's work to do."

Bowing slightly, the old man motioned to his fellow priests, who set off across the stone floor. As he was about to disappear through a narrow door, he turned back to the group in the chancel.

"My church has served as your sanctuary long enough," he said. "Please gather your arms and disturb us no more."

Gildan glared after him. "What of that?" she said to her sister. "He denies us sanctuary—and calls this his church. Come Bronwen, let's depart this dank and odorous place."

Bronwen caught her sister's arm. "Listen to me, Gildan. You act as though we are in control of our destinies. But you must consider our position. We have nothing—not one single thing. We have only Enit and the clothing we wear. So stop behaving as though you're the daughter of a lord. You are not—and I am a widow who hasn't even a mourning dress to wear."

Gildan appeared stunned at her sister's words. Then her expression hardened. "I thought you would be the last to abandon hope, Bronwen. You have always been the one to tell me everything would work out well. Have you grown weak and spineless now—just when we need your courage?"

"Your sister is hardly spineless, Gildan," Jacques said. "At Warbreck, she very nearly took off my head."

For the first time since they had met again, the hint of a smile tipped the corners of Bronwen's mouth. "You well deserved any fright I gave you, sir. Your Norman army stole a large portion of an ancient and vital land. You violated Amounderness, and I weep for our loss."

"Whether you believe it or not, dear lady, your small wedge of swampland already belongs to another people. Aeschby is merely a caretaker of a holding that will soon belong to Henry Plantagenet."

He had gone too far, Jacques knew. Bronwen turned away from him and spoke to her sister. But as he listened to her words, he sensed she intended them for him.

"You say I lack courage, Gildan," she said. "You are wrong. I've not lost my dream of happiness and the boldness to strive for it. But one thing I learned in my marriage is that life—and the people you meet in it—are not always as you may expect or hope them to be. You cannot depend on things to turn out the way you plan—and you can never be certain people are who you thought."

Jacques could not let that rest. "You avow that people are not what they seem," he said, taking her elbow and forcing her to meet his eyes. "You think of me as nothing more than a Norman conqueror. Allow me to prove you wrong. Again, I offer my protection and care at Warbreck Castle. For you, your sister and your nursemaid."

"Who is this knight, Bronwen?" Gildan asked.

"Jacques Le Brun is the man who took Warbreck from my husband. He is a Norman under fealty to Henry Plantagenet."

Gildan's lips parted in astonishment. "We want neither protection nor care from Normans. Your people are nothing but scavenging dogs, devouring everything in sight. I beg of you—depart our company at once."

Jacques studied the bruised and ragged woman. Then he turned his attention to her proud sister. "I'm learning firsthand of Briton prejudice and hatred," he told them. "I've done nothing to deserve your ill will. Though I took your husband's lands for Henry Plantagenet, I treated you fairly, Bronwen. You will find Henry to be a just man, as well—far more intelligent, capable and respectful than the Briton who left this church moments ago. Upon my honor, I believe you would much prefer Norman lordship to that of any other."

Bronwen moistened her lips as if preparing to speak, but he no longer had patience for her injustice and defiance. Beautiful and spirited though she was, the woman clearly had no desire to know him more intimately. Though her kiss had been filled with yearning and her eyes spoke of deep longing, she always chose her family and her heritage over him. The doors to her heart were locked tight, and he did not have the key with which to open them.

"I offered you my protection once, and I have offered it again. Though spurned twice, I remain constant. Only say the word."

With that, he turned and strode down the aisle and out into the day.

Bronwen stood rooted to the floor, staring after him. With all her inner self she wanted to run after Jacques— to fall into his strong arms, to tell him she was sorry, to go with him back to Warbreck. But how could she allow herself to trust a man again? And especially a Norman.

At the sound of a door opening, the women's attention was drawn to the young priest, who was walking toward them.

"Ladies," the man addressed them in a near whisper. "There are several nunneries near London. A merchant I know—he comes often to Preston to trade in spices and silks from the Holy Land—sets sail for London this very day. He is a pious Christian. If I spoke to him, perhaps he would take you there free of charge."

Bronwen glanced at her sister and then at Enit. Both looked aghast at the very idea of traveling so far from home. But what other options did they have?

"Please go and ask the merchant on our behalf," she told the priest. "We'll await you."

As the women followed him to the door, Bronwen

considered what their tutor had told them of Christian nuns—women who served God, read holy books, prayed in silence. The idea flooded her with unexpected serenity. Perhaps this was the life for her, after all. Perhaps this one God, this unknown deity, wanted her to become His servant.

Fearful that Aeschby lingered nearby, Bronwen peered around the church door into the crowded market. A gentle gust bore a heady mixture of smells—the musky scent of new wool, the pungent odor of fresh fish and newly slaughtered lamb, the sweet aroma of honey and cakes. Cries of the fishmongers and fruit sellers filled the air over the sounds of earnest bartering. Great round orange cheeses lay piled in pyramids, brightly dyed fabrics—blues, yellows and reds—flapped in the summer breeze.

Mounds of fruit—red and green apples, golden pears, berries and grapes—filled the stalls and flowed out onto small tables. Piles of nuts, brown and white eggs, jugs of fresh cream and bunches of vegetables—beans, peas, parsnips, cabbages, turnips, carrots, celery, beets and onions—crowded other small stands.

It was a magical place, and she longed to explore it. But she spotted the young priest running toward them. "Come! Come!" he shouted. "The ship departs even now."

Bronwen grabbed one of Enit's hands, Gildan took the other and they started after the priest. In short order, they caught sight of the water lapping against a dock where a sturdy-looking ship was taking on the last of its cargo.

Bidding the young man farewell, they crossed a ramp to the vessel's deck where a short, weather-beaten man stood calling out orders.

"Three of you?" he said on noting them. "The priest told me two."

"This is our nurse, Captain," Bronwen told him.

"My name is Muldrew." The old man studied Enit. "You've been at sea before, woman?"

Enit squared her shoulders. "Of course. Scratch a Welshman, find a seaman, as they say."

"You hail from Wales! I, too—from the north, just past the isle of Anglesey."

"Upon my word—my home was very near there."

"Welcome then. Excuse me, ladies, for I must see that we cast off." With a jaunty bow, the captain strode away.

Bronwen turned to her nurse. "Enit, you hate the sea. You cursed the *snekkar*. What is this about scratching—"

"Whist, Bronwen. Mind your tongue. He has taken me aboard. Don't endanger my passage."

At that moment, the sound of clattering hooves drew Bronwen's attention, and she spotted Aeschby riding toward the wharf with Haakon at his side. Gildan screamed and hid behind her sister.

"Cast off!" Captain Muldrew shouted. "Cast off!"

The ship began to drift away from the dock, but Aeschby brandished his sword. "You'll not escape me, Bronwen!" Aeschby roared. "I'll have my wife back, and I'll keep my holdings! And I shall see you dead!"

A nearby movement caught Bronwen's eye and she turned to find Jacques Le Brun's gray steed thundering down the wharf.

"Aeschby!" the dark Norman shouted, drawing his sword. "Stand by, man! You have driven the women from this land—let them go in peace."

Aeschby whirled his horse. "This is none of your affair, Norman!"

Jacques reined his mount. "I defend the honor of Bronwen the Briton. Pay your insults and threats to me, knave."

At once, Aeschby spurred his horse and drew his sword.

"Bronwen, he means to kill you!" Gildan wailed. "And now he'll murder the man who saved you at the church."

Bronwen held her breath as the men galloped toward each other. At the first clash, she wrapped her arms around her sister and closed her eyes. "We will escape Aeschby. He'll never find us again. The Norman is bold and able. I pray he can defend himself."

"But there are two of them against him." Sniffling, Gildan pivoted her sister toward the fracas on the wharf where Haakon had joined Aeschby in attacking Jacques.

For all her confidence in Jacques's skills as a swordsman, Bronwen's heart quaked. She had seen Viking bloodlust, and she knew with what fervor a Briton could do battle. Could the Norman hold them back? Would he survive their assault?

As the ship made its way toward the sea, the figures on shore grew faint. "Why is the Norman fighting Aeschby?" Gildan asked. "What did he mean when he said he had come to defend your honor, Bronwen? I cannot understand it."

"Nor can I, Gildan," her sister said softly. "Nor can I."

Chapter Nine

After a few days and Gildan's endless complaints over the ship's tight and smelly quarters, Bronwen decided to venture to the deck and speak in earnest with Captain Muldrew. He was well traveled and would have good advice for three lone women on their way to London. Clutching the rigging to keep her balance, she picked her way through coils of rope and buckets of pitch. The old vessel creaked and groaned with every wave. A stench of bilge water wafted up from below deck, and the tall mast overhead swayed like a willow in the breeze.

Bronwen much preferred the *snekkar* with its long narrow body and deep secure seats to this creaky old sieve. At last she spied the captain talking with two of his crew.

"Ah, madam," he called as she approached. He dismissed the men. "I'm happy to see you on deck. I began to fear I'd dreamed the lot of you."

She smiled. "My sister labors to accustom herself to sea travel."

"Tell her we'll be on dry land soon enough. Tomorrow evening, we weigh anchor at Chester where I'll be taking on a load of cheeses. Then we'll stop in Bangor, and after that Cardiff."

"When will we arrive in London?"

"Exeter and Southampton will be our final ports before the great city. You'll see France when we pass Dover, but it won't be long before we're sailing up the old Thames. We should be at sea no more than two weeks. I'm bound to arrive before the first of August. I've a load to pick up from a merchant who wants it shipped to the Holy Land."

"You go there often, sir?"

"It's my regular route. The crusades have brought much interest in trade between England and the east."

"Do you know of Antioch?" she asked.

"A beautiful place!" he exclaimed. "Antioch is a walled city that sits between a river and a mountain range. Never have you seen such homes as those in Antioch, madam—marble walls, painted ceilings, floors inlaid with mosaics. The homes of the wealthy have great wide windows to let in the fresh air, and gardens and orchards filled with oranges, lemons and fruits you've never seen. Their baths use water piped in through aqueducts from the springs of Daphne. The people lay large tapestries they call carpets on their floors, instead of rushes as the English do. Antioch is fairyland indeed, madam."

Bronwen tried to make his words form pictures in her mind, but she could not even imagine such things. "Do you know many merchants in Antioch, Captain Muldrew?"

"Every one, madam."

"Have you heard of a man, Charles, who went with Robert of Normandy on the First Crusade?"

The captain nodded. "Indeed, he is one of the wealthiest merchants in Antioch. He married a local woman, and they have several children. How do you know him?"

"I met his son, Jacques Le Brun."

"You must mean young Jacob, the second son. Does he call himself by his Norman name now? Then I suppose he has left his homeland. It stands to reason. His older brother was to inherit the father's business. The last I heard of Jacob, he was a student of law at the college in Antioch—a fine intellectual and very bold as well. He studied swordsmanship under a great master. When did you meet him?"

"He usurped my husband's lands, and I was widowed during the battle. Your young Jacob has become a knight in the service of Henry Plantagenet. He is now lord of Warbreck Castle in Amounderness."

"Fancy that," the old man muttered.

The gnarled seaman and the young woman stood in silence on the deck. Bronwen supposed the captain was trying to envision the youth he had known as Jacob, now a powerful Norman lord. And Bronwen was trying to see the Norman as a boy.

What had it been like to grow up in a city such as Antioch? she wondered. What was a college—and how could one study law? And how had the second son felt, knowing his older brother would inherit the family's trade, and he would have nothing? Perhaps that had driven him to embrace his father's Norman heritage and serve Henry Plantagenet—a man who also struggled to gain power in a world that would deny it to him.

Nothing was as it had seemed to her in the fire-lit chamber inside Rossall, Bronwen realized. People could be very different than she had been taught. Vikings were not all cruel barbarians. Rossall was not a great hall, and though Warbreck had seemed a mighty keep, the castles she had seen along the English coast-line were far grander.

Preston had been an enormous town but she knew Chester was much larger. London would be bigger still. Marriage had appeared to be a secure, orderly tradi-tion—until Bronwen had learned that husbands could be treacherous, deceitful and cruel. The gods she wor-shipped had seemed all-powerful, but believers of the one God and His Son had conquered much of the world. As she leaned on the ship's rail, Bronwen wondered how many new ideas she must accept before she could be at peace with herself again.

"I have a proposal," Bronwen said. The three women—all on deck at last—took in the sights as the old boat slipped down the estuary of the River Dee toward Ches-ter. "Gildan, you must trade one of your gold rings for fabric. On our way to London, we shall sew new tunics for you and Enit. I would like to wear black mourning garb, for I have not given proper homage to my husband."

The plan breathed life into Gildan at once. "A wid-ow's dress must have wide sleeves and hang loosely to the floor. We'll make a short black veil and then fash-ion a guimpe."

The white fabric would cover the upper part of Bron-wen's chest, encircle her throat and join the veil. Would this sign of grief be just a farce? she wondered. Had she any real desire to honor the old man she had barely known? Since leaving Warbreck, Bronwen had tried to picture Olaf Lothbrok, but she found it difficult to re-call any distinguishing features. She could only form the image of a great bulk of a man, standing like a shadow over her.

"We'll cut the instep of your stockings, too," Gildan said, as though she were creating a costume for a mummer's play. "Then you'll look like a proper widow in mourning."

The sun rising behind them cast soft pinks and oranges across the purple waters of the River Dee—one bank of which was Wales, the other England. Trees were still black silhouettes, while snow-white gulls wheeled and dipped above the ship. In the distance, a great old walled city began to emerge from shadow as men gradually filled the wharf and set to the day's tasks....

"'Tis a lovely city, Chester," Captain Muldrew said as he joined the women. "The Romans built her more than a thousand years ago—named her Deva and put one of their main forts up on that high sandstone ridge you see there where the river bends."

"Romans?" Bronwen said. "How strange to imagine Romans living on our land."

"Land is owned by God," he said. "Men may fight and die for it, but they never truly possess it. The Romans came and went. Saxons took their place. Aethelflaeda, daughter of the Saxon king Alfred the Great, refortified the old city. She built some of those very walls you see in order to keep out the Vikings. That was more than two hundred years ago, when they were at their worst. Vikings. One never hears of that forgotten race these days."

Gildan was about to speak up when Enit nudged her into silence.

"You must go into the city and have a look," Muldrew went on. "You'll find three churches—St. Werburgh's, St. Peter's and St. John's—and the Roman amphitheatre. The great castle begun by William the Conqueror is now home to the Earl of Chester, a Norman of course."

As the captain wandered off to begin preparations for weighing anchor, Enit spoke up. "Perhaps we should not leave the ship. What if *he* is here?"

"Aeschby? He'll be back at Rossall, fearful that the Norman will usurp his holding if he stays away too long."

"We must be careful, though," Enit said. "Your husband may have slain the Norman."

"That handsome fellow has twice the strength of Aeschby," Gildan returned. "Though he's a Norman dog, I thought him beautiful beyond measure. Did you see his eyes? They never left Bronwen once. Frankly, I cannot help but wonder how you managed to draw his attention, sister. It is obvious he feels great affection for you."

Bronwen's heart ached at the reference to Jacques Le Brun. How cruel she had been to him—insulting the man and his entire people, spurning his offers of protection, accusing him of every manner of evil and treachery. And yet he had left his newly taken holding and ridden to her rescue—speaking of honor, defending her name. The man was a mystery she could not begin to unravel.

Her last memory saw him battling the hate-filled Aeschby, who had vowed to take her life. Haakon, too, had joined in the fracas. The thought of Jacques lying dead on the wharf filled her with unspeakable dread. From their first meeting, the man had been with her constantly—his gentle touch and admiring words always in her thoughts.

Surely she would have been wise to accept the Norman's offer to go back to Warbreck. Had he not proven his honor when he came to defend her on the wharf?

She pulled the black mantle around her shoulders and touched the dagger at her side. Why had she scorned him? What had led her to believe without question in the villainy of England's Norman conquerors? Captain Muldrew had spoken truth about the land she held so dear. Tradition held that Britons had populated Amounderness—indeed all England—since time began. But the old seaman had recounted the rule of Romans, Saxons, Vikings and now Normans.

Who did own the land? Perhaps all her father's dreams of reuniting England under Briton rule had been nothing but wisps in the wind. Perhaps Jacques Le Brun's chosen king, Henry Plantagenet, would be as capable as any Briton. But such musings had no value now. Jacques was far away, possibly lying dead, and all because of her.

Confirming the women's freedom from pursuit at last, their journey into Chester proved uneventful. They purchased fabrics and other necessities, and then they returned to the ship in time to settle in for the remainder of their journey.

In the following days they sailed around the rugged green coast of Wales. At Bangor, the crew unloaded the cheeses in exchange for woolen blankets. At Cardiff, they took on boxes of fishing nets. Next the ship rounded Cornwall, a stormy finger of land protruding into the blustery Atlantic, and sailed along the southern coast of England to Exeter and Southampton. By the time they passed through the Strait of Dover—with tall white cliffs rising from the sea on one side and the distant shore of France on the other—the ship was laden with all manner of goods.

"A good day to you, ladies," Captain Muldrew said as he crossed the deck to the bench where Bronwen, Gildan and Enit had taken up regular residence. "Come up to have a look at the old city, have you?"

All three stood at once. "Is it London?" Gildan asked.

"'Tis Canterbury, the center of church power in England. The School of Canterbury, under Theobald, has pledged itself to the succession of Henry Plantagenet."

"That man again," Gildan said. "Everywhere I go, I hear of Henry Plantagenet. Everyone adores him."

"Not everyone," the captain said with a chuckle. "King Stephen has a loyal following. Indeed, I fear this blood-soaked civil war will continue for years."

"Who do you favor in the struggle for the throne, Captain Muldrew?" Bronwen asked.

"I support the man who'll do the best for trade. His name is Henry Plantagenet."

While Bronwen absorbed this information, Enit was questioning the captain about where they might find a nunnery when they arrived in London. The man found the idea of himself even associating with such pious women highly amusing and declared that he had no idea. As they could not pay for a room at an inn, he suggested they visit the home of Gregory, Lord Whittaker. He was a wealthy Norman merchant with whom Captain Muldrew often traded, and they were friends.

The thought of beseeching this stranger—an enemy to her father's cause—for food and shelter distressed Bronwen. She suggested they find an almshouse instead.

"Never!" Gildan exclaimed. "I'll not set foot in such

a place. We aren't beggars who must depend upon the charity of others."

"Be reasonable, Gildan," Bronwen admonished her sister. "We have no money and nothing to recommend us."

"The almshouse nearest the wharf is named after St. Nicholas," the captain said. "I'll give you directions if you wish, but I do believe Sir Gregory would welcome you."

At the mention of St. Nicholas, whose symbol appeared on her mantle's crest, Bronwen's heart stumbled. Throughout the journey from Preston, she had done her best not to worry about what had become of Jacques Le Brun in his battle with Aeschby and Haakon. Indeed, she had tried to forget him altogether and concentrate on the freedom of the sea and the future that stretched out before her.

But once again, the man's glossy black curls and high cheekbones formed in her mind. At her final refusal of his offer, his eyes had gone a liquid brown, and she'd felt the sting her words had inflicted. Expecting him to despise her, she had been astonished beyond measure to see him riding along the wharf and declaring himself her defender.

Had she made the gravest error of her life in setting sail for London? Or was her action honorable—a deed about which her father would have boasted to his men?

It seemed the ship had barely passed Canterbury when the old captain stretched out a knobby finger. "Look there in the distance," he said. "There's your destiny, ladies—'tis London."

After much discussion and argument, Gildan finally persuaded Bronwen to go to Lord Whittaker's house and make inquiry. But now on the wharf, the two young

women stood hand in hand, afraid to move. Enit had
gone as pale as a frog's belly. The vast city with its in-
numerable chimneys, rows of wooden houses and endless winding streets all but overwhelmed them.

Bronwen could not count the ships of all shapes and
sizes moored along the brown river. Every sort of food,
drink and spice that could be made was rolled in bar-
rels down long planks, or packed in timber crates and
burlap sacks ready for export. In the shops that supplied
the wharfsmen lay dried cod, whiting, hake and eel.
The aroma of freshly baked breads, cakes and puddings
mingled with cinnamon, chives, garlic, mint and thyme.

"Madam, I had hoped to see you before you went,
and now I have."

To Bronwen's surprise, she discovered that Captain
Muldrew was addressing Enit. The nursemaid's cheeks
flushed a brilliant pink as the elderly man removed his
hat and gave her a bandy-legged bow.

"May your stay in London prove pleasant," he said.
"I shall look in upon you—and your charges—when I
return from the Holy Land. Perhaps you would like to
journey on my ship to your home in the north of Wales."

Enit nodded, suddenly as shy as a young rabbit. "Certainly, Captain. I'll look forward to it."

Before Gildan could open her mouth to remark on
this unexpected exchange between the two, Bronwen
spoke up. "Thank you, sir, for your kindness in bringing us here. If we could, we would reward you well."

"No trouble," he said, giving Enit a last glance. "No
trouble at all."

As he hurried away, Bronwen turned the other two
women toward the city. Taking their hands, she set off
through a confusing array of alleys and streets. They

soon spotted St. Nicholas Almshouse not far from the river. The bells rang in the tower, and a nun who stood outside the front door beckoned the women.

"The bells signal the time for prayer. You are welcome to join us."

Bronwen made a quick survey of the place in case they must return. It was clean but barren of all furnishings save a bench and a cross hanging over the arched entry to the main hall. Inside that unlit chamber, long rows of narrow straw pallets were already occupied by resting women.

"Do you make a schedule of your prayer?" Bronwen asked the woman.

"We nuns pause throughout the day to offer praise and petition to the Lord. Matins, Terce, Sung Mass, Sext, Vespers, Nocturnes—bells announce each of these special services. But as Christians, we are free to kneel before God at any time we choose. Will you come in?"

"No," Gildan said firmly. "We're on our way to Lord Whittaker's house."

"Lord Whittaker is our patron," the nun exclaimed. "You'll find him a generous and kind man."

"Thank you for welcoming us," Bronwen told her. "But we must be on our way."

As the women set off through the city again, Bronwen pondered the many differences between this world and the one she had known all her life. Normans, Christians, nuns and church bells—what would her father think if he could see his daughters now? He had so carefully planned out their futures, but fortune's wheel, it seemed, had spun them into the hands of the One God and His whims.

Bronwen found it hard to imagine that a God so great

as Jacques Le Brun had portrayed would turn His eye on three impoverished women in the midst of the great city of London. What could He want with her, after all? As she hurried toward the merchant's home, she heard Jacques's deep voice in her heart. *And now you have your own crusade,* he had told her.

Almost as if God Himself had answered her query, Bronwen realized that crusade—her pursuit to regain control of Rossall—must be uppermost in her thoughts. She would settle Gildan into a nunnery. Then she must find a way to return to Rossall and take the holding. But how? How could she ever hope to succeed?

As they finally found the street on which the merchant lived, the clash of swords and the cries of angry combatants suddenly rang out nearby. A man racing toward the fracas had already drawn his blade. "Henry Plantagenet has returned to London from a *chevauchée* around the countryside to raise support," he said to the frightened women as he hurried by. "King Stephen doesn't want him back in the city, and so our battle rages anew."

A contingent of armed knights thundered down the street. Weapons at the ready, they shouted their loyalty to Stephen, the king. Gildan began to cry, and Enit pressed Bronwen to return to the almshouse before they were caught up in the melee. But she spotted a young man running down the steps of his home toward an iron gate. He, too, had drawn his blade for the skirmish.

"Sir," Bronwen called out to him. "Good sir, we seek the home of Gregory, Lord Whittaker. Can you tell us how to find him?"

Tall and sandy-haired, the man halted. "*This* is the home of Sir Gregory. I'm his son, Chacier. What would you have of my father?"

"We are sent at the commendation of Captain Muldrew. He told us that Lord Whittaker might hear our plight and offer us refuge."

Clearly eager to join the swordplay down the street, Chacier wavered for a moment. Finally, he opened the iron gate and ushered them inside. "My sisters will greet you. Mention the captain, and you'll be welcomed."

Before they could speak further, he raised his sword and bolted through the gate. Bronwen hurried Gildan and Enit toward the large home. They were nearing the top of the steps when the door fell open and two young Norman women stepped outside.

"Has he gone?" one of them demanded of Bronwen. "Did you see our brother go out just now?"

"If your brother is Sir Chacier, son of Lord Whittaker, he left us moments ago."

"Father will be furious," the elder lady said to the younger. "But who are you? Did Chacier let you in?"

One of the Norman girls appeared to be about Gildan's age, while the other was several years younger. Both had dimpled smiles and turned-up noses. Each had flaxen hair that had been twisted into rolls on either side of her head and held in place with a net. Rather than veils and circlets, they wore cloth bands beneath their chins to secure colorful round, flat-topped hats. Their embroidered tunics glittered in the last of the evening sunlight.

Bronwen repeated the information she had given their brother, and at the name of Captain Muldrew, the two ladies brought them quickly into the house. Though their journey from the gate to the front door had been hasty, Bronwen had noted that the house stood three stories high with a sharply pointed roof housing a fourth level. The front courtyard contained intricate beds of bright flowers and shrubs. Numerous windows of various shapes and sizes faced the gate. It could never be called a castle, but this home certainly outshone anything at Warbreck.

"Captain Muldrew is our dear friend," the elder sister said as they gathered inside a candlelit room. "He brings us gifts each time he visits. May we have your names?"

After hearing Bronwen's introductions, the woman presented her younger sister, Lady Caresse. She was called Lady Linette. "But are you truly noblewomen?" Caresse asked. "You are oddly garbed, and where are your guards?"

"We are of noble blood, madam," Bronwen explained. "Our father, Edgard of Rossall, died this summer. Soon after, an enemy usurped his lands. We fled for our lives."

"Such tragedy! Then you must agree to be our guests. With Captain Muldrew's good word, you are surely honorable women. Please follow us."

They led their visitors into an even larger chamber with yet more lights. Wide-eyed, Gildan finally managed to speak. "This is your home? How magical!"

The Whittaker sisters giggled. "We love it," Linette said. "And you must not fret about the disturbance in the street. We are accustomed to such incidents now. Soon Henry will attain the crown, and England will be at peace."

"You said your father has died," Caresse spoke up, "and I see by your mourning tunic that you must be a widow, Lady Bronwen."

"My husband was killed in battle. We had not been married long."

"Did you love him?"

Bronwen glanced at Enit in consternation at the unusual question. "He was my husband. I respected him."

"Had you many young suitors to sing you ballads and steal kisses in the halls of your northern castle?"

Bronwen hardly knew how to respond to such a query. "Upon my honor, I was a faithful wife."

Lady Linette and her sister elbowed each other as they snickered behind their hands. "We are an amorous people here in London," Linette said. "You'll soon learn our ways. We shall take you all about London and introduce you to our friends, for we are cheerful all the year long."

At this announcement, Bronwen noticed her sister's face beginning to regain its color. But their hostesses sobered when an elderly gentleman stepped into the room.

"Girls, who is here? And what has become of my son?"

The elder spoke. "Papa, Captain Muldrew sent these women to you with his commendation. They are noblewomen from the north. As for Chacier—the last we saw, he was racing out the door into a fray at the end of the street."

The old man's face grew grim. "I must send him reinforcement. Go to the guard, good man." He motioned to a servitor standing in the shadows. "Linette, will you please remember your manners and make introductions?"

"Ladies, this is our father, Gregory, Lord Whittaker. Papa, these are Lady Bronwen and Lady Gildan, along with their nurse. They've fallen on difficult times—the loss of a dear father and husband."

"Then consider this your home until you have sorted out your affairs," Sir Gregory told them. "Take your time and be in no great hurry to depart. It is often the hasty decisions that we most regret."

"Thank you, Sir Gregory," Bronwen said. "Your generosity is more than we had ever hoped for."

He lifted a hand. "Think no more of it. Linette, Caresse—take these women to your mother."

"Yes, Papa," the sisters said as one. In a moment the door had shut behind him.

"That is our father's counting room," Linette explained, pointing out a closed door as she led the others through the chamber. "Near the stair is the storeroom where the wares are kept. Across the hall is the merchants' room, where Father meets with tradesmen."

They climbed a steep flight of stairs, and Linette pushed open a door that led to a room with many windows and a great fireplace. Instead of a circular area in the center of the hall with smoke vents in the roof, as at Rossall, this fireplace stood against a back wall, and smoke rose through a hidden pipe or tunnel. Dismantled tables had been propped against another wall on which hung tapestries embroidered with battle scenes.

"Here is the *solar* where we eat," Linette announced. "Caresse, do go across the hall and find Mother. She is probably speaking to the cook."

"Is your kitchen *inside* the house?" Gildan asked.

"Of course! Where else could it be?"

Before Gildan could reply, a small red-cheeked woman rushed in, followed by Caresse. Flinging her arms toward the ceiling, she cried, "Oh, you poor dears! Come, come—we must draw you a bath at once. Do you like salmon pie? The cook has just brought one out of the oven."

"Allow me to introduce the ladies Bronwen and Gildan," Linette said. "This is Lady Mignonette."

When Bronwen and Gildan curtsied, the woman

urged her daughters to see to the welfare of their guests. After ascending to a third floor, the group emerged from the stairwell into a long hallway. Linette walked down it, calling out occupants of each room.

"Here dwell Chacier, Roussel and Gilbert—our brothers. And here is the garderobe."

"Garderobe?" Gildan asked.

"The room for privacy, of course," Linette explained. Bronwen peered inside to find a wooden platform containing an oblong hole. How barbaric, she thought, to have both your kitchen and your privy inside the house!

"Did you not have garderobes in the north?" Caresse wanted to know.

"Certainly not," Gildan replied. "Our privy stood near the stables. Do you not fear infections?"

The Whittaker sisters laughed at the very idea. "Here sleep my mother and father, and here is our chamber," Linette said. Much like the parents' room, theirs contained a row of bright garments that hung from a pole near the ceiling. Each bed likewise was suspended from the ceiling beams by four thick ropes, and they were covered with blankets and furs. At the foot of each bed sat a large brass-studded chest and a washstand.

The guest room was across the hall. Gildan paused to admire an embroidered hanging of an outdoor scene with several ladies serenaded by gentlemen who played pipes and lutes as they all lounged in the grass.

"How marvelous," she remarked. "Your home is so different from ours. Our father slept in the great hall with his men. We never imagined building chambers one on top of the other, did we, Bronwen?"

"No, but Sir Gregory is a merchant and has no need for a great hall with many warriors."

A knock at the door brought in three servants. One bore a large oaken tub, and the others each carried buckets of warm water. They filled the tub and emptied a pouch of herbs into it. Bronwen frowned at the idea of stepping into an entire vat of water. But Linette and Caresse would hear of nothing but that both guests must strip off their clothes and enter the tub. Gildan shivered as she shook her head. "I shall die of frogs and worms that will eat my flesh!"

Lest her sister protest further, Bronwen slipped into the tub and discovered that the water was not only warm and fragrant, but relaxing. Gildan finally joined her, but she sat trembling and clearly at the verge of tears.

"How often do you take baths here?" Enit asked from the corner where she stood warily observing the event.

"Two or three times a month in summer," Linette said. "Less often in winter, for it is cold and damp in London. Crusaders started the fashion of bathing, and we adore it."

After much discussion of their different customs, the women dressed and entered the solar. Sir Gregory met them with a somber face. "Chacier is wounded," he reported. "He lies below, tended by the leech."

His sisters gasped and fled down the stairs, Gildan trailing behind. "Are your son's wounds grave?" Bronwen asked. "Our nurse is a healer. Perhaps she can help."

"Sit please." Sir Gregory pointed to a pair of chairs and joined Bronwen near a window. "My son will live. His arm is slashed below the elbow, and he may never draw sword again—but that is well with me. He stands to inherit my trade, and I do not endorse these youthful adventures."

He paused and assessed his guest. "Tell me of your situation, Lady Bronwen. I wish to be of service."

"My sister's plight is the greater, sir. She was married to the man who usurped my father's lands after his death. Her husband was cruel and the church condemned their consanguineous relationship. If Gildan gains funds to press the issue in a church court, it will be permanently annulled. But her husband means to have his wife back—and to take my life."

He scowled. "You? But you are a widow of no means. What harm can you do him?"

"My father willed his lands to me, sir, and I intend to have them."

Sir Gregory leaned back in his chair. "We have two issues before us, then. First, annulment. I do not favor the dissolution of marriage, yet I know Henry Plantagenet's own wife made use of it. My lady, I am a wealthy man, and in this city wealth means power. I can give your sister counsel, and I'll use my connections with the church to make her lot easier. Now what of you and this quest?"

Bronwen squared her shoulders. "I will not give it up. I seek a young man who came here to enter a monastery. He is good and just. He knows the customs of the north and has met my enemy. And…and he is a Christian. I find this religion to have more power than I supposed. I wish to find my friend, Martin, and ask his guidance."

Sir Gregory smiled. "In two days' time, I will make rounds of these holy institutions to deliver alms for the poor they support. You may go with me."

Bronwen grasped the old man's hands in her own. "Thank you, sir," she said. "You are more than kind."

As promised, two days later Bronwen set out with Sir Gregory in his carriage, surrounded by a train of mounted guards. In seeking Martin, she felt she had a chance at finding answers. Perhaps he would be able to advise her of a suitable nunnery where Gildan would be content—and safe from Aeschby. He might also have words of wisdom about her father's will. Should she seek to follow it, as her heart led her—or should she abandon it, as her mind argued?

Invigorated by the throbbing, bustling life in the city, Bronwen stared from the carriage window at the fabled White Tower of London, built by William the Conqueror on a hill near the river. She saw the royal buildings where nobles and knights met with King Stephen and worked their plots against Matilda and her son Henry. On narrow streets, the carriage rolled beneath thatched and tiled roofs of leaning timber houses. Along the river, they passed stalls displaying oil, iron and clay pots from Spain; spices, glass vessels and silks from the Holy Land; and linens and cottons from Flanders.

Never had she seen so many different shops. Fly-coated sides of beef and tubs of fresh fish filled the butcheries, while strolling vendors hawked oysters and mussels. Along St. Margaret's Place in Bridge Street, she saw eels and Thames fish for sale. At the various almshouses, monasteries and churches, Sir Gregory descended from the carriage to donate his money. Each time, he returned to say that Martin was not there.

Passing Ledenhall, Bronwen saw swans, geese, pigeons, hens and ducks for sale, alive or already dressed. She observed cloth sellers, charcoal makers, barrel makers, barbers, furriers, shoemakers and glove makers. The sights and smells of the marketplace intrigued Bronwen, but she knew a growing disappointment with each stop.

As the sun began to set, Sir Gregory told her they

would visit Charter House. The carriage left the streets of Old London through a gate in the ancient wall. Along the straighter roads of the new city, they rode between neat houses with tiny garden plots until at last they spotted a building enclosed by a high stone wall.

Sir Gregory pulled at a bell rope and a small window in the gate slid open. The monk inside spoke with him for a moment, then the window closed again. Certain of another disappointment, Bronwen was startled to hear the rusty iron gate creak open. In the soft orange glow of the setting sun stood a thin man whose head had been shaved but whose eyes she could not mistake.

"Sir Martin," she cried, climbing down from the carriage and hurrying toward him. "Is it you?"

"It is I," he said with a quiet smile.

"Do you remember me at all?" she asked.

"Of course. You are the dark woman of the north, wife to the Viking. How could I forget you? From that beach to the walls of this sanctuary, I heard of little else. Each time my master spoke to me in private, it was to consult about a lady whose eyes had captured him. You are Bronwen the Briton."

At the memory of a time and place so far away, she clutched the iron bars of the gate. "I last saw Le Brun in Preston where he dueled against Aeschby and Haakon. Have you heard of him in recent weeks? How fares your master?"

"You will have to ask him yourself," Martin said. "He is here—inside the antechamber. Come, the two of you must speak."

Chapter Ten

Wordless with disbelief, Bronwen signaled to Sir Gregory, who called out that he would wait for her in the carriage. Martin bade her enter and led her toward the door to a small chamber inside the monastery wall.

"I never expected to see you in London," he said as they crossed the courtyard. "What has become of you since the night you defended me against Haakon's wrath?"

As Bronwen related the events of the past months, the tears that had been threatening all day spilled from her eyes. Laying a hand on his arm, she begged him to stop. The very idea of an encounter with Jacques Le Brun on this evening was more than she could bear.

"I have learned nothing in my life, Martin," she confessed, "except that my judgments are usually wrong. People I expect to trust deceive me. And those I disdain turn out to be kind and gentle. The world is filled with too many confusing ideas, too many religions, too much war. Oh, sir—"

"Martin, what is taking so long?" The deep voice could belong to only one man. "I am expected back before dark, and it is already…"

His voice trailed off as his eyes focused on the woman at Martin's side. "Bronwen the Briton."

"As you see."

A flood of relief washed through her at seeing Jacques alive and well. But she could not stay. She had come to seek counsel of Martin, and Jacques would only confuse and distract her. The monk was clearly unaware of the chaos in Bronwen's heart as he ushered her into the chamber. A single lit candle sat on a rough shelf beside the door.

Jacques looked so like he had on the beach in Amounderness—yet his face registered as much surprise as hers. Her heart beating quickly, Bronwen turned to the fair monk.

"I must go," she told Martin. "I came to ask your guidance, and I see you have a guest already."

"One moment, madam." Jacques placed a hand on Bronwen's elbow to prevent her departure. "I have news of Rossall."

"Rossall!" Bronwen's breath caught. "Tell me."

"Martin, will you leave us for a moment, please?"

"Let him stay," Bronwen said. "What can you say that your friend should not hear?"

Jacques spoke firmly. "I would speak with you alone."

Martin glanced from one to the other. "Madam, I shall greet the gentleman who brought you here—and I'll rejoin you in a moment."

With a nod, Martin shut the door. At once, Jacques took Bronwen's hand. "Tell me you are well."

"I am. My sister and our nurse stay at the home of a good family. They treat us well."

"What has befallen you since that day in Preston? I confess I have feared for your life."

"As I have feared for yours." Bronwen knew she should draw her hand away, but the warmth of his fingers as they entwined hers left her weak. "Our journey to London was uneventful. The ship's captain referred us to the home of his friend, and there we stay. Gildan will enter a nunnery, and I… My plans are uncertain. What news of Rossall?"

"Aeschby remains there. You are safe for now. My spies tell me he plots to take Warbreck."

"Warbreck? Surely he does not have the strength."

"His closest adviser is the son of your late husband."

"Haakon," she said. "Of course he would press for an invasion of his father's castle. Together they may be able to amass a sizable army."

"Aeschby lusts for land. I believe I can avert their schemes and overpower them, but not from this distance."

"Why did you come to London?"

"I have business here. Henry Plantagenet is newly arrived from a *chevauchée,* and he has called a meeting of his supporters. I must return to the north as soon as may be. But you? Do you mean to stay here?"

She looked away. "Why do you suppose I sought out Martin? My gods played havoc with me in Amounderness, and yours gives me little guidance here."

His hand touched her shoulder and stroked down the length of her arm. "Is your hatred for Normans and our Christian faith as strong as ever it was?" he asked.

"I am certain of nothing now." She sensed him moving closer in the darkness. "Rossall is my home, and I shall always be a Briton. But…"

"Bronwen, permit me to meet you in another place than this. I must see you again."

"How can I say yes?"

"How can you say no?" His arms slipped around her. "Please woman, do not keep me in this agony forever. I can conquer many things, but not this! It plagues me."

"I cannot see you, sir. My sister—"

"Where do you stay?"

Martin opened the door again, and Jacques released Bronwen at once. She quickly stepped out into the night. "I shall come to consult with you another time, Martin," she told the monk. "My carriage awaits."

Martin pursed his lips as Jacques ducked to avoid the low doorway and joined him in the monastery courtyard. Awhirl with tears, joy, fear, so much emotion she could hardly hold it in, Bronwen started for the gate. But at the thought of turning her back on Jacques Le Brun once again, she halted.

"I stay at the home of Gregory, Lord Whittaker," she said, meeting his dark eyes. "They are Normans and supporters of Henry Plantagenet. I am sure they would make you welcome."

Before he could answer, she slipped through the gate and hurried to the carriage.

Bronwen and Sir Gregory were seated in the *solar* discussing the political atmosphere in England when the door burst open, and the chamber filled with giggles.

"Oh, Papa!" Linette sang out. "Poor Chacier is quite smitten with our dear Gildan. You must see the look in his eyes—as if he's in a trance."

Caresse chimed in. "You should hear his honeyed words, Papa. True love, true *amour,* true romance!"

Bronwen turned to her sister, who stood beaming beside her friends. Gildan's cheeks had flushed a bright red, and her blue eyes twinkled. Trembling ever so slightly, she adjusted her jaunty hat and straightened her gloves.

"Now daughters, enough of that," Sir Gregory scolded. "You are always imagining Chacier in love. Let him be. He is wounded, and cannot hope to parry your teasing."

At their father's reproach, the girls captured Gildan and hurried off again. Nearly a week had passed since Bronwen's visit to the monastery, and she had seen nothing of Jacques Le Brun. Though her memory of his words of passion played constantly through her mind, she felt a sense of relief that he had not come to Lord Whittaker's home. He must be taken with labors on behalf of Henry Plantagenet's cause. And with Aeschby threatening Warbreck, Jacques would certainly be eager to depart London.

She was grateful to Sir Gregory for his wide-ranging knowledge, which she drank from him like cold water on a summer day. Though she still had no idea or plan as to how she might regain Rossall, she knew the information he gave her would be useful.

Even more, she had come to enjoy the Whittaker family. They were a unit, interested in each others' lives, asking questions, offering comments. How strange it was—and how pleasant—to live like this, Bronwen thought. There were no rows of onlooking guards at mealtimes. There were no roaming pigs or chickens underfoot. There were only good smells, delicious food and cordial conversation.

She and Gildan had settled easily into the comfortable life of the burgher's home. Even Enit seemed relaxed. The Norman sisters took joy in adorning Gildan with their most colorful garments. And she, in turn, made frequent trips in their company to visit Chacier. The young man's wounds were healing well, and Bronwen could see that he was smitten with Gildan. She hovered about his bed chittering and smoothing his blankets. Chacier's eyes followed her everywhere and at each witty comment she made, he laughed.

With the departure of his daughters, Sir Gregory chuckled. *"Amour,"* he said. "Such silliness."

"Can you enlighten me on this subject, sir?" Bronwen asked. "In the north we do not know of *amour.*"

He smiled. "It is a French fashion that will surely pass as all this sort of nonsense does. I am told *amour* begins when a man sees a woman more beautiful than the sun and the moon together. It strikes his heart like a blow. If the object of his affection spurns him, he often grows ill unto death."

"Indeed," Bronwen remarked, thinking she had never heard a more ridiculous idea.

"The man truly in love sends his beloved all manner of gifts and trinkets to turn her eyes favorably upon him. At seeing her, he feels as if his heart has never beaten so fast. He nearly swoons for joy at her every smile."

"And what becomes of this wild emotion in time? Do the lovers marry?"

"Usually not. Often the woman is already married." Sir Gregory sighed. "Marie de Champagne—daughter of Henry's wife, Eleanor of Aquitaine—has declared that love and marriage are incompatible. Men and women marry whom they must—but love whom they will. We hear rumors that her mother has many lovers besides her husband."

Uncomfortable at the realization that Jacques Le Brun's profession of desire for her so closely matched this drivel, Bronwen spoke again. "What becomes of the love if the woman accepts the man who has pursued her?"

"According to my daughters," Sir Gregory said, "there are two kinds of love. *Pure love* exists when the amorous pair meets to kiss and caress, but the woman remains faithful to her husband. *Mixed love* occurs when the passion is carried to its completion."

"Mixed love?" Bronwen said. "In the north, we call that *infidelity,* and we punish it."

"We call it *adultery*—a vile sin. But don't fear this dalliance between your sister and my son. Gildan's marriage is not dissolved, and Chacier is no fool."

"But I do fear it," Bronwen said. "Gildan easily falls into traps set by her own need for admiration. She knows nothing of *pure love* and *mixed love.* I cannot allow your son to ruin her chance to annul her marriage and continue with her life because he has seduced her and perhaps gotten her with child. Though I can't control Gildan's life, I shall do my best to protect her from misfortune—even at well-intentioned hands."

Sir Gregory nodded. "You are wiser than your age would give you credit. Chacier intends no harm—you must believe me. But you are right to protect your sister and want the best for her."

"Will you speak to your son?"

"I already have," he said. "He knows of my concern, but he avows that he has lost his heart to Gildan's beauty and sweet nature. He begs me not to deny their love simply because you and I have not experienced it ourselves."

Bronwen searched the man's gray eyes and saw written in them a measure of her own ache. Perhaps he, too, had once felt the stirrings of the heart. Maybe some woman had captured him as surely as Jacques Le Brun had captured Bronwen. Could either deny the power and beauty of such passion? Yet, dare they allow it to continue?

On hearing that Henry Plantagenet's meeting with his supporters was ended and his allies had returned to their posts, Bronwen realized Jacques must have seen the error in his desire to meet with her again. Though it pained her to think that her hesitation had rebuffed him at last, she convinced herself it was for the best. Sir Gregory told her that Henry's resolve to defeat King Stephen and see that his son never sat upon England's throne had increased in the past months. The civil war would continue unabated.

Though news of the continuing strife was important to Bronwen, she must make plans of her own. The affection between Chacier and Gildan grew stronger by the day, and it had become imperative that the golden-haired beauty be taken to a nunnery as soon as possible.

Deciding it was safe to seek Martin's counsel with no danger of meeting Jacques again, Bronwen asked Sir Gregory if she might take his carriage to the monastery. He agreed at once and provided her with a full contingent of guards.

The monk greeted her warmly at the gate, and again they walked together to the small chamber built into the wall. As Bronwen expressed her confusion and lack of direction, Martin led her inside and saw her seated across from him on a low stool.

"You are deeply distressed," Martin said, "yet, God can use things you are learning here to your benefit."

"In what way? I am more confused than ever before."

"You've begun to open your mind and see people as they really are—not as you had been taught to think of them. And you now understand that God's plans for us may not be the ones we made for ourselves. Once I thought that I would live my life in service to Jacques Le Brun—the best and most intelligent man on this earth. Never once did I suppose I would find peace as a monk, devoted only to God. But when I felt His calling, I knew I must answer."

Bronwen listened carefully. Perhaps Martin was right. Perhaps she was learning new things. But she had no direction in life, as he had.

"I can find no sense of purpose to my existence, Martin," she told him. "Should I join Gildan and become a nun?"

"What do you think?"

"That I do not know your God well enough to give over my future to His service. But I want to know Him, Martin. I want to understand Him as you do. I need the peace that you have found."

"Peace comes when we seek God, worship Him and do His bidding."

"Sir Gregory tells me that God and His Son are one with the Holy Spirit. Three in one? I cannot fathom it."

"Nor can I. If there were nothing unfathomable about God, why would we need faith? There is much of majesty, glory and mystery to our Father. How did the womb of a virgin—a created being—contain the essence of the Creator? How could Jesus have risen to life after His violent death on the cross? Where is heaven and where is hell? Why would our holy God permit evil to have such power on this earth? Madam, there are more questions in Christianity than we will ever have answers."

"Then what use is it?"

"When one puts full trust in Christ, allowing Him to reign over desire, will and the impulse to do evil, He fills the heart with His Spirit. Such peace, such joy as that, is beyond explanation. It gives life meaning and purpose. The goal becomes to please Him and do good to others. Self is lost, utterly lost."

Bronwen shook her head. "I have always been driven by my father's will. It is hard to hear God speak."

"Forsake the gods of your youth, madam. They are false. Instead, pray and worship only the one God, the Creator King of heaven and earth. Go to church and listen to what is said. Study what is written in the Holy Scripture. Then you will hear Him."

"But that must take many years, sir. I cannot sit at Sir Gregory's house forever. My sister's virtue is at risk. My own life has no purpose. And what of Rossall?"

"What of it? Do you feel God pressing you there?"

"I do, Martin. I must go back to Rossall. I have known it all along. I must find a way to reclaim my father's lands. It is my duty—and my desire."

The monk smiled at her. "Of course you must go back to Rossall. Your sister must make her own path. God brought you to London to show Himself to you. Now it is time for you to return home with a new heart and a soul committed to Him."

For the first time in many weeks, Bronwen felt the dark clouds roll back and the path before her grow plain. "Rossall needs me. My people have so much to learn.

Not only do they need the power and comfort of the Christian God, but they must have knowledge of this new world or it will overwhelm them. But how can I reclaim my lands? I have no knights and no husband. And I left the box containing my father's will at Warbreck."

Martin sat up. "Your father left a written will?"

"Yes, as a safeguard against just such treachery as has been committed against me. But what use is it? No one can read it, not even I. And who will honor a piece of parchment against the word of so strong a man as Aeschby?"

"There is great value in the written word, my lady. I am a scribe. All my days are spent copying the Holy Scriptures onto parchment. The written Word of God is the foundation of our faith. As more men learn to read, the value of the written document increases. Even now, a court of Norman law places more trust in a piece of writing than in what a man may say. You must go to Warbreck. Jacques will give you the box."

"How can I trust a man who took my husband's lands?" Bronwen asked. "His dream is to acquire Amounderness for Henry Plantagenet. Surely he has already set his eye upon Rossall. We are enemies."

"You do not know his heart, my lady."

"I know men of battle. You are a man of God, and I implore you not to speak of our conversation to Le Brun. You must not tell him about my father's written will."

The monk's deep gray eyes regarded her. "If you wish to learn to put your faith in God, madam, you would do well to begin by finding at least one human you can trust. Jacques Le Brun could be that man. He cares for you. Truly, he would never betray you."

"Martin, you may trust him, but I cannot! Swear you will tell him nothing of this exchange between us."

"I will never speak of it. You have my word. But you are going to need your father's will to regain your lands. Of that you can be certain." He paused for a moment. "Before I joined this monastery, Jacques and our retinue made a journey to Canterbury. There we met a young churchman who is influential in legal, political and religious matters. We became fast friends, and he often comes here to visit me."

"Is he trustworthy?" Bronwen asked.

"I don't believe the man to be always correct in his actions—but he is wise and well respected. People flock to his home for counsel, and he finds time for each one. I believe he could make your decision easier. He will tell you whether your document has value and advise you on ways to regain your lands."

"Who is this man?"

"He calls himself Thomas of London, but others know him as Thomas à Becket."

Bronwen stepped down from the carriage and crossed to the gate that protected Sir Gregory's home. London's streets were not safe even by day, and she was relieved to have arrived before the sun was fully set. As she slid back the hasp, something brushed her elbow. She had seen no one nearby when she'd left the carriage, and she started at the touch.

"Bronwen the Briton," Jacques spoke. "You are as difficult to pin down as a feather in the wind."

He stood beside her, garbed not in mail but in the clothes of a London gentleman. In the fading light, his dark gaze settled on her face, and he smiled. "You thought I had returned to Warbreck—and you were pleased."

She glanced at the door to Sir Gregory's home, praying that no one could see her. "I could not imagine you would stay away so long with Aeschby and Haakon threatening."

"I left good men to hold my castle. My best, in fact. If Aeschby and I continue to live, I imagine we'll threaten each other forever. Men spend much time at battle, and leave too little opportunity for more important things."

"Your friend Martin chooses wisely. He spends his time at prayer."

"And copying Scripture. A worthy cause."

"Yes, for those who can read." She reached for the hasp again. "I must go inside. My sister will wonder about me."

"I wonder about you more," he said. Taking her arm, he tucked it under his and turned her away from the house. "Come, let us stroll."

"Sir, I cannot!" She struggled to free herself. "This is unseemly."

"I have come to see you, waited nearly an hour behind that blasted shrubbery and will not be denied." He laid his free hand on her arm, effectively preventing any hope of escape. "We have spoken rarely, yet you refuse to leave my thoughts. Why is that?"

"I cannot say, sir. Perhaps your brain is faulty."

At that, Jacques gave a hearty laugh. "Madam, you delight me. At this moment, in the most loathsome of cities and weighted by demands I cannot hope to meet, I find myself happier than I've been in years."

Wondering where he was taking her, Bronwen fought

to steady her breath. "If you dislike London, you should leave it. You are needed at Warbreck."

"And you? Will you stay here?"

"No," she told him. "I intend to settle my sister and return to Rossall. It is my home."

"Rossall is rightfully yours, but what of the Viking? It is you he most dreads, and he means to see you dead. I fear greatly for you, my lady."

He turned them onto a path that led up to a fine house, not as tall as Sir Gregory's but more sturdily built. Grand stone steps rose to a wooden door studded with brass and iron. Jacques fitted a key into the lock, turned it and held out a hand to welcome Bronwen inside.

"Where is this?" she asked. "I have never been to this house before. Who lives here?"

"I do. My father owned it before he joined the Crusade, and now it is mine. Will you come in?"

"The two of us, alone together? Sir—"

"Bronwen, I mean you no harm. Surely you know that by now. Come and sit. Take refreshment and speak with me. Merely speak, that is all I ask."

Trying to listen for the will of God as Martin had encouraged her to do, Bronwen could hear nothing but the urging of her heart. Lifting her skirt, she stepped into the foyer and saw that candles had already been lit. It was a comely chamber with a marble floor, tapestried walls and a blazing fire. The scent of some exotic spice lingered in the room, and she drifted toward the fire as if in a dream.

"I have sat here many an evening," Jacques said as he followed her across the room. "The hearth at Warbreck, too, has been my comfort. But my idle thoughts turn always to you. I picture you here in London—alone. You have nothing. No one."

"Why do you think of me at all? I am nothing to you. I am no more than the widow of a vanquished lord. I cannot understand why you pursue me—why you care."

He reached out and touched the side of her neck with his fingertips. "I cannot explain it. I only know that when I see you, I long to hold you. When I think of you, I remember your bold spirit, your tenderness, your dark beauty."

Bronwen laid one hand on the mantelpiece, struggling for some measure of reason to prevail. Were these words of passion true? Or did the man have guile behind his avowals of desire? She thought of Sir Gregory and his explanation of Norman *amour.* She knew Amounderness was a large area that Jacques intended to possess for Henry Plantagenet. Surely this speech of his reeked of falsehood, luring her into a trap from which she could not escape.

"I know by your silence that you think me unworthy of you," he said. For a moment he could not speak. Then he raked his fingers through his hair. "It is true what you said—I am a half-breed. Many have taunted my heritage of mixed blood. My skin is the deeply tan shade of my mother's land, and I was given the name Le Brun because of it. You are a Briton, lily-white, a woman of noble ancestry, the proud bearer of an ancient bloodline."

"Jacques," she said carefully. "Please… Please know that I was wrong to judge you by your lineage. I was unfair. Thoughtless. Cruel. My father brought me up with the belief that Britons were superior to all and must eventually once again rule this isle. I was taught to hate and mistrust anyone who didn't share my heritage. Though I respect and honor my father, in this he was wrong. I have learned that some good may be found in a Viking, a Welshman, a Norman. And in a man whose life represents a blending of people."

"You speak of me." He paced away from the fire and then back again. "Have you learned not to hate me?"

"I am wary of you, sir. But I see the admiration you have earned from many others, and I trust it."

"Even if you can accept that I am not Briton, Norman or Viking, I am no nobleman. I am the son of a merchant. My Norman name is a symbol of what I have tried to become."

"Once you were called Jacob," she said softly. "Captain Muldrew who brought us to London knew your father. He told me of your home in Antioch."

"I was Jacob there, but now I am Jacques. It is what I want in life—to be a Norman lord, a knight in service to Henry Plantagenet, king of England. And yet all I am and want to be causes you pain. Please, Bronwen, you must accept me as I am."

He captured her arm and drew her close. Before Bronwen could hold him back, he slipped his arms around her and pressed her against his chest. His breath stirred the wisps of hair on her forehead. She resisted his embrace, desperately trying to think, to protect herself, to keep herself from this man. But his warmth and strength were too much. She let her hands slide across his back as she laid her cheek on his shoulder. Why had he uttered such words of confession and pain? What could they mean? She must make some sense of this madness between them.

"My lord—" she began.

"No, do not speak. I fear what you must say, my dearest lady. Too many barriers stand between us. I know that. I see them all as clearly as you do. Just let me hold you now, and deceive myself into believing that you are mine."

Bronwen felt tears well. How she longed to tell Jacques everything in her heart—every dream, every joy, every fear. She ached to stay in his arms, to be held forever by this strong yet gentle man. He spoke so openly to her. She wanted to believe him, to trust him. How could she doubt his motives? And yet she must. To become a pawn in some game he played would ruin her forever.

As the tumult of emotion spun within her heart, Bronwen tried to pull away from the man whose very existence threatened her purpose in life. But when she tried to draw away, he slid his arms more tightly about her. When she lifted her focus to his face, his lips brushed hers, robbing them of purpose. He kissed her again, this time with greater urgency, and his fingers slipped beneath her veil into the dark locks of hair that tumbled around her shoulders. Unable to resist, she drew her own hands up his broad back and across his shoulders.

"Bronwen, please," he murmured against her ear. "Do not leave me."

"I must go." She could hardly find breath to form the words. "I don't know what you want of me, Jacques."

"Give me a chance to prove myself. Allow me to defend and protect you. Let me stand up for the honor of your name against Aeschby. Permit me to give you all that is in my heart to give. The seeds of love grow between us, my lady. Let us nurture them, I beg you."

Defend…protect…honor…love. Frightened of the very words, Bronwen drew away from him and bent to retrieve her veil. "You confuse me, sir," she said. "Your words make no sense. I should go."

She started toward the door, but he caught her and turned her toward him again. "Bronwen, you have said my heritage no longer repels you, and I have offered you my protection and aid. Why do you continue to reject me?"

"You speak of love, my lord. *Pure love, mixed love, amour*—is this what you mean? If so, I must refuse it. I revile these French games of immorality and sin."

"Games? Upon my honor, I—"

"When you hold and kiss me, I can only assume you desire something from me. I shall not cast myself at your feet to be used by you and then tossed aside should you get me with child. Or do you want Rossall? Is that the object of your charade? But you know Aeschby has taken it. You know I am a widow. Indeed, I have nothing to give you. I have no lands, no wealth, no dowry. What do you want of me? What?"

"Bronwen—"

"Leave me in peace, sir. Do not torment me again."

She swept her veil over her head and fumbled for the latch. At last her fingers found the cold metal and she opened the door. Stepping out into the night, she ran down the street. Fleeing the cry of her heart…and his… she ran until she found the gate to Sir Gregory's house. When she stepped into the warm foyer, she buried her head in her hands and wept.

Chapter Eleven

Exhausted, Bronwen climbed the stairs that night to find Gildan seated on the second landing. The younger woman rose and drew her mantle about her shoulders.

"Are you not abed, Gildan?" Bronwen greeted her.

"How can I sleep when I think what you have done to me? Why did you go to see the monk? Had it something to do with my marriage to Aeschby? Did you tell him about Chacier? I know you spoke to Sir Gregory about us."

"Calm yourself, sister," she said, as Gildan rose to meet her. "The monk gave advice about my own life—not yours."

"Why did you talk to Sir Gregory, Bronwen?" Gildan stamped her foot in anger. "Now Chacier has learned I am married, and you have ruined all my happiness!"

"Both Sir Gregory and I know the admiration Chacier holds for you—and the dangers that entails."

"Chacier loves me! My life is changing for the better, and it is all because of him. Perhaps I don't understand this *amour* of which he speaks, but I want to, Bronwen.

Unlike you, I refuse to close myself off from all affection and become a sour, bitter, heartless old woman."

Bronwen grew hot with anger at Gildan's words. "Very well, then. Go about this illicit affair your own way. But be aware that Sir Gregory has his eyes on you. Chacier is his heir, and you are nothing but a dowerless, poverty-stricken married woman."

Gildan's blue eyes brimmed with tears of fury and dismay. "Well, Bronwen, you think you know so much about people. But you're wrong about Chacier and me. You've closed your mind to new ideas and your heart to tenderness—and I pity you. Just because you're miserable does not mean I must be condemned to unhappiness also. Stay out of my affairs, Bronwen. Out."

Gildan turned on her heel and stomped up the stairs, weeping. Bronwen started after her, then stopped as tears spilled down once again. How could Gildan say her sister was doomed to be a sour, bitter, lonely old woman? Yet, as Bronwen sat wiping her damp cheeks, she saw a picture of herself—her dark widow's robes, her often angry eyes, her tight lips. Was Gildan right? What had happened to that carefree young girl exploring the riverbank near Rossall?

Should she have let herself believe the words Jacques had spoken to her by the fireplace of his London home? Dare she have given herself to his touch, to his fire?

More unsettled than ever, Bronwen climbed into bed beside her sister without even discarding her tunic. Gildan would not look at her, but lay curled into a ball with the blankets over her head.

The next morning at breakfast, Lady Mignonette and her daughters pressed Bronwen for news of her meeting with the monk. Sir Gregory frowned at the three from across the table. He had led Chacier into the *solar* for the first time since his son's injury, and he motioned for silence. "Bronwen has no desire to discuss personal affairs at the breakfast table. Do let us have a moment's peace, girls."

"But this friendship between our friend and a monk is fascinating, Father," Chacier said with a smile on his lips. "Let us hear something of it."

Bronwen was still getting used to the family's habit of mealtime discussion. Chacier, she soon learned, was an eager and intelligent debater. When she declined to describe her experience, the young man gave a detailed history of the monastery. Gildan sat mesmerized, her breakfast untouched and her pink lips open.

"They live like hermits," Chacier told the women.

"How boring," Gildan commented.

"But dear lady," he said, "I understand you are to become a nun...if your sister has her way."

"Chacier, don't speak nonsense!" Caresse cried as Gildan blushed a vivid pink. "She is too lively for a nunnery. Perhaps you can think of better employment for her, brother."

"Indeed, I am certain of it." Chacier leaned back in his chair. His long blond mustache cut a fine and noble outline on his narrow face. His hazel eyes were full of merriment as he glanced around the table and drew the conversation away from Gildan.

Bronwen drifted in and out of the discussion. She hated it when Gildan was angry with her, and she wanted to be done with this lengthy breakfast. But she did have one mission to accomplish.

"Do you know of Thomas à Becket?" she asked Chacier during a lull.

"But of course," Chacier said. "He holds a school in his home for the ambitious young nobles of the city. The king may reside in Bermondsey, but it is from the house of Thomas à Becket that emissaries are sent with state secrets to the pope and the kings of Europe."

"How did he gain such respect and position?" Bronwen inquired, beginning to doubt Martin's advice about taking her petty mission to such a great man.

"He was born of an Anglo-Saxon mother and a Norman father—citizens of London. Becket takes pride in being a native-born Englishman and Londoner. His father, called Gilbert à Becket, was a merchant but they lived humbly. It was his mother who urged her son to greatness. Indeed, some say she dreams he will one day be called a saint. Mothers always have high hopes for their sons—but Becket has shown what a merchant's son can do for himself."

Sir Gregory laughed and proudly clapped his son on the shoulder. But Bronwen was remembering Jacques's words to her the night before. He had called himself unworthy, lower than she. Yet in Norman England, a merchant's son could become great and powerful.

"Becket was schooled in Merton, London and Paris," Sir Gregory told Bronwen. "He learned the merchant trade, the life of a knight, and the duties of a sheriff—all by apprenticeship. And he studied church law and common law in Italy. He has been made the prebendary of the churches of Mary-le-Strand, Otford in Kent and St. Paul's. With that, he has enough money to live in comfort the rest of his life. If Henry becomes king, who can tell to what position he may aspire?"

"Enough of politics," Lady Mignonette put in as soon as she saw a break in the conversation. She quickly turned the talk to plans and preparations for the coming fall and winter festivities. Bronwen could not bring herself to join in the merriment over events she did not plan to attend. By winter's start, she planned to be back at Rossall tending to her duties as lady of the holding.

Days slipped by, and Bronwen had no message from Martin regarding an appointment to meet with Thomas à Becket. Gildan, meanwhile, continued to blossom in the bustle of city life. Assisted by the Whittaker sisters, she garbed herself in colorful, fashionable gowns and hats. It seemed to Bronwen that as the days grew more chilly and damp, Gildan's beauty became all the more brilliant.

She and Chacier became nearly inseparable from morning until night. Gildan confided that they exchanged furtive kisses in the stairwell and tender caresses as they passed in the hall. Forgetting her anger at her sister, she eagerly shared the flowering emotion and the tumult of passion she knew in the man's embrace. She felt her life reborn as Chacier treated her with the gentleness and affection her husband never had.

No matter how apprehensive these confessions made Bronwen, her heart softened when she saw her sister's eyes brimming with joy. For her own part, she was certain she had at last driven Jacques away. She and the other young ladies often passed his house as they visited friends, but she saw no sign of the man. He never returned to Sir Gregory's home or sent her tokens of affection like the ones Gildan received from Chacier several times a day.

All the same, Bronwen longed for the touch of Jacques's hands, and she ached to be near him again.

As she sat in the window of her chamber and peered out at the changing leaves, she stroked her fingers along the silken lining of his mantle. The three gold balls of his crest glimmered in the dim light of the afternoon sun.

A knock at her door one afternoon brought Sir Gregory into the room. "Madam, I have been on my almsgiving rounds today. Your monk has sent you a message."

The merchant held out a scrolled parchment. Bronwen took it and broke the seal. Unrolling the paper, she saw that a short note had been inscribed. "Please, sir," she said. "Will you tell me what it says?"

"To Bronwen of Rossall," Sir Gregory read. "From Martin of Charter House, London, 13 October, 1153. The interview with Thomas of London, called Thomas à Becket, is scheduled one week from this date upon the bells of None at his home. I have kept your confidences to me. Now I make one request in return. Please treat my friend with grace and fairness. He means well in all things."

Bronwen took the note from Sir Gregory and pored over the unfamiliar script. If only she could read and write. Then she would be able to explain her thoughts to the monk. She would be able to send messages of her own. And she would be able to read her father's will.

"Madam." Sir Gregory broke into her thoughts. "You do well to speak with Thomas à Becket. He gives wise counsel. But more important, pray about these matters. Follow the leadings of God, and you cannot go wrong."

The night before Bronwen was to meet with Thomas à Becket, Gildan woke her with a rough shake. "What is it, sister?" Bronwen whispered. "Why are you not abed?"

"I must speak with you, Bronwen. Tomorrow I want you to ask Becket to annul my marriage to Aeschby. Please! Surely he can do it—everyone says he has great influence in the church court."

"But he's only a deacon and a prebendary. He has no power to do what you ask."

Gildan's face fell. "Then, I must tell you what Chacier plans. He will ask his father to see me converted and to pay the court fees that I may have the marriage ended."

"And then what?"

"And then he plans to wed me."

Bronwen stiffened at her sister's words. "Wed you? Sir Gregory will never allow it."

"I know I have nothing to offer. But I care for Chacier so much and he for me. Oh Bronwen, you cannot imagine how I feel when he holds and kisses me! Aeschby was so cruel, so vicious. Chacier makes me feel like a woman again. He says he loves me. And I love him, too."

As Bronwen listened to her sister's words, she considered scolding Gildan for even considering the notion of a marriage based on the fleeting emotion of *amour*— nothing but a French whim. But recalling the genuine joy she had seen on her sister's face in the past weeks, she decided she must give a more considered response.

"Gildan, let us think carefully. If Sir Gregory agrees to pay for the court, and if you are granted your annulment, and if Sir Gregory consents to allow his son to marry you, what then? Gildan, one day Chacier may need the fortune that a wealthy wife could have brought him. Can you live, knowing he may regret his decision?"

Wiping tears, Gildan shook her head. "What shall I do, sister? I love him so much that I would give him up rather than see him disgraced. But I long to be his wife. I want to manage a fine household like this, and I want to bear his children. Oh Bronwen, I feel that my body will give him children. Fine, beautiful English children."

Bronwen had to smile. "So you are English now, and no longer Briton?"

"I don't care what I am. When you're in love, it cannot matter. I just want to be Chacier's wife."

"Then let us wait to see how Sir Gregory acts. If he does what Chacier asks, then you'll know that he has pondered the situation carefully and feels you will not harm his son's reputation or future. Chacier's father is a wise man to have built so prosperous a business. He is not likely to make a mistake in the choice of his son's bride."

"Oh, dear! When you put it that way, I can see there is little chance of him allowing it. But I would rather die than be forced to submit to Aeschby again."

Bronwen hugged her sister gently. "Stop your tears, now. It is not as dire as that. You'll never belong to Aeschby again, and Sir Gregory has allowed your *amour* with Chacier to continue. He must not be so set against it as we fear."

At this, Gildan's face lit up. "Dear Bronwen, you are my strength and my wisdom. I do love you so much."

"Enough of love for one night, please." Bronwen laughed. "Now go to sleep at once, you silly goose."

Gildan giggled and slipped beneath the thick fur blankets of their bed. Nestling against Bronwen, she heaved a deep sigh. Before long the two of them were fast asleep.

* * *

As she set out in the carriage, Bronwen seemed to see before her—not the street to Becket's house—but the road to Rossall. Still wearing her mourning garb, she walked through the ornately carved doors of the man's magnificent home and realized she was viewing a way of life she had never imagined. A servitor led her down marble hallways into a great arched chamber lined with tables. Though it was well past the luncheon hour, the tables were crowded with knights, merchants and scholars who leaned to converse across platters piled with food.

A second servitor led her to a vacant chair, and a third presented her with an array of exotic fruits, most of which she had never seen before, and a selection of cheeses. She was lifting a slice of fruit to her plate when a hand reached out to steady her.

"Take care, Bronwen the Briton. You have chosen a rare delicacy." Jacques Le Brun drew out a chair and seated himself beside her.

At the sight of him so near, she quaked and the piece of fruit tumbled into her lap. Pinning it between her knees, she felt it burst against the fabric of her tunic.

"Well caught!" he said with a laugh.

"You startled me," she retorted. Cheeks afire, she retrieved the fruit and dabbed at her gown with a napkin.

"I came to observe you among the intellectuals of London, dear lady. When Martin told me he had directed you here, I could not resist joining you. Your keen wit can only be sharpened in the presence of these minds."

Bronwen bristled. "Why did Martin tell you of our conversation? I asked him to keep my confidence."

"As he did. He refused to utter a word of your conversation. His only confession was his advice to send you here. You see, he needed my help to arrange the interview."

The Norman smiled and bit into a piece of the same fruit. In contrast to their last meeting, his mood was light and friendly. Bronwen recalled Martin's message asking her to treat his friend with grace and fairness. Though Jacques's presence at the house only added to her anxiety, she was determined to honor the monk's request.

"This is called an orange," Jacques told her as he handed her a freshly cut slice. "From the Holy Land."

Expecting the bitterness of a lemon, Bronwen slipped the fruit into her mouth, bit down, and instead discovered a sweet, tangy treat. "How lovely it is! Do they grow near your home in Antioch—these oranges?"

"Everywhere. We pluck and eat them just as you might eat a raspberry."

"I cannot imagine such a place." She chewed a moment in silence as she studied the busy chamber. "Please, sir, can you tell me which man is Thomas à Becket?"

Jacques settled back in his chair. "He is in another chamber speaking with some priests. He'll see you in time. Today perhaps, or tomorrow—certainly this week."

"But I was told to come at the bells of None."

The scholar at Bronwen's other elbow leaned over and patted her arm. "You cannot expect a man as busy as Thomas à Becket to keep every appointment he makes with widows and beggars. He has been known to keep kings waiting."

Bronwen stiffened at the implication. "I am a noble-woman, sir. I came at his invitation."

"Madam," the scholar said. "Where Thomas à Becket is concerned, we are all beggars. We are supplicants for his favor, his advice, his money or his power. Everyone here has come to plead for something. Do not take offense."

Bronwen let out a breath and tried to calm her nerves. Animated banter among the scholars at her table drew her attention. They were discussing whether the earth was flat or round. Most believed it as round as the sun and stars.

"But if so," Bronwen could not help but interrupt, "might a man not set sail from England journeying westward, and continuing westward arrive back at England?"

"Precisely," Jacques confirmed. "But here is the dilemma—who will undertake such a journey?"

The men began to discuss this question as Bronwen found her ears drawn to the exchange at her left.

"If, as we all believe," one man was saying, "matter is made of various combinations of the four elements—earth, air, fire and water—then can one type of matter be completely re-created from another?"

Another man spoke up. "For example, could gold be produced from some mixture of other base metals?"

"In Europe," Jacques said in his deep voice, "I learned that in order to transmute one substance into another, a special ingredient must be present. This is called the *lapis philosophorum*—the philosopher's stone. No one has yet discovered it."

"But where do they look for it?" Bronwen asked.

"It is believed to be found in water. Anyone drinking this liquid gold will obtain eternal youth."

As the hours passed, Bronwen found herself absorbed in one discussion after another. Often Jacques asked for her opinion or listened to her questions. Her mind reeled with ideas, thoughts she had never before entertained, words she had never heard spoken, theories she could not have imagined. Seated on the edge of her chair, she leaned forward, enthralled at the debates before her. So intent was she that she hardly noticed when a servitor touched her shoulder.

"Bronwen of Rossall? Sir Thomas will see you now. Please follow me."

"I see your request has a speedy response," Jacques said, rising to help her from her seat. As he took her hand, their eyes met. "I've enjoyed this afternoon. You have proven what I suspected—that you have a quick mind and an able tongue. It pleases me that there has been no strife between us on this day."

Bronwen smiled up at him. "Indeed it has been pleasant. I regret that life cannot be filled with such days as this. Thank you for your assistance in procuring my interview. Perhaps it will help to ease my path ahead."

"I hope so, Bronwen."

With a nod, she drew away from him and followed the servitor out of the bustling chamber and down the long hall to a tall wooden door. The man announced her presence.

"Bronwen of Rossall in Amounderness. Referred by Jacques Le Brun of Warbreck and Martin of Charter House."

Bronwen stepped into the dim room. For a moment she was breathless at the opulence around her. On every

wall hung vivid tapestries depicting scenes of the hunt,
or moments in the life of Christ. Expensive beeswax
candles burned in each corner and sent a sweet aroma
into the room. The floors, like the walls, were covered
with cloths. Bronwen feared to walk lest she tread on
some sacred scene. Most astonishing of all was a great
window constructed of bits of colored glass fitted together to form an intricate picture. The late sun shone
through the glass and cast colored shadows that danced
like jewels on the carpets.

"Good afternoon, madam," a quiet voice said.

Bronwen scanned the room until she located a soli-
tary shadowed figure standing beside a wooden chair.
She dropped a deep curtsy and bowed her head.

"Please be seated." The man extended his arm toward another large chair. "I am Thomas of London, and
I see you have two fine references—good, honorable
men. How may I serve you, dear lady?"

Bronwen studied the pallid face and deep frank eyes
of the churchman. His dark hair framed a wide forehead
and a long narrow nose. For all his power and wealth,
Thomas à Becket looked young indeed.

She swallowed. "Thank you for your time, sir."

"At the moment, fortunately, I am free of kings,
kings-to-be and holy men. And in my own home, I
may choose to see whom I wish."

"I seek your advice in a personal and legal matter,"
she said. "But I must ask for your oath of confidence."

"You have it. Speak plainly."

"Before my father died, he engaged a scribe to write
out his will concerning his possessions. The will is unusual—no one in our country has ever known of such a
thing. Our spoken word is our oath. In this document,

all my father's lands and half of his treasure were endowed to me. Though he arranged for my marriage, he stipulated that nothing of his would ever belong to my husband. Rather, it must go to our firstborn son. If my husband were to die, I should remarry at once, especially if I had no son. My sister was to receive the other half of my father's treasure, and it would belong to her husband—as is the normal custom."

The man's face registered nothing. "And what has happened?"

"I married at the end of last year. Soon my father died, but before I could claim the land, my new husband's holding was attacked. He was slain and his property taken. During this time of chaos, my brother-in-law usurped my father's lands. Now I have no husband or son to avenge me, yet I feel it is my duty to do my father's will."

As she spoke, Becket rose and walked around his chair. Standing in the gloom, he paused with his head bent and his brow creased. After a short time, he returned to his seat.

"Whom do you support for the throne—Stephen or Henry?" he asked.

Bronwen could not answer at first. As a Briton, she would prefer one of her own people to become king. But she soon realized the purpose of Becket's question. Normans believed that all lands belonged to the king. He distributed properties to his barons according to their merit. Each baron then divided his lands among lesser lords. Despite all this allocation, the land yet belonged to the king. Bronwen knew she must answer, and she found it easy to choose between the two men Becket proposed.

"I support Henry Plantagenet," she said.

"And which baron usurped your father's lands?"

"A man who supports neither Henry nor Stephen," she told him. "Amounderness is in dispute. King Stephen has awarded it to the Scots, but they give it no heed and never set foot there. The original lords revile the Scots."

"If Henry were to become king and restore the lands to their original lords, would all serve him gladly?"

"I have not spoken with each man, sir. But this I do know. My brother-in-law serves only himself."

"But you—if you were to regain your father's holding—would you place yourself under the guardianship of the pretender to the throne, Henry Plantagenet? And would you then marry the man he selected for you, that your lands might be held securely for the king?"

Now Bronwen realized she had made a fearful mistake in coming to see this man. She had no intention of becoming a ward to Henry Plantagenet—of placing her life and Briton property in the hands of a man she did not even know, and a Norman at that. But Becket had trapped her. She had no option but to agree with him or show herself loyal to King Stephen.

"I would accept the authority of Henry Plantagenet," she answered at last.

It was a lie, and even as she spoke it, Bronwen begged forgiveness from God. The many deities of her youth permitted curse-casting, spell-making, fortune-telling, sacrifices and many other things the Christian faith forbade. Since meeting with Martin, Bronwen had visited the nearby church and discussed religion with Sir Gregory many times. God the Father, she had learned, found a great list of behaviors reprehensible and termed them *sin.* But He was also eager to forgive and filled with compassion for His creation. Indeed, He had sent His only Son to a sacrificial death in order to build a bridge between Himself and mankind.

Bronwen knew she still had much to learn, but at this moment, she placed her trust in God's willingness to pardon her lie.

"Hear this, madam," Becket told her. "Your father's will is not as unusual as you suppose. Perhaps he didn't school you well in the history of Norman royalty. Indeed, the very dispute which has caused this bloody civil war between Henry's mother, Matilda, and King Stephen rests in part on just such a will. You see, Henry I—son of William the Conqueror—left all his dominions to his daughter Matilda to the exclusion of her husband Geoffrey Plantagenet. And upon the birth of a son, all those dominions were to go directly to that son."

"Oh, my," Bronwen whispered. "I did not know."

"Henry Plantagenet is Matilda's son," he continued. "He claims the throne by direct descent. Stephen, son of one of Henry I's other daughters, asserts that Plantagenet has no claim and that his own son, Eustace, deserves the crown. But, of course, due to the will of Henry I, his grandson—Henry Plantagenet—is the rightful king of England. Were Henry to become king, no doubt he would support your cause over your brother-in-law's. And he would aid you in any way possible."

Bronwen sat back in shock. She had no idea that Henry's quest was so like her own. "But Henry is not king," she pointed out.

"No, madam, he is not. But as you're eager to claim your rightful possessions, and as they're already in dispute, here's my advice. Take your father's written will to Henry Plantagenet. Declare your loyalty and agree to become his ward and wed the man he selects. Henry will then either give you the troops with which to battle for your lands, or he will go to Amounderness with you and there hold trial against your brother-in-law."

"Which is more likely?" Bronwen asked.

"I believe he'll give you troops," Becket answered, "though he will make certain you're married first. After all, he's not yet king and has no authority to hold trial. If he becomes king, however, you can take comfort in knowing that Henry places more importance on the written law than any man I've ever known."

Bronwen stood trembling. All this wise counsel would do only one thing—put Rossall in Norman hands. That was the very thing her father had wanted to prevent. "Your advice has opened my eyes, sir," she said, trying to control her voice. "I thank you."

Becket acknowledged her words with a brief bow and led her out into the hall. As he handed her back into the charge of a servitor, he said in a low voice, "When you have made your decision, please inform me. I'll gladly arrange an interview for you with our future king." With that, he wished her good night and strolled back into his chamber, his crimson robes swishing behind him and the jewels on his fingers twinkling in the candlelight.

Bronwen stared after him. Why had she been such a fool to consult with this Norman? Now he knew everything. No doubt he would tell Henry Plantagenet, and all hope would be gone. She had ruined what small chance she ever had of regaining her home.

Hurrying down the hall, she saw Jacques Le Brun waiting for her beside the front door. He joined her as she made her way to the carriage. "I hope your mourning is near an end, madam."

Bronwen paused. "I shall be in mourning until the last Norman leaves our land. If you will excuse me now, I must prepare for a journey."

"So the churchman gave you unhappy counsel," Jacques said. "I feared as much. Becket knows more than anyone about current politics—but you must follow where your heart leads you."

"Is that all you Normans think of—your hearts? I'm sorry, but I cannot follow emotion. I must do what is right by my father's training and discipline. Now let me go."

"You cannot mean you plan to face Aeschby alone. I beg of you, stay here in London with the merchant's family. At least here you're safe."

"Safely out of your way while you take my father's lands for Henry Plantagenet? No, sir. I shall fight Aeschby or any man who tries to take my home. Even you."

Chapter Twelve

As Bronwen entered Sir Gregory's house, she heard laughter floating down from the *solar*.

"Ho, Bronwen! Come at once!" Gildan cried.

Met halfway up the staircase by her sister, Bronwen was crushed in an embrace and then pulled into the brightly lit chamber. The family had gathered to enjoy cups of hot spiced cider and bread still warm from the oven. As Bronwen sank onto a chair, a servitor pressed a steaming mug into her cold hands. She took a sip and looked up to see Gildan, Linette and Caresse dancing hand in hand about the room while Chacier stood watching by the fire.

"Bronwen, what do you suppose has happened?" Gildan teased. "Sir Gregory has agreed to everything!"

"Is that so?" Bronwen responded, turning to the elderly man who sat beside his wife.

"Your sister speaks the truth. I have arranged with my partner, Firmin of Troyes, to accept you and Gildan as his wards for six months. In France, you will be converted to Christianity, and the court will proceed with the marriage annulment. Firmin will then arrange for the wedding of his ward, Gildan, to my son, Chacier. It will be a more than proper alignment. As we are partners, it's sensible to consolidate our business union with a marriage. And I'm certain he will arrange a profitable marriage for you as well, my dear Bronwen."

She frowned with the effort of grasping the implications of this new development. "Sir Gregory," she asked, "who will provide my sister's dowry?"

"It will be arranged," he replied.

Bronwen suspected that he planned to provide the dowry to his partner in exchange for the six months' lodging.

"Bronwen, how can you worry about such things as a dowry?" Gildan asked. "We're going to France tomorrow! In six months, I shall wed my beloved Chacier and return to London to become a proper wife. You must marry as well and live very close to us. We shall visit one another, and our children will play, and everything will be lovely."

"France?" Bronwen asked Sir Gregory.

"Troyes is a city in eastern France," he confirmed. "It is the cultural center of Western Europe."

"They have two grand fairs in Troyes, Bronwen," Gildan added. "We'll see goods from all over the world. It's going to be marvelous. Though I shall long for my wedding day to arrive, I'll learn to be a proper Norman—in a city even more exciting than London."

As all eyes studied her, Bronwen considered the news. If she went with Gildan to France, she might have a deeper drink of the vast fountain of knowledge that she had tasted today at Becket's house. Perhaps she might marry a scholar or merchant and find joy in a life far from England and Rossall—and a certain dark Norman lord bent on conquest.

She had told Jacques she planned to take Rossall, but could she ever hope to succeed? It would be far easier to follow her sister to France and allow her future to be molded there than to submit to the leading of the one God to whom she now prayed.

Though the choice was difficult, Bronwen knew what she must say. "I'll leave for Rossall in the morning," she told the family. "In speaking with Becket today, I saw the importance of returning home. My sister's future has been accounted for—thanks to Chacier's love and Sir Gregory's great kindness—and I have no cause to linger in London."

Gildan squealed in disbelief. "No, Bronwen, you cannot go back to Rossall! How can you even consider trying to overpower Aeschby? Are you as blind as our father to believe Rossall will stay Briton?"

Lady Mignonette patted Gildan's hand as she spoke to her sister. "Truly my dear, you would be unwise to set out across the country as winter begins. You would have to go by land, for the seas are not to be trusted till spring."

Sir Gregory cleared his throat. "I agree with my wife. Madam, where is the logic in this idea? Has Sir Thomas à Becket really given you such dubious advice? Where does he suppose you can find arms for your cause?"

"Becket did not suggest that I go to Rossall. It is my own plan and my only choice."

"But who'll protect you against Aeschby, Bronwen?" Gildan asked, her blue eyes filled with tears.

Bronwen rose and hugged her sister. "God will protect me, Gildan, if He chooses. My life is in His hands. I must try to recapture Rossall. Surely you understand."

Gildan nodded as she dabbed at her cheeks. "I do understand, Bronwen. You are bound by our father's dream of preserving Rossall as a Briton holding. That's why he willed Rossall to you. But I'll miss you so. Oh Bronwen, if you go against Aeschby alone, you go to your death!"

Early the next morning, Bronwen was supplied with two horses, a cart carrying food and blankets, and an entourage of four armed guards. Enit had decided against all protest that she would return to Rossall with Bronwen.

With Enit driving the cart, the two sisters rode together in a carriage down a row of quays along the Thames to a large old trading ship. There they met Sir Firmin of Troyes, an elderly white-haired gentleman who warmly welcomed Gildan as his ward. She hugged everyone and burst into tears as Chacier kissed her farewell. Soon the ship weighed anchor and Bronwen watched her fair-haired sister waving a pink handkerchief and blowing kisses until she was a speck on the horizon.

Finding Sir Gregory alone for a moment, Bronwen made her way over to him and touched his shoulder.

"Why did you do it?" she asked.

The old man looked up. "Do what, madam?"

"Why did you agree to help my sister get an annulment so she can marry your son?"

The gentleman thought for a moment. "In truth, I cannot be certain. I suppose it was something in Chacier's eyes as he pleaded with me for the girl. He offered to give up his birthright in the business that he might wed her and not shame me. Dear lady, your sister brought my son to life. I've never seen him so happy. I believe there seems to be something in this *amour* that is all the fashion. Indeed, I begin to take to the idea myself."

Bronwen had to smile. "Gildan is happier, too, Sir Gregory. I am pleased for them both."

He chuckled. "Come Mignonette, girls. Do you want to miss the opening of market?"

At this, his daughters turned and ran toward him, leaving their lovelorn brother still gazing off toward the horizon. As Bronwen embraced the family one by one, she knew she would miss them dreadfully. But her sorrow turned to consternation when she lifted her head to find Jacques Le Brun and a full contingent of armed horsemen nearby.

"Ah, yes," Sir Gregory spoke up before Bronwen could utter a word. "In all the madness of the morning, I forgot to mention an occurrence of great import to you, madam. May I introduce Sir Jacques Le Brun, a nobleman and a loyal supporter of Henry Plantagenet. I know his father well, for we have engaged in much trade through the years. Indeed, Captain Muldrew often carries cargo between our warehouses. Sir Jacques owns a London home not far from my own, and he overheard you yesterday at Becket's house."

"Did he?" Bronwen said, eyeing the dark-haired Norman.

"Le Brun came to see me late last night. He told me that he has been given charge of a holding in Amounderness, and that Henry Plantagenet himself journeys even now by ship to inspect loyal fortresses along the west coast—including Le Brun's castle. Can you imagine?"

"Hardly," she replied.

"Le Brun travels overland to Amounderness to meet our future king," Sir Gregory continued. "Hearing of your plans, he generously offered to accompany and protect you, and of course I agreed at once. You'll not regret this, I assure you. He is among the finest of men."

The thought of traveling so many miles in the company of Jacques Le Brun—of trying to elude his touch, avoid his gaze, focus on her mission and not on the man whose presence even now sent her heart skittering— left Bronwen in a quandary. She should refuse his help. She knew that beyond doubt. But what excuse could she give Sir Gregory? And, in truth, such a large company of men-at-arms would speed her journey.

"You have always treated me well," she told Sir Gregory, giving him another hug. "May God bless you."

Then with a last glance at Jacques, she walked to the cart. "Are you comfortable, Enit?"

"Dear girl, I'm as happy as a mule eating a nettle in early spring. Let's be off. I can't wait to see my home."

Bronwen smiled and mounted her horse. Just as she had settled herself on the gelding's saddle, the first snowflakes of winter began to fall. Pulling the hood of the black mantle over her head, she urged the horse forward away from the river. As the travelers started for the road that led out of London, Bronwen noted the sandy-haired young man standing alone at the edge of the water, bent and weeping for his lost love so lately sailed away to France.

Jacques rode well to the front of the company, ensuring that Bronwen and the cart with her nursemaid and their supplies remained safely surrounded by his men. They would make haste for the city of Coventry, for the road was frequented by outlaws. Jacques had no desire to expend valuable weapons on such wastrels. He had little doubt that his men and their arms would be needed once they neared Amounderness, especially with Henry Plantagenet expected at Warbreck not long after Jacques arrived.

Remote inns would provide secure lodging for the nights their journey must entail. After Coventry, the next town was Lichfield, and after that, Chester. The route would take them past few villages or castles, for the country remained wild and open with vast expanses of virgin forest always threatening to close over the road.

As they set out across the white moorland, Jacques turned to see how Bronwen fared. She rode her horse alongside the cart, and he could not make out her features beneath the hood of his mantle. That she still wore the gift pleased him beyond measure.

Her tongue was sharp and her will strongly set against him, but her heart had softened the moment they'd met. The few times he had held her in his arms, she'd yielded willingly to his touch. Her kisses matched his in ardor. Her eyes pleaded for more. Even as she pushed him away, the expression on her face beckoned him to return. And he would.

The old nursemaid, just visible under piles of blankets, lifted her grizzled head and smiled at him. He knew that despite the unexpected company, both women could not deny their joy in starting for home at last. He, too, anticipated his return to Warbreck. Before leaving, he had commissioned many improvements to the battlements and refurbishments to the hall, and he was eager to see how his workmen had fared.

Looking about at the stark black trees with withered brown leaves still clinging to the branches, Jacques wondered how long it would take to reach their destination. The safest place in England must be Amounderness, he thought. It was a land so marshy and so heavily forested that hardly anyone lived there. Not even kings could bother themselves to count the population.

Yet Amounderness had come to the attention of Henry Plantagenet, and Jacques was happy to begin the quest of taking it bit by bit for England and the throne. If Edgard of Rossall had known the political situation his daughter understood now, what would he have done? Could he still have believed it possible to return the entire island to Briton rule? If the father was anything like his daughter, Jacques thought, not a single dream would have changed.

That evening as the sun slanted across the dusting of snow, the travelers came to an inn at the edge of the forest. Determined to cause Bronwen no discomfort in the presence of his men or her nurse, Jacques said little to her as he arranged for rooms. The night passed swiftly, and soon dawn was upon them.

The track wound around small hills and beneath great silent oaks and beeches on to Coventry. That night and the next, the party managed to find inns able to welcome them for a few coins. Each day the track grew more crooked and rugged. Never once did they meet another traveler.

On the evening of their third day, Jacques realized they must make do in open air as best they could. Needing to feed an entire contingent of hungry men, he decided to lead a large hunting party into the forest in search of deer and small game. He left four guards to protect Bronwen and her nurse, who were spreading their blankets on the cart to wait for his return.

The hunt took him to the top of the nearest hill, where he spotted a fine buck standing alone in a clearing. With one arrow, he took the deer through the heart. Several of his men joined him in dressing the meat, for they did not wish to leave the offal near their camp.

Tired but satisfied, Jacques was returning to his horse when a shout rang out from the vale below.

"Lord have mercy on us! Help! Help!"

He instantly recognized the voice of Enit, the nurse-maid. Turning his steed, Jacques saw a band of shapes ride out of the trees and surround the cart.

"Where is she?" a man shouted over Enit's screams. "Get her!"

In an instant they swarmed the two women. As Jacques called out to his men, he saw the glint of steel and heard the sound of clashing weapons below. Thundering down the hill on his horse, he caught sight of Bronwen standing on the cart and fighting with the dagger he had given her.

A familiar figure stood out among the rest. *Aeschby.* His golden hair whipped about in the chilling wind, and his mantle gleamed a blood-red. Jacques realized the man had not yet reached Bronwen, and he was shouting to Haakon, who was still on horseback.

"'Tis a black witch!" someone screamed in agony. "The woman has sliced my arm nearly in twain!"

As Jacques's steed finally broke out of the forest, he saw Bronwen slashing and stabbing at the men who reached for her. His own guards did battle with others, sword against sword, ax, mace and knife. Drawing his own blade, Jacques began to cut his way toward Bronwen. But before he reached her, Haakon leaped from his horse and threw the woman from the cart into the wet snow.

"I have her!" the Viking yelled. "Aeschby! I have the wench!"

Gritting his teeth, Jacques hacked an enemy's ax handle in two as he made for the woman. Wielding her dagger, Bronwen fought Haakon until he slammed her face with the back of his mail-clad hand.

Now Jacques was at her side, but Haakon bellowed in rage and clubbed her again. As her eyes rolled back in her head, Jacques's sword found its mark.

With great effort, Bronwen summoned a breath. She lay cheek down in the snow, her arms twisted and her body pressed by a great weight. All she could see was the silver moon hanging just above a rim of black trees. Except for the stamping of horses' hooves and the hiss of swords sheathed, the air was silent.

"Here's one," she heard a voice say.

"Dead?" another voice asked. "Bring him along then. We've got four here."

Bronwen heard the crunch of boots on the snow beside her head, but she could not lift her face to look. She sensed a figure kneeling at her side.

"Dear God, help me now, I beg You," a man said under his breath.

The weight lifted from her chest, and a blanket slipped beneath her frozen cheek. A sword that had been thrust into the ground beside her was drawn away. Gentle hands turned her, but a sharp pain knifed into her ribs and she cried out.

"She lives," the man breathed. "Thanks be to God!"

Bronwen blinked through the milky clouds across her eyes and tried to focus on the face before her. Two dark eyes, black hair curling down chiseled cheekbones, a noble nose above a pair of familiar lips.

"Jacques," she murmured.

"My dearest lady." The Norman lifted her in his arms and wrapped the black mantle close about her shivering body. She could feel the tension in his arms as he carried her to the cart and placed her into a cocoon of blankets.

"I was almost too late," he muttered as he smoothed her hair.

"Enit," Bronwen croaked. "Where is she?"

"Your nurse lies beside you. I fear she has taken a grave blow to the head."

With a cry of dismay, Bronwen struggled to sit up. "You must let me help her. Fetch the healing bag."

"Rest, Bronwen, I beg you," Jacques said as he found the pouch. "You're injured yourself. Tell me what to do."

She reached for the old woman and found Enit's hand. Holding it, she spoke to the Norman. "Build a fire and heat water for washing."

He shouted at his men to set about it at once. Indeed they must have built a fire already, Bronwen realized, for soon a bowl of steaming water sat on the cart floor.

"Lift her head and bathe the wound," she told Jacques. "There will be much blood."

"Yes, and her breath is shallow."

Bronwen nodded. "God has sent His gift of darkness so she feels no pain. Now find the container of comfrey-root poultice in the bag."

"Smell this. Is it the one?"

Bronwen sniffed the jar he held beneath her nose. She shook her head. He tried two more. The third was comfrey root. "Smooth it across her head, directly on the wound. Now bind it tightly so the bleeding will cease."

Looking up in the moonlight, she could see the man's furrowed brow as he worked on Enit. His mail glimmered a silver-white. A small muscle flickered in his jaw, and the grim line of his mouth turned to a frown at each corner.

When the binding was done, he turned his attention to Bronwen. "Your face is bruised and torn," he said, stroking his fingers down her cheek. "Aeschby did this—and Haakon, his henchman."

Bronwen lifted a hand to her swollen cheekbone and felt the tender skin around her eye. "Aeschby intended to kill me. Haakon did his best."

"Aeschby fled, Haakon is dead and you live."

"How could they have found me?"

"Aeschby has spies," he reminded her. "And after all, there are few roads between London and Amounderness. It wouldn't have been difficult for him to guess your path." He bent and kissed her forehead. "Where do you have pain?"

"My side," she said. "My ribs are broken."

Biting back an oath, he pulled Bronwen's blankets aside, tore the mantle clasp from her neck and spread the cloak apart. He probed gently, but Bronwen winced in pain as his fingers brushed the fractured bones.

"This injury I have had myself," he growled.

Tearing a strip from the hem of a thin blanket, he lifted her and wrapped the cloth tightly about her ribs. Chill wind whipped across the vale as he worked to secure the ends of the bandage. With her chest bound, Bronwen knew instant relief, and she relaxed in his arms.

"Are you better?" he asked softly.

"Well enough," she murmured. Drowsy in the warmth of his chest against her cheek and his arms about her, Bronwen closed her eyes again.

The next days Bronwen spent in the jolting cart, tending to Enit and trying to rest her own aching body. The days grew a little warmer and no snow fell, so the road turned to mud and slush.

As she watched the bone-thin tree branches lacing across the blue sky, Bronwen wondered if Aeschby now believed her dead. He had seen Haakon throw her from the cart and would think she could never survive such an attack. Perhaps he felt himself secure in Rossall—secure enough to lay plans against Warbreck. This was all to her advantage, she realized. During the long journey, she had at last formulated three possible means of regaining her father's holding.

The guard she had met near the river pledged an oath of service should she need it. With effort, she might assemble a small force of armed men still loyal to Edgard the Briton. The old butler knew secret ways to enter the hall, and he would help Bronwen and her allies slip inside and take Aeschby by surprise.

If that failed, she would have no choice but to enter Rossall in disguise and face Aeschby one-on-one. Untrained in weaponry, she feared she must surely be vanquished—even slain. Yet if she lived, she could resort to her final option. She would show her father's will to Henry Plantagenet and beg him to honor it. Vowing to support his cause, she would plead for an army to conquer Aeschby.

If it came to this, Rossall would then become a part

of the Norman fold, and her father's dream would be dashed forever. Yet, some hope remained, for the holding would remain in Briton hands. Perhaps she might make a marriage to one of her countrymen and bear him a Briton son—and through that child a flicker of the dream would live on.

Nights arrived quickly in the winter forest. When the party stopped, Bronwen would clamber down from the cart and join the men by the fire in their evening meal. Enit barely stirred, and Bronwen worried that she would starve. Little nourishment had slipped between those torn lips in the days since the attack. Bronwen and Jacques spent no time alone together in the camp. He made a point to ask after her well-being every evening, but they had no other exchange. She slept beside Enit in the cart.

During the day, Jacques continued to ride ahead, so far ahead that Bronwen rarely caught sight of his broad back and the black waves of his hair. She understood his haste, for his men often spoke of their eagerness to meet Henry Plantagenet.

One night while seated beside the fire, Bronwen heard a soft moan coming from the cart. She hurried to Enit's side and saw the papery eyelids slide open.

"Oh, Enit, you wake!" Bronwen said softly. "No, don't turn your head—you've had a terrible blow."

The old woman's thin lips opened. "Where am I?"

"We travel to Rossall. Aeschby and his men attacked, but we were saved. Come now, can you sip a bit of broth?"

Jacques appeared at her side. "Enit wakes at last."

"Esyllt," the old woman rasped.

Bronwen turned to her nurse. "What did you say?"

"Esyllt, your hair needs a combing, child."

"But I am Bronwen. Esyllt was my mother."

The blue eyes wandered across Bronwen's face for a moment. "Esyllt, your hair is a mess. Come, bring the ivory comb and let me plait it up for you."

Her eyes filling with tears, Bronwen tucked the blanket beneath Enit's chin. As she wiped her cheek, she felt the Norman's hand touch her back.

"Look, she sleeps again," he said. "Her sense must surely return soon. All is not lost. She is alive."

Bronwen drew a deep breath. "Yes, she is alive. And I have more reason than ever to regain Rossall. I must take Enit home."

The Norman stood still for a moment, then turned and strode away toward the fire.

Winter had set in for good when Jacques announced that at last they were drawing near Amounderness. The following evening the party would prepare to ride for Warbreck.

In the passing days, Enit had grown haler. She ate of the pigeon, hare and quail Jacques's men roasted each night. By day, she sat up in the cart and looked about. Sometimes she knew Bronwen and remembered their stay in London. She recalled that Gildan had gone to France and that she and Bronwen were returning home. Other times she thought Bronwen was Esyllt on her way to wed Edgard.

Feeling sad and lonely one night, Bronwen covered her slumbering nursemaid with blankets and climbed out of the cart. She needed time to think, to be alone. Four guards stood on alert, but Jacques and his men slept by the fire.

Walking along the edge of the track, Bronwen gazed at the mighty trees swaying overhead. She lifted her widow's skirts and stepped onto a thick carpet of musky-smelling fallen leaves on the forest floor. A full moon lightened the night, and she could see the bare branches and thorny brakes that crossed her path. Cold, fresh air filled her lungs as the sound of limbs clicked in the breeze.

Bronwen threw back the hood of her mantle and tilted her face to the sky. *Dear God, it is good to be alive,* she lifted up in prayer. *Please aid me. Teach me what I need to know. Make me Your servant and—* At the sound of footsteps behind her, Bronwen reached for her dagger.

"You wander unguarded, Bronwen," came a deep voice.

A sigh of relief escaped her lips. "You frightened me. I'm not alone. Your men can see me well enough."

"Yet you must be careful." Jacques pulled back his own hood. Bronwen gazed at the angle of his jaw and the curl of his raven hair. His tunic was a royal-blue, embroidered with a fine silver border. It fell from a straight neckline across his wide chest to the thick leather belt at his waist. From there it hung to his knees. His leggings and boots were a deep black.

Jacques was at least a head taller than her father had been, Bronwen realized. He was even taller and more broad-shouldered than Aeschby, whom she and Gildan had once thought magnificent. Jacques's legs, powerful and long, had hardened with the riding and training that were part of his daily life. His large hands were taut and lean as he hooked his thumbs on his belt.

"You look upon me as though you've never seen me before." The quiet voice interrupted Bronwen's musings.

"Forgive me," she stammered. "I didn't realize I was staring."

The Norman smiled. "Our meetings often have taken place in dim light, and we battle far more than we speak in peace. At Warbreck, we'll have time to know one another better. There will be walks in the orchard and evenings of quiet talk beside the fire. I'm eager for you to meet Plantagenet. He'll take great delight in your intellect."

Bronwen listened to his words, her heart in her throat. "Sir, you must know I intend to be about my business of regaining Rossall. I'll not stay at Warbreck more than a day or two."

Her purpose would be to find and secure the small box containing her father's written will. But of course she must say nothing of that to Jacques.

"You speak always of regaining your father's land," the Norman said in a tone of frustration. "Bronwen, are you so blind that you do not see what is already yours for the taking? Why will you not see *me?*"

With one arm, he captured her at the waist. "I offer you my home, my protection. I trail you here and there, trying my best to keep you safe from yourself and your enemies. Yet you treat me like a stranger. You behave as if you've never seen me—as if I don't even exist."

Bronwen looked up into the flashing eyes. "But, sir—"

"I do exist. I'm here, Bronwen. Look at me. Feel my arms about you. Hear the words I speak. I am a man, Bronwen."

He bent his head and covered her mouth with a kiss

that swept the air from her lungs. She could do nothing to resist, and why should she? Each day, she had followed him with her eyes, her focus riveted to his broad back and her eyes drawn to every gust of breeze that lifted the hair from his forehead. Each night, she had watched him settle near the fire and ached to be lying beside him. Every word he spoke to her and each time their eyes met became treasures that she stored like precious jewels in her mind. Resting near Enit at night, she took them out and examined them, recalling each precious word, savoring every glance.

He turned her into the shadows of the forest, and she slid her arms about him. "Oh, Jacques," she said drinking in the scent of his neck and the brush of his hair against her cheek. "You make me weak when I should be strong. I cannot let you do this."

"Hold you in my arms? Kiss your lips when I know they long for mine? Bring you a life you cannot have known?"

"You know precious little of my past life. Why must you torment me? Can you not leave me in peace?"

Without replying, he turned his back on her and stared at the moon. His jet hair fell in waves on his shoulders.

"Jacques Le Brun," Bronwen said. The Norman glanced back at her, his eyes a fierce black. "You and I are different. You have education, lands, wealth. You are a Norman—a conqueror. I am a Briton. I have nothing but a dream. And every time we come together in this way, I fear the loss of that dream."

She hugged herself, fighting for words that might make him understand. "When we first met, I knew nothing of you—yet you kissed me then and spoke words of such affection that when we parted I was able to think of little else. What is it you want of me? Why do you pursue me? You must know our differences are too great."

"That is it, then," he said. "You reject me because you cannot bear the differences between us—my mixed blood, my uncertain pedigree must never be mingled with your purity. Why not say it outright? You would never deign to think of me as husband."

"Husband?" she breathed.

"That night at Rossall when I first saw your dark hair, your skin—so like my own—I thought you would not care about my lineage. But I was mistaken." He paused a moment. "Have no fear, madam. I'll not come to you again in hopes of tenderness and a meeting of the soul."

With that, the man turned from her and strode back to the fire. For some minutes Bronwen could do nothing but stand rooted to the ground, her body stiff with shock. What had he said? What had he meant?

Husband!

But how? She had no father to arrange a marriage. She had no dowry, no land or gold to offer. How could he see them as a match?

Bronwen shook her head in confusion. His kisses were so passionate, so filled with desire. Was that what he had meant—that he wanted her as a husband craves his wife, but without the bond of matrimony? Did she think she might join him in a dalliance of *amour?*

A lonely widow. In need of aid and protection. She would be perfect for such an arrangement.

Torment raging through her, Bronwen lifted her head and returned to her prayers.

Chapter Thirteen

As the sun lit the tops of the golden trees, the party rounded the final bend in the road. Bronwen gasped at the sight that met her eyes. Warbreck Castle was a full level higher than it had been when she'd lived there. A third story rose above the first two, and at the corner facing the river an even taller tower loomed against the purple sky. Along the parapet surrounding the stronghold, newly built notched battlements allowed the knights to shoot arrows through slotted windows. Around the tower's top a machicolation extended out from the expanse of wall to protect the men who dropped missiles or hot oil through it.

A new stone wall now extended across the river and back again—enclosing the village and ensuring a water supply for the moat that had been dug around the castle. Though the wall was not yet complete, Bronwen could see it was far stronger than the wooden palisade at Rossall.

The tall gate that the party now approached had been built of wood, but it was studded with iron spikes to deter a battering ram. When they neared, a formation of guards opened the gate, allowing the group to enter.

Again Bronwen caught her breath at the changes. The village had grown. Huts had been built against the base of the inner wall. The lanes running between the houses were paved with cobblestone. A market area had been cleared, and a white stone cross designated its center.

As she rode toward the castle, Bronwen saw that not everything was altered. There stood the kitchen, just as she remembered it. And there were the stables looking much as they had before. She recalled the care she had taken to improve the place for her husband.

Olaf Lothbrok…now joined by his son. Did they walk the halls of Valhalla, as they had believed? Bronwen's new understanding of the one God and the teachings in His holy book led her to fear that Olaf had been sadly mistaken.

"May I take your horse, madam?" a stable hand asked.

She did not recognize the man, but Enit knew him at once. Before Bronwen could dismount and smooth out her rumpled skirts, he had invited the old woman to join his family for dinner that very evening. Unable to resist her nursemaid's glee, Bronwen dismissed her into his care.

Jacques had already vanished, surrounded by men eager to acquaint their lord with everything that had happened in his absence. Bronwen was relieved. Their final encounter had left her in great turmoil. She felt she should speak to him alone again—try to explain how she felt about him, attempt to make him see that it was not his heritage that separated them. It was her own.

Approaching the castle door, Bronwen gathered up

her courage and stepped inside. Just as she remembered, the long stone staircase rose at her left toward the guardroom and her former bedchamber. But through the archway before her, she saw not the familiar hall with its rush-strewn floor and bare walls, but a changed room. Thick carpets of bright color and pattern were echoed on walls hung with tapestries that had been adorned with scenes of battles, flowers, trees, unicorns and dragons.

Each table was covered with cloths dyed in brilliant peacock-blue. The fireplace, no longer in the center of the room, now stood against the far wall. The dais was in its accustomed place, but over it hung a baldachuin made of blue silk and ornamented with gold balls. On a newly erected minstrel's gallery above the canopied dais, a large group of musicians played a lively tune.

Already servitors prepared for the evening meal, rushing about with silver trays, golden goblets, and yes—even ewers that diners might wash their hands. Feeling almost as though she was in a different place altogether, Bronwen at last recalled her mission at Warbreck. She must find the small box she and Enit had hidden. She was hurrying toward the staircase and her old chamber when Jacques stepped through the front door.

"Madam?" he called out. "Do you climb to the guard tower for some malevolent purpose…or are you gone astray in your own home?"

As his men chuckled, Bronwen faced the man whose eyes even now beckoned her. "My bedchamber is upstairs," she told him. "I'm weary, and I mean to retire for the night."

"You may have stayed there once, but that stair now

leads to weapons storage and sleeping quarters for my men."

"The entire floor?"

"Indeed. My workmen have constructed more comfortable chambers just down the corridor. Will you accompany me?"

He held out an arm, and she could do nothing but slip her hand around it. As he escorted her toward a second newly built staircase with carved wood newel posts and a fine banister, Bronwen spoke in a low voice.

"Sir, may I be so bold as to ask for a moment of your time? I wish to shed light on our previous conversation."

"You spoke clearly enough for me to see your heart," he said. "Any further exchange between us is unnecessary."

"But that is not true. You misunderstood me."

"Did I? I think not. If I may boast, I'm known as a man of high intellect, and I rarely mistake anything."

Followed by his men, Jacques accompanied her up the steps to a door that opened into a chamber far grander than the one at Sir Gregory's house—and she had believed that one to be more magnificent than anything possible. The windows were covered with blue silk curtains, while matching hangings surrounded a large sumptuous bed.

"Nevertheless," she murmured as he led her into the room, "you have mistaken my words. Please may we speak?"

"I assume this will be suitable, madam," he said loudly enough for his men to hear. "I shall see that the chests of clothing you left here previously will be brought up, and a meal provided. You have my invitation to stay as long as you wish—though I would encourage you to remain at least one more day. Henry Plantagenet's ships have been sighted not far from Warbreck Wash, and I expect him to arrive on the morrow. I'm sure he would take great interest in your view of current politics."

Before Bronwen could respond, Jacques and his men left the room, shutting the door on her. A curl of pain crept through her chest at the echo of their footfalls down the corridor. She had, indeed, rejected Jacques Le Brun for the last time. His dismissal of her was obvious, his disdain palpable.

Crossing the room, she drew aside a curtain. The small window looked out on the forests, once verdant and thriving. Now they appeared as dark and lifeless as her own spirit. Retrieving her father's written will from a guarded armory seemed futile and pointless. Opposing Aeschby was a vain dream that must surely end in her death. But the ache that caused her the greatest agony was the certainty that her own pride and selfishness had driven away the one thing that might truly fill the rest of her days with peace and joy.

She would never again know Jacques's passion. His words of love were ended. Now she had only herself and God. Martin had promised that His Spirit would fill her if she honored the Christian deity above all gods. She had chosen to obey that calling. Now she must trust in Him to bring her peace.

"Henry Plantagenet is to be king!"

"King Stephen signed a compromise."

"The civil war is at an end."

Jacques heard the rumble of excited discussion from the knights who surrounded him as he waited outside the great hall. Earlier that afternoon, Plantagenet and his attachment had arrived at Warbreck Castle. Henry had given Jacques the good news at once. Soon exaltation and merriment had broken out from the village to the castle towers. Everyone from knight to peasant rejoiced.

Jacques, too, was delighted at his lord's triumph over Stephen. Even more, he felt pleased at Henry's public acknowledgment of the presence of Amounderness in his future kingdom. The swampy forest land had been hard won, and Jacques knew his men were proud to present it to their sovereign. The one thing that dampened Jacques's joy was the knowledge that Bronwen had made her distaste for him undeniable. No matter how wealthy or powerful he became, no matter how passionate or tender his love, she hated him.

She was a proud Briton. He was a Norman dog— worse than that, he was of mixed blood. A cur. A mongrel.

On this night, if she deigned, Bronwen would enter his hall and observe the very best he had to offer. And then she would leave him—marching away in stony silence to confront her enemy. Still driven by the obsolete notion that her people might one day rule the island, she would defy her kinsman, and he would kill her.

"Sir? May I have a word?"

One of the younger men stood before Jacques. The lad had followed Jacques from his knighthood, through the battle for Warbreck, to this victory. "Sir, some of us are wondering. Why did Stephen sign the treaty?"

Jacques smiled. "He saw he had no chance against us, of course. Henry Plantagenet is God's man for the throne."

"But what of Eustace, Stephen's son?"

The answer would soon become a source of glee, he knew. Yet it had to be told. "Eustace choked to death while eating a plate of eels."

"Eels?" the young man repeated. "He choked on eels?"

"Yes, and we would do well to remember that Stephen yet lives. Only when he dies will Henry become king."

When the minstrels ceased their song, Jacques drank down a breath and squared his shoulders.

"Presenting Jacques Le Brun, lord of Warbreck," the ward-corn announced.

Jacques strode into the hall and allowed his men to gather beside him as the crowd bowed and began to applaud. Within an instant, he spotted Bronwen among the throng. She stood at a table some distance from the dais, but her beauty radiated as if a fine emerald had suddenly been revealed on a swath of dark velvet.

At last the woman had decided to remove her widow's garb. Tonight she wore a green gown that revealed her lovely figure to great advantage. Discreet but well-fitted, it served only to remind Jacques of what he had so desired…and lost. Though a white veil covered her head, he could see that she had plaited her dark hair into two long ropes woven with green ribbon.

Their eyes met, and she looked away.

He fought the rising tide of anguish that welled inside him at her rejection. It mattered not what the woman thought, he told himself. Tonight he was lord of Warbreck Castle. Beneath his fur-lined black mantle, he wore a crimson tunic embroidered in gold. A ruby-encrusted gold belt loosely cinched his waist and a magnificent sword hung at his side. His boots and leggings were of black leather and had been polished to a high sheen, and a golden circlet crowned his head.

The horn sounded again. "Presenting Henry Plantagenet—Duke of Normandy, Anjou, Touraine, Maine and Aquitaine...and future king of England!"

The crowd burst into a cheer and knelt to the floor as the man entered the room. He stood for a moment on the threshold and looked about. Jacques knew that although the man was stocky, even tending toward corpulence, the impression would soon be dismissed by his air of kingliness. Indeed, everyone in the room grew silent as the young man strode to the platform. They seemed to understand they were in the presence of a man who knew himself completely, who had a great sense of mission, who bore the stamp of nobility on his forehead.

The feast began with a prayer offered by Henry himself. Once he had been seated, everyone else followed. The servitors then circled the room bearing ewers that the guests might wash their hands. Platter upon platter of meat, poultry and fish were carried into the room. Jacques noted with pleasure that his lord sampled every dish presented—spiced tripe, marrow-and-fruit tart, smoked pike salad in pastry, swan-neck pudding and artichokes with blueberry rice. He spooned up mouthfuls of pheasant in lemon wine sauce, and savored the giblet pie. Bronwen ate also, Jacques noted, but her attention was trained on her plate. Those seated beside her tried to engage her in conversation without success. And each time she glanced at Jacques and found him looking back at her, she shrank and turned away.

Entertainers performed between each course. Henry roared with pleasure at the tumblers and jugglers. The live bear delighted him so much that the creature's owners were obliged to present it several times. Singers gathered before the dais and performed a local melody without the accompaniment of musicians. Bronwen seemed especially pleased with this, Jacques noted. But of course, these were her people, singing in her native tongue.

At the instigation of a dance tune performed in the gallery, many knights rose and escorted ladies toward the center of the room. As they arranged themselves into a circle and began a rhythmic, swaying dance, Jacques looked toward Bronwen's table once again.

This time, she was gone.

With Jacques's attention drawn to the musicians in the gallery, Bronwen rose and slipped behind the tables of feasters. Mesmerized at the brilliance before them, no one took note of the lone figure making her way out of the hall. Guards, busy with a game of snapdragon, barely looked up. She watched as they covered a bowl of raisins with brandy and set it ablaze to remove the alcohol. Then, when one of the guards snatched a raisin from the fire and popped the burning treat into his mouth—to the great mirth of his friends—Bronwen started up the staircase.

The passageway was lit with torches, and she found that a door had been built into the opening of the guardroom where there had been none before. Taking the iron handle, she turned it and the door swung open. Her fear that she might meet someone there was eased at once. Everyone, it seemed, was enjoying the feast.

As it had been before, the large room was filled with weapons—row after row of spears, shields, swords, knives and maces. She hurried across it in the dark and pushed open the door to the chamber where she once had slept.

Empty cots and several chairs stood about a low fire, while carved chests lay along its perimeter. A thick curtain covered the slotted window from which she had gazed and thought of Jacques. This drape blocked the wind and allowed the blaze to warm the room. Her heart hammered as she approached the window, for she knew that beneath the floorboards lay the small box containing her father's will.

Downstairs the song ended and another began. Bronwen knelt and lifted the curtain. Just as she touched the floor, she heard the sound of footsteps. Someone was coming up the stairs. Low voices told her that several men were crossing the guardroom.

Reaching for her dagger, she realized that for the first time in these many months it was not at her side. Wanting Jacques to notice her, perhaps admire her and maybe speak with her, she had worn her loveliest gown. The dagger and black mantle lay abandoned in her bedchamber.

As the door opened and two rushlights brightened the chamber, she slipped behind the curtain.

"You have fine minstrels here in the north."

"Thank you, my lord. I'm pleased you approve." Bronwen knew that voice too well. Jacques himself was in the room.

"This chamber is where my guards may sleep between watches," he said. "It's small but adequate."

"Your weapons room is amply stocked, and this one is remote and quiet enough for the men to rest. I'm impressed with what I've seen thus far. Thank you for this tour, my friend. The castle is well fortified."

"When the outer wall is complete, I'll be satisfied. The place was in disrepair when I conquered it. My workmen have followed my instructions with diligence, sir."

"Of course! Who would defy such a man as you? And please—call me Henry. After all, we are old friends."

Bronwen pressed against the wall. *Henry...* The future king of England stood not five paces from her hiding place!

"Do you remember when we met as boys?" Jacques asked. "You told me you would become a king."

"Did I?" Henry chuckled. "You always listened to my dreams. In this dark, silent room beside a warm fire, I can almost imagine we are children again. How carefree those days seem to me now."

"Indeed they were."

"Come, Jacques, let us sit a moment. No servitors lurk in the shadows here, and my guards stand outside the door. We can speak freely."

The sound of a breath exhaling told Bronwen that one of the men had elected to seat himself on a chair near the fire. A squeak indicated the other man had joined him. Her heart sinking, Bronwen realized she was now listening to the private conversation of England's future king. She could be executed for this—and rightly so.

"Now tell me," Henry said. "What are your plans for Warbreck?"

"What are your plans for England—specifically Amounderness?" the deep voice returned. "My plans depend on yours."

"Ah, England. Did you know that my grandfather and great grandfather cared nothing for this isle? But I love her. I see greatness in this rough country and her plain, solid natives. Saxon blood flows in my veins, you know."

At this revelation, Bronwen stifled a gasp.

"How did it come about?" Jacques asked.

"My grandmother was niece to Edgar Atheling, a descendant of England's Saxon kings. A remote connection—but I feel sure it has influenced my character. If I had a drop or two of Briton blood, I'd be satisfied indeed. King Arthur—now there was a leader of men."

A chill ran through Bronwen as she listened to the man. Was this true? Did he honor her Briton forebears? Through a small hole in the curtain, she could see Jacques. Leaning back, he had stretched his long legs before the fire. For the first time, he appeared truly at peace.

Henry, on the other hand, moved constantly. His fingers slid along the smooth chair arm, stroked his own fine tunic, tugged at his beard. Beginning to speak again, he rose and began to wander about the room, lifting objects, weighing them, even opening chests and sorting through their contents. It was as though his brain demanded constant stimulation. Clearly curious and inquisitive, he spoke with great understanding.

"I'm grateful for my Saxon ancestors," he said. "Using their principle of *King's Peace,* I plan to revolutionize England's judicial system. My royal court of law will use a jury of the defendant's peers to decide a case. The judge will pass sentence based on recommendation of this jury. All laws must be set down in writing, and no man may defy them without consequence."

"You may encounter trouble with that," Jacques said. "People here place no value on written documents, Henry. Only a few scribes and priests in the larger cities can read. In Amounderness, the spoken oath and law hold sway."

"I mean to change that, Jacques. The English now live in a dark age. When I'm king, I'll encourage education."

"We shall have our hands full in Amounderness," Jacques replied with a chuckle. "My people are wise but unlearned. What do you intend for us, Henry? By treaty, we belong to Scotland. Will you leave us beholden to a foreign power—or will you reclaim us for England?"

"You should know the answer to that. A true Norman— and certainly a Plantagenet—never willingly parts with any land."

"I'm glad to hear it. Amounderness may be no jewel, but I love her deeply. I have dreams for her as well."

"Tell me your dreams, my friend?"

Bronwen could see Jacques leaning toward the fire, warming his hands. "I want my people to be happy and to labor profitably for me—and therefore for you," he said. "But my dream is to develop this land into a place worthy of respect and admiration. Already the village has grown. It's clean now, and I've had a marketplace built. Soon, I'll introduce coinage to encourage trade, and I may drain some of the marshes for plowing. In my mind, Henry, I see ripe fields and heavy orchards, hives flowing with honey, sacks of salted fish, wool and grain. I see traders, roads, churches and schools all filling Amounderness with bounty beyond belief."

"We might be boys again for all our dreaming." Henry laughed as he clapped Jacques on the shoulder. "But I do fear for you, my friend. How long can you hold Warbreck? You've never married and have no heirs. I'm only twenty and already I'm wedded to Eleanor who has given me my first son. Why have you no interest in matrimony?"

"I do care about this matter, Henry." Jacques's face was pained. "But my ancestry makes me unfit for Norman women. Even in Antioch I'm known as a *poulain*— a half-caste. Only one woman can satisfy my desire for a wife, but she has refused me."

Wife? At that, Bronwen caught her breath.

"Impossible!" Henry cried. "You're the finest among men! How can—"

"One moment," Jacques cut in. He held up a hand, and Plantagenet fell silent.

Bronwen stiffened at the whisper of a sword drawn from its scabbard. Catching her breath, she drew back against the wall. A knife left its sheath. Heart thudding, Bronwen heard two sets of footsteps move toward the window.

Just as she closed her eyes in panic, the curtain flew open and a flash of cold steel slid beneath her chin, stopping just above her pulsing vein. She clenched her teeth and waited for death to take her.

When it did not come, she looked up the length of the long sword into the flashing eyes of Jacques Le Brun.

"But who is this?" Henry asked in surprise.

"Bronwen the Briton," Jacques said.

"You know this woman?" Henry asked.

"Tell him," Jacques ordered. "Reveal your identity and purpose to the future king of England on whom you spy."

For the first time, he saw fear in the woman's gaze. "I am no spy. I never meant to hear your conversation."

"Jacques, put away your sword," Henry suggested. "She seems harmless enough."

Pleased to see that she immediately made a deep curtsy before his friend and master, Jacques sheathed his sword.

"Sir, I am Bronwen of Rossall." Her hands trembled as she knotted them together, and her words came softly. "My husband was Olaf Lothbrok, lord of Warbreck Castle. Jacques Le Brun took it from him, and I was widowed."

"What treason do you mean to work?" Jacques asked.

Bronwen lowered her eyes. "I intend no treason, sir. When I lived at Warbreck, this was my bedchamber. I returned tonight to retrieve a possession."

"Where is that possession?"

"It is yet where I hid it when I fled the castle."

Henry touched Jacques's arm. "Why speak to her with such animosity, my friend? She can work us no harm."

"This woman reviles Normans, my lord. Her intentions toward you are questionable at best. She has made it clear that she despises me."

"Upon my honor," Henry said, "I observe great passion between the two of you, and my insight is never wrong."

"Indeed, sir. It is the passion of enemies." Jacques studied Bronwen's face. Though Henry's intuition was accurate, Jacques would never divulge the truth of his emotion. In the past, he had read every feeling plainly written in the woman's eyes. But now he could not tell whether she spoke the truth or lied to protect herself.

"Retrieve your possession, then," he told her. "We eagerly await you."

Bronwen looked toward the wooden door as if willing it to open that she might flee. Then with a sigh of resignation, she knelt and ran her hands over the plank floor beneath the window. With the tips of her fingers she grasped an edge and pulled one of the boards. It lifted easily, and she laid it aside. Reaching into the hole, she felt around for a moment and then removed a small box.

"My father gave this to me the last time I saw him alive," she said softly as she stood.

"What does it contain?" Jacques asked.

"Trinkets, I'm sure," Henry said. "Leave the poor creature in peace."

Jacques shook his head. "Trinkets? My lord, you do not know this woman as I do. Madam, open the box and let us see its contents."

Bronwen's dark eyes met his, and this time he read her agony as she clutched the box to her chest. Finally, she drew a necklace from the bodice of her gown. A small key dangled from it, and she used it to unlock the lid.

Before either man could see what was inside, she spoke in a rush. "Henry Plantagenet, future king of all England, this is my father's written will that Rossall holding in Amounderness belongs to me. Please do not take the will from me, I beg you. Allow me to keep it, for this is all that I have of my family and my home."

"A *will?*" Henry's voice was incredulous. "Jacques, not moments ago, you told me these people placed no value on the written word. Yet this woman insists that her father penned a document containing his resolve to give his daughter all his lands. Madam, let me have it."

With obvious reluctance, Bronwen took the manuscript from the box and handed it to Henry.

"Now, then," he said, stepping toward the fire and reading aloud. "Edgard of Rossall in Amounderness, the son of Sigeric, the grandson of Ulfcetel the Briton, doth herein declare his final will and testament upon this thirteenth day of December in the year of our Lord 1152."

Henry paused. "Edgard was your father?"

"Yes, my lord."

He continued reading. "Upon my death, all my lands, Rossall Hall and half of my treasures must go to my elder daughter Bronwen. They will not pass into the possession of any husband she may wed, but must remain in her hands until that day when her firstborn son may come of age."

Henry looked at Bronwen again. "Your father thought very highly of you, dear lady. But perhaps he was not as fond of your husband as you were."

"I had never met my husband until my wedding day, sir," Bronwen told him. "The will is testimony to my father's faith in me."

"And his desire to keep his land under Briton rule," Jacques added. "You see, Henry, this woman labors under the misguided belief that a ghost of King Arthur may someday rise from the mists and reunite all England."

"Perhaps Edgard was right, Jacques." The corners of Henry's mouth turned up. "It could well be that the spirit of King Arthur stands before you even now."

As Henry continued reading the will, Jacques studied Bronwen's luminous brown eyes, now focused on his face. He told himself she was consumed with the document being perused. That flickering fire he saw was passion for her land and her people. But how could he mistake her look of desire, for he had seen it so clearly when he'd held her in his arms? Her eyes pleaded with him, beckoning, luring him toward her.

With one word of longing, she would have his heart again in an instant. The fortress he had built to protect himself crumbled as if made of sand. Why did she do this? What could it mean that she always gazed at him in such a way—and then spoke words of rejection and denial? How could he conquer the yearning she roused inside him?

"Fascinating," Henry said, handing the document to Jacques. "Her father had great foresight, and I believe the manuscript is genuine. Madam, have you any witnesses to guarantee it?"

"I heard Edgard's vow, Henry." Jacques spoke in a low voice. "Her father did bequeath Rossall to his daughter."

Bronwen's eyes softened into liquid pools. "Thank you, sir."

"Excellent, then," Henry exclaimed. "Jacques, you can vouch for her. Bronwen of Rossall, you came to this room with the intent to regain the will and use it to your advantage. What was your aim?"

"My aim has not altered since the day I understood my father's plan. It is my duty to administer the keep at Rossall, her lands and her people."

She swallowed before continuing. "When I spoke with Thomas à Becket in London, my lord, he urged me to place myself under your guardianship. He assured me that when you become king, you will set my appeal before the court. If I were to submit to you, sir, what would you do?"

Henry turned to Jacques with a broad smile. "By George, you must be wary of this woman, my friend. She has an ample measure of intelligence."

"Believe me, sir, I am more than wary."

Henry took Bronwen's hand. "If you become my ward, Bronwen of Rossall, I'll do exactly as Becket recommended. Your document will be your primary evidence in court. Le Brun will be your witness. With two valid testimonies, you'll easily win your land again. If the present holder refuses to surrender it, I'll send an army against him."

"To what end?" she asked. "Will you then give my land to a Norman, perhaps a faithful knight like this man—Jacques Le Brun? To do so would be a grave injustice to me, sir. My father intended the land to remain in his family, and he taught me to manage it faithfully."

"I believe you would make a good manager," Henry said. "I do, indeed. Thus, I shall say that if everything we have discussed here tonight should come about, I will see that you're given your family's land, Bronwen of Rossall. So it remains to you, now? Will you become my ward?"

Jacques could almost feel Bronwen's anguish. She knew full well that Henry Plantagenet was a Norman. If she placed herself in his hands, then ultimately Rossall would belong to him.

"Yes," she replied at last. "I accept your guardianship, Henry Plantagenet. I shall serve you faithfully and obey your commands. But I caution you to remember that Briton blood flows through my veins. I'll honor you as lord and king, but if I see the need to act against the usurper of my land, I will do it with or without your help. It may be many years before you become king, and I cannot wait long."

"Very well. I accept this affiliation between us. I'm pleased to have the loyalty of a woman of King Arthur's tribe."

Bronwen curtsied. "And now, I must apologize for my imposition on your privacy, sir." She looked at Jacques. "May I have my document, please?"

He returned it to her, and as she locked the box and tucked away the key, he realized he might not see her again for many a month. Perhaps longer. She started for the door, but he touched her elbow.

"One moment, my lady," he said. "Where will you dwell? If you intend to wait for King Stephen to die, you must stay somewhere."

She gazed down at the box as if it held the answers she sought. And perhaps it did.

"I'll stay with Enit," she told him. "My nursemaid needs my care."

"Bring her here. I have chambers enough for both of you. I'll spare no expense to see that she's comfortable and well fed. As Henry's ward, you may take your leisure in the castle and be certain of my respect and generosity."

Bronwen searched his eyes. For a moment, he felt certain she would agree. Her answer hung suspended between them, and he found he could not draw breath. Then she spoke.

"I must go home to Rossall, Jacques," she told him. "I made Enit a promise."

"But Aeschby will find you there. Bronwen, he'll have you killed—you know that. The risk is too great.

Even Warbreck village would be unsafe, for the man has as many spies as I. You must remain inside this castle. I insist upon it."

Reaching out, she laid her hand on his. Her fingers touched his palm, and he closed his hand around them. "I was wrong about you, Jacques," she murmured. "Wrong in every way. I beg your forgiveness, and I plead with you to accept my gratitude for all you've done on my behalf. Without you, I am nothing. I draw from your strength, and I honor your faithfulness. It is because of you, sir, that I have no choice but to go to Rossall. Please understand."

With that, she bent and kissed his hand. Pressing the small box to her chest, she hurried from the room. Jacques stared at the open door, watching her cross the guardroom, her gown an emerald glow in the firelight. And then she was gone, slipping down the stairs to another life in another place. He had no doubt Aeschby would kill her, and the life they might have shared would be lost forever.

"My word," Henry muttered. "Such a creature. No wonder you love her, Jacques. And no wonder she loves you, too."

Chapter Fourteen

"You'll not go into the village again today, will you?" Enit asked as Bronwen sat up from the straw pallet on which she had slept. "I have little doubt Aeschby knows you're here, child. If one of his henchmen sees you, he'll take you to his master, and that will mean your death."

"You're in a cheery humor this morning, Enit."

Bronwen had woken to the scent of fresh fish frying. As she slipped a tunic over her head and fastened on the black mantle Jacques had given her, she noted Enit studying her from the fireside in their small hut.

Nearly a month had passed since they'd departed Warbreck Castle and traveled by horse and cart to Rossall. Ogden, the butler who had served Edgard, and his wife, Ebba, had been delighted to see them again. Well aware of the danger Bronwen faced should she be discovered by Aeschby, they'd led her and Enit to a stream in the midst of the forest where a hovel had stood untouched for many years. There, Ogden and Ebba had settled the two women with blankets, firewood, a good black kettle and provisions to tide them through the winter.

"Of course I go to the village," Bronwen told her nurse. "I'm to speak to Malcolm at the butchery just after sunset."

Though she did not like to share too much with her nurse, Bronwen had been pleased to locate the guard she had met while leaving Rossall with Gildan and Enit nearly a year before. On that black day, Malcolm had professed his loyalty to her and had given her his bow and a quiver of arrows. He'd assured her that if she ever returned, he and many others would support her cause against Aeschby.

Now she was back, and Malcolm had been steadily gathering a small force of men. At first, Bronwen had intended to wait until she heard of King Stephen's death before pursuing her rights. But word of Aeschby's mismanagement of the land and his exploitation and abuse of Rossall's people spurred her to action.

Within days of Bronwen's decision to oppose the usurper, faithful men—some of them Edgard's former guards and others loyal peasants—had begun gathering by night at Malcolm's hut to lay out a plan of action. Bronwen had joined them in their plotting, and this evening, they would put the final pieces in place.

"I suppose fish will do for your final meal on this earth, then," Enit said. "I'll save some of this batch for your pocket. When Aeschby imprisons you tonight, at least you'll have a bite to eat before his sword severs your head from your neck."

"Enit, please!" Bronwen laughed. "You are too dire."

The winter chill seeped through the wattle-and-daub hut, and the women huddled together as they ate. Though their lives had sunk to a point lower than Bronwen could ever have imagined, at least she could take joy in knowing that Enit was well again. Or nearly so. Now and then, the old woman confused people's names or told a tale in the wrong order. She forgot the words to songs and sometimes left an ingredient out of a loaf of bread. But all in all, she had healed from the head injury she'd suffered during Aeschby's attack, and Bronwen thanked God daily.

"I must go to the stream," she told the old woman. They had eaten a little of the fish and shared an apple. Now water must be drawn for drinking and pot scrubbing. "I'll see to our nets, too. Perhaps we've captured a nice fat trout. Do not go outside until my return."

Enit had begun singing and paid little heed as Bronwen left the hut. Setting out through the woods with the water pail, she tried to squelch her discomfort about the events to come. Not only did she feel almost certain of failure, but she had no confidence that God approved of her plot. Had He not ordained peasants to live beneath lords? Edgard had told his daughter that the common people must never be allowed to revolt. *Do the stones rise up against the grass?* he had asked. *Does the fly attack the hawk?*

At a Christian church in London, Bronwen had heard the tale of God's creation of the heavens and the earth. When the angel Lucifer had defied God, he had been cast into eternal darkness. No, she should not urge the peasants to attack their lord. Yet, if she sat by and did nothing, what would become of the keep, the land, the people? How would her father advise her if he knew what Aeschby had done to Gildan and to Rossall?

Kneeling on the stream's bank, Bronwen dipped her pail into the water. Enit was right to worry. It was safe enough here in the forest, but Bronwen had no doubt that with each passing day her chances of exposure grew. She kept Jacques's dagger at her side at all times, and when she walked alone, she searched the trees and listened for rustling in the brush.

As she bent over the brook to lift out the water, that very sound caught her ears. At once, she let go of the pail and reached for her knife. As she turned, Jacques Le Brun stepped out onto the sand.

"You frightened me!" she exclaimed.

"And you've lost your bucket." He sprinted downstream, grabbed the pail and carried it back to her filled with water.

"There," he said, setting it beside her. "My misdeed is corrected."

At the sight of the man, garbed in mail and carrying his sword and bright blue shield, Bronwen made an awkward effort to tidy her hair. How she must look to him—as a peasant in the humblest garb with charcoal-smudged cheeks and not even a braid or a ribbon. She smoothed down her skirt, the same green gown she had worn when she'd left him. Its hem had been peppered with holes by embers popping from the fire, and her sleeves had been tattered by brambles.

"Truly, you should not be here, sir," she told him. "You endanger us both. I insist that you leave at once."

"As I recall, you made yourself welcome in my private chambers without permission or regard as to my wishes."

Bronwen lowered her eyes. He was right, of course. She had hidden in his guards' sleeping quarters and listened to a conversation not meant for her ears.

"How did you find me?" she asked. "I am well hid."

"Madam, you might as well be standing on a London

street corner. My spies brought news of your where-abouts *and* your plot against Aeschby. Frankly, I am surprised to see you in one piece."

Mortified, Bronwen cast a worried glance about her. If Jacques knew all this, Aeschby must be aware, too. "Why have you come, then?" she asked. "Surely you were followed."

"It's possible, but I think not. I came away without a guard. I have brought you a letter." He stepped toward her. "It's from your sister."

"A letter from Gildan? But how did you get it? When did it arrive? Is she all right?"

Jacques held out the document. "A messenger brought it this morning. I suppose she sent it to me on the assumption that you were living safely at Warbreck, as you should be. What the letter says, I do not know. It is sealed."

"Then open it, I beg you! Please, read it to me."

Jacques broke the seal. "To Bronwen, Edgard's Daughter of Rossall Hall, Widow of Olaf Lothbrok of Warbreck," he read. "From Gildan, Ward of Firmin of Troyes, France. Beloved sister, I pray all is well. The annulment of my marriage to Aeschby has been completed in good order. Chacier and I plan to wed in May soon after I return from France. We shall dwell near his family. Even now, Chacier takes control over much of his father's trade, so our lives will be filled with ease and contentment. My greatest desire now, dear Bronwen, is that you might attend my wedding. I long for the comfort of your presence. I miss you sorely, my dearest Bronwen. Come quickly!"

"They will wed in May," Bronwen said, her thoughts filled with images of her beautiful sister. "Thank God."

"I would ask if you intend to go to her in London, but I know the answer. Gildan is destined to hear sad news of her sister's demise before her wedding day."

"You and Enit are harbingers of doom." Bronwen picked up the pail. "I am not as confident of my death as you."

She started for the hovel, but Jacques bent and took the water from her hand. "Walk with me," he said. "On our last encounter, you asked to speak to me. I refused to hear you. Let me atone for my ill behavior."

Unwilling to deny herself this moment with him, she nodded. He set the pail on the sand again, took her hand and settled it over his arm. As they walked along the bank, he spoke. "Our dispute has continued far too long, Bronwen. We have misunderstood one another and judged unfairly. I should like to begin our acquaintance anew."

"Begin again?" she asked. "But you have just predicted my end."

"I fear it greatly. Will you not give up this quest? Go to your sister. Assume your rightful role in society. Please tell me this is not our final meeting. Our lives are woven together, Bronwen. Surely you see that."

"I have never understood how or why God allowed us to meet. Are we enemies? Your kisses belie that." She decided to speak her heart. "Sir, I have believed you wanted to make me your paramour…that I should become your lover. Perhaps I am sunk so low now that I seem to have no other choice, but I cannot do that."

"Is that what you think of me? Upon my honor, I mean no such thing. I am a Christian and a gentleman. My faith in the person and the teachings of Jesus Christ utterly prohibits such behavior. Bronwen, I am neither your foe nor your conqueror. Your blood makes you a noblewoman, and I would never treat you otherwise."

Bronwen gazed down at the ferns by the path. "How can you think of me as a noblewoman? Look at me. I live no better than a peasant—and worse than most. I have no land, no home, no father, nothing to make me noble."

"One only has to look at you to see your intelligence, strength and character. Henry sensed your nobility at once. Indeed, your heritage is far above my own."

"That subject is what I wished to discuss with you at Warbreck," she said. "Jacques, you misunderstood my words on the road. I care nothing about your heritage. It matters not to me that your blood is mixed. Indeed, your mother's church at Antioch is more purely rooted and uncorrupted than mine can ever be. If God reigns above lords—and He does—then your blood is nobler than that of any Norman."

"If my lineage doesn't matter, why do you continue to despise me for being Norman?"

"Normans took England from us. You yourself took—"

"I took the lands of a Viking, Bronwen. See the truth—England was no Briton stronghold when we came here. It was a mixture of weak tribal kingdoms held by Vikings, Saxons and a few Britons. Normans have united this country. We've built roads, cities, markets, castles. Please, open your eyes and use your keen wit, my lady. For once, admit what you know in your heart is right. You loved your father—but he was *wrong*."

Bronwen paused on the riverbank and covered her eyes with her hands. She could not accept that. She had struggled and fought and lived her very life in order to fulfill her father's dream.

But Jacques was right…and she had known it all along.

"Please don't look so downcast," he said gently. "I only want to make you see me as I am. I'm not your enemy. I have no desire to take what is yours—to rob you of anything. Like Henry, I'm honored to know a woman of your noble Briton blood. Your race is no less glorious than his simply because he's your conqueror. Can we not forget our differences and speak as man to woman?"

They had reached a place where the water bubbled down into a small pool. Bronwen walked to its edge and drew her mantle close about her shoulders. "Your words are true," she told him. "I'm glad to have the confusion and anger between us erased."

He lifted her hand to his lips. As he kissed her fingertips, his eyes met hers and held them.

"Bronwen, I have thought of you day and night since you left Warbreck," he whispered, tilting her chin with a finger.

The Norman's dark eyes gazed into her own until she could see nothing but him. How she had longed for his touch and how lonely she had been since their parting. She looked now at his hair, and her hands ached to touch the locks that curled about his neck. His lips— how close they were. She could almost taste his kiss.

In the space of a breath, she might forget her purpose in these woods. She might cast aside her father's dream and place her heart in this man's hands. Trembling, she stepped away from him.

"I cannot stay here any longer," she told him. "No matter your heritage or mine, Aeschby is a cruel overlord who has taken the soul of my people and crushed it. I cannot stand by and watch our land wither and our spirits turn to dust. If you love Henry as you say…if you care at all about Warbreck…you must understand this."

"It is Henry who makes us one, Bronwen. You are his ward, and therefore I stand ready to assist in your attempt to regain your inheritance. Our future king has declared that the land will belong to no one but you. Will you reject my aid?"

Bronwen shook her head. "I'm trying to trust what you say, Jacques. It is difficult. All my life, I was taught to see you as the enemy. Aeschby is Briton and Henry is Norman. Is it right for me to unite with my foe to defeat my kinsman?"

"Henry's will is to end the enmity between us. He wishes Briton and Norman to form an alliance, a camaraderie, even a friendship."

"Friendship," she murmured. "Enit always told Gildan and me, 'Be slow to fall into friendship—but when thou art in, continue firm and constant.'"

Jacques chuckled. "That is an old saying indeed. It was first uttered by Socrates, a Greek philosopher. I studied his teachings in Antioch."

Bronwen noticed a large flat stone beside the pool and took a place on it. Jacques sat beside her. "You have had much education. My father brought a tutor to teach us French, but Gildan and I know little else. We cannot read or write. We knew nothing but Amounderness until we traveled to London." She gave a low laugh. "We had never even seen a town until we went to Preston."

"Antioch is hardly larger than that," he told her. "But we did have schools. My father insisted that my elder brother and I attend. We studied law, science and literature. At fifteen, I left my homeland and went to France for further studies and training as a knight. There I met Geoffrey Plantagenet and his son, Henry."

"You are fast friends."

"We have much in common—a love of learning, hawking, playing at chess. He is far more ambitious than I, and he has the funds to support his campaigns."

Bronwen considered his words, musing on the differences in their upbringing. "If you have such a great love of learning, why did you not become a churchman like Thomas à Becket? Since you never planned to marry, why become a knight and seek to own land? You cannot pass it on to your heirs."

Jacques shook his head in amusement as he stretched his long legs out before him. "Did nothing escape you in your hiding place behind my curtain? What other secrets did I bare? Here are your answers then—I did not become a churchman because I am a man of action. I could never fit into the world of the church as my friend Martin has."

"Then what was the purpose of your education? Surely a knight doesn't need knowledge of literature and science."

"Be he king, baron or knight, every man must learn about the world as he is able."

"And what of every woman? Should I not have learning, too?"

"You have natural wit. Education would sharpen it further, and could only be good. But you were trained to accept your father's beliefs without question—and that's a grave error. The wise question everything."

"Even the existence of God? That is heresy, is it not? No one can prove He is real, Jacques."

"How shall I know Him if I don't seek Him? The

one who asks questions of God and studies diligently to learn the answers must, in the end, have a far greater and deeper understanding of Him than the one who accepts Him blindly. I seek to know God—and my belief in Him grows deeper."

Bronwen sighed. "But what is the use of that for me? You have books and can learn everything you long to know."

"Then you must learn to read and write."

"How? I have no school, no house of learning like Becket's."

"I'll teach you," Jacques said. "It should be simple enough. Return to Warbreck with me and study in my library."

Bronwen could barely breathe at the thought. To be able to read! To examine her father's will with her own eyes. To study the Holy Scriptures at her leisure. To write letters to Gildan. How wonderful!

But what of Rossall?

"Tempt me no more," she cried, standing. "I must return to Enit. On this night, my faithful army gathers to set the final plans for an attack on Aeschby. How can I think of abandoning them in order to study books at Warbreck? It is impossible."

"Woman, your quest is impossible."

Bronwen looked at Jacques as he stood beside the pool. His massive frame stood highlighted in the morning sun. A very giant of a man he was, a man of bold desires, bold words, bold actions. She longed for him with all her being—and yet she knew that if she listened to her heart, she would never be able to leave him.

He stepped to her and caught her about the waist. "Do not go to Aeschby. If I lose you from my life, Bronwen, it has no meaning. I long for you now as I have since our first kiss. Hear reason, I beg you. Hear *me*."

"But your words are torment."

"Oh, Bronwen, my lady," he said. "Then know my touch."

Drawing her close, he brushed her lips lightly with his own. Then, as though the contact had merely teased a flame, he kissed her again. This time his mouth burned like the coals of an all-consuming fire.

Bronwen's senses reeled as he pulled her nearer still. Closing her eyes, she reveled in the scent of his skin and the rough plane of his cheek against her downy skin.

"Allow me to love you," he whispered. "And love me in return."

"Love?" she asked. "You speak of *amour*—a passing French fancy. Is that what you want of me?"

"True love is more than that, Bronwen. I saw it in my parents as they looked into each other's eyes. I know it in the church when I bow humbly before my God. It fills my chest when I gaze at Warbreck and hear the laughter in the market. Love is affection, humility, pride, passion, the sacrifice of oneself for another. Surely you know that."

She reflected on his words. "I love Enit," she told him. "I love my sister."

"And your husband? You were married once. Was there no feeling between you and Olaf Lothbrok?"

Bronwen bit her lip and looked away. How could she tell him that no man had ever touched her? Though a widow, she had not known her husband's arms or the blessing of the marriage bed. Dare she tell him of her utter betrayal at Olaf's hands?

"What are your eyes telling me, Bronwen?" he asked. "Please. Speak what is in your heart."

Shivering, she backed away from him. "I was married," she began brokenly. "I was married to the Viking."

"What did he do to you? Did he harm you?"

"No, no. Indeed, he did not lay a finger upon me."

At her words, his face registered confusion. "But then you are untouched?"

"I am a maiden," she said. "Olaf stayed away from me all the months of our marriage, for he had vowed not to get me with child. He wanted Rossall for Haakon, you see."

"Haakon?"

"Haakon knew of his father's treachery against me. Why do you suppose he joined Aeschby after Olaf's death? Haakon would have killed his ally and taken Rossall as soon as opportunity presented itself. Warbreck would be next."

The clearing fell silent.

At last Jacques faced her. "Your husband wronged you."

"He did, indeed. It was my right and my duty to bear a child. Now you understand my surprise to learn of your patron. Though we knew little of Jesus when I was a child, we had heard of Christmas and also the tale of St. Nicholas. He placed golden balls in the stockings of three virgins—allowing them to prevent their greedy father from wedding them to rich but cruel husbands. I had always thought well of St. Nicholas for his protection of maidens. After I met you and saw your crest, I began to wonder if some holy force had led a dreaming young adventurer and a timid maid toward one another until they met on the seashore one winter night."

"Bronwen, it is God Himself who brought us together. You must believe that." Roughly drawing her to him, he crushed her against his chest. "I cannot bear this existence any longer. Every time we meet I grow to love you more. For months, I've lived in agony, longing for you without hope. Tell me you love me as I love you. Speak the words now."

"I do love you," she whispered without hesitation.

"Thanks be to God!" he ground out. Sealing her lips with a searing kiss, he wove his fingers through her hair. "Bronwen, what do you want of me? I will give you a home, lands, whatever you desire. I'll protect you and care for you always."

Laying her head against his chest, Bronwen reveled in the warmth of his embrace. It was true. She knew it beyond doubt. She loved this man—this Norman—as fully as it was possible to love. He was more than her ally, more than her friend, more than her conqueror. Indeed their hearts were wedded more closely than she knew two hearts could be.

Every sense awakened, she felt the imprint of the man's hand on her back. She could feel each separate finger, the thumb, the burning palm. Unable to stop the sudden rush of tears to her eyes, she met his kiss again. Oh, to have found such a love—and now to give him up for a quest that would end her life!

"Why do you weep?" he asked as he brushed the tears from her cheeks. "It's this land, isn't it? Rossall beckons you. Your blood demands it and your heart cries out for it."

"I'm so sorry," she murmured. "Jacques, you are my

great passion, my new desire, my dream and my love. But Rossall calls to me from a time older than memory, and I cannot deny her. I am torn in twain."

"No," he said, silencing her with another kiss. "Say no more. You tell me you love me—do you trust me? If so, let me join in your quest. I'll ride for Warbreck this night. Within the week, I'll return with my men. Then we shall mount an assault on Aeschby. When Rossall is taken, it will be yours again. Yours alone."

Silenced by his offer, she lifted his hand and held it against her damp cheek. Such love…such sacrifice…such beauty.

"I trust you," she whispered. "I shall trust you always."

He groaned as he drew her close once again. Then he set her aside and without a word, he leaped the brook and vanished into the forest.

As she walked resolutely toward the village that night, Bronwen willed her thoughts away from the man whose soul had fused with hers. Now she must speak to the loyal men gathered at the butchery. They would rejoice in the news that Warbreck intended to come to their aid. What a day of celebration Rossall would know when Aeschby was defeated and Edgard's will was done.

She gazed up at the fingernail moon as it climbed across the sky and reached its zenith. Stars winked down on her, but she knew it would be a dark night. Indeed, the sky was a deep black when Bronwen at last caught sight of the familiar rise on the horizon. The timber palisade stood as it always had, guarding the ancient keep of her father and his fathers before him.

A lump formed in Bronwen's throat as she slipped into the village and down a rutted lane. Nearing the butchery, she saw lights and knew the men were gathering. Ogden, Malcolm and the others would welcome her. Using a lump of charcoal, they had mapped out the palisade and the keep on a plank of wood. Malcolm and the other guards had marked weak areas where the wall might be breached. The butler had told of a tunnel, a secret door and several hiding places throughout the hall.

With so few men, Bronwen had cherished little hope that their scheme to enter the keep and vanquish Aeschby would succeed. But with Jacques's armed knights to lead the way, they could hardly fail.

Happier than she had been since she'd left Rossall so long ago, Bronwen stepped to the door of the butchery. As she reached to knock, a hand clamped across her mouth. Someone threw a hood over her head. Her feet were swept out from under her and tied together with a rough rope. Her hands were bound behind her back. Before she realized what was occurring, she had been thrown into the back of a cart that began rolling up the hill toward Rossall Hall.

Chapter Fifteen

"I am Bronwen—rightful mistress of Rossall. Sheath your sword, sir."

She faced Aeschby, who was drawing his weapon from its scabbard. He sneered at her. "You are Bronwen, mistress of *nothing*. I have you now, and here you'll stay. You thought you could plot against me. Bah! Your schemes are at an end. By morning those traitors will be strung up from the gates."

"No!" she cried. "Leave them be. This was my doing. The men were only following my instruction, for I have always planned to take Rossall from you. The moment I heard you had stolen it from me, I began to contrive a means of wresting it away. I've been to London and spoken with men of law and wisdom. Indeed, Henry Plantagenet, England's future king, has advised me."

"I know everything you mean to say before you speak the words, wench." Aeschby strode across the floor of the wool storage room where he had imprisoned Bronwen. Though the door had been barred, she was free of the ropes that had bound her.

"Henry is now your guardian," Aeschby spat. "He

plans to send troops against me when he gains the throne. My spies told me this weeks ago. What would Edgard say to his dear daughter? You betrayed him, Bronwen. You gave your life to one Norman and your heart to another."

"The world has changed, Aeschby. Norman authority in England is absolute. My obedience to Henry guarantees that Rossall will stay in Briton hands. You have no hope against him."

"No?" Aeschby said. "On what do you place such confidence?" He held up the small gold box she had worn at her waist. "I have your father's will. Why don't you remind me what it says, Bronwen, while I part your haughty head from your shoulders."

She gasped and stood back as he leveled his sword at her heart. "Aeschby! Let us speak like the civilized Britons we are. What need is there to battle like animals? We are kinsmen, after all."

"We are no longer kinsmen. You took your sister to London and had our marriage annulled in a church court. You plan to see her wedded again…this time to a Norman."

"Chacier is good to her. I saw what you had done to Gildan. You would have killed her."

"She was worthless. A spoiled child."

"Then you are better off without her. And set me free, as well. You foiled my scheme. I can harm you no more."

"Not until your dear Henry takes the throne. But see? Here is the end of that alliance, too."

He opened the box, took out Edgard's will and cast it into the fire. The dry parchment burst into flame and crumbled into ashes.

"No," Bronwen cried. "You heard my father's words. You know what he wanted for this land. Why have you destroyed all that was left of him, Aeschby? He was your friend and supporter."

"Edgard held land that I coveted. And why should I not have Rossall?" Aeschby began to stalk Bronwen around the storeroom. "Can you not see that this keep is mine and you will never possess it? How can a woman hold lands? It is impossible, and your father was a fool. I have despised you from the moment you stole my wife away. And I will kill you for that deed if for no other!"

Bronwen swallowed and lifted her chin. "You wanted Gildan only to give you children that you might pretend your claim was valid. You never cared for my sister."

"I care for nothing but my own gain. I have my father's land, and now I have Rossall. In time, I shall have Warbreck, too."

"What do you mean?"

"The Norman dog will come to your rescue. Have no fear on that account. My spies tell me of your union. Once Le Brun learns I hold you, he'll march here with his men to save you. But you see, Bronwen, I've been scheming, too. I plan to lure the Norman to Rossall with you as my bait. I could never wrest Warbreck from him if I had to storm it myself. But from this keep, I can wage war against him until his men are all dead. Warbreck was held by a Viking, and it fell easily. But I am a Briton, and I will never give over my land. I'll kill your knight and make Warbreck mine."

"You make me rue my Briton blood, Aeschby," she flung out. "You disgrace our tribe and shame us all."

"And see how much I care?" He spat at her feet, sheathed his sword and strode from the room. The door swung shut behind him, and the guards dropped the bar across it.

* * *

Bronwen told herself that Aeschby's words were nothing but empty threats. But as the night passed and the morning light dawned, she could no longer deny the truth. Rossall Hall had never been taken. From its construction to this day, the keep had stood as a beacon of safety and protection. The moment an enemy threatened, peasants flooded through the gates of the palisade. It was made of wood that had all but turned to stone in the passage of years.

Again and again, rivals had tried to take the hall by warfare, by siege or by subterfuge. Nothing had succeeded. No one could recall when it had been built, but all knew it had never left the hands of Bronwen's family until the moment of Edgard's death.

Remembering the catapult and the rolling tower, Bronwen tried to comfort herself in the belief that Jacques could outwit Aeschby and maneuver him into surrender. But in the end, her confidence failed. If the Norman had ridden straight for Warbreck after leaving her, he might return to Rossall in less than a week— especially if he learned she had been captured.

Finally unwilling to allow Jacques to face Aeschby on Rossall land, Bronwen decided she must do all she could to defeat the man herself. To her surprise, she discovered that although her foe had taken the will box, his men had declined the improper task of searching a woman. Her kidnappers were Briton guards, and their tradition forbade such a thing. Thus, beneath her green gown, she still had the jewel-encrusted dagger that Jacques had given her. Ogden had clearly mapped the wool storage room. And so she formulated a plan.

Once darkness crept over the room again that night,

Bronwen knelt near the window and lifted up a prayer. The wool in the room had been shorn in the summer, but it had not yet been spun or woven. As she leaned into the soft cushion, it seemed to whisper words of hope. The familiar musky scent of the wool bags and the smell of dyes from the bolts of fabric along one wall comforted her. This was her home. If God willed, she would return it to her family.

Standing, she removed a length of rope from a hook on the wall and wrapped it around her waist. She guessed that Aeschby would be inside the chamber where she and Gildan had slept. She ran her hands along the storeroom wall until she found the stones Ogden had specified. Removing them soundlessly, she set them on the floor. With a deep breath, she crouched and slid through the opening.

It was almost too easy. She stood in the deep shadow near the wooden palisade and studied the roofline until she spotted a corner post standing above the others like a sentinel. She tied a loop in her rope, cast it over the post and pulled it tight. Holding the rope in both her fists, she began to scale the wall.

It was not high, but the post's rough bark tore at her knees, and the rope burned her hands. At last she reached the top. She threw one arm around the post and pulled herself onto the roof.

After she caught her breath, she crawled to the smoke louvers above the fire. Peering down into the gloom, she could just make out the glowing coals beneath her. She slipped three long wooden slats out of their grooves and tied the rope around two others.

The eastern sky was lightening, and she knew she had to work quickly. Gripping the rope, she began lowering herself into the room. As she slid toward the floor, she saw that she was indeed entering her enemy's room. In one corner sat the great old bed and on it lay the fair-haired Briton lord.

As her feet touched down, Aeschby sat up in the bed. Bronwen drew her dagger.

"Who's there?" the man called into the darkness. "Guard!"

"You've barred them from your room," she said.

"You!" Aeschby threw back the furs and scrambled from the bed.

At that moment, Bronwen saw that the end of the rope had touched the coals and ignited a scattering of dried rushes. The flames curled upward as she leaped between Aeschby and his sword.

"Surrender to me," she ordered. "Kneel and submit to the rightful mistress of this hall."

Aeschby spat and lunged past her. Bronwen's dagger made a quick stabbing thrust that caught him in the arm and sent a spurt of blood across his chest. With a cry of rage, he grabbed his sword and turned on her.

Light had grown stronger in the room now, and Bronwen knew it came from the flickering fire creeping slowly across the timber floor. "Surrender, Aeschby," she shouted. "Admit defeat before we both go up in flames!"

"Never!" he cried.

He whirled about and lunged at Bronwen, but he was too far, and she parried the stroke with her dagger. Surprised, he paused, and this time she slipped the blade into his right side. His nostrils flared and his face reddened with pain.

"I'll kill you!" he shouted.

Drawing back his sword, he swung it with a stroke that could have hewn Bronwen in two. But she grabbed her black mantle, yanked it from her neck, and threw it over the weapon. The blade clattered to the floor, buried in folds of woolen fabric.

With a roar of rage, Aeschby ran at Bronwen. She backed away, throwing chairs, stools, burning bedding—anything she could reach—in front of him. If he stumbled, she struck out at him with the dagger.

"Aeschby, you are defeated," she said as she circled a chest of flaming clothing. "You know Rossall is mine. You cannot win."

"You will die!" he panted, throwing himself at her again.

This time, he wrenched the knife from her hand and slashed at her. It caught her shoulder, and with a cry of pain, she dropped to the floor in search of the sword.

From outside, Aeschby's men hammered on the door. A ringing of swords and clash of mail filtered through the exhaustion in Bronwen's brain. Flames now began to consume the curtains, the bedding—even the shutters so that they hung as cinders in the dawn air. Her head throbbed and her lungs ached in the smoke-filled room. From somewhere deep inside her, she felt a prayer rise up to God, and she called on the Lord Jesus to protect her and thwart her enemy.

Aeschby stepped toward her just as Bronwen found Jacques's mantle. Knowing Aeschby's men would break through at any second, she kicked over a table. As he leaped across it, she drew the sword from the folds of fabric. Then she rolled onto her back with the sword's hilt at her chest. The blade glittered as Aeschby fell onto it, his eyes wide with disbelief.

His knees buckled beneath him, and he sank slowly to the floor. A dull gray cast crossed his eyes and the dagger fell from his hand.

Shaking, Bronwen curled onto the mantle. Coughing, unable to breathe, she barely heard the crack of the door as it splintered. As the first of Aeschby's men rushed toward her, Bronwen staggered to her feet.

"Halt!" she shouted hoarsely. "I have slain your lord, and you now owe homage to me—Bronwen of Rossall."

The men checked their steps and fell back bewildered at the scene before their eyes. For several seconds no one moved. The guards glanced at the shambles of the chamber. Their confusion changed to shock at the sight of Aeschby lying in a bloody heap at Bronwen's feet.

"Your lord is dead," she told them. "I have avenged my father, and now I claim my heritage."

The men stared at Bronwen from beneath their helms. Then the mob began to part as a husky guard shoved his way to the front and fell to his knees before her.

"Malcolm!" Bronwen let out a breath of relief at the sight of her ally.

"I pledge my allegiance to the house of Edgard the Briton," he said. "And to Bronwen, mistress of Rossall Hall."

The warrior rose. Drawing his sword, he came to stand beside Bronwen. Two more men stepped clear and knelt before her.

"Brian. Robin. Welcome," she said.

Then three came. Then five. As she called their names, they stood and walked to her side.

"Enough!" shouted one of Aeschby's men. "We owe no allegiance to this woman!"

"Slay me and you will have neither master nor mistress," Bronwen said. "The pretender lies dead at my feet. Surrender, and you'll have safe passage back to your families."

Before she finished speaking, the men began pushing through the staunch front line and coming forward to pay obeisance. Bronwen recognized many of them and called them by name. But several fell before her who had been Aeschby's men, and she welcomed them as well.

It seemed to Bronwen that these moments were in a dream. The cloying smoke, the dead man at her feet, the bloody sword, the kneeling guards. She could hear only the pumping of her blood as it rushed in her ears. And now the last few of Aeschby's men dropped their swords and came to acknowledge her dominion. The blood running from the wound on her shoulder dripped from her hand as she stretched it out to the kneeling men.

"Rise," she said. "You will be treated fairly. You may remove the body of your lord."

The fog before her thickened. She swallowed and licked her lips. The formless shapes of men moved before her eyes, and she blinked, trying to focus. Her head swam, and it seemed she heard shouts coming from the grounds as she took several swaying steps forward. And then the darkness swallowed her.

A warm, wet rag passed over Bronwen's forehead. She felt a trickle of water run down into her hair and course onto the pillow. Yes, it was a pillow. And blankets covered her. But somehow stars shone overhead, and the moon gleamed a bright silver in the night.

The wet rag dabbed her forehead again and Bronwen tried to open her eyes.

"Where am I?" she said, her voice a croak.

"Quiet, Bronwen. You must rest now." The deep voice could belong to none other than Jacques.

"You are safe!" she managed to say. "Thanks be to God."

The face before her broke into a familiar smile as Jacques's warm hands stroked her hair.

"And you're at home, Bronwen. Here you lie beside the sea where first we met. I arrived with my men during your struggle with Aeschby. Could you not hear the battle below?"

Bronwen lay back and closed her eyes. Pieces began to fall into place, and then she remembered Aeschby coming at her with his sword. She sat up and cried out, but Jacques folded her into his arms.

"Bronwen, the victory is secure," he said as he cradled her against his chest. "Aeschby's men have departed, driven away by a band of loyal knights."

She turned her head and looked up again at the cascade of stars in the night sky. A thin trail of smoke floated across them like a veil.

"I lie on the beach," she whispered. "Rossall is lost. Burned—is it not?"

Jacques nodded as she blinked back tears. "Bronwen, why did you face Aeschby alone?" he asked. "He might have killed you. You had only to stay in the room where he held you prisoner, and I would have come."

"Don't speak of it now," Bronwen whispered. "It all seems a dream to me."

At her words he turned his head to the stars. Bronwen gazed at the familiar profile framed in dark curls.

"Jacques. Rossall is gone." She spoke quietly yet firmly. "Not just burned. Gone from my life. When I knew I would die for her, I saw she no longer mattered. Lands and castles are fleeting. They stand…or fall… and we pass on without them. It is the life we live that means something. The God we serve. The friends we cherish. The ones we love."

"Bronwen—"

"Let me finish, Jacques. I must say it all. I give you Rossall holding—and Aeschby's land with it, now that he lies dead. Take the lands for Henry and rule them well. I have no need of them."

Jacques bent and kissed Bronwen lightly on the brow. "I have a message from Henry," he said.

"One day I shall read it myself. But for now, tell me what our future king has written."

He took out the folded parchment and opened it.

"To Jacques Le Brun of Warbreck," he read. "And to Bronwen of Rossall. From Henry Plantagenet, Duke of Normandy and heir apparent to the throne of England.

"On this twelfth day of January in the year of our Lord 1154, I do herein state my will as your master and guardian. Jacques, you must win this woman's loyalty to you and to my kingdom. Bronwen, you have captured this man's heart, now take his hand in marriage. Bear sons and daughters that they may hold this land one day."

Bronwen looked up. "January? But that was when he was at Warbreck."

"The letter was in his room when he left." Jacques paused. Brushing a wisp of hair from her bandaged shoulder, he bent and kissed her forehead. "I believe

Henry liked you very much, Bronwen. I think he was drawn to your spirit—and he wanted us together."

"But why did you not tell me sooner?"

"He commanded me to win you, Bronwen. That became my quest. I wanted your love more than I wanted a marriage arranged by a king."

Bronwen slipped her fingers into his hair and drew him to her lips. For a moment, she lost herself in him, wanting nothing more than to curl against his chest and feel his arms around her.

"One more piece of news," he murmured, "and then you shall sleep again. Stephen is dead, and Henry is to be crowned."

"When?" she gasped.

"Stephen died a few weeks ago. I received word yesterday. Henry is in Normandy and has been unable to cross the channel due to the winter seas. Knowing him, I imagine he'll be too anxious to claim his throne—and he will brave the weather with Eleanor, despite the fact that she is again with child."

Bronwen's heart leaped. "Is Henry to be crowned in London?"

Jacques nodded. "Will you accompany me to the coronation, Bronwen? We shall see the king crowned and your sister wed. Will you be baptized so we can be married in church before we go? Will you go as Bronwen Le Brun of Warbreck and Rossall? Will you go as my wife?"

Bronwen looked up, her heart full. "We shall go together."

* * * * *

Evicted from her home, Joanna Nelson and her two children seek refuge on the harsh Montana plains— which leads her to rancher Aidan McKaslin's property. When outside forces threaten their blossoming friendship, Aidan decides to take action. Can he convince Joanna to bind herself to him permanently or will it drive her away forever?

Read on for a sneak preview of
High Country Bride *by Jillian Hart!*

"Where are you going to go?"

His tone was flat, his jaw tensed, as if he was still fighting his temper. His blue eyes glanced past her to where the children were going about their chore.

"I don't know." Her throat went dry. Her tongue felt thick as she answered. She trembled, not from fear of him—she truly didn't believe he would strike her—but from the unknown.

Of being forced to take the frightening step off the only safe spot she'd found since she'd lost Pa's house.

When you were homeless, everything seemed so fragile, so easily off balance. It was a big, unkind world for a woman alone with her children. She had no one to protect her. No one to care. The truth was, Joanna had never had those things in her husband. How could she expect them from any stranger? Especially this man she hardly knew, who seemed harsh, cold and hard-hearted?

And, worse, what if he brought in the law?

"Let me guess. If you leave here, you don't know where you're going and you have no money to get there with?"

She nodded. "Yes, sir."

"Then get you and your kids into the wagon. I'll hitch up your horses for you." His eyes were cold and yet not unfeeling as he fastened his gaze on hers. "I have a shanty out back of my house that no one's living in. You can stay there for the night."

"What?" She stumbled back, and the solid wood of the tailgate bit into the small of her back. "But—"

"There will be no argument," he snapped, interrupting her. "None at all. I buried a wife and son years ago, what was most precious to me, and to see you and them neglected like this—with no one to care…" His jaw clenched again, and his eyes were no longer cold.

Joanna didn't think she'd ever seen anything sadder than Aiden McKaslin standing there in the slanting rays of the setting sun.

Without another word, he turned on his heel and walked away, melting into the thick shadows of the summer evening.

Don't miss
High Country Bride *by Jillian Hart,*
available October 2018.

www.LoveInspired.com

LIHEXP89584

Love Inspired®

Save $1.00

on the purchase of ANY
Love Inspired® book.

Available wherever books are sold,
including most bookstores, supermarkets,
drugstores and discount stores.

Save $1.00

on the purchase of ANY Love Inspired® book.

Coupon valid until October 31, 2018.
Redeemable at participating retail outlets in the U.S. and Canada only.
Limit one coupon per customer.

52615896

5 65373 00076 2   (8100)0 12379

Love Inspired®

Inspirational Romance to Warm Your Heart and Soul

Join our social communities to connect with other readers who share your love!

Sign up for the Love Inspired newsletter at **www.LoveInspired.com** to be the first to find out about upcoming titles, special promotions and exclusive content.

CONNECT WITH US AT:

Harlequin.com/Community

 Facebook.com/LoveInspiredBooks

 Twitter.com/LoveInspiredBks

LISOCIAL2017